The Gilded Cuff

Surrender Series, Book #1

LAUREN SMITH

New York   Boston

Copyright © 2015 by Lauren Smith
Excerpt from *The Gilded Cage* copyright © 2015 by Lauren Smith
Cover design by Elizabeth Turner
Cover copyright © 2015 by Hachette Book Group, Inc.

Forever Yours
Hachette Book Group
1290 Avenue of the Americas
New York, NY 10104

hachettebookgroup.com
twitter.com/foreverromance

First ebook and print on demand edition: February 2015

Forever Yours is an imprint of Grand Central Publishing.
The Forever Yours name and logo are trademarks of Hachette Book Group, Inc.

The publisher is not responsible for websites (or their content) that are not owned by the publisher.

The Hachette Speakers Bureau provides a wide range of authors for speaking events. To find out more, go to www.hachettespeakersbureau.com or call (866) 376-6591.

ISBN 978-1-4555-3274-2 (ebook edition)
ISBN 978-1-4555-3275-9 (print on demand edition)

*For Kaylan. The world is dimmer without your
light shining in it.*

Acknowledgments

I'd like to thank Aimee, Laurie and Jeanne, my wonderful beta readers and the ladies of the White Car Book Club who remind me that books should inspire discussion and be fun. For my street team members of Lauren Smith's League, you guys are wonderful and keep me inspired to write every day with your enthusiasm and joy for my stories. Thank you to Amanda and my parents, steadfast supporters who always help make my dreams a reality. And finally, I have to thank my amazing editor, Lauren Plude, who changed my life when she fell in love with the Gilded Cuff series and its bad boy heroes.

The Gilded Cuff

Chapter 1

EMERY LOCKWOOD AND FENN LOCKWOOD, EIGHT-YEAR-OLD TWIN SONS OF ELLIOT AND MIRANDA LOCKWOOD, WERE ABDUCTED FROM THEIR FAMILY RESIDENCE ON LONG ISLAND BETWEEN SEVEN AND EIGHT P.M. THE KIDNAPPING OCCURRED DURING A SUMMER PARTY HOSTED BY THE LOCKWOODS.
—*New York Times*, June 10, 1990

Long Island, New York

This is absolutely the stupidest thing I've ever done.

Sophie Ryder tugged the hem of her short skirt down over her legs a few more inches. It was still way too high. But she couldn't have worn something modest, per her usual style. Not at an elite underground BDSM club on Long Island's Gold Coast. Sophie had never been to any club before, let alone one like this. She'd had to borrow the black mini-skirt and the red lace-up corset from her friend Hayden Thorne, who was a member of the club and knew what she should wear.

The Gilded Cuff. It was *the* place for those who enjoyed their kink and could afford to pay.

Sophie sighed. A journalist's salary wasn't enough to afford anything like what the people around her wore, and she was definitely feeling less sexy in her practical black flats with a bit of sparkle on the tips. Sensuality rippled off every person in the room as they brushed against her in their Armani suits and Dior gowns, and she was wary of getting too close. Their cultured voices echoed off the craggy gray stone walls as they chatted and gossiped. Although she was uneasy with the frank way the people around her touched and teased each other with looks and light caresses, even while patiently waiting in line, a stirring of nervousness skittered through her chest and her abdomen. Half of it had to do with the sexual chemistry of her surroundings, and the rest of it had to do with the story that would make her career, if she could only find who she was looking for and save his life in time. Her editor at the Kansas newspaper she wrote for had given her one week to break the story. What she didn't know was how long she had to save the life of a man who at this very moment was in the club somewhere. She swallowed hard and tried to focus her thoughts.

Following the crowd, she joined the line leading up to a single walnut wood desk with gilt edges. A woman in a tailored gray suit over a red silk blouse stood there checking names off a list with a feather pen. Sophie fought to restrain her frantic pulse and the flutter of rebellious butterflies in her stomach as she finally reached the desk.

"Name, please?" The woman peered over wide, black-rimmed glasses. She looked a cross between a sexy librarian and a no-nonsense lawyer.

A flicker of panic darted through Sophie. She hoped her inside source would come through. Not just anyone could get into the club. You had to be referred by an existing member as a guest.

"My name's Sophie Ryder. I'm Hayden Thorne's guest." At the mention of her new friend's name the other woman instantly smiled, warmth filling her gaze.

"Yes, of course. She called and mentioned you'd be coming. Welcome to the Gilded Cuff, Sophie." She reached for a small glossy pamphlet and handed it over. "These are the club rules. Read over them carefully before you go inside. Come to me if you have any questions. You can also go to anyone wearing a red armband. They are our club monitors. If you get in too deep and you get panicked, say the word "red" and that will make the game or the scene stop. It's the common safe word. Any doms inside should respect that. If they don't, they face our monitors."

"Okay," Sophie sucked in a breath, trying not to think about what sort of scene would make her use a safe word. This really was the most stupid thing she'd ever done. Her heart drummed a staccato beat as a wave of dread swept through her. She should leave…No. She had to stay at least a few more minutes. A life could hang in the balance, a life she could save.

"There's just one more thing. I need to know if you are a domme or a sub." The woman trailed the feather tip end of her pen under the tip of her chin, considering Sophie, measuring her.

"A domme or sub?" Sophie knew the words. Dominant and submissive. Just another part of the BDSM world, a lifestyle she knew so little about. Sophie definitely wasn't a domme. Dommes were the feminine dominants in a D/s relationship. She certainly had no urge to whip her bed partner.

She liked control, yes, but only when it came to her life and doing what she needed to do. In bed? Well…she'd always liked to think of an aggressive man as one who took what he wanted, gave her what she needed. Not that she'd ever had a man like that before. Until now, every bedroom encounter had been a stunning lesson in disappointment.

The woman suddenly smiled again, as though she'd been privy to Sophie's inner thoughts. "You're definitely not a domme." Amusement twitched the corners of her mouth. "I sense you would enjoy an *aggressive* partner."

How in the hell? Sophie quivered. The flash of a teasing image, a man pinning her to the mattress, ruthlessly pumping into her until she exploded with pleasure. Heat flooded her face.

"Ahh, there's the sub. Here, take these." The woman captured Sophie's wrists and clamped a pair of supple leather cuffs around each wrist. Sewn into the leather, a red satin ribbon ran the length of each cuff. The woman at the desk didn't secure Sophie's wrists together, but merely ensured she had cuffs ready to be cinched together should she find a partner inside. The feel of the cuffs around her wrists sent a ripple of excitement through her. How was it possible to feel already bound and trapped? They constrained her, but didn't cut off her circulation, like wearing a choker necklace. She wanted to tug at the cuffs the way she would a tight necklace, because she was unused to the restriction.

"These tell the doms inside that you're a sub, but you're unclaimed and new to the lifestyle. Other subs will be wearing cuffs; some won't. It depends on if they are currently connected with a particular dom and whether that dom wishes to show an ownership. Since you're not with anyone, the red ribbons tell everyone you're new and learning the lifestyle. They'll know to go easy on you and to ask permission before doing or trying anything with you. The monitors will keep a close eye on you."

Relief coursed through Sophie. Thank heavens. She was only here to pursue a story. Part of the job was to get information however she could, do whatever it took. But she wasn't sure she would be ready to do the things she guessed went on behind the heavy oak doors. Still, for the story, she would probably have to do something out of her comfort zone. It was the nature of writing about criminal stories. Of course, tonight wasn't about a crime, but rather a victim—and this victim was the answer to everything she'd spent years hoping to learn. And she was positive he was in danger.

When she'd gone to the local police with her suspicions, they'd turned a blind eye and run her off with the usual assurances that they kept a close eye on their community. But they didn't see patterns like she did. They hadn't read thousands of articles about crimes and noticed what she did. Somewhere inside this club, a man's life was hanging by a thread and she would save him and get the story of the century.

"Cuffs please." A heavily muscled man reached for her wrists as she approached the door that led deeper into the club. He wore an expensive suit with a red armband on his bicep, but his sheer brawny power was actually accented, rather than hidden, by his attire. It surprised her. She'd expected men to be running around in black leather and women fully naked, surrounded by chains, whips, and the whole shebang.

The man looked at her wrists, then up at her face. "You know the safe word, little sub?"

"Red."

"Good girl. Go on in and have a good time." The man's mouth broke into a wide smile, but it vanished just as quickly. She smiled back, and bowed her head slightly in a nod as she passed by him.

She moved through the open door into another world. Instead of a dungeon with walls fitted with iron chains, Sophie found the Gilded Cuff was the opposite of what she'd anticipated.

Music and darkness ruled the landscape of the club, engulfing her senses. She halted abruptly, her heart skittering in a brief flare of panic at not being able to see anything around her.

The dungeons and screams she'd expected weren't there. Was this typical for a BDSM atmosphere? Her initial research had clearly led her astray. It wasn't like her to be unprepared and The Gilded Cuff certainly surprised her. Every scenario she'd planned for in her head now seemed silly and ineffective. This place and these people weren't anything like what'd she'd imagined they would be and that frightened her more than the cuffs did. Being unprepared could get you killed. It was a lesson she'd learned the hard way and she had the scars to prove it. The club's rule pamphlet the woman at the desk had given her was still in her hands and a slight layer of sweat marked the glossy paper's surface.

I probably should have glanced at it. What if I break a rule by accident?

The last thing she needed to do was end up in trouble or worse, get kicked out and not have a chance to do what she'd come to do. It might be her *only* chance to save the man who'd become her obsession.

Sophie made her way through an expansive room bordered with rope-tied crimson velvet drapes that kept prying eyes away from the large beds beyond them when the curtains were untied. Only the sounds coming from behind the draperies hinted at what was happening there. Her body reacted to the sounds, and she became aroused despite her intention to remain aloof. Around here, people lounged on gothic-style, brocade-upholstered couches. Old portraits hung along the walls, imperious images of beautiful men and women from ages past watching coldly from their frames. Sophie had the feeling that she'd stepped into another time and place entirely removed from the cozy streets of the small town of Weston, on the north shore of Long Island.

The slow pulse of a bass beat and a singer's husky crooning wrapped around Sophie like an erotic blanket. As if she were in a dark dream, moving shadows and music filled her, and she breathed deeply, teased by hints of sex and expensive perfume. Awareness of the world outside wavered, rippling in her mind like a mirage. Someone bumped into her from behind, trying to pass by her to go deeper into the club. The sudden movement jerked her back to herself and out of the club's dark spell.

"Sorry!" she gasped and stepped out of the way.

As her eyes adjusted to the dim light, bodies manifested in twisting shapes. The sounds of sexual exploration were an odd compliment to the song being played. A heavy blush flooded Sophie's cheeks, heating her entire face. Her own sexual experiences had been awkward and brief. The memories of those nights were unwanted, uncomfortable, and passionless. Merely reliving them in her mind made her feel like a stranger in her own skin. She raised her chin and focused on her goal again.

The cuffs on her wrists made her feel vulnerable. At any moment a dom could come and clip her wrists together and haul her into a dark corner to show her true passion at his hands. The idea made her body hum to life in a way she hadn't thought possible. Every cell in her seemed to yearn now toward an encounter with a stranger in this place of sins and secrets. She trailed her fingertips over the backs of velveteen couches and the slightly rough texture of the fabric made her wonder how it would feel against her bare skin as she was stretched out beneath a hard masculine body.

The oppressive sensual darkness that slithered around the edges of her own control was too much. There was a low-lit lamp not too far away, and Sophie headed for it, drawn by the promise of its comfort. Light was safe; you could see what was happening. It was the dark that set her on edge. If she couldn't see what was going on around her, she was vulnerable. There was barely enough light for her to see where she was headed. She needed to calm down, regain her composure and remind herself why she was here.

Her heart trampled a wild beat against her ribs as she realized it would be so easy for any one of the strong, muscular doms in the club to slide a hand inside her bodice and discover the thing she'd hidden there, an object that had become precious to her over the last few years.

Her hand came to rest on the copy of an old photograph. She knew taking it out would be a risk, but she couldn't fight the need to steal the quick glance the dim light would allow her.

Unfolding the picture gently, her lips pursed as she studied the face of the eight-year-old boy in the picture. This was the childhood photo of the man she'd come to meet tonight.

The black and white photo had been on the front page of the *New York Times* twenty-five years ago. The boy was dressed in rags, and bruises marred his angelic face; his haunted eyes gazed at the camera. A bloody cut traced the line of his jaw from chin to neck. Eyes wide, he clasped a thick woolen blanket to his body as a policeman held out a hand to him.

Emery Lockwood. The sole survivor of the most notorious child abduction in American history since that of the Lindbergh baby. And he was somewhere in the Gilded Cuff tonight.

Over the last year she'd become obsessed with the photo and had taken to looking at it when she needed reassurance. Its subject had been kidnapped but survived and escaped, when so many children like him over the years had not been so lucky. Sophie's throat constricted, and shards of invisible glass dug into her throat as she tried to shrug off her own awful memories. Her best friend Rachel, the playground, that man with the gray van…

The photo was creased in places and its edges were worn. The defiance in Emery's face compelled her in a way nothing else in her life had. Compelled with an intensity that scared her. She had to see him, had to talk to him and understand him and the tragedy he'd survived. She was afraid he might be the target of another attempt on his life and she had to warn him. It wouldn't be fair for him to die, not after everything he'd survived. She had to help him. But it wasn't just that. It was the only way she could ease the guilt she'd felt at not being able to help catch the man who'd taken her friend. She had to talk to Emery. Even though she knew it wouldn't bring Rachel back, something inside her felt like meeting him would bring closure.

With a forced shrug of her shoulders, she relaxed and focused on Emery's face. After years of studying kidnapping cases she'd noticed something crucial in a certain style of kidnappings, a tendency by the predators to repeat patterns of behavior. When she'd started digging through Emery's case and read the hundreds of articles and police reports, she'd sensed it. That prickling sensation at the back of her mind that warned her that what had been started twenty-five years ago wasn't over yet. She hadn't been able to save Rachel, but she would save Emery.

I have to. She owed it to Rachel, owed it to herself and to everyone who'd lost someone to the darkness, to evil. Guilt stained her deep inside but when she saw Emery's face in that photograph, it reminded her that not every stolen child died. A part of her, one she knowingly buried in her heart, was convinced that talking to him, hearing his story, would ease the old wounds from her own past that never seemed to heal. And in return, she might be the one to solve his kidnapping and rescue him from a threat she was convinced still existed.

She wasn't the boldest woman—at least not naturally—but the quest for truth always gave her that added level of bravery. Sometimes she felt, when in the grips of pursuing a story, that she became the person she ought to be, someone brave enough to fight the evil in the world. Not the tortured girl from Kansas who'd lost her best friend to a pedophile when she was seven years old.

Sophie would have preferred to conduct an interview somewhere less intimate, preferably wearing more clothing. But Emery was nearly impossible to reach—he avoided the press, apparently despising their efforts to get him to tell his story. She didn't blame him. Retelling his story could be traumatic for him, but she didn't have a choice. If what she suspected was true, she needed the details she was sure he'd kept from the police because they might be the keys to figuring out who'd kidnapped him and why.

She'd made calls to his company, but the front desk there had refused to transfer her to his line, probably because of his "no press" rule. Thanks to Hayden she knew Emery rarely left the Lockwood estate but he came to the Gilded Cuff a few times a month. This was the only opportunity she might have to reach him.

Emery ran his father's company from a vast mansion on the

Lockwood estate, nestled in the thick woods of Long Island's Gold Coast. No visitors were permitted and he left the house only when in the company of private guards.

Sophie tucked the photo back into her corset and looked around, peering at the faces of the doms walking past her. More than once their gazes dropped to the cuffs on her wrists, possessively assessing her body. Her face scorched with an irremovable blush at their perusal. Whenever she made eye contact with a dom, he would frown and she'd instantly drop her gaze.

Respect; must remember to respect the doms and not make eye contact unless they command it. Otherwise she might end up bent over a spanking bench. Her corset seemed to shrink, making it hard to breathe, and heat flashed from her head to her toes.

Men and women—submissives judging by the cuffs they bore on their wrists—were wearing even less than she was as they walked around with drink trays, carrying glasses to doms on couches. Several doms had subs kneeling at their feet, heads bowed. A man sitting on a nearby love seat was watching her with hooded eyes. He had a sub at his feet, his hand stroking her long blond hair. The woman's eyes were half closed, cheeks flushed with pleasure. The dom's cobalt blue eyes measured her—not with sexual interest, but seemingly with mere curiosity—the way a sated mountain lion might watch a plump rabbit crossing its path.

Sophie pulled her eyes away from the redheaded dom and his ensnaring gaze. The club was almost too much to take in. Collars, leashes, the occasional pole with chains hanging from it, and a giant cross were all there, part of the fantasy world created amid the glitz and old world décor.

Sliding past entwined bodies and expensive furniture, she saw more that intrigued her. The club itself was this one large room with several halls splitting off the main room. Hayden had explained earlier that morning the layout of the club. She had pointed out that no matter which hall you went down you had to come back to the main room to exit the club. A handy safety feature. A little exhalation of relief escaped her lips. How deep did a man like Emery Lockwood live this lifestyle? Would she find him in one of the private rooms or would he be part of a public scene like the ones she was witnessing now?

She was nearly halfway across the room when a man caught her by her arm and spun her to face him. Her lips parted, ready to scream the word "red", but when she met his gaze she froze, the shout dying at the back of her throat. He raised her wrists, fingering the red ribbon around her leather cuffs. His gray eyes were as silver as moonlight, and openly interested. Sophie tried to jerk free of his hold. He held tight. The arousal that had been slowly building in her body flashed cold and sharp. She could use the safe word. She knew that. But after one deep breath, she forced herself to relax. Part of the job tonight was to blend in, to find Emery. She couldn't do that if she ran off and cried for help at the first contact. It would be smarter to let this play out a bit; maybe she could squeeze the dom for information about Emery later if she didn't find him soon. For Sophie, not being able to get to Emery was more frightening than anything this man might try to do to her.

"I see your cuffs, little sub. I'm not going to hurt you."

His russet hair fell across his eyes and he flicked his head: power, possession, dominance. He was raw masculinity. A natural dom. He was the sort of good-looking man that she would have mooned over when she was a teenager. Hell, even now at twenty-four she should have been melting into a puddle at this man's feet. His gaze bit into her. A stab of sudden apprehension made her stomach pitch, but she needed to find Emery and going along with this guy might be the best way to get information. He tugged her wrists, jerking her body against his as he regarded her hungrily. "I need an unclaimed sub for a contest. Tonight is your lucky night, sweetheart."

Chapter 2

ELLIOT AND MIRANDA LOCKWOOD WERE
VISIBLE DURING THE TIME THE KIDNAPPING IS
SPECULATED TO HAVE OCCURRED. THE TWINS
WERE LAST SEEN IN THE KITCHEN BY THEIR
HIRED NANNY FRANCESCA ESPINA, AGE FIFTY-
FOUR YEARS, WHO HAD SUMMONED THE BOYS
TO THE KITCHEN FOR DINNER.
—*New York Times*, June 10, 1990

Sophie barely had time to protest at the dom's tight hold on her wrist before he dragged her across the room to where a group of people circled a couch against the wall. She could have said "red" and stopped whatever game he'd intended to play so she could keep searching for Emery, but the word died on her lips. A large crowd of people all turned to face her, amusement flashing in their eyes. The crowd's focus on her was not comforting in the slightest. She was prey, for a so-called contest, in a BDSM club. Searching the faces for Emery's, she prayed she'd be lucky enough to find him. If not, she'd use her safe word and get free of the man and his "contest."

Holding her, he grinned darkly at the onlookers. "Found a new-bie. She'll be perfect."

Sophie again jerked to get her wrist back and failed. She stifled a gasp as he promptly smacked her bottom with an open hand. Her gaze darted across the crowd, trying to seek out Emery's familiar face. He had to be here somewhere. Most of the club members had moved in to watch her and this dom.

"Stand still, bow your head," he commanded.

To her shock she obeyed instantly—not because she naturally bowed to anyone who shoved her around, but because something inside her responded to the commanding tone he'd just used on her. He seemed like a man who would enjoy punishing her, and she knew enough about this lifestyle to know she never wanted to end up over a spanking bench, even if the idea did make her insides flare to life.

"Bring her here, Royce." A cool, rich voice spoke, pouring over her skin like whisky—slightly rough, with an intoxicating bite to it. When this man spoke, the voices murmuring around her stopped and a hush fell over the area.

The crowd around her and the man, Royce, parted. Another man, sitting on the blue brocaded couch, watched them. His large hands rested on his thighs, fingers impatiently drumming a clipped beat. Royce shoved Sophie none too gently, sending her to her knees right at the man's feet. She reacted instinctively, throwing her hands out to balance herself, and her palms fell on his thighs and her chest collided with his knees.

Air rushed out of her lungs in a soft *whoosh*. For a few seconds she fought to regain her breath as she leaned against the stranger for support. The large muscles beneath his charcoal pants jumped and tensed beneath her hands, and she whipped her palms off him as though burned. She'd practically been in the man's lap, the heat of his body warming her, tempting her with his close proximity. Hastily she dropped her head and rested her hands on her own thighs, waiting. It took every ounce of her willpower to concentrate on breathing.

She still didn't look at his face, focusing instead on his expensive black shoes, the precision cuffs of his dark charcoal pants. Her eyes then tracked up his body, noting the crisp white shirt and thin, blood red tie he wore. It was loosened beneath the undone top button of his dress shirt. She had the sudden urge to crawl into his lap and trail kisses down his neck and taste him.

"Raise your eyes," the voice demanded.

Sophie drew a deep breath, letting air fill her, making her almost light-headed. And then she looked up.

Her heart leapt into her throat and her brain short-circuited.

Emery Lockwood, the object of her darkest fantasies, the ones she'd buried deep in her heart in the hours just before dawn, was looking down at her, predatory curiosity gleaming in his gaze. He trapped her with a magnetic pull, an air of mystery. She was caught in invisible strands of a spell woven around her body and soul.

The boy's soft angelic features were there, hidden beneath the surface of the man before her. He was the most devastatingly, sensual man she'd ever seen. His high cheekbones, full lips, and aquiline nose were all parts of the face of a man in his early thirties. But his eyes—the color of nutmeg and framed with long dark lashes any woman would kill to have—were the same as those of the wounded eight-year-old boy in her photo. Although she could see that they'd hardened with two decades of grief.

He was masculine perfection, except for the thin, almost invisible scar that ran the length of his sharp jaw line. Even after twenty-five years, he still bore the marks of his suffering. She ached with every cell in her body to press her mouth to his, to steal fevered kisses from his lips. Her fingertips tingled with the need to stroke over the scar on his face, to smooth away the hurt he must have endured.

"Do you know the rules of our game?" Emery asked. As he spoke, his gaze still held her in place, like a butterfly caught beneath a pin and encased in glass. Hands trembling, she pursed her lips and tried to remain calm and collected. It was nearly impossible. The heat of his intense regard only increased as the corners of his mouth curved in a slow, wicked smile. Oh, the man knew just how he affected her!

Emery leaned forward, caught her chin in his palm, and tilted her face up to look at him. Her skin burned deliciously where his palm touched her. He pulled her, like the moon calling to the tides, demanding devotion and obedience with the promise of something great, something she couldn't understand. Her senses hummed with eagerness, ready to explore his touch, his taste. Like a minnow caught in a vast current, she was pulled out to deeper waters, helpless to resist. In any other situation, she wouldn't have been so off balance, and wouldn't be letting herself get sucked into this strange game she sensed she was about to play. But here in this dark fantasy of the Gilded Cuff, she didn't want to look away from him.

"The rules are as follows: I give you a command, you obey. I have to make you come in less than two minutes. I cannot do more than stroke any part of your body covered by cloth—no touching between your legs and no touching of your bare breasts. You are to look into my eyes and do whatever I say so long as my commands are within the rules. If you come, I win; if you don't, Royce wins."

Sophie struggled to think clearly. There was no way she would have agreed to this anywhere else, but in the club, this was the sort of game the doms played…the sort of game Emery played, and he wanted to play with her. A shiver of desire shot through her, making her clit pulse. How could she refuse?

"Uh…permission to speak?"

"You will call me Sir, or Master Emery."

"Sir," Sophie corrected. She wanted to kick herself. She had read enough about this lifestyle that she should have remembered to address him formally, but in all honesty the way he was looking at her—like something he wanted to eat—she couldn't remain entirely rational.

"Permission to speak granted." Emery's voice dropped into a softer tone, approval warming his hazel eyes.

"What happens to me, Sir? Only one of you can win."

Royce shared a glance with Emery.

"She's a smart one, this little sub. Well, Emery? What do you think?"

Both men focused their intense gazes on her. It took everything in her not to look away.

"Punishment by the one who loses. But what form? Flogging?" Royce suggested.

Sophie flinched.

"No whips," Emery seemed to conclude, his eyes reading her tiniest reaction.

Emery ran a palm over his jaw, which was shadowed with night stubble. The look gave him a rugged edge, reminding her of the men back home in Kansas.

The tension in the crowd seemed to heighten as the subject of punishment continued. Emery continued to stare at her, his eyes seemingly unlocking the puzzle she presented. "She's new. Why not a spanking?" he murmured softly.

That caught her attention. Her clit thrummed to life, pulsing in a faint beat along with her heart. The twinge of uncomfortable pain in her knees was temporarily abated by this new distraction. Her eyes immediately settled on Emery's large, capable hands. She could practically feel the width of his palm striking her bottom...Trouble. She was in so much trouble.

"Definitely spanking." Emery smiled. "My favorite form of punishment. It will be a disappointment when you come in my arms, and I shall have to allow Royce the pleasure of laying his palm to your flesh."

"Cocky bastard," Royce retorted. "She might resist you. I bet she's far less submissive than she looks, and given her clothes, far too self-conscious to come in front of people. When I win, you'll owe me your best case of bourbon."

Her knees were aching, pain flaring like sharp little needles through her skin and deep into her bones. She shifted on them, trying to favor one over the other, and then hastily switched, but it didn't help. There was no way she was going to make it much longer on her knees.

Emery's hazel eyes lit up with the challenge. "Like hell! When she comes, and she will, you'll owe me your best case of scotch."

As the men continued to posture and argue, Sophie sat back on her heels, her knees aching something fierce. Like metal rods were jabbing up between her knees into her nerves.

Screw this. I'm getting up. Surging to her feet, she breathed a sigh of relief as blood flow pumped through her legs.

The people gathered around her gasped. Both men stopped arguing and turned to face her, gazes dark with anger. It wasn't the lethal sort of anger she'd come across before, not like the murderers she'd interviewed for her crime stories. That anger was a terrifying anger, pure hatred. It rolled off those criminals in waves. The kind of anger that truly good people never felt, it was the sort of rage that consumed the soul and blackened the heart until only a killing machine was left its place.

With Royce and Emery, however, it was merely the anger of a parent or a mentor at a charge who'd clearly disobeyed a direct order. She knew the outcome. Punishment. She could read it on their faces, and it aroused them both. Hell, it aroused her.

"You weren't given permission to rise." Emery spoke slowly, as though trying to decide whether he would give her a chance to apologize or to just skip straight to the punishment.

Even as she opened her mouth she knew it was a bad idea.

"My knees hurt. This isn't carpet; it's rock. *Hard* rock."

Emery's jaw dropped. The people around them stepped back.

Royce was silent for a long moment, and then burst into long, hooting laughter. He doubled over, palms on his thighs, as he struggled to catch his breath. "Damn, this is going to be fun."

"Fun," Emery muttered and shook his head. "Back on your knees, until we decide what to do with you."

"Yeah…no thank you, Sir." Sophie challenged. "I'll stay on my feet until you're done."

He was up and on his feet and before she could react he had turned her to face the crowd and bent her over.

Whack! His palm landed on her butt. The impact stung, but it faded almost instantly to a warm, achy feeling. Her legs turned to jelly and she trembled helplessly against a shocking wave of pleasure that began to build inside her abdomen.

The glare she launched in Emery's direction had no effect. When he released her and took his seat again, she spun to face him. His narrowed eyes shot her pulse into overdrive.

"You have a safe word, little sub?" Royce asked.

She wracked her brain for one, knowing it had to be something she could remember when she was panicking because it was the word that would get the doms to stop whatever they were doing if the interaction became too unbearable.

"Apricot," she decided. Being highly allergic to the fruit made it a word she wouldn't forget easily.

Her unusual choice of safe word had both men raising their brows. In that instant they could have been brothers. They mirrored each other the way only true friends could. A pang of envious longing cut through Sophie's heart and she sucked in a breath as she thought of Rachel.

"What's your name, little sub?"

"Sophie Ryder." When his brows lowered she hastily added, "Sir."

Emery patted his thigh with one palm. "Let us begin the contest. You will come and sit on my lap and I will command you."

Sophie's stomach pitched so deep it felt like it hit her toes. Emery leaned back, his arms rested on the back of the couch. He looked every bit a prince, a leader of a pride of lions, merely waiting for his conquest, his prey. His relaxed position only made her feel more helpless. She knew he could move fast, catch her in his arms and have her bent for punishment again in seconds if she dared to resist him. Her nipples pearled beneath the unforgiving leather of the corset, rubbing until they ached. She clenched her hands to stop them from shaking.

Here we go, you can do this. Sophie approached him and sat across his lap. She wriggled, trying to find a comfortable position, unable to ignore the feel of his muscular thighs beneath her.

He cocked one eyebrow imperiously, as though her restlessness had somehow offended him.

"Do not *squirm*." He issued his first command.

She stilled instantly. Her only movement was her breasts rising and falling with her breaths.

"Look at my eyes, *only* my eyes." His tone softened, but the rough edge still scraped over her, making her hungry for the promise she found in his gaze. The voices around them faded and she slipped deeper and deeper into his dark spell.

He would be a rough lover; carnal, quiet. He wouldn't whisper sweet words, wouldn't utter harsh arousing statements. He'd simply take her, take her again and again, the grinding, the pounding. The soft silence punctuated by uneven breaths, the stroke of rough hands over her sensitive skin. Everything a sensible, modern woman shouldn't want from a man in bed. He'd be all animal in all the right ways.

She'd never been with someone like him before, might never be again, and the thought was an intoxicating one. To be at the mercy of such power, such electrifying sexual control and surrender it all to him…Her mouth was suddenly dry, her pulse tapping Morse code for help as she tried to maintain a semblance of calm. Would she be able to give in to him? To let him guide her through the dark lust that so often took hold of her when she had no way of releasing it? Yes…She could let go with him, and the uncertainty of what would happen when she did was half of the excitement that lit a fire in her veins.

His hands settled on her hips, fingers slowly stroking back and forth, teasing her skin beneath the leather mini-skirt. What would it be like to have his hands on her bare flesh? Fingers exploring between her legs.

"Tell me what you'd like, Sophie." Emery leaned his head down, his brow touching hers, eyes still locked on her face.

She gulped, her mouth dryer than the Gobi Desert.

"What would it take to make you lose control? Do you want a hard fuck? A desperate pounding? Or would you like to have your hands bound, lying facedown on a large bed, softness against your belly and my hardness above you, in you?" His erotic whispers were so soft, so low that no one nearby could hear what he was saying to her. The images he painted were wild, vivid, yet blurry—like a strange combination between Van Gogh and Monet. Sweet and sensual, then dark, exotic and barely comprehendible. Emery was an artist in his own way, an erotic painter of words and pictures.

"I'd take you slow, so slow you'd lose all sense of time. You'd focus only on me, on my cock gliding between your thighs, possessing you." His words were slow and deliberate, as though he'd given them years of thought, but the slight breathless quality to the whisper made her realize she was not the only one affected.

The first quiver between her thighs was inevitable. She shifted, restless on his legs, despite his command not to move.

His breath fanned her lips. "Oh, god," she murmured.

He smiled, unblinking, and licked his lips. She wanted that tongue in her mouth, tangling with her own. She craved his hands on her bare flesh.

"Please…" she moaned. He moved his hands down from her hips, to her outer thighs, barely exerting any real pressure. That made it worse. The hint of his touch, the promise of the pressure she craved. Sophie wanted him digging his fingers into her skin, holding her legs apart as he slammed deep into her.

"Take a deep breath," he issued another command.

She obeyed. Her heartbeat seemed to expand outward from her chest until the pulse pounded through her entire body so hard she swore he could feel it beat through her skin wherever he touched her. The throb between her thighs nearly stung now—her need so great, his effect so potent.

"When I take you, no matter the position, you will like it. I'll bend you over a couch." He stroked one finger on her outer thigh, made circular patterns. "I'll push you up against a wall."

With little panting breaths she wriggled, trying to rock her hips against his lap, but he held her still. She nearly screamed in frustration at being denied what her body frantically needed.

The finger moved higher, past her hip, up to her ribcage. "Spread and bound open on my bed." His fingertip quested up past the laces of her corset. "You'll twist and writhe, unable to get free. At my mercy, Sophie, my mercy. You will beg and when I'm ready, I will grant your every desire, just as I take mine."

She couldn't breathe. The orgasm was so close. She could feel it, like a shadow inside her body, breathing, panting, waiting to be set free. She was ready; she wanted to climax in his arms, wanted to forge that connection which would tie her to him. Terrifying, shocking, intimate, but damn if she didn't want it more than anything in the world at that moment. Wanted it more than her story, more than the interview, more than easing her pain from the past. She needed pleasure. His pleasure.

The feathering touch of his fingers, Emery's erotic murmurs now incoherent with breathless anticipation against her neck as they both strained toward the great cliff, eagerly craving the fall back to earth. Why wouldn't he touch her where she needed it? The slightest pressure on her inner thighs, the rhythmic stroke of his hand against her clit, anything would do it if he could only…

"Time!" Royce's triumphant call shattered the glass bubble that had cocooned them for the last two minutes. Murmurs of shock from the surrounding crowd broke through.

"Damn." Emery's eyes darkened. Anger, but not at her, flared at the lines of his mouth. He bent to press his lips against her ear. "You were close, weren't you, darling? So close I almost had you." His body was trembling beneath hers, the little movements wracking his arms and chest. The press of his arousal beneath her bottom far too evident. He'd been there, right alongside her, dying to come.

Together. And it hadn't happened for either of them; two minutes hadn't been enough time.

Sophie's legs shook as cold reality slashed through her. The climax her body had been prepared to give Emery faded away. In its wake little tremors reverberated along her limbs, made worse by the tension in her entire body that hadn't found release. She tried to breathe, to let her shoulders drop and her muscles relax. It was going to take a while to come down from this.

Almost had her? No. He definitely had her, practically wrapped up with a bow on top, totally and completely his. No question.

Chapter 3

THE KITCHEN IS NOW THE OFFICIAL CRIME SCENE WHERE THE ABDUCTION IS BELIEVED TO HAVE OCCURRED. THE CRIME SCENE WAS LITTERED WITH BROKEN COKE BOTTLES, BLOOD, AND HALF-EATEN SANDWICHES ON THE BOYS' PLATES.

—*New York Times*, June 10, 1990

So, my best case of bourbon?" Emery raised his face to look at Royce, who stood in front of the couch.

"If you don't mind." Royce's eyes twinkled with devilish merriment, but he clapped a palm on Emery's shoulder with gentle camaraderie. "I'll be by the house later to pick it up."

"I'll have it ready for you," Emery assured him, and then turned his attention back to Sophie. "Now, little sub, let's see about that punishment."

A sensuous light flickered at the back of his eyes, like a lighthouse's beacon fighting to shine through the depths of a storm. Every emotion—a thousand of them—shuttered and then exploded behind his gaze. To Sophie it felt as if she was seeing the entire world captured in one rapid blink...and then it was gone. His eyes were heavy with desire and nothing else.

Oh dear. "I…uh…" How inadequate words were! What could she say to persuade him against punishing her?

Emery rose from the couch in a fluid movement with Sophie still clasped in his arms. She had only a moment to marvel that her weight didn't seem to bother him at all before he was carrying her through the group of people. There was a door ajar halfway down one of the halls that branched off the center room. He nudged it open with his foot. It was completely empty save for a thick rug spanning the entire room and a wooden piece of furniture that she knew from her research was a spanking bench.

At the sight of the bench Sophie went rigid; her limbs locked up, her hands balled into fists. Only a sliver of her panic came from fear. The rest of her wanted to know too badly how it felt to be bent over that, with his hand smacking her ass until she cried out. *That* scared her: how much she wanted to experience something so dark and sinful. Emery set her down and started to close the door. He left it open about an inch or two. Someone could come in, could get to her if she needed help. Still…Sophie shot a glance at the bench. There was no way in hell she was going to bend over that and…and…let herself go with him. She'd never been able to do that with anyone and she couldn't start with someone like him. He was tall, blond, and brooding. She'd make a fool of herself if she gave in to him. What would he think of her if she got aroused by a punishment? That she was just like any other woman in the club? The thought stopped her cold.

She didn't want to be just another woman to him. She wanted to be something more; she wanted him to trust her, to open up to her. Letting him spank the hell out of her might not be the best way to earn his trust…

Then again, maybe it would.

I wish I knew what I was doing. She cursed inwardly. With men, she was always awkward and unsure of herself, and now her typical failings seemed magnified because he affected her too strongly.

"Look, I'm sorry, but this whole scene just isn't for me. I shouldn't have come here." She edged toward the door. Maybe if she got far enough from the bench, he'd forget about punishing her and she could talk to him about the abduction. If he thought she was scared enough to leave, he might back off in his determination to spank her and she'd have her chance to speak.

Emery sidestepped, blocking her access to the exit. She saw the outline of well-defined muscles; he was much bigger and stronger than she was. To her sheer humiliation, something inside her started to purr with delight at the thought of that strength and size directed at her, for her protection and more importantly, her pleasure.

He placed a hand on the side of her neck where it connected to her shoulder. His thumb moved slowly back and forth against the base of her throat, as though questing for the frantic drum of her pulse. His lips moved, flirting at the tips with a smile.

She couldn't take much more of this. If she didn't get away, she'd let him take her over to that bench and she'd surrender to him. That couldn't happen.

"Please, let me leave." Her tone, thankfully, sounded stronger than the whimpering inside her which begged to stay, to let him bend her over the bench and do wicked things to her.

"If you want out, say your safe word." His sharp tone was edged with a challenge. Something deep inside her responded.

She knew enough of D/s relationships to know that subs weren't powerless; surrendering to a dom was their choice, one that had to be based on trust. Emery's challenge for her to surrender was tempting, too tempting if she was honest with herself. She'd never wanted to surrender to a man, but the idea of willingly letting one overpower her? Her thighs clenched together, her sensitive nerves inside jumping to life. Could she give in? Gain power by giving him power?

"I'm waiting for your answer."

When Sophie hesitated, Emery threaded his fingers through the black satin ribbons that laced the front of her corset. He tugged one bow's string with careless ease, so at odds with the cool, dispassionate expression on his face as he began to loosen the laces and peel her corset apart. A haze of heat settled over her skin and fogged her mind. Sophie prayed he'd keep going, would pull her corset open like they were in some torrid romance novel, and bend his head to her breasts to…

His fingers caressed the tip of the folded up photo. She jolted back, the memory of where she'd tucked his photo slamming into her. He couldn't see it; he'd never understand. Emery's hand shot out, caught her wrists, and lifted them above her head. In a move as smooth as the steps of a slow dance, he maneuvered her back against the wall by the door. One thick, muscled thigh pressed between hers, and he kept her wrists trapped above her. His other hand moved back to her corset, dipped between her breasts and retrieved the photo. His thumb and index finger deftly unfolded it and the wide-eyed interest of natural curiosity on his face morphed to an expression of narrowed suspicion.

He released her wrists, stepped back several feet and stared at the image in his hand. He was so still he could have been carved from marble — his eyes dark with horror, his tanned skin now alabaster white.

A long moment later he drew a deep measured breath and raised his eyes to hers.

"Where did you get this picture?" Each word seemed dragged out between his clenched teeth. He changed before her eyes, the prince transforming into a beast. Wounded rage filled his eyes, morphing with the promise of vengeance.

The pit of her stomach seemed to have dropped out. She felt as if she was falling, that awful sensation of losing control, of being seconds away from a sickening crash. This was what she'd come to talk about, come to warn him about, and she wasn't ready. It would hurt him to drag this out in the open again and she wasn't prepared, not after the way they'd been so close just seconds before. The truth was, she didn't want to lose him, not this sexy, addictive man. And she would lose him if she brought up the past. Like all victims he'd retreat into himself and pull away from her even as she tried to help him.

"The newspaper," Sophie replied breathlessly.

Emery continued to stare at her, his long elegant fingers curling around the photo, crumpling it. "Why do you have a picture of me from twenty-five years ago?" When Sophie opened her mouth he waved a hand at her. "Think carefully how you answer, Ms. Ryder. I'm not above lawsuits, and I have a very, very good lawyer."

Sophie bit her lip, tasted a drop of blood and licked at the sore spot before she replied. She'd only rehearsed this a thousand times yet now she didn't know where to begin.

"I wanted to be able to recognize you, because I wanted to interview you. I'm a freelance investigative journalist. I specialize in crime stories, primarily those about kidnappings." She knew she'd made a mistake the moment the words left her mouth. She felt incredibly small in that moment, like a mouse cornered in a lion's cage. Should she have started with the part where she thought his life was in danger? That would've made her sound crazy, and she needed his trust more than anything.

Emery's eyes turned dark as wood that had been consumed by flames and burnt to ash.

"You people are all the same." His tone was deadly calm. Quiet. The hand holding the photo started to shake. His fingers clenched so tightly that his knuckles whitened. The shaking spread outward; his shoulders visibly vibrated with his rage.

Sophie sucked in a breath. He wasn't withdrawing…He was going to lash out. The oppressive wave of guilt that cut off her air warred with a new, unexpected apprehension. This looked bad, she knew it. The sneaky reporter trying to get the scoop on a story that defined this man's worst moment in his life. God, she'd been an idiot to think she could waltz in here and start chatting about his kidnapping.

Goosebumps rippled along her bare arms and her muscles tensed. Despite the anger she could feel rolling off him in waves, he seemed to rein in that silken thread of self-control and loosened his fingers. The photo stayed crinkled in a tight ball, completely destroyed. When she swallowed, it felt like knives sliced her throat.

Emery spoke again, much to Sophie's dread. "Invade my life, my privacy. You know nothing of what I've endured or what happened to me and my…" the words faded but Sophie sensed he nearly said "brother."

Her eyes burned with a sudden rush of tears. His pain was so clear on his face, and it made her think of herself, of the way she felt when she thought of Rachel.

"Mr. Lockwood—" She had to explain, to show him she only wanted to help.

He threw the crumpled photo at her feet. He might as well have slapped her. Would he be more willing to listen if he knew she was here to save him? But how could she get him to listen long enough to explain everything?

Summoning her strength, she stepped toward him. "But you survived. I think people want to know the truth, know how strong you are." Why couldn't he see what a miracle his escape was? He'd survived a horrific experience and was stronger, stronger than she was. Losing Rachel had destroyed her innocence and shattered her world.

A ruthless laugh broke from his lips. "Strong? Strong?" He shook his head from side to side, a wild smile splitting his face suddenly. "I'm strong now. I *wasn't* strong then. If I had been strong, Fenn would be here." When his eyes grew hollow Sophie realized how much that admission must have cost him. He blamed himself for whatever had happened to his brother, thought Fenn Lockwood's death was his fault. And she'd played right into reinforcing his delusion that an eight-year-old boy should have been able to stop kidnappers. That was ludicrous.

"At least you're here. You're alive and you have a good life." The words were hollow; Sophie didn't know what else to say so she repeated what her therapist had told her years ago, after Rachel was taken.

"It's a half-life, nothing more." Emery's soft utterance cut open her soul. He understood, felt the same way she did, if not more.

She'd poured her heart into what little life she felt she had left, but it wasn't enough to fill the empty space where Rachel should have been. She couldn't imagine what it must be like for Emery to have lost his twin. A sibling, a person he'd shared a womb with, had been raised alongside for eight years. Whatever had been between them had been destroyed, one life ended, the other haunted.

"I'm not going to agree to an interview. Your homework should've told you that. Now if you'll excuse me, I've had enough of the club tonight."

Sophie's heart cracked down the middle. She'd failed. But there was more to it—the loss of something else, something deeper and infinitely more important: his trust. She'd never met this man before today, didn't fully trust her, yet she hated that she'd let him down, abused what little trust he'd started to give her. It was like losing him, even though she sensed he'd never belong to anyone. He seemed so distant, buried beneath the past and that made him dangerous. A wildness emanated from him that made him seem like the sort of a man a woman couldn't own, couldn't claim, not matter how hard she wanted to or tried to. Her grandmother used to say you could never harness the wind.

Foolish woman that she was, Sophie just had to try. She waited a breathless moment that seemed to hang on the edge of forever. He needed her to submit to him; he needed the control between them. She could give it to him, right now, even if it was only temporary.

"Mr. Lockwood, please." Guided by some instinct, she grabbed his hand and fell to her knees at his feet, head bowed. "Please…" She knew the second his gaze shifted to her. The hairs on the back of her neck rose, her skin prickled, and arousal flooded through her, making her damp, and her breathing shallow. Even though he was upset with her, his focus heated her blood.

There was a long pause before he spoke. "Please, what?" Emery's voice was dom-like—cool, calm, commanding, not hard or biting like moments before. He shifted his feet, angling his body toward her—a few inches only, but it was enough to show she was getting through to him again. There might still be a chance.

She swallowed thickly. "Please, Sir."

"And what do you request of me?" He pulled the hand that she clutched free of her grasp, but moved it to the crown of her hair, stroking. His palm moved down to her neck, fingers threading and pulling tightly enough to make her arch her back to ease the pressure. It forced her face upward, and she had to look into his eyes. He stood over her now, his towering posture not threatening but completely dominating. She didn't cower but kept herself submissive, giving him what he needed.

No one understood. No one knew the agonizing grip of pain at losing someone you loved. But Emery did. And she wanted him to talk to her, to tell her how he'd survived with a broken heart. But when he turned to look at her, eyes so full of echoing pain, she came to a realization. He wasn't stronger, at least not in this. He was just as wounded as she. They were both lost. He without his brother, she without Rachel. Lives taken from them that could never come back. Memories tarnished by other men's evil, leaving them with nothing more than a child's fear of loss and death.

She didn't think he could give her the answers she needed. But he could give her the story, provide the details which might give her enough information to solve who was behind his kidnapping. She was so close to figuring it out. She could catch whoever was responsible and prevent them from harming Emery or anyone else ever again. It would have to be enough.

"I want your help to make the monster who did this to you pay. He's still out there. You know that." She paused, licking her lips. "And he could come after you again. It's why you've kept bodyguards and security high for the last twenty-five years," she guessed. Her reports always showed the same man shadowing Emery the few times he'd been photographed outside his home.

Emery's lips pursed into a thin line and his brows drew down over his eyes, which were more the color of chocolate-kissed honey now.

"You think you can catch a man who's eluded police and the FBI?"

Her heart jolted. He'd just admitted his captor had been a man. The reports said three masked men, but he made it sound like only one man was involved. What had happened to the other two? More puzzle pieces shifted.

"I'm a skilled reporter. I've focused on criminal stories for years, Sir. If you let me, I can use whatever you tell me to solve the case. I *know* I can." She prayed he'd hear the sincerity and resolve in her tone. She meant every word. She'd protect him and catch the bastard who'd hurt him. As penance for Rachel. As penance for every child she couldn't save.

He seemed to consider her request.

"What would you do for me in return?" His eyes promised he meant something sexual. Something that might shatter her lonely world into pieces and leave her craving him for the rest of her life.

"D-do for you?" Sophie stuttered. That was becoming an irritating habit she needed to fix. The man had the ability to tie her in knots when he got her thinking of other things besides her job.

"I'm a dom, darling. Your needs should involve me, and your thoughts should be about what I need and want. If I am nice and give you what you need, you must give me something in return. And no...I'm not talking about money or anything as trivial as that. My story, as you call it, is worth something beyond money. I will need something just as important from you in return."

She hesitated. What could she give him? She had nothing to offer. Nothing but...herself. She could give herself to him. A scolding voice in her head warned her that it would be a devil's bargain. But she silenced the voice. Damn the consequences; her body wanted him. Never had she crossed a line before, never had she wanted to. She was tired of being the good girl, tired of playing it safe. The hint of danger and the thrill of dark passion in Emery's eyes was an escape, one she needed more than her next breath.

"I'll give you anything. Name it and it's yours. I came here knowing what to expect." She threw a glance around the room, eyes touching briefly on the spanking bench before settling back on him.

He chuckled and brushed the pad of one thumb over her lips. "That's a dangerous offer." His hand dropped to her neck, his fingers curling around her throat, the touch a warning, but he didn't hurt her.

"What if I demand you strip completely and I tie you to a St. Andrews cross and fuck you senseless? Or if I require you to walk through the main room and accept any intimate touch another dom wishes to give you? Would you agree to that? There are a thousand things I could ask of you that would not just push your limits but break them. You were spooked at the sight of one little bench, and that tells me everything I need to know. You may have studied domination and submission, but you haven't lived it. The importance of this particular lifestyle is that one must always be safe, sane and consensual. Your offer shows no consideration for any of those, and half the doms outside would do things you might not consent to. You have natural submissive tendencies. It's clear from the way you responded to my commands, but we aren't in a vanilla sex world, Sophie. While this life demands trust, it is a dark world, full of fire, passion, loss of control. Are you truly ready for that?" The bite to his tone made her arousal sharp; her womb clenched in eagerness, even as she felt a cold sweat dew on her body as trepidation set in.

Sophie breathed deeply. He'd warned her, hadn't just accepted her blanket offer. *Trust*. Even as scary as what he'd mentioned sounded, she also longed for a taste of that forbidden passion. She was hungry for it. But she needed to trust him in return.

"Would you really do those things?" She glanced away then forced her eyes back. He was watching her, the way a hawk at the tallest branches of a tree might survey a rabbit in the field below. Yet he was close, so incredibly close to her he could have kissed her.

With a sigh, Emery shook his head. "Absolutely, unless of course that fell within your hard limits. I'm not a saint, and I have only the semblance of being a gentleman, but I would respect your safe word. Sharing my bed would push you right to the edge of your limits. Lucky for you, I'm in no mood to bed a woman who inherently denies her submissive nature."

"You think I'm a real submissive?" Sophie could hear the shock in her own voice. Was she truly? More importantly, could she trust him to keep his word and respect her safe word if she needed to use it?

"You are submissive. To the right man, you are. When I held you in my arms and commanded you to focus only on me, you did it without hesitation, without question. You submitted to me and it was a beautiful thing to behold. You're too strong for most, but you still crave submission. Being a sub doesn't mean you're weak. It only means you need to surrender. Many weak people crave power, crave to hurt others, to take control, but they are still inherently weak individuals."

Sophie knew that was the truth. She had met killers and murderers—pathetic examples of humanity. They were too weak to stand up for themselves when it mattered, and the resulting loss of power or control turned them toward paths of violent retribution on innocents. Such behavior was more common than it should be.

A sudden thought struck her. "What if...I let you teach me how to surrender?"

Curiosity flitted shadowlike in his eyes, but his wariness was stronger.

"I'm not sure I come out on top in this bargain. You might prove to be too much trouble." Emery moved over to the spanking bench and sat down on the edge, seemingly unbothered by its real purpose. Sophie's face heated with a treacherous blush.

It should have surprised her how much she did want to please him. He seemed an intricate puzzle and knowing her behavior was a partial key; she couldn't help but wonder what doing his bidding would unlock.

He leaned back, crossing his legs at the ankles, and looked at her. She was still on her knees, hands clenched together, fingers knotted. Sophie studied him, traced the perfectly tailored suit that clung to his body like a second skin. He was every inch the rich recluse she'd heard him to be.

People spoke of him in sad whispers, their eyes full of pity. But when Sophie met Emery's gaze, she couldn't pity him. Sympathize? Yes. Pity? No. His expression of domination demanded obedience, respect, and not one second had passed where he'd let that expression falter, except when he'd stared at the picture from his past. Only then had she seen the other Emery, the one trapped in childhood memories. The one she had to save. For that was clear. Part of this man before her needed to be saved.

"I'm not sure bedding you is worth my tale of woe." His tone sounded almost taunting, rather like he was reciting Shakespeare. He was mocking her!

Embarrassment flooded her face with heat, but her pride was pricked. Without a second thought she slipped off one shoe and threw it at him.

Thunk! It bounced off the solid wall of his muscular chest and dropped to the floor. He didn't move an inch except to drop his eyes to the shoe, and then raise his gaze again. She could feel it passing over her body as he did so.

"You just threw a shoe at me." His eyes flashed fire, but his lips twitched.

"Yeah? Well, you just implied I'm not good in bed!" Muttering to herself, she bent to remove her second shoe, wanting nothing more than to chuck that one at him too. She was completely unprepared for his reaction.

One second she had her hand on her remaining shoe, the next he'd spun her around to face the wall, his body pressing tight against hers from behind. Both her wrists were caught in one of his hands at her lower back. He rolled his hips, rubbing against her bottom, grinding a very hard erection against her miniskirt. Emery put his free hand on her stomach, his large palm making her feel incredibly small.

"You have an unusual way of expressing your temper." His low growl summoned deep shivers from the base of her spine. "Some doms like to paddle that temper out of their subs, then they pound the sub into delicious submission until the sub is dying of pleasure." He punctuated this with a sharp arch of his hips again. Her clit throbbed and her breath quickened.

Images rose in her mind—him dragging her skirt up to her waist, tearing away underwear and taking her hard from behind. Sophie jerked when her knees smacked together and she wobbled. Emery held her upright, rubbing her stomach, the pressure arousing rather than soothing.

"Don't tell me I've struck you speechless." His husky laugh was rich as scotch and burned her to the core.

He nuzzled her ear, then nipped at it. An explosion went off somewhere below her waist and Sophie sucked in a breath. Her blood pounded in her ears, and a dark mist seemed to roll across her vision as she sank into him and his teasing kisses and touches.

"I'm having trouble…thinking," she admitted through the fog that seemed to curl around the logical part of her mind. All she could focus on was his breath on her cheek, his tongue flicking inside her ear and the stinging jabs of arousal that spiked though her lower spine and zoomed straight to her clit. She was empty, and needed something inside her, needed him. Her body actually hurt with the wild craving to have him. All it would take was his thrusting into her softness and giving it to her hard enough, and she'd die from the pleasure.

"You respond well to me. Perhaps you are worth a few nights." He licked a path up from her shoulder to a spot beneath her ear, and then feathered kisses before blowing softly on the now sensitive shell of her ear. Her hands shook violently in his hold.

Then he was gone. He'd released her and stepped back. Sophie fell forward a few inches, her body resting against the wall as she fought to regain her composure. The stone against her cheek was cool and slightly rough, like the craggy rocks of a castle's keep. It lent a dungeonlike atmosphere to their sparse surroundings, more than chains and whips and other objects might have. She was at his mercy, his to torture or to pleasure, or perhaps a combination. Her clit pulsed to life at the thought of both.

"Very well. Unlace your corset."

The command was so abrupt that Sophie balked instantly. There was no way she'd do that, and it didn't have anything to do with modesty.

"You can't obey a simple command?" One golden brow arched over his eye.

"It's not that I don't want to obey…"

"Are you plagued by modesty?" His lips tilted down, but a glimmer of amusement danced briefly across his face.

"I'm not plagued, I'm naturally modest. But that's not why I can't unlace the corset."

Emery sighed and crossed his arms. "I suppose I'll give you one easy out today. Tell me why you won't open your corset and I will release you of the command to actually unlace it. Can you do that without issue?"

"Just tell you?" She could do that, couldn't she?

"For now. Someday you will show me." He raised one hand to his hair, raking his fingers through it, mussing the blond waves. It made her ache to do the same. To lie beside him in bed and know that she mussed up his hair, that she had grasped the thick shimmering strands and tugged while in the midst of passion.

"I don't like delays, Sophie," he warned.

Swallowing a shivery breath, she nodded, more for herself than him. "I've got scars." There. It was out. No going back.

"What kind of scars?" Emery's voice was soft, velvety, like he wanted to soothe her.

His question confused her.

"Scars. There isn't any other kind."

Emery's eyes trained on her. "I mean, are they scars from abuse? From an accident?"

"No abuse. Surgery."

"What did you have surgery for?"

"Explaining that isn't part of the bargain," Sophie replied. She'd agreed to submit, not tell him her every secret.

Emery stood up and left the bench to come toward her. He moved so fast she had no time to react. He snatched her wrists and dragged her over to the bench, bending her over it and spreading her knees with one thigh. He pulled her wrists back behind her body and pinned them there with one of his hands. When he pushed his leg up against the apex of her thighs beneath the skirt she whimpered. The soft, expensive fabric of his suit rubbed erotically against the sensitive skin of her thighs.

"Lesson one: Never lie to your dom, or any dom. Punishment is always the result, or worse, the dom severs the relationship and releases the sub. Now, let's try this again. What was the surgery for?"

"All right!" Sophie hissed. She was madder than a wet cat, but she knew he had her beat. Still, she jerked and jostled against the bench, testing his hold. Tight. No way to get out of this.

"Stop." His bark made her flinch and go slack. "Tell the truth. I have ways of making you talk if you think to keep quiet."

Did he mean he'd spank it out of her? She wish she knew, then again, maybe she didn't want to know. Her eyelashes fell against her cheeks and darkness captured her vision, thankfully making her feel alone enough to utter the truth. "I had an accident and got cut. The surgery was to sew the cuts back together. Is that a personal enough answer for you?" She flinched, waiting for a blow.

"I didn't want a personal answer, only a truthful one. And I don't *ever* beat answers of anyone, especially a sub who surrenders to my care." Although his words suggested a chastisement, he didn't seem angry, rather puzzled and hurt that she'd assumed he'd beat it out of her.

"How did you know I was afraid you would hit me?" she whispered.

"You flinched after you lashed out verbally. I've seen that before in other submissives. You expected me to spank you, but know this, I don't ever react with violence, only with erotic punishment. There is a difference and I will teach you."

Very slowly, he withdrew his leg from between her thighs and released her wrists. Sophie lay for a moment, unsure of what to do. But rather than standing, Emery sat on the floor and reached for her. He took her in his arms and laid her on the floor beside him. Sophie gasped as he settled over her. If she hadn't been so distracted by his close proximity she might have laughed. Emery Lockwood did not strike her as the type of man to prefer the missionary position.

But Sophie was distracted; he invaded her space, gently took hold of her wrists again and secured them to the floor above her head. He slid one hand down her ribs, over her belly and then between her knees, parting them so his hips could sink into the cradle of her legs. He rocked his pelvis forward, rubbing against her, showing her she couldn't shift, couldn't move unless he wished her to.

It had been ages since she'd been this close to a man, with every inch of their bodies touching except their lips, and his were so temptingly close. The last time hadn't affected her like this. Her universe was shrinking around this one single moment, to just the two of them. Their gazes locked.

"This is personal. My past is personal, Sophie. Everything you want from me and what I want from you is personal." His free hand slid up from her hip to rest on her lower ribcage. He toyed with the loose ribbon of her corset. She could feel him tug, tease, but not undo the laces any further. Still, he could if he wished; he could pry the corset open and see her scars, her ugliness.

Sophie's breath hitched, her breasts rising rapidly as she struggled to breathe.

Concern darkened his eyes. "You're like a frightened little sparrow, your chest heaving as you beat against the cat's paw holding you down. *Relax*, Sophie," he murmured. "Otherwise I might lose my already tenuous control. As a dom, I am aroused by your apprehension. I love bringing a woman to the fine edge between trust and fear. I'd never hurt you, but still I'm determined to push your boundaries, test your limits, and I know that scares you just as much as it arouses you." His once silky tone was now gruff and a little ragged.

The truth of his words was like a whip cracking in her mind, more sharp and agonizing than anything she'd ever felt on her skin.

Sophie bucked her hips, trying to dislodge him. "Damn you!" His large erection dug into her, making her womb throb.

As though he could sense her rising need and frustration, Emery's eyes swirled with lust and hunger.

"So you have scars and they upset you," he observed.

She raised her chin, glowering at him. "Well, it's humiliating. Men don't like my…my…." To her own shame, her voice wavered.

"They don't like your breasts?" The sheer look of incredulity on his face startled her.

"Uh huh." Sophie shut her eyes, shame smashing her insides like a sledgehammer through fine china.

God, let this humiliation be over quickly. Every other man had left her alone after hearing this. Emery wouldn't be any different. He was too sexy, too gorgeous to ever settle for a scarred woman like her, not when he could have his pick.

Emery held still, didn't make a sound or move until she opened her eyes. When she did finally look up at him, he dropped his head a few inches, his nose touching hers, nuzzling her cheek.

"I'm not like other men, Sophie. Scars are a sign of strength, survival. Someday you'll be brave enough to show me, and I'll prove you have nothing to be ashamed of. Now, I am willing to accept the deal you proposed. Are you willing in return?"

She bit her lip. It had been her idea; she had to see it through. She wanted to see it through, even if it scared the living daylights out of her.

"Yes. I'll do it. Your story, my submission."

Chapter 4

AUTHORITIES ARE CONVINCED THE STRUGGLE
BETWEEN THE NANNY AND THE ABDUCTORS
OCCURRED IN THE KITCHEN. FRANCESCA
ESPINA SUFFERED SEVERE INJURIES FROM A
HEAD WOUND DEALT BY ONE OF THE
KIDNAPPERS.

—*New York Times*, June 10, 1990

He kissed her with raw possession, his mouth showing her how wicked it would be between them. Wild, dark, and completely free. She wanted that more than anything, the freedom to let go, to give in to the erotic dreams she'd spent years ignoring but never had felt safe enough to give in to before. His kiss broke down every barrier, obliterated every part of herself she tried to hide. Sophie lifted her chin, offering him her mouth, pleading for him. Emery drew a quick breath, eyes widening before his lashes fell to half-mast, his gaze drawn to her lips.

When he took her lips, he dominated her with the depth of his claiming. She breathed him in, like drawing the first heavy breath upon waking from a thousand-year sleep. Sophie came alive in that single moment. The woman she'd been all these years since losing Rachel, the scared little girl fighting against the evils in the world, was gone. In her place was the woman she'd always wanted to be, a woman not afraid to live her life. She couldn't shut this man out like she had her other friends or her family. No. He demanded she give in to him. Electric tingles pulsed outward from the places they touched, setting her senses on fire, fogging her mind. His kiss consumed her—enveloping her until she was lost, set adrift in a haze of desire, longing, and aching.

She felt his mouth tremble against hers; he seemed to strain to keep his possession under control, to bank the fires of his passion. His tongue slipped between her lips, thrusting in time with the rocking of his hips against hers in tiny circles. He gave up his control and took her over. His body weighed hers down, his hips rocking into hers. He could have done anything to her in that moment, and she'd have agreed to it. Sophie's inner muscles clenched, empty and wet, yearning for him, but it was his kiss that was her downfall—almost brutal with craving, as though he was a thirsty man savoring his first sip of water from her mouth. All his focus, all his energy seemed to be on her, on her lips.

He tore his mouth from hers, panting roughly. He cursed savagely and withdrew his hands from her body. She blinked in surprise when she realized his hot hands had slid up her outer thighs beneath the mini-skirt. Her chest heaved, her breasts dangerously close to escaping the confines of her corset. Emery's eyes slowly tracked down from her mouth to her breasts. With a rakish grin he pressed his mouth lightly on the tops of the creamy swells, his tongue darting out as he licked and nibbled a path back up to her lips. He paused, then feathered his lips at the corner of her mouth and brushed his nose against hers playfully.

Sophie whimpered at the loss when he finally drew his head back. It felt like good-bye, but that was foolish; she'd only just met him and agreed to surrender to him. They couldn't be done.

Emery sighed, his breath uneven against her temple. His body stiffened above hers.

"Go home, Sophie. Forget me, this place. Let it be a peculiar dream, nothing more. I'm not the man for you." His voice was harsh.

"No," she whispered fiercely, but she wasn't as sure of herself as she had been. She'd expected a spanking, some rough kissing. She hadn't expected to feel so vulnerable and exposed by a man taking control of her body and owning her completely in a mere few minutes.

"You think you can really survive this lifestyle for even one minute? You're vanilla, sweetheart. You wouldn't ever let me tie you up and take you the thousand ways I'd like to. You'd cry when my hand came down on your ass in punishment. You're not ready for this."

She shook her head, furiously fighting off the swell of tears as her throat constricted. He and he alone had offered her what her secret dreams and longings had called for night after night. The phantom lovers that had tormented her to the brink of violent need in her dreams could never compare to the very real and very heavy weight of his body on hers at that moment. The devastation of that perfect kiss couldn't be undone. The story could wait…but the *need*…the desperation to feel alive again…she couldn't let go of that, not yet.

"No. Take me home with you." She paused, calculating each word. "*Please*, Sir." She was begging. There was no doubt about it for either of them, and as shocked as she was by her own impulse to beg, she prayed he'd let her go with him.

Emery's lips twisted into a crooked smile. For a moment, she saw the boy in him, the one he'd been before his world had been utterly destroyed. The child wasn't gone, wasn't dead. Buried yes, but not dead. He threaded a hand through his hair and remained silent for moment. Shadows of doubt and indecision danced across his face before he finally replied.

"How can I resist?" Emery lifted himself and hauled her to her feet.

Sophie winced. Her back was bruised after lying on the stone floor beneath him. She hadn't minded at the time—her body had been distracted by a thousand other things. But now her shoulder blades and hips screamed in protest. Emery took her into his arms, rubbing her back, massaging it with knowing hands.

"Come, I'll summon my driver."

"Okay." She tried to remain calm. She was going home with Emery Lockwood. One of the richest men in America. Yet it wasn't his wealth that made her fight off the rippling tremors at the base of her spine and in her womb. No, it was the fact that she was going home with a man who kissed her like she was the last woman on earth and time was ending. If he kissed like that, sex with him would be the Apocalypse. She'd never survive it.

* * *

What the hell am I doing? Emery held the little journalist's hand trapped between his. They were seated in the backseat of his black Mercedes while his bodyguard, Hans Brummer, drove them back to Lockwood Manor, his childhood home.

His parents had long since abandoned the house, but not him. He'd wanted to leave but couldn't. Something kept him there, like a tree with deep roots. He couldn't live, couldn't breathe anywhere else. He was bound to the soil of the estate as much as the trees that lined the mile-long drive leading up to the house. It was his castle, his fortress against the harsh world, and yet he was bringing Sophie inside. A journalist with the intent to expose his soul. He really was a fool to let her in. What would she think when she saw the endless empty rooms and dark halls? Would she wonder if he was the same deep inside? He didn't want to be empty, but a sinister, creeping fear warned him that he might be after all these years. What was a twin without his other half? Incomplete. A woman would never want half of a man, not a woman like Sophie.

He'd never dared to bring a woman home before, had never wanted to. There was something about Sophie that made him want to risk everything even though there was every chance that she'd turn her back on him or betray him. She was a journalist after all. Telling stories was what they did best, often at others' expense. He hadn't forgotten that she'd claimed she could save him and solve the kidnapping. It didn't need solving. He knew the man who'd taken him, would never forget that face for as long as he lived. But he was curious to know what this intrepid little creature thought she could show him about the past.

"We're almost there." He rubbed his thumb on Sophie's palm, reveling in her responding tremor.

She was unpredictable. He'd spent years avoiding people in her line of work, but there was something irresistible about Sophie. The way she'd defended herself, tried to hide her weaknesses as she met him head on. But then she'd knelt at his feet and surrendered herself to earn his trust. On some level she was submissive, but she was also a warrior, not a timid mouse. Earning complete trust and surrender from such an equal would be a sweet prize, one he had to taste again soon or he'd go mad.

That dangerous kiss. He shouldn't have done it, shouldn't have given in to his need so soon, but he was unable to deny her offering. She'd raised her lips and he'd just taken them. Her kiss heated him, like the first step on hot sand after months of winter. The pleasure of the heat, the scorching blaze, barely controlled and yet incredibly soft for all its intensity.

"Oh my god." Sophie sat up on the edge of the seat, peering through the car's windshield to see where they were headed.

The headlights struck the black wrought-iron gates of the entrance to Lockwood. Hans tapped a small device on the visor above and the latticework of the iron broke apart to allow them passage. A gravel drive cut a white path through the well-manicured lawns. Trees loomed along the road's path, just visible at the edge of the beams from the Mercedes' headlights, lining the drive like walls of brown steel. Even at night the sight was impressive beneath the bright moon's glow.

The house was still a ways off, but the moonlight accented the columns of white marble, while its red brick blended into the night. Hans guided the car up the drive that curved around to the back entrance of the house. No servant waited for them. Emery kept the house empty; a cleaning crew came in once a week to take care of the necessities. He preferred the house empty, empty as his heart. It was a fitting punishment, after all these years. He allowed the specters of those golden days to seep out of the walls and haunt him with the sound of his brother's laughter, the sunny remembrances of hours spent in the gardens playing the games only children could dream up.

Emery's eyes traced the night breeze as it rippled through the thick ivy that crawled up the brick walls. Like a lady's evening gown stirred on the dance floor during a gentle waltz, the house's walls seemed to shiver and roll with the light wind. The house was a ghost, a shell of its former glory in so many ways. Even though he'd updated the plumbing, and electricity and given it an impressive security system, it didn't feel the same. Not since…then. Emery shut his eyes as a headache swamped him.

A low husky laugh. The burn of scotch in his throat. The strains of a country song teased his ears.

"Hans, turn off the radio," he said, and opened his eyes.

"It's not on, sir." His guard raised his gaze in the rearview mirror and met Emery's stare.

"Oh, right." He fought off a wave of dizziness and confusion. Sometimes he got headaches, sometimes not, but every so often he seemed to slip somewhere else. He was pretty sure he was going crazy—probably all the strain of running his father's company, among other things. There was also the stress from his nightmares. He never left his back exposed to an open door. The doctors said he suffered from some form of PTSD. Maybe he did. After everything he'd…

Emery shook his head, jostling the unsettling thoughts and memories, shoving them into the dark box inside his head and locking them up. The sense of otherness, the awareness of that external part of himself he could have sworn died twenty-five years ago, faded. The clean scent of trees wet with recent rain filled him and he drew a breath upon the cool air, letting it clear his head.

"It's so beautiful." Sophie seemed unaware of the dark path his thoughts had traveled. She pressed a palm against the window, peering out at the monolithic home. She unknowingly teased him with the close proximity of her body. It took every ounce of control not to drag her into his arms and claim her with the hunger that gnawed at him.

Emery wasn't looking at the house, but at her. She had a luscious figure: wide hips, a trim waist, muscled legs and sculpted arms. She was on the delicious edge of plumpness that made his body ache to be cushioned in its softness. She wasn't tall, couldn't be more than five-foot-three inches, but she was a perfect size. Small enough to be cuddled and held, but strong enough to handle his sensual appetite.

Unable to resist, he curled his fingers around the back of her neck and rubbed. She tensed instantly, and then slowly relaxed. He'd practiced this move, perfected it over the past several years and it never failed to make a woman melt. He stifled a chuckle as Sophie sighed and leaned back against him, resting in the crook of his arm.

"I'm not normally like this, you know." Sophie's gray eyes flicked up to his. They reminded him of tarnished silver, dark and mysterious.

"Like what?" He knew what she was going to say. He'd broken the first wall of her defenses, made her accept his touch, however innocent.

Sophie waved a hand in the air. "This. I'm not easy, but you make me do the stupidest things."

Emery cupped her cheek in one palm, nuzzled her neck and then kissed the corner of her mouth.

"When we're through, you'll do many things you wouldn't have done before. Being with me is about testing your limits."

The car rolled to a stop. Hans slid out and walked around to Sophie's door and opened it for her. Emery followed her, eyes fixed on her curves, on the way her skirt hugged her bottom and her hips swayed as she walked.

She was probably just out of college and her energy appealed to him. Normally he avoided much younger women. Their innocence wasn't alluring. He'd only slept with jaded women, who mistrusted emotional connections and wanted sex and nothing more. They knew the score and didn't fall asleep dreaming of sunny futures with children and happily ever afters.

There was something about Sophie, though. A passion for her goals, a healthy ambition rooted in her desire to be good at something she loved. He knew so little about her, but he did know that once he discovered her every secret, he'd be even more impressed. Even though he despised journalists as a rule because they couldn't keep their noses out of his life, Sophie seemed different. It wasn't morbid curiosity that had her begging for his story. There was pain and fear in her eyes, something he recognized all too well because he was forced to look at it in the mirror every day. This was the secret he wished to know most about her. What had driven her to seek him out; what reason could she have for needing his story, needing to know how he'd survived?

He slid an arm around her waist as they went up the steps to the door.

"Sophie, where are you staying in town?"

"The Brighton Bed and Breakfast. Why?" She raised a delicate brow.

Emery tightened his grip on her waist. "Hans, go to the Brighton and retrieve Sophie's things. Settle her bill while you're there."

She jerked out of his grip. "Hey! You can't do that!"

"Are you objecting to the removal of your luggage or my paying the bill?"

Her hesitation told him everything. She was afraid of ceding control to him. A small bump in the road, one he'd have to smooth over quickly.

Sophie sighed, eyes drifting up as though beseeching the heavens to spare her from him.

"You can't just…" Her fists clenched against her thighs.

"You forget about our bargain. I set the limits and the terms. You get your story."

He didn't leave room for her to argue. He simply tucked her arm through his and escorted her into his home. Emery didn't miss the flicker of amusement in Hans's eyes. Unable to resist, he flashed a small smile at his bodyguard. Hans was a good friend, a mentor, and one of the few people outside his family and his two friends Royce and Wes who he trusted implicitly, without question. Emery kept his distance from the rest of the staff at Lockwood, which was really only a small weekly cleaning crew, but Hans was never kept at arm's length. A man's bodyguard had to know his charge well enough to anticipate his needs and, more importantly, any life-threatening circumstances that could develop. He and Hans had been together a long time.

He covered her lips with a fingertip. "Let's get any objections out of the way right now. You'll sleep in my room, my bed. Unless of course you're afraid of me…or is it that you're afraid of yourself, of the passions you hide?" Outside his home, he couldn't afford to demand such intimacy with a woman; it was too dangerous for him. But here…inside these walls he could breathe and just…*be.*

She narrowed her eyes, the angry expression only making her more irresistible to him. Her stubbornness was going to give him so much pleasure.

"When you glare at me, it only reminds me I owe you a punishment." Her eyes darkened with rebellious heat as he teased her. Never had he craved fire as he did in that moment. His little warrior liked the idea of a spanking. He'd certainly remember that.

Sophie opened her mouth beneath his finger and moved to bite him. He moved faster, catching her chin and pulling her head up, forcing her up on tiptoe to steal a kiss. He gave it to her hard, focusing every bit of himself on her mouth, the way she tasted like strawberries, her retreating, hesitant tongue when he took control. He opened her mouth further, distracting her while he captured her wrists behind her back. He loved restraints, and couldn't wait to get her beneath him, tied to his bed. Someday he'd allow her to touch him, to stroke those lovely hands all over his body. But the need to have her powerless and trusting in his bed, awaiting the fulfillment of her every desire, was a potent need that made him nearly blind with hunger.

She melted in his arms, a little purr escaping her mouth between kisses. There was nothing better than getting a strong, intelligent, beautiful woman to surrender. It wasn't about force, wasn't about breaking someone down. It was about gaining trust, and getting a woman like Sophie to submit fully would be like nothing else he'd ever done. A true achievement. Never in his life had he wanted to accept a challenge like dominating her.

When he drew back to look at her, her silver gray eyes were soft, warm, like polished moonstones.

"Your mouth is dangerous." He feathered another kiss across her lips. Was it insane to feel he couldn't get enough of her mouth? He almost dreaded the thought of how desperate he'd been to bury himself inside her and never leave.

"Dangerous?" she murmured against his lips.

"Hmmm, yes…" He licked at her lips, savoring the taste. "I can't stop thinking about what you could do to me with it, what I want to do to it."

"Really?" Her surprise shocked him. Did she have no idea what effect she was having on him? His cock was so hard he'd be lucky to get upstairs without any serious pain.

Emery's hand tightened on her trapped wrists. "How many men have you been with?"

"Hmm?"

Sophie was smiling dazedly, as though his last kiss had addled her mind and left her happily drunk on passion.

"How. Many. Men? How many times? And don't lie. The truth, Sophie."

Finally his words seemed to sink in. "Two men. Two times each."

So few? How had men not been beating down her doors to share her bed? Emery decided the men, wherever she was from, were idiots.

"While you're with me, no one else, understand? I'm the possessive type."

She scowled, her eyes narrowed to slits.

"The same goes for you. I don't share and I don't want you eyeing any other women. I hate that. Every man I've dated has never been able to keep his eyes off other women. Can you promise to be better?"

Emery swept his gaze over her tantalizing body, trying not to indulge in fantasies of all the things he would soon to do her. "You're all mine, and I haven't been able to look away since Royce brought you to me."

Truth. Scary, confusing, truth. Sure, she wasn't gorgeous, wasn't slender. Sophie was the opposite of most women he met on a daily basis. And that made her fascinating, an odd mixture of warrior tigress and kittenish innocence. He knew with the right man, a good dom, she'd explode and burn like a wildfire in bed. Damn if he didn't want the blaze to consume him.

* * *

Sophie let him lead her through a maze of corridors lined with paintings hung on the richly painted walls. This had to be a dream: to be escorted through a mansion lit by dim golden lamps and pools of moonlight spilling through windows, leaving pearly puddles of light across the floors. Her hand was tucked securely in Emery's, the contact comforting. She'd never been one for touching, hugging, any of that. But Emery's large elegant hand curled around hers was soothing and yet completely mystifying.

Emery was like a phantom of the past, a gentleman whisking his lady toward a distant bedchamber. Sophie was only too eager for his seduction, but everything around her was a distraction. There were statues and art in odd places. She couldn't help stopping in front of carved marble figures or running her fingertips over the glossy polished wood of what had to be priceless antiques. After she paused for the tenth time, Emery sighed.

"What is all of this?" Sophie stood transfixed by a marble figure of Poseidon that was tucked into a corner.

"Over the years I've collected and rescued many pieces from original houses built in the first half of the last century on the island."

"Why?" Sophie turned her face up to his.

He was silent for a long moment, his gaze crossing the expanse of years. "Back before the Depression, this coast was covered with castles and palaces. American fortunes were lavishly spent on homes that rivaled those of the European royals. But after the Depression and every decade since, those same houses have slowly decayed, been destroyed, sold. Just last year some developer beat me out in an auction. He bought one of the houses four miles from here." Emery's eyes sharpened, the lines of his face tightening as he popped his jaw. "He bulldozed the whole place and built some cheap condominiums. Americans have never respected history." Emery spat the last few words. Irritation tinged with a hint of despair consumed his hazel eyes.

How true it was. Too many landmarks, too many places with history had been destroyed in the wake of American growth.

Emery tightened his grip on her hand. "I've devoted much time and personal resources to preserving any land I can and I rescue everything possible from demolition sites and bring it here."

Shock rippled through her at the thought of this man hunting for bits of Americana, that he could care so much for the broken dreams of a golden age long past. Her heart clenched tight. He was unlike anything she'd expected. He was haunted, yes; tortured, yes. But whatever hold his past had on him, he seemed determined to protect it. Like a king in a bewitched land where time could never move forward and he never aged. There was something sad and beautiful in seeing this about him. She couldn't help but wonder if he thought his preservation of the past in some way preserved his brother, too.

"It seems like you're a romantic, Emery." She gripped his hand tighter, squeezing his palm.

His hands suddenly curled around her arms, shaking her a little. Fine lines around his eyes creased as his gaze hardened.

"Never mistake me for a romantic, Sophie. Especially not when I am fighting off the desire to bend you over my bed, naked and open for my possession. I've done nothing but devise a thousand ways in which I'd like to take you, restrain you, own you. Does that sound romantic to you?"

Sophie's mouth went dry. Rather than be repulsed, his words shot fire straight to her womb, and she blinked slowly, barely able to move.

"Any more of those delightful little hungry looks of yours, and I'll forget the bed and take you against the wall right here," he warned.

"Promises, promises," she muttered, inwardly amused she could find air to breathe. At twenty-four years old she'd never been all that interested in sex, had actually dreaded intimacy of any kind. Yet, here she was panting like a cat in heat after a stranger, wanting him to make love to her until she forgot her name, until her legs gave out and her vision hazed.

I'm shameless, completely shameless and I don't even care.

Was it possible to go from prude to wanton in a mere hour? Apparently it was.

She eyed Emery with open hunger, the way his dark suit molded to his muscles and clung to him as he moved. He was like a leopard: sleek, graceful, powerful. He could corrupt a legion of the purest angels, have them tearing their wings from their backs and throwing themselves prostrate at his feet for just a touch or a husky whisper. The devil could make bargains with the body of this man, and she was more than willing to sign on the dotted line to give her soul up for another of his all-consuming, soul-stealing kisses.

It was only after a moment that she caught him watching her. His eyes shimmered with summer heat, scorching and dangerous.

"I think we'll save a tour for later. You look too tempting and I don't think my great Uncle Timsworth—" he pointed to a painting over her shoulder, of a gray-haired, solemn-looking man seated in a chair, cigar in hand— "would appreciate me fucking you against the wall next to him."

Sophie blushed; her breath halted for a second. Why did the idea of that make her want to melt into a puddle on the floor?

"Are you hungry?" He raised her hand to his mouth, feathered his lips over her knuckles, locked his eyes on her the way an artist might focus on a blank canvas. Visions, dreams, each step of a masterpiece placed in the artist's mind's eye all before he set a brush to canvas. Sophie wondered what he saw in her, what masterpiece he sought to create.

Please let it be something dark, carnal, sinful.

As though able to read her thoughts, Emery smiled. It wasn't just any smile, but one that knocked her behind the knees, sent her tumbling into his arms. It was a smile that drove her to a place emptied of all else save need for him and what he promised with a simple look.

Trouble. She was in so much trouble. Sophie tilted her head back to look up at him, the heat of his chest against hers hot enough to make her sweat despite the fact that she should have been cold in her leather miniskirt and corset top. She sucked in a breath when his head descended toward hers.

Chapter 5

AFTER BEING TAKEN TO THE HOSPITAL AND
TREATED, FRANCESCA ESPINA, THE BOYS'
NANNY, RECOUNTED WHAT SHE COULD
REMEMBER OF THE CRIME. SHE STATED THERE
WERE AT LEAST THREE MEN IN BLACK MASKS
WHO CAME IN THROUGH THE BACK KITCHEN
DOOR. DURING THE FIGHT, ONE OF THE BOYS
TRIED TO DISTRACT ONE OF THE KIDNAPPERS
BUT WAS HURT. BLOOD SAMPLES FROM THE
SCENE WERE MATCHED TO THE YOUNG VICTIM
AS WELL AS TO THE NANNY.
—*New York Times*, June 10, 1990

Emery's lips brushed Sophie's ear. She angled her neck toward him, offering more of her skin, hoping desperately he would continue that wicked play of his mouth.

He gave a throaty laugh. "Are you hungry for *food*? We have plenty of time to satisfy your other hungers."

Disappointment at his stopping his kisses warred with the rumbling in her stomach.

"Food please," she replied, still a little breathless.

He laughed again, only this time the sound was louder, richer. She laughed too. It felt good.

"Food it is. This way."

He took her down several more corridors. As he led her on a winding trail through the massive labyrinth that was the Lockwood house, her eyes darted from the portraits on the walls back to Emery. His muscled body shifted and moved next to her, and the close tailoring of his suit displayed the finest figure of any man she'd ever seen. She licked her lips, ready to speak, to draw him into another sensual touch or kiss, but he stopped before a door and pushed it open.

"This is the original kitchen, built back in 1902 when the house still had over twenty servants and catered to huge parties."

Emery gestured to the large marble bar and even larger countertops that filled the room. Sophie could almost see into the past—the hustle and bustle of ill-tempered cooks shouting for scullery maids to bring fresh water to the stove. The steam curling from the soup and the smell of fresh bread and roasted chicken. Her mouth watered at the thought. What a grand thing it must have been to have lived in such an era. She continued her study of the kitchen, noting the wooden rack that hung above the center marble island where gleaming silver pots and pans were attached by handles and strings amid garlands of various spices.

Emery peeled off his suit jacket and tossed it over the surface of one bar stool. Sophie licked her lips at the sight of his muscled shoulders and slender hips. Perfect for fitting between her thighs…

Down, girl. She shook her head at the way her body kept trying to take over. She'd never seen a man so good-looking. He shot her a look over his shoulder, a mischievous grin on his face. He had to know he could kiss her senseless, but there was no bravado, no arrogance in his manner. He seemed to know his very presence had her hungry for him. She wanted him to take her now, hard and fast. It was as though she could barely wait another minute to have him touch her again.

"I can read your face," he teased. "Save those wicked thoughts for later tonight. Now, have you ever had breakfast for dinner?"

Sophie stifled a giggle as he spun to face her, wielding a spatula and carrying a big skillet. He waggled his eyebrows and smiled. Her breath caught. Gone was the tortured soul; in his place was a seductive man, all smiles and trouble. Despite her questions, her need to know his story, she wouldn't wreck the miracle of his good mood.

"Promise me there's bacon. I'll do just about anything for bacon." She meant it too. Bacon was one of her life's little pleasures, just like chocolate. Her hips hated her for it, but bacon couldn't be passed up.

Emery stalked toward her, eyes warm as honey. He circled behind her, wrapped his arms around her waist, and nipped her right earlobe. Sophie stiffened at the intimate contact despite the flood of wet heat between her legs. She wasn't used to physical contact from a man, especially one she desired.

"Rule number one, relax into my touch. Unless I'm punishing you. Then you may anticipate me all you like. Now…relax." He curled long, elegant fingers around her throat, not squeezing, merely holding her in place as he flicked his tongue into the shell of her ear. Sophie jolted up, only to be jerked back down by his arm around her stomach, to be held down, pinned helpless for his exploration of her sensitive spots…It was too much. She liked it far more than she should: the helpless feeling, the surrender to even so small a domination.

Sharp tingles stabbed her lower back, responding to the mind-bendingly erotic sensation of his tongue in her ear. He licked behind it, nibbled at the soft skin there, and she thrashed, desperate to get away, but wanting more at the same time.

"Mmm…," she moaned as he repeated the delicious torture, and her nerves seem to fray. She knew she wouldn't be able to take much more of this. Sophie dug her fingers into the skin of his arms, trying to alert him that she was at her wits' end.

Finally, slowly, he relented. Fire still licked up her spine and she shuddered, trying to shake off the arousal that had nearly soaked her underwear. Emery took her by the arm, forced her to stand up from the bar stool. She squeaked in sheer surprise when he swatted the metal spatula against her bottom and then sighed when he set the spatula aside and ran his palm over her bottom, rubbing soothingly at the place where he'd spanked her.

It only made her wetter, hotter.

"Sweetheart, with me, bacon is always guaranteed." Releasing her, he chuckled and walked over to the fridge. In rapid succession he tossed a stick of butter on the counter, slid a carton of eggs alongside it, and smacked down a package of bacon. He spun, nudged the fridge shut with the toe of his elegant dress shoe, and reached above his head to retrieve a grease splatter shield.

She gawked at him. He acted completely normal, as though he hadn't just brought her to her knees, desperate for sex, and then whacked her on the ass with a kitchen utensil.

Closing her eyes, she drew in a fortifying breath. Then she expelled it and opened her eyes again. "You do realize this is insane, right? We're total strangers...and this—" Sophie waved one hand in the air between them— "is crazy too. I don't sleep with guys I haven't dated and I definitely don't let strangers spank me." He raised one brow, that single action a challenge.

"Or boyfriends?" The soft stroke of his voice stirred honeyed desire in her.

"Not boyfriends either."

One corner of his mouth kicked up into a rakish smile. "I'll be the first man to lay my hand on you." He played with the spatula, eyeing it in serious contemplation. "Maybe not just my hand...but don't worry, sweetheart. You'll love it when I give it to you."

Her mouth dried up completely. And a heat wave flooded her from head to toe so badly that she braced herself on the counter to stop from toppling off the barstool.

Emery cracked two eggs over the skillet and flicked molten gold eyes on hers. "This was your idea, Sophie. You wanted to be my sub. Intimacy, both sexual and otherwise, is part of the bargain, at least for me."

Sophie flinched. Intimacy? Was she ready for that?

No. Hell no.

The last time she'd been intimate and let her guard down, a man had gotten inside her heart, and then nearly killed her when he walked away. That had been five years ago and the pain had only barely started to ease. She couldn't live through that again, couldn't bear to be on the end of a one-sided relationship at the end of the day. Sophie was convinced Unrequited Love was her middle name. And she had no intention of sharing herself so openly again. The last time she'd really cared about a guy, she'd made the mistake of sharing her job with him. Letting him see how important her work was hadn't brought them closer. Instead it had driven him away. She couldn't erase the look on his face from her mind, either, as though she'd lost her sanity when she tried to tell him she was helping to save lives by writing her articles and researching cold cases for patterns. He'd said her interest in the morbid subject was "unhealthy" and she should be writing articles about house decoration tips, or recipes for parties, as though her career was little more than a glorified hobby.

Sophie would never forget how she'd felt when he'd left: torn between rage and hurt, tears burning her eyes, and her throat so tight she couldn't breathe. The worst thing in the world was opening yourself up and being rejected. She couldn't let that happen again, not on Emery's terms, when he was demanding an emotional intimacy she couldn't give him.

It was time to leave. She'd get her story another way and figure out who had kidnapped him without risking herself in the process. She slid off the stool, her worn ballet flats silent as they touched the ground. Slowly she reached for her clutch purse on the counter, training her eyes on Emery's body as he kept his back to her, cooking the eggs. Her heart kicked into a panicked rhythm as she struggled to remain calm, stealthy in her escape.

The smell of his cooking was heavenly, wrapping around her, teasing her stomach to the point that it grumbled. *Loudly.* Sophie froze. But Emery must not have heard her stomach because he didn't turn around. Thank God, she thought and quickly tiptoed toward the kitchen door. With one longing glance over her shoulder at Emery, she didn't see the hulking mass blocking her path until it was too late.

Whump!

She collided with solid muscle and large hands fell to her shoulders, rooting her in place as she prepared to struggle.

"Say, Emery, your little sub's making a run for it," announced a familiar voice.

The man who held her still was none other than Royce, Emery's friend from the club, the one who'd brought her right to Emery and practically shoved her into his lap.

Emery didn't even turn around. He merely laughed. Cocky bastard.

"Thanks Royce. That saves my bodyguard the trouble of tracking her down before I unleashed the pack of wild dogs on her."

Wild dogs? He's kidding, he's totally kidding. Sophie bit her lip and tried to push Royce's hands off her shoulders. Emery rotated halfway to face her, oven mitt on his hand as he held a skillet on the stove.

"She's too sweet to feed to your wolf pack. Let me take her home. I'll make her behave. A good twenty whacks on the ass will put her to rights. She'll be on her knees, eyes all adoring and asking what would please her Master," Royce boasted.

"Yeah, not likely." Sophie bristled and kicked his knee. He didn't show even a hint of pain, and she'd kicked him hard, hard enough that any other man would have been hopping around the kitchen clutching his shin and moaning. Royce just gave her a wolfish smile and a devious wink.

"I'll cuff her for you," Royce said to Emery, sliding a hand into his pants pocket and retrieving a set of handcuffs. He hauled her back over to her stool and plopped her down on the seat. Before she even had time to react, he'd clicked a cuff around her ankle and its twin around the bar stool leg above the footrest bar so she couldn't lift the stool and slide the cuff off.

"Who the hell do you think you are?" She cut him off when he opened his mouth to answer. "And what the hell are you doing here?"

"That's a lot of 'hell's, sweetheart. I'm betting you have no idea what hell is. I'm Royce Devereaux. Emery's known me as long as…" Royce's gaze shuttered and he shrugged off the sudden heavy shadows of emotion. He was silent a moment before he noticed the kitchen and food on the counter.

"Breakfast for dinner? Wow, Emery must really want you in his bed. I'd sleep with anyone who cooks like he does." Royce flashed her a cocky grin.

"Are you…" she paused, unsure of whether she grasped the dynamic between the two men.

"Into men? Nope. I'm only for the ladies. But Emery has serious kitchen skills. You'll let him do anything to you once you've had a taste. I guarantee it."

Emery spooned some scrambled eggs onto a plate then slid it across the counter to Sophie before speaking to Royce. "You know, you're ruining my surprises. Now she'll be demanding a taste every day, and I have to figure out what to make her do in return."

"Well, I've got some new toys, if you're interested…I bet she'd like some clamps, a bit of pain; maybe you'd like to borrow my cross? I've got a great new spreader bar for the legs."

She didn't know much of clamps, crosses and spreaders, but it sounded medieval. The handcuffs she could deal with. She even still wore the leather cuffs from the club around her wrists, but those felt more like a badge of ownership than a torture device. Sophie shuddered and jerked her ankle, trying to get free. The metal cuff on her ankle bit warningly into her skin and clanked sharply. Both men zeroed in on the sound instantly. She felt like a fox with her paw in a poacher's metal trap.

Emery's pupils dilated and he drew a slow breath between barely parted lips. "I love that sound." His voice was whisky rough, and sent riotous shivers through her. He liked the sound of her struggling? Wetness pooled between her thighs and she clamped them together, mortified that the idea of her being helpless at his hands continued to do this to her, melt her inside completely until she could only think about him and his domination.

"I know," Royce agreed, his voice just as low. "I love to hear a woman testing her restraints."

Emery nodded. "The best ones are fighters. It takes someone aggressive to give them pleasure." As he spoke, he abandoned the bacon and the pan to reach over the marble counter to her. His palm cupped her cheek, the pad of his thumb smoothing over her cheekbone, the touch affectionate, tender, but the fire in his eyes melted her insides. "Wouldn't you like that?" he asked. "To wrestle on the bed before I finally pin you down and—"

Sophie's lungs burned. The image he painted—god, how she wanted him to do just that—prove he was stronger and then give her such pleasure that she'd almost die. How could she not want that?

"I think we're scaring her," Royce said.

"Sophie, darling. Breathe." Emery's command was sharp, drawing her out of the haze of her world of desire.

Good God, she'd forgotten to breathe.

"This little one is too much fun." Royce captured her hand, brought it to his lips and kissed her knuckles. There was nothing innocent in his gesture, especially when his tongue flicked out over her skin.

"Hands off, Royce. She's mine." The rumbling noise coming from Emery made Sophie's pulse skitter wildly and her body hum.

"We could share…she could handle two at once. She's a strong little thing, just made for a double fu—"

In an instant her lungs were searing and she had to remind herself to breathe. "Share?" Sophie cringed at the squeak in her voice.

"Hmm, yes. I'd take you from behind, Emery from the front, in and out, again and again, harder and harder... *Two* is so much better than one." Royce still held her hand, and he punctuated his words with slow, pressured rubs against her palm.

Sophie's ears started ringing; her chest tightened. She couldn't think...two men...two...Was that even possible? She knew logically a big bed could hold three people, but was a woman capable of withstanding that much...passion? A secret dark part of her entertained the idea, briefly, hungrily, but she shut it back down.

Emery's voice cut through the tide of arousal before it could overwhelm her. "Normally I'd be tempted, Royce. But I find myself more possessive over my little journalist than other women."

Royce jerked back from her as though she were a poisonous viper. "Journalist? Emery, you knowingly brought a reporter to your home?"

His words sounded like an accusation, as though she'd committed a crime just by being here. Irritation at his assumption that she'd hurt Emery prickled uncomfortably beneath her skin like tiny little sparks of electricity.

"She's fine. For now. I'm having Cody run an extensive background check on her. Hans is getting her luggage and searching it for bugs. She'll be moving in here until I'm through with her."

Through with her? Sophie didn't like the sound of that. Like he could just toss her aside when he was tired of her. She had to leave, but her mouth started to water as the aroma of bacon drifted beneath her nose. She'd leave just as soon as she had some of that bacon.

Royce turned his attention back to her and Emery resumed cooking. Royce wrapped his fingers around her arm, squeezing.

"Hurt him, betray him, do anything that upsets him..."

"You'll kill me?" she prompted sarcastically.

"I don't hurt women unless they ask for it, and even then it's about pleasure. But if you hurt Emery, *I'll destroy you.* You'll never write another article again; you'll be a pariah even in your hometown."

She wasn't the sort of person to betray anyone and she didn't like being accused of something she hadn't done yet, or ever planned to do. When she wrote her articles she told the truth; she even warned her interviewees of that before proceeding. But she never ever betrayed anyone.

Emery finished preparing breakfast, or dinner, and Royce kept up a conversation, but Sophie didn't feel like talking. Her stomach knotted and twisted. She had to force herself to eat the eggs, bacon, and toast. The man could cook. No question, the taste of it was beyond words. But even the fantastic, melt-in-your-mouth food couldn't erase the unease creeping along her skin.

She'd always been logical in her decisions, but this plan to get Emery's story was rash. Too rash. Now she'd gotten all tangled up in a mess. He'd hired someone to research her? The thought made her shiver and not in a good way. She should have expected him to dig into her background but she'd been so focused on him and finding out who'd kidnapped him, that she'd lost perspective. Now she might lose her chance to warn him, to protect him from what she was convinced would happen again, all because he'd dig into her past and find out about Rachel. He wouldn't understand. Hell, he might even blame her for what had happened to her friend. With a deep breath, she tried to feign a sense of calm.

"Who's Cody?" she finally asked.

"She speaks at last," Royce taunted, but his tone was playful, no hint of malice.

Ignoring Royce, she continued to look at Emery. "So who is this guy digging into my life?" She pushed her plate away and settled her chin in her hands, resting her elbows on the counter.

Emery eased back on his stool across from her, his eyes flitting to the kitchen door and back again. The movement of his gaze was constant; nearly every thirty seconds he scanned the room as if he might come under attack at any moment, but he seemed unaware of the habit, as though he did it so often it had become second nature.

What have you been through, Emery?

"Cody is my technological assistant at the house. He has rooms here and helps me run Lockwood Industries. He also supervises my personal security system, among other things. He's a kid, only twenty-four, but he's brilliant." Genuine warmth filled his tone, and Sophie's tension eased slightly.

"Twenty-four? He's my age. I'm not a kid."

Emery raked her body with his gaze and so did Royce.

"No, you certainly aren't. I will promise to prove that to you over and over again." The confidence in his voice made Sophie shiver. She knew if she stayed, he would do exactly as he promised.

Royce cleared his throat. "Again, I'd like to throw my hat into the ring for a ménage."

Emery picked up a dishtowel and without taking his eyes off Sophie, chucked it at Royce's face.

"So possessive," Royce *tsk*ed and lobbed the towel back at Emery.

"Yep." He didn't even bother to argue. "This is one woman I refuse to share, even with you."

Royce set his dishes in the sink. "Well, that's unfortunate," he chuckled wryly. "Could have been fun." He checked his watch and grimaced. "I ought to head out. My students' term papers won't grade themselves, and my new TA is giving me hell."

"TA?"

"Teacher's Assistant," he clarified with a little smirk. "It's a…"

"I know what a TA is. You're a teacher?" Sophie blurted out, then covered her mouth with a hand, embarrassed.

"College Professor at Hampstead University. It's a small college, but I like it. I teach Paleontology."

Sophie snorted. "Like Indiana Jones?" She giggled. The idea had merit. Royce was sexy, dominating, and funny. He'd give Harrison Ford a run for his money.

"Something like that. Only Indy is an archeologist. He handles artifacts from human cultures. I deal with dinosaurs."

Sophie sat up straighter in her seat, completely fascinated. "Do you actually go on digs and stuff?"

"As much as possible." Royce studied her with a new gleam in his eyes. "You want to come on a dig sometime?"

A low growl broke through their conversation. "She's busy, Royce. Why don't you go find Hans and have him get the case of bourbon?" Emery cut in as he came around the bar. He slid his arms around her hips and placed his chin on her shoulder to gaze at his friend warningly.

Royce's lips twitched. "Well, I see how it is. Sophie, sweetheart, when you and he aren't…shacking up anymore, you give me a call. We'll go *digging*." The way he said the word "digging" had her biting her lip and containing a breathless sigh. And with that, Royce smiled and left the kitchen.

Emery released her only after Royce was gone. Sophie attempted to get off the stool, but her ankle clanked sharply against the bar stool leg.

"Oh crap! He's got the key. Go get him!" Sophie demanded. Emery only shook his head, grinning.

"I've got a spare key." He retrieved it from a kitchen drawer. A fact that for some reason disturbed Sophie. Was handcuffing women to bar stools normal for him? She didn't like the idea of Emery with other women—not that she had any right to be possessive about his past, and it wasn't like they would be exclusive for long in this strange bargain they'd made. Once he found out her secrets, he'd kick her out immediately.

"Is there any special reason you have handcuff keys in your kitchen?"

"Sometimes I like a midnight snack, and I have to chain her to a counter."

A wicked image of her restrained on the counter, spread wide like a feast, burst into bloom. Emery's golden head between her thighs, his tongue thrusting in and out, his lips sucking on her clit...

"Now that looks like an interesting thought you just had. Care to share?"

"Nope, not sharing." She was on fire, and he was just standing there putting dishes in the dishwasher. Ridiculous. This was all absolutely ridiculous. And yet, if he asked her to strip and get on the counter and spread her legs, she'd do it without a second thought.

He leaned back against the counter, arms crossed over his chest as he studied her. "Pity. It looked like it might have been fun to try whatever you were thinking."

"Can you just uncuff me now?" The handcuff jangled and *thunk*ed against the wood leg of the stool when she jerked her ankle.

His eyes softened with amusement and the hard lines bracketing his mouth smoothed for a moment. "And let you break our bargain by running off? Not a chance." Something buzzed and Emery dug into his pants pocket. He pulled out a sleek black smartphone and put it to his ear.

"Lockwood." His tone was clipped.

Silence.

Sophie cocked her head, straining to listen.

"Brant, I told you that we are ready to issue the press release on the latest GPS locator...The kinks have been eliminated...You want me to go where? You know I don't like Manhattan...No, if the board wants to meet, I'll fly them out here...Being stubborn?" Emery laughed, but Sophie flinched at the edge of bitterness layered beneath the rich sound. "Of course I'm stubborn. Quit arguing with me. Tell the board I'll have a jet waiting for them tomorrow morning. Eleven a.m. No sooner. I've got—" Emery paused, his eyes roving over Sophie's body— "things that require my attention. Very important things and I cannot be bothered before then. See you tomorrow." He returned the cellphone to his pocket and closed the dishwasher.

"Who's Brant?" Sophie leaned forward, admiring the view of his backside as he bent to pick up a towel from the floor. The muscles of his thighs were large and beautiful outlined through the dark suit pants. He looked strong, and the thought of all of that power directed at the sensitive spot between her legs, straining, pounding...

"Brant is my cousin." Emery straightened and was now viewing her with an amused expression. She realized she'd been daydreaming as she stared at his butt and legs. Sophie clamped her eyes shut, feeling like a total idiot.

"Older or younger than you?" She opened her eyes again, blushing when she caught a knowing smirk flitting across his sensual mouth.

"You really are a reporter. Got to have all the facts, huh?"

She didn't miss the slight edge to his words.

Sophie's face flamed even more. How could he make her feel like an obnoxious fly even when she was just doing her job?

"Brant is my Uncle Rand's only son, my father's older brother. Uncle Rand died when I was eight years old, and Brant was just eighteen. He had pancreatic cancer. My father bought back my uncle's share of the family business just before Rand died. Brant took that a little personally, and bought his way into the company a few years later. He's been on me about the company ever since I took over for my father...Brant's a nosy bastard. Pushy too."

"Why's that?" Curiosity buzzed inside her like a veritable hive of bees.

Emery shrugged, the action smooth and natural. He was so at home in his own body. Sophie envied him that comfort. She felt like a stranger in her own skin half the time and didn't like her body enough to get to know it better. It was easy for Emery, though, she suspected. How could it not, when he was so perfect, so beautiful?

"Brant's ten years older than me. He wishes he had control of Lockwood Industries, but he has no sense of vision. He's completely motivated by dollar signs. Don't get me wrong; he's family, and he's a decent guy, but I have a short attention span for people who seem to be born with habits that I loathe or desires I spurn. Brant loves New York. I can't stand the thought of leaving Long Island. In fact, I don't leave the island unless it's an absolute emergency."

His declaration raised a thousand questions, but Sophie bit her lip, keeping silent. As a journalist, you had to learn how to interview. The best journalists knew when to wait and let their interviewees pace themselves and reveal everything at the right time. Her instincts told her there were many things Emery wasn't prepared to discuss.

"You're not asking me why?" Emery raised a brow, almost challenging.

"Nope."

"Huh. Unpredictable," Emery murmured.

He retrieved a set of tiny keys from a drawer and walked over to her. He knelt, unlocked the cuff at her ankle, stroking her calf upward as he stood, and then he slipped the cuffs into his pocket. That one little caress promised so much that she bit her lip to stifle a sigh of longing.

"We'll use them later," he promised with a wolfish grin. He took her hand in his and led her from kitchen.

* * *

There was a beautiful grandfather clock at the base of the grand stairs and Sophie touched its gleaming wooden surface.

"Emery, this is beautiful. Does it still work?"

Emery froze, his languorous movements ceasing as he turned to face her. Behind him, at the top of the beautiful stairway hung a massive portrait. Two young boys, twins, with fair hair and ready smiles, stood frozen, gazing out through the layers of dried oil. Sophie stared up at Emery, his face just beneath the two children from where she stood. The same eyes...eyes that followed her in dreams of empty halls and lonely graveyards. The boy on the right, half an inch shorter than the boy on the left, the one with a crooked smile, had to be Emery. Such mischief, such wonder, all captured in that innocent gaze. Sophie's heart clenched and her eyes burned. That child would come to lose all he held dear.

"The clock hasn't worked in years." He flicked his fingers in an impatient gesture and she quickly dashed up the steps, taking his open hand. He grasped hers tightly, but not in a way that hurt. The long walk down the hall, with the silence stretching between them, made her nervous and edgy. When they reached his bedroom, he pushed the door open.

She wasn't surprised by the room; it was just like him. Elegant and simple with a massive, beautiful, ornately carved bed frame, a dresser, nightstand, and large walk-in closet. Sophie balked just inside the door.

"What's the matter?" He turned around to face her, a challenge glinting in his eyes.

She swallowed hard, her gaze darting between him and the bed.

"This is part of our bargain. My story for your submission. I want you in *my* bed tonight with *me*." He closed the distance and reached around her to pull the door shut behind her. She leaned back instantly, pressing herself into it, relying on the wood's steady support.

"Tonight is not about sex. A dominant/submissive relationship isn't always carnal. Sometimes a dom just needs to hold his submissive close at night, and the sub's need to be held is just as strong. The best relationships are symbiotic." As he spoke he slid his hands behind her back and gently pried her away from the door.

"The first lesson tonight is about trust and caring. I want you to undress me." He stepped back a few feet until he was close to the foot of his bed.

"Undress you?" Sophie remained frozen, her body vibrating with nerves and anticipation.

Emery's full lips curved into that bad boy smile she was starting to love and hate. It made her want to sigh and rub up against him, and she hated how it affected her so strongly.

He crooked a finger. "Come here, little sub." His tone was teasing, but his command was strong and her knee-jerk reaction at his command had her approaching him. His jacket was already off, but other than that he was still fully dressed.

"Untie my shoes." He put a hand on her shoulder and with a faint pressure there, he showed her he wanted her to kneel. Sophie gritted her teeth, not liking the subservience of the position, but once she was on her knees, she focused on the task, unlacing the expensive, Italian leather shoes.

"Thank you," he praised in a low soft voice that made her inner wanton purr. Then he toed out of his shoes.

"Stand." He curled one finger under her chin and tilted her head back as she got to her feet. Normally she wouldn't have liked being ordered around, but it did make it easy to have him tell her exactly what he wanted her to do. It was actually freeing, not to worry about what she was supposed to do. Would it be that easy in bed?

"You're doing very well, Sophie. Now unbutton my shirt." He waited patiently.

Sophie tried to bury the riotous emotions exploding through her—disgust at herself for enjoying his praise, curiosity about his naked body, shock that she was actually undressing the man when she'd never done that before. Her hasty couplings in the past had never amounted to much and they'd always been in the dark. There was no exploration of bodies, no admiration of the human form. She'd never even really climaxed before, at least not compared to what she'd felt on Emery's lap at the club. She'd been so close to something great, something truly life altering. That had been a first for her and she couldn't imagine what it would be like when she finally slept with him. Would it be as wonderful and exciting as those brief moments in the club had promised? She wanted to know, but she was *afraid*, too.

Maybe if I got this over real quick… Her fingers shook as she reached for the top button of his shirt. She got three buttons undone before he grasped one of her hands by the wrist and palm, trapping it.

"Easy, little sub. Go slow. The best things in life should be enjoyed, not rushed." He held her hand, clasping it gently to his chest above his heart. Through the expensive dress shirt, she could feel his heart beat against her skin. A strong, steady beat. The *thump-thump* lulled her into a haze of sensual awareness as he finally let her hand go.

She continued to unbutton the shirt, savoring the experience of baring inch after inch of his lightly tanned flesh. She was in control of him now, removing his clothes, and that did make her feel more certain of herself. When the shirt was fully open, she slid her hands up his chest under the fabric before she peeled it off his shoulders. The action brought her unbearably close to his hot body, and her arms slid around him as she pulled the shirt down off his back and arms, as if she was embracing him as she undressed him. Then the shirt fluttered to the floor and he was standing there in just those expensive trousers that hugged his lean hips. The muscles of his abs were like corded steel and she stared at them in shock and hunger. She reached toward him without thinking and placed one palm flat on his abs. The muscles jumped beneath her touch and she could have sworn they both held their breath. Unable to resist, she raised her head just as he leaned down. Their lips feathered in a ghost of a kiss—so delicate, yet potent, like an addictive drug. She shivered, aching for more, needing his lips on hers, but he didn't press her.

"Not so fast, my little Sophie. Pants next." The corner of his mouth quirked into a little grin and she focused on breathing as she dropped her head again, staring at the silver button and the zipper on his pants. Was she really doing this?

Pants. She could handle pants. Oh god, she was unzipping his pants!

The top button slipped out of the slit and she had to coax the zipper down. There was no mistaking the massive bulge of his cock barely concealed behind black cotton briefs. She tugged the pants off his hips and they dropped to the floor. He stepped out of them and removed his socks. She raked her gaze over him, admiring the lean muscled calves, powerful thighs, and sculpted chest. The man was beautiful. There was no denying that. And she…she wasn't. The negative thought had her retreating back a step but he caught her by the upper arms, stilling her retreat.

"Sophie, sweetheart," he murmured, as though he sensed her fear. "We're just sleeping tonight. Now, tell me, since your bag hasn't arrived yet, what do you like to sleep in?"

The intensity of his eyes had softened and his hands were warm on her cold skin, and it was comforting, not frightening. Was this how a normal woman was supposed to feel? A woman not ashamed of her body?

"I like big t-shirts and boxers," she said.

With a little approving nod, he walked over to a dark wooden dresser and opened the top drawer, pulling out a pair of boxers and a large shirt. When he came to her, he set the items on the bed and twirled a finger.

"Turn around. It is time to undress you."

She gave him her back and had to fight the urge to close her eyes. He wouldn't see the scars from behind; was that why he'd insisted she face away? Was it out of respect for her desire to hide them, or his own desire to avoid them?

"Stop thinking so hard. I can almost hear your thoughts, little sub. I know you're sensitive about your body. I told you how I feel about scars, but I'm allowing you some privacy while we get to know each other." He reached around from behind, his fingers tracing playful patterns up the front of her corset, almost plucking the satin ribbons like the strings of a cello. When he reached the top of the bodice, the tips of his fingers innocently—or perhaps not so innocently—stroked the tops of her breasts before they unfastened the bow and began to unlace the ribbons. The corset loosened and when it was almost ready to fall off her, he reached for the shirt.

"Lift your arms," he murmured in her ear.

Her hands shot up and he slid the shirt over and down her upper body. Then he completely removed the corset from beneath her shirt and let it drop to the carpet. She turned around to face him and he pulled her into his arms. The heat of his bare chest sank through his shirt to touch her barely covered breasts. She liked this feeling of closeness, but she feared it would end all too soon.

"There, that wasn't so hard, was it?" The smile on his lips reached his eyes and she couldn't resist smiling back, until he unzipped the mini skirt and tugged it down. Then his hands were on her bottom. She wriggled, trying to get free, but he swatted her ass with his hand.

"You're itching for a spanking, sweetheart." He bent his head and gave her a nibbling little kiss, meant to tease more than seduce. Only after she'd calmed did he hand her the boxers.

"Thanks," she whispered, still shy as she tugged them on.

"You're welcome." He captured her wrists and unfastened the leather cuffs, setting them on the nightstand. "Now get into bed. I've had a long day, as have you, I imagine. We'll talk more about our bargain tomorrow." He waited until she'd climbed into bed before he flicked off the lights and got into bed with her.

Sophie didn't mean to go completely rigid, but she did. Like a piece of wood planking, she was stiff, and jerked when he reached for her.

"You haven't slept with many men, have you?" he asked. In the darkness she couldn't see much of him. But the faint light of the moon from the distant window reflected in his eyes.

"I've slept with men. I've just never had any of them stay the night before." Why she admitted that to him, she wasn't sure. It was easier in the dark to speak the truth, and she could hide her face, the shame that no doubt colored her cheeks.

"I've never let a woman come home with me either." His admission shocked her, and yet it felt like he'd evened the playing field. This was new for both of them.

"Really?"

"Really." His strong arms curled around her waist and she slid a few inches closer as he tucked her against his side. After several long seconds, she relaxed bit by bit and then nuzzled her face into the pillow, letting her body absorb his heat and his strength. A woman could get used to this...

* * *

The clock chime was heavy, sharp, and ominous. Sophie jerked awake as Emery abruptly sat up in bed. Outside the moon was still bright, which meant they'd only been asleep a short while.

"Emery? What's that matter?" Sleep fogged her brain, but she tried to focus on the fact that he was getting out of bed and walking toward the door. He opened it without a word to her and started down the hall. The patter of rain outside was steady, and the occasional rumble warned her that a storm front was moving through.

Was he sleepwalking? She followed him, wondering where he was going as he reached the top of the main stairs. Just as Sophie put her foot on the top red-carpeted step, the grandfather clock chimed again and thunder growled menacingly from overhead.

The grandfather clock continued to chime, and the sound rang clear, striking the pale yellow marble of the walls.

"It's midnight," Emery murmured almost absently. "The clock shouldn't work." He gave a strange little shake of his head. It chimed again and he tensed. "Hate that sound, *hate* it."

He looked over her head to something behind her and blinked, but the cloudy cast to his gaze spoke of his seeing something from the past, or perhaps the future. Sophie only knew he was gone in that moment. Something or perhaps someone had captured his head and heart, leaving her with a shell, a mere body.

"Emery? What's wrong?" Her gaze darted between him and the grandfather clock, confused.

"Shadows…always shadows." He kept staring out the window next to the huge door. "Told you they were there. I told you…but I didn't tell her. I stopped you from telling her."

Sophie thought about asking him what he was talking about, but she sensed he wasn't talking to her, wasn't even seeing her.

The electric lamps lighting the gilded hall dimmed to a lower setting simultaneously. Shadows blossomed, growing pregnant from the loss of light.

"Emery?" Sophie tugged on his hand, apprehension coiled tight in her stomach. Emery seemed to be frozen in place.

The clock, which continued to chime its full beats, suddenly went silent save for the heavy ticking—counting hours, days, measuring the ghostly sense of the Lockwood house. A clock that wasn't supposed to work. Unable to resist, she turned her head toward the massive grandfather clock, eyes locking on the gold pendulum that swung back and fourth behind the clear glass.

Her grandmother's voice intruded on her mind, a whisper of ghoulish tales and scary stories. Granny Belinda, or Bells as everyone called her, had been born in Boston, and swore her roots dated back to the days of the Salem witch trials. And on more than one night Granny Bells had sat in her great wing-backed chair by the fire, a soot colored cat in her lap, and told Sophie stories.

"You must take care, Sophie. When the clock strikes twelve, 'tis the witching hour."

"What's so bad about that?" six year-old Sophie had asked.

"'Tis the time when you're most vulnerable to darkness, to the evil that can steal your soul. The witches ride their black-winged horses, helping the devil claim wandering souls."

Sophie blinked, and the strange lethargy of watching the pendulum swing was broken at last. She looked up at Emery, saw his mouth moving as though he was whispering. She drew closer, standing up on tiptoe, still clutching his hand. Finally, she stood close enough to hear the words leaving his lips.

"Fenn, listen to me…you can't make me go. I'm not leaving you behind."

Emery repeated the words over and over, a hurried, breathless mantra. Horror filled Sophie, swallowing her like a black cloud. Her heart clenched. He had to be having some kind of relapse. She needed to get him out of the past. She had to rescue him. Without a second thought, she wound her hand back and slapped him.

He collapsed, crumpling on the stairs behind him. Sophie eased down next to him, cupped his chin.

"What are we doing down here, Fenn?" he asked. The look on his face was that of a young boy, frightened and hurt. He raised a hand to his cheek and touched the reddening mark. "Did you hit me?"

Sophie winced. He didn't recognize her, still caught up in the flashback.

"Why did you hit me? I'm frightened; he won't let us go, you heard him. We have to escape!" Emery pushed away from the step and got to his feet. He leaned heavily on the polished walnut railing and gazed at her, wounded mistrust in his eyes.

"The clock chimed, Emery. It triggered some sort of flashback. You have to snap out of it. Fenn's not here." Sophie's brows drew together when he ripped his hand away from hers. She hated losing physical contact with him. In the few short hours since she'd known him, she'd grown accustomed to his touch, to his hand enveloping hers and the safe feeling that came from being surrounded by him. Being bereft of him left her hollow.

"Don't lie to me, Fenn. You can't convince me this is a dream. I know he's going to kill us." Emery's voice was low but his tone was clipped.

Outside the snarling thunder continued. Rain began to pelt the roof and ping against the windows. Sophie glanced over her shoulder, seeing the heavy clouds packed tight, like hundreds of clenched fists punching the air over the treetops. When the next thunder rolled, the mansion shivered beneath her feet.

Suddenly Emery grabbed her arm, spun her to face him and pinned her back against the stair railing. His eyes were wild, almost glowing.

"I heard them talking. I know they said someone allowed them into the grounds. Who was it?"

"Emery, stop! I'm not Fenn."

Emery's eyes fogged again, confusion blurring the anger on his face. He released her, panting.

"Leave me alone." He started to climb the stairs as though to escape.

Sophie ignored his command and started up the stairs after him. He was too pale, too upset to be left alone, clearly still stuck in some delusion. She put a palm on his shoulder but he recoiled at her touch, stiffening and whirling on her like a wounded animal.

"Get out! Leave my house now!" He waved an arm at her, as though to ward her off, and Sophie stumbled down a few steps to escape the wide arc of his reach. He pursued her. In less than a minute he'd caught her arm and propelled her out the large wooden door.

"I'm safe now, you can't ever get in again," he growled. "Ever." The door slammed and locked behind her, the sound more threatening than the thunder.

"Emery!" She smacked her hands on the wooden door, but he didn't come back. "Damn it!" She cursed and pressed her face against the door. Where the hell was Hans? Maybe he could let her in. Using her fists, she continued to beat on the door for a few more minutes, but no one came to let her in. Had Emery ordered his bodyguard to keep her out even in this weather? She sneezed and rubbed her arms. The icy water seemed to sink straight through her skin, deep into her bones. All she wore were those boxers and the t-shirt and they were now completely soaked through.

He'd just kicked her out in the middle of a freezing rainstorm. That was not good. But more importantly, he'd thought she was Fenn, and that he'd betrayed her because of something he'd heard while kidnapped. It was just as she'd expected; he'd overheard things during his captivity, things that could tell her who was the person behind this. As soon as she figured out what to do about being locked out, she'd think about what to do with this new information. The question was whether he'd let her come back tomorrow, assuming she could manage to find her way back to the Brighton Bed and Breakfast during the storm.

Shivering, she walked across the marble patio, slipping every few steps, her arms flailing as she struggled to find her balance. Cold water squelched against the soles of her bare feet as she straightened. Rain sluiced down her back, soaked her hair, t-shirt and boxers.

"Damn." She walked back to the door and huddled against it for a moment, feeling stupid for hoping Emery was on the other side ready to let her back in. The rain was cold on her skin, soaking through to her bones. It came in heavy waves across the yard and up along the patio. It bent the grass in ripples and splashed on the marble steps ahead of her.

She could walk back to the B&B, but wasn't Hans supposed to have picked up her stuff and settled her account? And her clutch. She'd dropped it in the hall, so she had no money to pay for another room. Staring glumly out at the rain-soaked forest before her, she vowed never to surrender to a rich man's whims again. They had no concept of money, no understanding of survival. He'd taken away her ability to care for herself, and she despised him in that moment. She didn't hate him, would never be able to hate him, but she was angry enough to wring his neck for doing this to her.

The gates were ahead of her, a mile off, black lacy specters silhouetted by moonlight as they rose from the thick mist. She'd probably have to climb over. What a pleasant thought. Sophie grimaced as she glanced down at the thin boxers. It was too bad the house seemed servant-less, otherwise she could have knocked on the door and gotten someone else to let her back in, at least until morning. If only she had her cell, she could call Hayden to come pick her up and she could bunk down with her for the night.

Sophie hugged her arms around her waist, keeping herself as warm as possible, and left the miniscule comfort of the overhang by the door. Rain clung to her hair, her lashes, sinking deep into her clothes. A shudder wracked her body and she chastised herself for getting into this mess. It was October. The air was far too cold during a thunderstorm for boxers and a t-shirt. She took her time descending the marble steps. Tension made her limbs ache as she navigated the slick marble.

When she finally got to the bottom she crossed the lawn and headed toward the distant gates. Her nose started to run and she coughed once, twice, trying to clear her throat. What a night. She'd never experienced such an amazing high as being in Emery's arms, nor the low of being shouted at and kicked out like an unwanted stray cat. It certainly ranked as one of the top worst and best nights of her life and she'd had plenty of bad nights.

Snap!

Sophie spun at the sudden crack of something breaking in the woods off to the right. She squinted through the rain, seeing only flickering shadows from the trees swaying in the wind. For an instant she could have sworn she'd seen a person.

Chapter 6

AFTER BEING KNOCKED UNCONSCIOUS, FRANCESCA ESPINA, THE NANNY, CAME AROUND ONLY TO FIND BOTH CHILDREN GONE. SHE FLED TO THE OUTSIDE, WHERE THE LOCKWOODS WERE HOSTING THE PARTY, SHOUTING FOR HELP AND TO CALL THE POLICE.
—*New York Times*, June 10, 1990

Emery reached the top of the stairs before he had to sit down. His chest expanded and flattened with each hasty inhalation. He'd done it again: flashed back to that awful moment when Fenn had demanded that Emery leave him behind and escape.

He dropped his head, pressing the heels of his hands into his eyes so hard he saw stars. "I should have stayed." His whispered confession echoed off the marble floors. He should have died alongside his brother; at least then they'd be together.

Emery remained at the top of the stairs for several long minutes. Something was wrong. Something was missing.

"Mr. Lockwood?" A voice intruded on his dark thoughts.

A young man stood at the foot of the stairs, running his hand through surfer blond hair, pushing it out of his pale blue eyes. Cody Larson. Ever casual in a t-shirt and jeans, Cody looked at him in concern. His lips were pursed, brows drawn together.

"Yes, Cody?"

"You know that woman you brought home? I saw her wandering down toward the gates on my monitors. I wasn't sure if she was supposed to be out there. Given the weather, and the fact that she's only wearing boxers and a t-shirt, she could get pneumonia or something."

A horrid buzzing started up in Emery's ears, like the drone of a thousand bees.

"Sophie!"

He'd blanked out and hadn't realized she'd gone. Then it all flooded back: his shouts, tossing her out of the house. He'd been near mindless with rage and misery at reliving the worst moment of his life.

The price? He'd shoved Sophie out into the darkness and the rain. Danger was out there. Maybe not in the same creatures he'd feared as a child, but danger was behind every tree, beneath every rock. He had to get her back inside, keep her warm and safe.

He ran down the stairs and called to Cody. "Call Hans, tell him to return with Sophie's luggage immediately. If I haven't returned with her by the time he gets back, send him out to find us."

"You might need some pants. I grabbed these from your room before coming down here." Cody held out a pair of blue jeans. "I saw on the cameras when you left your room you didn't have anything on. I figured you might need them to go after her."

"Fuck," Emery snapped, and jerked the pants on before running to the door.

He left Cody and flung open the door, darting out into the rain. He cursed as he slid on the rain-slicked marble patio.

The wide green lawn leading to the gates was nearly black by night. The lowering skies were dark and heavy with rain clouds. Blood pounded in Emery's ears as he ran. Flashes of memory blasted him like lightning strikes, but he shielded himself with the image of Sophie. She could be hurt, or have become ill from the weather and the chill. A thousand worries and fears sliced him again and again as he sprinted toward the gates.

Where was she?

"Sophie! Where are you?" His eyes sank into the darkness, seeking any sign of her. Sophie!" he bellowed.

Something near the gates moved. A trembling ball shifted, revealing bare arms and legs.

"Emery?" The sound of her voice, the frightened trill, knifed his heart. "The gates were locked…I couldn't leave. I'm sorry."

"Sophie. Oh thank God."

He fought off a wave of self-revulsion when she shied away from him. She looked like a half-drowned kitten, shaky and wet. Emery knelt and wrapped his arms behind her back and under her knees. She wasn't light, but she wasn't heavy either. A perfect weight. He hugged her close to his chest, dropping his chin over her head to keep her face tucked into the groove of his neck. Once she was secure in his arms, he started the long walk back to the mansion. He fought off the panic of being outdoors without Hans beside him.

"You came for me." Sophie's breath warmed his skin. Her hands curled into fists, clenching and unclenching. He quickened his steps, anxious to get her inside.

"Of course." His reply was gruff. He wasn't one for eloquent speeches. He didn't wish to remind her it was his fault she was out there. Guilt stirred restlessly in him, slithering beneath his skin like a poisonous snake. He didn't want to feel responsible for her, but he'd let her come and had agreed to be a dominant in some fashion toward her. She was his responsibility whether he wished to accept it or not.

Of course I'd come for you. No matter where, or how far. You're mine. The thought was oddly right, the need to connect with someone whose way of life, way of thinking was so opposite his own. He was a recluse with secrets wanting to bed a determined re-

porter...dangerous, yet inevitable. Emery was forced to acknowledge that he and Sophie were an inevitable disaster.

* * *

Antonio D'Angelo stood just inside the gates of Lockwood Estate,
his lean muscular frame hidden by a massive oak. His eyes locked on
the sight of Emery carrying the woman.

Almost had him. Antonio had been ready to finish what he'd
started twenty-five years ago. He'd kill Emery and have everything
he'd ever wanted. But it was a hard thing to get inside the gates, let
alone into Emery's house. The man kept an almost religiously perfect schedule of alarms, passwords, and codes. No servants stayed in
the house overnight and those that came during the day couldn't be
bought off easily.

The wireless bug he'd planted in the office of Emery's resident
hacker provided Antonio with a constant stream of information. He
knew each new passcode the second Emery did. Tonight would have
been perfect; the thunder would have covered the sound of his gun-
shots. But the girl had ruined it. The plan had been flawless: he'd
managed to bribe a maid to reinstall the working pieces of the clock
to make sure it chimed. Emery would have had a breakdown and
Antonio would have gotten to him while the bodyguard was out.
If it hadn't been for the woman...There couldn't be witnesses. He
would have to take care of her, too. She'd been dead the moment
she'd gone home with Emery. Antonio would not let her live once
he'd handled his true target.

A sly smile stretched his lips. He could kill Emery and the girl together and make it look like a lovers' quarrel.

But he would not kill them tonight. His clothes were soaked
clear through, and he had important matters to see to tomorrow. He
slipped his phone out of his pocket and dialed a number. When Antonio heard the click on the line, he knew his master was listening.

"I missed tonight. A girl got in the way."

There was silence save for the faint sounds of someone breathing.

"But I have an idea," Antonio added hastily.

Finally the other voice spoke. It was rich and cultured. "Good. I like ideas. See that it's done." With that the line disconnected.

He pocketed the phone, entered the new code for the front gate and slipped out, cloaked in storms and shadows.

* * *

Emery was never so happy to see Hans and Cody as when they were waiting by the door to help him. Hans took Sophie from him so Emery could catch his breath after the mile-long walk. Cody held out a fleece blanket and helped Hans wrap it around Sophie's shaking shoulders.

"Where was she?" Hans asked in a low voice.

"By the gate." Emery waved a hand, indicating the other men should go upstairs. "I'll put her in my room on the bed. Hans, run her a bath. Cody, fix some hot tea. Put honey in it."

Hans climbed the stairs and walked down the corridor ahead of Emery. When they reached Emery's room, Hans laid Sophie down on the massive bed. Her wet pajamas bled rainwater onto the comforter, but Emery didn't care. She curled up in a ball beneath the fleece blanket still wrapped around her. Emery paused in the doorway of the bathroom to look back at her. She faced him, eyes half-closed, and nuzzled the comforter like an exhausted kitten. Hans patted her on the back and nodded at Emery.

"I'll do a perimeter check and head in for the night. Call if you need me."

"Thank you, Hans."

Once Emery was alone with Sophie, he left the bedroom and entered the bathroom. A massive porcelain tub was embedded into the wall. He plugged the drain and turned the polished taps, lingering a moment to test the temperature before he poured in several table-spoons of bubble bath. He'd never had occasion to use it but was thankful he had some on hand. Sophie would want to hide her body beneath the bubbles and he'd let her. For now.

When he returned to his bedroom Sophie's eyes were closed, her hands curled into loose fists tucked close to her chin. He pulled the blanket back from her face and she shivered and opened her eyes.

"Well, aren't you a wet dream." He couldn't resist teasing.

"Ha, ha," she muttered.

"Come on, I've drawn a hot bath for you." He helped her stand and walked with her to the door.

"Undress and get in. I'll be back in a moment." He'd let her undress alone, but he'd keep her company while she bathed. It was time for her to learn that as part of their bargain she had to give herself up to him, even if he just required her companionship.

While he waited to hear sounds of splashing water, he retrieved one of his other t-shirts. She could wear this tonight; no boxers. He wasn't entirely a gentleman; she made him want to be bad, so bad. He smiled. She'd fall asleep getting used to him, his scent, his clothes. He wouldn't have her body tonight, but clothing her soothed some of that possessive need. She was driving him wild with it. Every breath, every look, every little sigh she made even when he didn't touch her, was a devastation to his control. He could practically feel it fraying. He wanted her on her stomach beneath him, creamy skinned bottom in the air, legs spread for him to take her from behind…

Christ…He'd never get rid of this perpetual hard-on if he kept letting his imagination get the better of him.

The faint sounds of water lapping against porcelain and her soft little moan of pure relief told him she'd gotten in the tub. Emery laid the shirt on the bed and strolled back into his bathroom. Sophie lay chin deep in bubbles, cheek resting against the porcelain tub's edge, her long dark brown lashes fanned out over her cheeks. Not moving.

"Sophie!" She didn't stir. He put his hand to her throat, his fingers seeking a pulse. It was strong. She sighed and leaned into his touch, asleep. No doubt she was worn out. She'd fallen asleep fully naked with him in the next room. As much as she acted like she didn't fully trust him, on some subconscious level she must. A warmth blossomed in the center of his chest, the feeling oddly fuzzy, like fleece wrapped around his heart and lungs. What a strange sensation. One he hadn't felt in years.

* * *

Bliss. Sweet, wondrous bliss. Sophie purred as strong hands caressed her arms and shoulders. Those same hands moved up and down her legs, rubbing something soft and silky against her skin.

What a lovely dream! Unable to resist, she curled her toes and shifted her legs toward where it felt like the hands were coming from. The touch felt so good. Touching had never been good before, but it was heavenly now. The few men she'd dated before had never treated her with such sensual tenderness. She could spend the next century letting these hands strum her senses to life and lull her into dreams at the same time.

I've been missing this. This is what my friends must feel when their men hold them close. I would kill to have this, keep this feeling forever.

She rubbed her cheek against a hot, slowly moving surface. It smelled so good, like rich spices and musk. Sophie pressed her lips to the surface and flicked her tongue out, tasting delicious skin.

"Greedy little kitten," a rough voice rumbled—so hot, so dark it made her thighs clench together.

Greedy? He had no idea.

She froze. Her sense of self returned enough to realize she'd been kissing Emery's chest. She opened her eyes and tensed as she realized she was lying on a bed, wearing just a t-shirt, and Emery was beside her, hands stroking her body over the cotton fabric.

"What?" It was the only word she could get out. When she struggled to pull back, to put precious distance between them, he wrapped an arm around her shoulders.

"No, no, Sophie," he said firmly as though she were a child. "I want you close, to feel you're safe and well." He cupped her chin and raised her face. "Can you forgive me for...throwing you out? I wasn't myself."

For a long moment she couldn't speak. He'd had some sort of reaction, an emotional one that had made him unable to recognize her, and he'd cast her out of his house into the dark during a storm. He hadn't threatened her, not really; but there was an undeniable level of danger associated with his presence that she hadn't known she'd have to face. Was finding the answers she looked for worth the risk? There was only one answer.

"Yes, I forgive you."

The darkness formed an ever present shadow to the pain lingering behind the warmth of his eyes. She knew it so well. It was there in the mirror every day when she woke and faced the day. If she could forgive him, why couldn't she forgive herself? If only she'd been quicker to scream for help when the man had grabbed Rachel on the playground. If only she'd been able to memorize the numbers on the license plate of the truck. If only...

Emery paused, his lips parted as though he wanted to say more, but he seemed to struggle to find the words to express himself. "Sophie...I...." He shut his eyes tight and then opened them.

She was lost in the hazel-honey world she found there.

"What?" she pressed.

"I want so badly to make you mine, but I don't trust myself not to have another lapse. They happen sometimes. Usually they fade out and I'm okay. Normally I'm alone, so it doesn't make much of a difference. With you here, I'm terrified I'm going to hurt you."

"But you've been with other women..." She let the words fall between them.

"Yes. But I've never brought them home. I've kept my activities confined to the club. I never seem to lose myself there. But here…"

"Shh." Sophie placed a finger on his lips, warmed to the very core of her being by his worry. "You didn't hurt me, and I'll know to leave you be next time. So don't think you can get rid of me that easily. I didn't exactly help you. I sort of slapped you. "

"That explains why my face hurts," he laughed softly, but the tone was more melancholy than merry.

"I'm sorry. I was just trying to get you to snap out of it. I want to help you," she pleaded.

One side of his mouth kicked up into a charming crooked smile. "Okay. You've persuaded me. Should I reward you for your bravery?"

Sophie arched a brow. "What type of reward?"

"Hmm, hot tea for my little hellion, perhaps?" The second the words left his lips, a young man walked through the door with a tray laden with a teapot and cups. Sophie studied the man, who appeared to be around her age.

"Let me guess. You're the infamous Cody?"

The man grinned. "I'm infamous? Well, the boss man must be improving his opinion of me. Nice to meet you, Sophie."

His casual demeanor, the rough and tumbled sandy blond hair—all of it put her at ease. He reminded her of the men back home—not rich or privileged, and not nearly as intimidating as Emery. While he was cute, he wasn't explode-your-body–from-the-inside-out sexy. Emery had that in spades.

Cody placed the tea tray on the large nightstand by the bed. "I'll be in my office if you need me, boss."

"Thanks, Cody."

The man winked at Sophie, bold but friendly, which earned a heavy frown from Emery and a growled "ahem."

"He's going to be in his office all night?" Sophie cringed at how dreadful that sounded. She hated her little office back in her tiny apartment in Kansas. She rarely spent time in it, preferring instead to chase her stories across the United States, living from hotel to hotel with her editor on speed-dial.

"Don't you dare pity Cody. I spent a fortune building him a suite of rooms connected to his office. He has a king-sized bed, a private kitchen and a bathroom to rival mine. Depending on his mood, he calls it his command center, or the bat cave."

Emery rolled over and reached for the tea, pouring two cups and handing one to her. She drank it gratefully. The chamomile tea was spiked with honey and deliciously smooth going down her throat.

"Bat cave, huh? Oh boy. How on earth did you find him?"

The smile that stole across Emery's lips seemed genuine, so very different from the practiced, seductive grin she'd come to expect from him. "I caught the rascal trying to hack my personal private computer system here at the house. He thought I had sensitive information about my company. He hoped to get trade secrets and patents. I do have sensitive information, but not the kind he was hoping to score. Luckily, I was a few steps ahead of him and I pinpointed his location and sent Hans to retrieve him."

Sophie raised her eyes to Emery's, secretly amused to find that she'd been staring at his lips. He cupped her cheek as he talked. The movement was natural, tender, and sensual at the same time. His thumb circled her chin as though the touch reassured him.

"What happened when Hans found him?"

"Hans got him here no worse for wear. My bodyguard is primarily a preserver of life, not a taker of one, and he has no interest in beating anyone to a bloody pulp, unless they deserve it, of course. But once he got here, I sat him down and we had a little talk. I straightened him out."

"How did you do that?"

Emery took her empty teacup set it on the table behind him. Then he angled her body, rolling her onto her back so he could lean over her, pressing his chest to hers. He kissed the tip of her nose then her cheeks, and then moved down to her lips, sucking the bottom one into his mouth for a slow decadent nibble. Sophie arched up into that erotic bite and tried to kiss him. He laughed huskily and pulled back, depriving her of the pleasure.

"I told Cody that he could work for me, rather than against me. He'd not only have a life of luxury but he'd get me, too."

Sophie struggled to focus on his words. Her hands settled on his chest, feeling the slow flex of his muscles as he shifted.

"I don't understand. Get you *how*?"

His eyes went dark, like rich chocolate with caramel swirls. "When I take someone in, I accept them. It's permanent. If Cody agreed to join forces with me, I'd play Superman to his Batman. A justice league, if you will. He was raised in the foster system. Trust doesn't come naturally to him, but he realized the depth of what I offered, and he agreed. He's been with me and Hans for the last eight years."

"How long has Hans been with you?" She regretted the question instantly, as pain ripped across his face.

"Hans has been with me for twenty-five years. My father hired him. The day after I came home, Hans showed up in my bedroom at the crack of dawn and didn't leave me alone for a second." Emery found an errant lock of her hair and curled it around his finger, staring fixedly at the strands. "I used to hate him."

"Why did you hate him?" Sophie rubbed her cheek against his knuckles, like a cat hungry for attention.

"He was there because I couldn't take care of myself. Seeing him was a reminder of my weakness. But after a few years, I was older and wiser. I realized he was there to protect me because I couldn't protect myself against forces that were unforeseeable. Whoever took me as a child would have succeeded no matter how strong I was. The numbers were against me. Once I accepted that certain scenarios had unavoidable outcomes, I began to value Hans on a whole new level. He kept me out of situations that could lead to such unavoidable outcomes. Friendship was inevitable."

"I like that," Sophie replied without thinking. *Blame it on the drugging kisses*, she thought.

"Like what?" He raised a quizzical brow.

"That you value loyalty and friendship. I don't know too many people who are like that these days." Unbidden thoughts of Rachel snuck past her barriers, like clever spies slipping beneath barbed-wire fences.

Rachel grinning, offering Sophie her pinkie. "Pinky swear, Sophie. It's sacred, you know." Her own pinkie curled around Rachel's, locking them together. Both girls laughing, the secret lighting up Rachel's eyes.

"Tell me something about your brother," she asked. Something in her tone must have gotten through to him because the hungry look in his eyes turned sad. "Please tell me," she encouraged.

"What do you wish to know?"

"Something happy. Something sweet." She put a fist in her mouth to stifle a yawn. Exhaustion battled her desire to stay awake.

"Happy?" His brows drew together; his perplexed expression cracked something deep in her chest. It was as though he hadn't thought of happiness in a long time.

She waited, holding her breath. He had to remember something happy, something good. During the darkest hours of her life, she survived on her happy memories, bathing in them as if they were sunlight.

"Every Sunday morning during the summer, we had tennis lessons. My father was convinced one of us would be a Wimbledon champion someday." His voice was rough at first, as if speaking pained him. The details must have been buried deep within him because he paused, closed his eyes, and after a moment began again.

"Fenn didn't like our instructor. He was a grouchy old man named Mr. Belkin, but he was quite the teacher. Still, as boys, Fenn and I didn't see the value in his lessons. Fenn used to get fed up with running laps around the courts. It was Fenn's idea for me to distract Belkin, and then Fenn would get out his penknife and puncture all of the new tennis balls. Every time Belkin hit a ball toward us, it dropped flat to the ground like a rock." Emery laughed softly, remembered joy lighting his eyes like distant stars.

Sophie tilted her face up, entranced by the sudden change. He looked boyish, mischievous.

"God, Belkin used to get so mad. He couldn't get a single ball to clear the net." Emery sniggered like a devious child. But all too soon the pleasure of that moment vanished like mist over a field as dawn gave way to morning.

She could almost see the walls closing around him, like metal gates slamming down. He was shutting her out.

"Hey!" she slapped his t-shirt-clad chest.

"What?" he growled back.

She nearly smiled, feeling like a small terrier barking at a Bengal tiger. It was only a matter of time before he made a meal out of her.

"You're shutting me out," she said. "I thought that was the bargain...I surrender, you talk. So far you've been all Mr. Grabby Hands, and I've gotten nothing in return."

His eyes turned that eerie shade of burnt umber, like tree bark in winter. Dead and cold. "We mustn't forget your story. Are you planning on a speech when my life's greatest tragedy wins you the Pulitzer?" His comment was a poison-tipped dart thrust deep between her ribs and not easily removed.

"You don't have to be so cruel." Sophie couldn't believe how much his words hurt. She rolled away from him, knocking his arm away to separate them.

Emery got up from the bed and headed toward the door. Sophie couldn't help looking him over. He was delectable in his black t-shirt and gray flannel pajama bottoms, which hung low on his hips. Even as angry as she was with him, she still wanted him to come back and put his hands on her. Despair lodged in her throat, nearly choking her. It wasn't fair of him to get mad at her for doing her job. She'd agreed to the bargain; he owed her. It wasn't as though she'd demanded details, or asked how Fenn died. No, she'd only asked that he not shut her out. Did that make her some sort of villain?

The soft snick of a light switch and the instant darkness in the room was almost as surprising as when Emery returned to the bed, drew back the covers and touched her shoulder.

"Get in."

She threw him a disgruntled look and was all for ignoring him until he swatted her ass.

"Mr. Grabby Hands has issued you an order."

Ahh, Emery, the dom, was back. Sophie bit off the caustic remark that singed the tip of her tongue and crawled under the sheets. Even the man's bedding made her hungry.

He joined her in the bed, and before she could protest he'd curled an arm around her waist and dragged her back into his arms. Her body spooned perfectly against his. It was impossible not to shiver when he placed a kiss on the back of her neck and nuzzled her ear.

"I give you permission to sleep." There was a ghost of a laugh in his whisper.

She bristled. "Thank you, your highness."

Silent laughter shook her body from behind. He bit the lobe of her left ear and electric pulses shot straight to her clit.

"You're most welcome, my dear."

She had every intention of giving him a snarky reply but when it came right down to it, she was too tired. She'd get him in the morning, though. She'd get him good.

* * *

Emery held Sophie in his arms and knew the exact moment she fell asleep. She fit against him perfectly, her rounded bottom snug against his groin, her hair teasing his nose and cheeks, the scent of it faintly floral.

So sweet. He'd never known someone like her. With that button nose and her bright eyes and pink cheeks. Most of all, he was mesmerized by the hungry look she got whenever she watched him, thinking he couldn't see. It did something funny to him. Rather than sleep with her and show her the door, he wanted…her companionship. He wanted to harness her desire for him and use it to give her blinding pleasure. But there was so much more. With her, he didn't feel that need to be reclusive, to hide away from the world.

Insanity. This woman was driving him mad. He almost felt free enough to leave the house, to go into town with Hans watching his back.

Frowning, he pulled her closer, even though he knew that come tomorrow he'd have to push her away. He mustn't let her get too close. She was a stranger with every intention of shining a bright light on his greatest tragedy, his greatest failure. He couldn't forget that for even one second.

Chapter 7

SEARCH DOGS AND LOCAL VOLUNTEERS FROM
SEVERAL PROMINENT FAMILIES IN THE
COMMUNITY CONDUCTED A DILIGENT SEARCH
OF THE VAST LOCKWOOD MANSION AND THE
EXTENSIVE GROUNDS OF THE ESTATE, LOOKING
FOR ANY SIGN OF THE BOYS OR THE MEN WHO
MAY HAVE TAKEN THEM. POLICE BELIEVE THE
SUSPECTS MAY HAVE HAD A VEHICLE WAITING
CLOSE BY AND USED IT TO ESCAPE THE ESTATE
MORE QUICKLY, LEAVING NO TRAIL FOR DOGS
OR THE AUTHORITIES TO FOLLOW.
—*New York Times*, June 10, 1990

Cody Larson propped his feet on the edge of his desk and steepled his fingers. The five thirty-inch HD screens in front of him showed key locations in the Lockwood estate. The one he was staring at with the most interest was the screen showing Emery's bedroom. Cody had witnessed the entire exchange between his employer and the hot little journalist. Emery had probably forgotten he'd had that fan camera installed years ago. There were so many cameras in the house and Cody only watched a few key points. Emery's bedroom was hardly a target for easy access by intruders and no one ever worried about privacy because Emery had *never* brought a woman home before. Cody knew it was only a matter of time before Emery remembered and would have that camera removed.

Cody glanced at the thick file he'd prepared for Emery on Sophie

Ryder. It had been a little surprising for his boss to ask for a background check on the journalist, but he couldn't blame Emery. Yet Emery hadn't yet asked for Cody to bring the report to him. He and the woman were far too busy cuddling like a pair of freaking bunnies. It was so unlike the Bossman to cuddle. Cody had seen enough over the years on his monitors to know that Emery didn't bring women home and he sure as hell didn't seem like the type of man who would snuggle with them.

The door to Cody's lavish office opened and Hans Brummer, Emery's personal bodyguard, strolled in carrying a suitcase. At fifty-one, Hans didn't look a day over thirty-five, yet it seemed like he had a hundred years of experience. The man could read a room quicker than anyone and point out threats and exit strategies immediately.

Cody nodded in greeting as Hans took a seat next to him at the large desk.

Technical gadgets were strewn over the desk like shiny space junk on a distant moon's surface. More than one device had been stripped of its motherboard or had wires thrusting out like multicolored intestines. Cody loved delving into each piece and figuring out what made it tick. Once he'd figured out their technical mysteries, though, he lost interest.

The bodyguard set the suitcase on a table and pulled up a chair next to Cody. He leaned forward, resting his elbows on his knees to stare at the screen showing Emery and the journalist. He flicked his glance toward Cody briefly before returning it to the screen. Hans's brown eyes were so dark they were nearly black, and they never missed a single detail.

"You finish the perimeter check?" Cody asked.

"Perimeters clear, but…"

Hans scrubbed one palm over his jaw, eyes still on the bossman lying in his bed like some giant tiger with a housecat tucked between his paws.

Cody didn't like the sound of that. "'But'?"

Hans was one scary guy. He'd kicked Cody's ass six ways from Sunday when they'd first met. Of course, that probably had to do with the fact that he'd tried to pull a gun on the bodyguard. Stupid move, that was. His body still hurt from just thinking about what had happened afterward. If Hans was edgy, that meant serious shit was going down.

"I found a size eleven hiking boot print by the main gate, only ten feet from the girl's prints."

"Just one print?" After a few years in Hans's company, Cody knew what that meant. The man out there had concealed signs of his passage pretty damned well. "So the guy's a pro. What are our options?"

Hans shut his eyes, rubbed his closed lids with his thumb and forefinger before he sat up sharply, alert once more. "We wait. No need to worry Emery." He picked up the file on the journalist. "So what did you dig up on her?"

"Believe it or not, this girl has led an apple pie life. Except for one incident in her childhood, she's squeaky clean. Boring, in fact. Well, besides her current job, that is. She's had a few nasty run-ins with criminals she was trying to write about, but she's proven useful to the police and solved a lot of cases."

"Really?" Hans's brows drew together. "No wonder she fascinates Emery. What happened in her past?"

Cody hesitated, then flipped open the file and pointed to one article.

Hans picked up the printed copy of the fading article. "Girl witnesses abduction of friend— No help to police in identifying suspect." He faced Cody, his mouth a grim line. "You understand what this means?"

Cody's mind was blank. "Not really. She saw her friend get taken by some perv and the police never recovered a body or made any arrests."

With a weary sigh, Hans returned his gaze to the monitor on Emery's bedroom.

"She wants more than his story. She wants answers he doesn't have."

"Thank you, Captain Cryptic. Care to explain?"

Hans flashed a smile.

"I mean, she thinks that by talking to Emery, she'll work out her own issues with her past, but it's not so simple. Emery isn't ready to move on yet and any answers he gives her won't help."

"How do you know all of this stuff?" Cody asked.

"I have a Masters in Psych from Princeton."

Cody's feet dropped to the floor. "No you don't. I ran an extensive background check on you after Emery hired me."

A corner of Hans's mouth lifted in a smile.

"I have three aliases you still don't know about."

Cody's jaw dropped and Hans laughed as he got to his feet.

"I need to check Ms. Ryder's bags for bugs and then I'm turning in. Don't watch that cam too closely. Emery would be displeased to discover you've turned his private life into a skin flick. He'll have your head for it if he finds out."

Cody snorted. "He's the one who installed the ceiling fan camera, not me."

"He did that to protect himself, not to give you a show."

"Wait a sec. Did you bring her phone?" Cody asked.

Hans slapped the slender cell phone into Cody's palm and he quickly plugged it into his computer, copying all of her data for later inspection. They had to be careful and thorough when checking out anyone Emery got involved with. If there was a fox in the henhouse, they needed to know about it before something bad went down. When the phone's memory was copied, he handed it back to the bodyguard who pocketed it. Hans picked up the suitcase and slipped into the hallway and Cody turned back to the monitors. He focused on the outdoor camera footage, and started scanning the video feed from when Sophie had been by the gate. Maybe he could see the owner of the single footprint.

Hans was right, though. No need to worry the Bossman. They'd had scares before—minor trespasses—and each time they'd dealt with it quietly, keeping Emery in the dark. He was too on edge to deal with the idea of people getting through his defenses. After what had happened when Emery was a kid, Cody couldn't blame him.

* * *

Emery awoke to the sound of a cell phone ringing. Tchaikovsky's Sleeping Beauty Waltz.

Lovely, haunting. The melody for a woman lost in a dreamless sleep. Very Sophie.

He rolled onto his back, surprised to find that Sophie moved with him. In the morning light he could see that the tension he'd seen earlier on her face had faded during sleep. He fought off the sudden urge to smooth a thumb over those spots, touch her soft skin and kiss her until she awoke.

The cell phone continued to ring and Emery finally disentangled himself from Sophie, who continued to sleep like the dead. He slipped out of bed, careful to tuck her back under the covers before he found her clutch purse by her luggage. Hans must have finished his sweep for bugs and slipped the bags in here sometime during the night.

Smooth plastic met his fingertips and he pulled the cell phone out of the purse, checking the caller ID.

Hayden Thorne. Wes Thorne's little sister.

"Figures," he muttered darkly.

He swiped a thumb over the glossy surface of the phone to answer. "Ms. Thorne, I should've known you'd be involved."

"Emery, where the hell is Sophie?" Hayden demanded. "You didn't do anything to her, did you? Sophie better not be locked up in some dungeon or I'll kick your ass!"

Emery didn't feel the least bit threatened. Hayden was around

Sophie's age, but she wasn't frightened of him, had never been. It was one of her few failings. But given she was concerned about Sophie, he'd forgive her.

Emery shot a glance at the woman in his bed and found he was almost smiling.

"I suppose I have you to thank for my new little submissive? She did very well last night at the club."

Silence on the other end stretched for several moments. Then Hayden said, "She doesn't know the rules, Emery. I didn't think she'd actually get your attention. I told her you *never* take women home."

Accusation weighted each word. Hayden had a temper, and Emery couldn't wait to see the man who'd someday take the pleasure in disciplining her temper and turning her aggression toward passion.

"People can change, Ms. Thorne. Ask your brother."

"Leave Wes out of this," she snapped.

He did his best not to laugh, but she was feisty attitude always amused him. It was too much fun.

"So I shouldn't tell Wes you recently purchased a membership at the Gilded Cuff? He was there last night with his sub Corrine."

Hayden took the bait. "Don't you dare tell him!"

"Are you threatening me?"

A soft inhalation on the other end of the line made him chuckle.

"Your new friend is here. Safe and sound, sleeping in my bed at this very moment. I'm not following the rulebook too closely. I know she's innocent of the ways of a true D/s relationship. I'm just giving her a taste and taking some pleasure of my own."

"Promise me you'll be good to her, Emery. I like this girl. She's different. You hurt her and I don't care who you are; I'll take you down. Doesn't matter to me if you are my brother's best friend. Got it?"

Emery was momentarily distracted by the sight of Sophie's restless turning in bed, the covers sliding over her body beneath the sheets. His groin tightened in anticipation.

"I got you, Hayden. As long as she's here, she's safe. But she has agreed to be my submissive. So if you interfere, we'll have a problem."

Hayden sighed. "Fine, deal. And you can't tell Wes about me joining the club."

The line went dead before he could say a word. He was getting ready to slide it back into her purse when it rang again. He didn't bother to look at the caller ID again, thinking it had to be Hayden. He answered it but before he could speak a woman started talking.

"Sophie, thank God. I hadn't heard from you all night. How did the club go? Did you find Lockwood and get him to agree to the exclusive interview?"

The phone cracked in Emery's hold as he squeezed it. He didn't say a word.

"Hello? Sophie? I know you don't like me calling when you're facing deadlines, but the paper can only give you a week. I told you that when you begged me for this story. If you can't get the Lockwood interview, it's done. You'll need to move on to a new subject if you want your next paycheck. I'm sorry, but that's the way it's got to be," the woman said.

"Don't worry. Ms. Ryder will get you an exclusive interview." He didn't care that his tone was cold enough to frost the entire island. He didn't give the woman a chance to respond. He hung up on her, then put the phone's ringer on silent and returned it to Sophie's purse.

His rebellious little reporter, determined to expose him. And he, the fool, was so hungry for her that he'd bargained his story for her surrender. Like a wolf lured by a hint of a crimson cloaked girl in the woods, he was desperate to devour her innocence. So he'd bargained for her. His story, her surrender. Only, she wasn't just surrendering her body; she was giving him something else, something softer yet stronger. Intangible. He could almost feel it curling around his cold heart, trying to warm him. Every survival instinct he had warned him to stay away. Even if she dared to fall for him, he'd not suffer the same mistake. He could and would remain distant. He would take his pleasure, slake his lust, and teach her to open herself up to the realm of passion she'd denied herself, but he would not go further.

He picked his watch up from the nightstand and checked the time. Nine a.m. He had two hours before the Board of Lockwood Industries arrived. They had their primary offices in Manhattan, but Emery rarely visited them and worked almost entirely from his home office at the house in Weston. He grabbed his own cell and called Hans.

"Yes sir?"

"Schedule my jet to pick up the LI board from and fly them out here by eleven. Order our usual catering service to prepare a light brunch and have it delivered in time for the meeting. I need you to run an errand in town for me, too. Sophie needs some clothes. I'll text you her measurements and the shop I want you to visit. Oh, and wake Cody up. I want to see him in my office at ten to eleven with two tennis rackets."

Hans's laugh echoed over the phone. "Let me guess: he's going to keep Ms. Ryder occupied while you handle the board?"

"Something like that." Emery couldn't believe he was smiling again. In the past few hours he'd smiled more, laughed more than he had in years. He'd also worried more. It was one thing to have anxiety over yourself when you'd been kidnapped before. But Sophie? The thought of anyone getting their hands on her…taking her away. His lungs exploded with pain, and he gasped for a quick breath. It would be fine. He'd protect her. She was safe. *Safe.* And she would be even safer in his bed. His worries vanished as thoughts of Sophie—warm, wet and waiting for him—took over. Emery's cock was suddenly hard enough that if he'd had her body under him at that moment he would have pounded her until the bed broke beneath them.

"I'll schedule the flight for the board." Hans hung up.

Emery set his phone on the nightstand and opened the drawer. It was time to start showing Sophie how to be submissive. The first lesson was about understanding who she belonged to. Inside the drawer a pair of delicate gilded cuff bracelets, perfect for Sophie's wrists, lay nestled on a black velvet cloth. He'd had the cuffs for a couple of years, hoping someday to have a woman to give them to. Yet, not a single woman he'd met before now had seemed…worthy of them.

He didn't really delve much into the D/s lifestyle. He didn't spend hours lecturing his subs on proper postures, or punish them for small things. For him, the true allure was control of a woman in bed. He never wanted to see Sophie bow her head to him when they were outside of it. He wanted her fiery, rebellious, completely free, save for those gold cuffs. Those had to be around her wrists. Proof to the world of his possession.

As though somehow aware of his thoughts, Sophie stretched, murmured something, and nuzzled her pillow. She didn't wake up even as he knelt next to her on the bed, brushed the hair back from her face, and peeled back the covers. He positioned one gold collar around her right wrist and clicked the clasp shut. Longing and hunger grasped hold of him. He clicked the second cuff around her left wrist. Fire licked at his veins, and an ache tore through his chest. The sight of the gold around her skin, marking her as his, was too much.

He put his knees on either side of her hips, keeping her pinned beneath the sheets. Sophie woke just as he grasped her wrists and moved them up by her ears.

"Emery, what—"

He took her mouth hard. She gasped against his lips, wriggling, but she couldn't move much. Her arm muscles tensed beneath his hands as she pushed, and then went limp. Sophie sighed into him, kissing him back. Her momentary struggle and surrender made him tense with the prolonged desire to claim her. She'd released her death grip on her mistrust and given him the submission he craved. The soft silk of her hair spilled out over the pillow, strands tickling the backs of his palms like condensed sunlight. Her plump, satin lips were perfect for kissing. So damned perfect.

Emery ground his hips into hers, trying to soothe his cock, which was so stiff it was ready to punch through his pants. He slid his hands up to her wrists then connected his palms to hers. She responded, lacing her fingers through his, squeezing gently. His throat tightened and his eyes burned.

The simple connection—so sweet, so innocent—bound him to her, like a shimmering web spun between them, unbreakable and inescapable. He lifted his head a few inches, needing to see her eyes.

They were luminous, her lashes at half-mast. He was lost. A world of unimaginable beauty existed in the crescent silver of her dreamy gaze. He felt like a man from the ancient world, gazing north at the distant star Polaris, finding his way home by the loyal light that shone there. She saw him, every part of her, her light penetrating the shadows stretching out from his soul. He was open, laid bare before her, a man prostrate before a goddess.

Completely and totally vulnerable.

A tremble racked his shoulders, his muscles clenching and tensing. Then pleasure swept through him. He was in control of this luscious, precious woman. He could take her, give her such ecstasy she'd never recover.

Sophie licked her lips, her breath slightly uneven.

"You have to stop doing that," she whispered in all seriousness, her nose wrinkling just a little.

He cocked a brow. "Doing what?"

"Kissing me like that."

"You don't like the way I kiss?" Her body told him otherwise as he shifted above her, the movement pressing his groin into hers. She raised her hips, seeking him, but the sheet and their clothes kept them worlds apart.

"I like it too much. That's the problem."

He rolled his hips again, reveling in the little hiss of frustration she made.

"What else do you like too much?" He dropped his head to her neck and nibbled on the underside of her throat. She shook slightly, her pulse leaping beneath his tongue. She was incredibly responsive and her inexperience made her reactions raw and pure. It was perfect. She was perfect.

"That. That's definitely too good." Her response was barely more than a breathless rush of words.

"Good. My sub has pleased me with her honest responses. You've earned a reward." He eased off her and lay down beside her on the bed.

Sophie's hands fluttered to her wrists, making contact with the gold cuffs.

"What are these?"

"Cuffs."

Sophie's lips twitched, even as she narrowed her eyes. "Yeah, I can see that. Why'd you put them on me?"

He propped himself up on one elbow and drew a finger along the sensitive skin of her inner right wrist by the cuff.

"It's part of our bargain. The cuffs remind you that you are mine."

"Okay, so what's my reward for allowing this?"

"You didn't allow it, Sophie. You surrendered to it. Never think being a submissive is about allowing your dom to do something. You surrender. You give me your power." Emery cupped her face and held her gaze, forcing her to confront his domination and accept it.

Her eyes—still wild, still free—darkened like a waning moon. "I surrender."

His smile was instant and overpowering. He couldn't have stopped it from happening. The promise of pleasure was there, in her gaze and his body. Sophie returned his smile.

"Now, your reward is to play tennis with Cody while I have a business meeting. I want you to get good and tired for later. Tired subs are less rebellious."

The look she gave him would have melted metal. "Oh yeah? Good to know." Sophie slipped free of him and caught sight of her luggage. A little squeal of joy escaped her lips as she darted over to it and began pulling items out. His eyes locked on the sight of her bottom as she bent over to dig through her suitcase.

Emery swallowed hard as desire struck a vibrant cord in him—pure, hard and ravenous to lay his hand to her bottom, to get her off on the faintest edge of pain.

"I can't wait to take a shower." She padded over to his bathroom. He should have let her clean up, but the desire to get his hands on her bottom was a siren call impossible to resist.

"Stop."

She froze, one bare foot on the marble bathroom floor, the other in the thick bedroom carpet.

He rose and crossed his arms, enjoying this far too much.

"Come here. Now." He pointed to the edge of his bed and tapped one foot.

She crept over, looking suspicious, and rightly so. He had every intention of spanking her.

"Bend over the bed." He pointed a finger at the spot he wished her to be.

Protest and outrage flashed in her lovely eyes, but she did as he commanded.

"Hands flat on the bed by your head. Good girl. Now, when you wish to ask me something and we're alone, you first acknowledge our relationship by addressing me as 'Sir'. For example, 'may I use your shower, Sir?' To which I reply, 'yes you may.' Because you are new to this, only five pats. Count them for me or I will start over. When I'm done, you will thank me for your punishment."

A heartbeat of silence, then, "Yes, Sir."

He was tempted to pull her boxers down, to feel satiny skin beneath his palm, but she wasn't ready for that. He put his hand on her, and she tensed. Then he swung his hand down on her bottom. He didn't strike hard at all, just gave her a little sting. He caressed each spot he struck, letting her count the gentle blows with trembling pants. When he reached five he smoothed his hand over her, delighted to feel her heated skin through the thin cotton of the boxers.

Was she ready for more? He moved his hand down between her legs and cupped her mound, pressing the heel of his palm against the soft fabric. Wetness seared him through the thin cloth. Sophie whimpered and jolted when he found her swollen clit and circled it with his index finger. The hardened bud of her arousal called to him, lured him, promising sweet release inside her body. But he couldn't take her yet; she wasn't ready for his type of sex—for the raw, savage need that blazed inside him like a wildfire devouring a dry forest.

"Take your pleasure. Push back, ride my hand." His voice scraped over his throat, almost guttural as he tried to rein in his own hunger.

She needed little urging to circle her hips, rubbing against his hand. She found a rhythm and when she came, it was with a strangled gasp as she buried her face in the comforter on the bed.

"Th-thank you, Sir." It was so quiet and muffled by the bed that he thought he might have imagined it. As though she was startled by the fact that she'd climaxed.

Emery's hand tingled as he stroked her soothingly. "There will be times, Sophie, when I punish you. I won't ever mark you, or hurt you. A slight taste of pain can heighten pleasure. Never think I mean to harm you. Do you understand? Sometimes a spanking isn't about punishment, but about pleasure."

It was crucial that she understood. He didn't indulge enough in the lifestyle to have many rules or expectations. He didn't want her cowering, head bowed. But he did want her to give up herself to him, for the pleasure they could share. If she could understand that, they would get along well.

"Yes, I understand." Sophie shifted, her bottom rolling restlessly beneath his touch.

He removed his hand and stepped back, focusing on breathing through his nose. He was so hard he could barely walk, but he had to see to her first. Helping her to stand on shaking legs, he led her to his shower. He gave her everything she needed to bathe and with a quick, rough kiss, left her alone.

The second he shut his bedroom door he leaned back against it, drawing in slow, deep breaths. His hands were shaking, his body tense and aching to finish what he'd started. Never before had a woman's body been so alluring, so irresistible, as Sophie's had. Her passion had unfurled like petals seeking the sun, all at the right pats and strokes from his hands, as though she were made for him.

Emery attempted to focus on the LI board as he dressed and left his room, on what he'd need to talk to them about, and how he'd handle Brant if his cousin decided to make trouble with the press release issue. But his thoughts continued to stray back to the woman he'd left behind. He wished thoughts of business would kill his sexual hunger for Sophie. But they didn't. She was on his mind, her scent on his skin, her cries of release still ringing in his ears. He wanted nothing more than to walk back into his room, drag Sophie into his arms and topple them both onto the bed. And that need, that ache to be with her and forget the rest of the world was the worst thing he could give in to.

The last person he'd dared to be close to had been his twin.

Fenn.

And he was gone. Everyone he cared about had left him. His parents had abandoned their family estate after Emery escaped and came home. They'd left the last place his brother and he had been together. Their leaving was a betrayal, one that cut soul deep. He'd been too young to argue when they'd made him go with them to their new home, but after college he'd moved back to the house by himself. It was so easy to hide away from the world, but it was lonely, so damn lonely. But better to stay here, protected and alone, than out there in the world losing everyone he cared about.

He shouldn't have given in to his need to bring Sophie here.

Emery couldn't allow himself to be so foolish with Sophie. She'd leave, and he'd be alone again, too afraid to go out into the world to be with her. Doomed always to be alone.

My penance, Fenn's sacrifice. His life for mine. Always.

Chapter 8

MIRANDA AND ELLIOT LOCKWOOD HAVE
OFFERED A $50,000 REWARD FOR ANY
INFORMATION THAT WILL LEAD TO THE RETURN
OF THEIR GOLDEN-HAIRED SONS. PICTURES OF
THE MISSING CHILDREN HAVE BEEN INCLUDED
WITH THIS ARTICLE IN HOPES THAT SOME
READER WILL HAVE SEEN THE TWINS AND THAT
SUCH INFORMATION WILL LEAD TO THEIR SAFE
AND SPEEDY RECOVERY.
—*New York Times*, June 10, 1990

Sophie leaned back against the shower wall for support. Her body was a stranger to her, betraying her with an orgasm so powerful she'd been unable to breathe, to speak. Her mind had blacked out. She'd been aroused by Emery's punishment, been on fire when he'd caressed her clit and massaged her mound.

It had turned her into some sort of wild animal, needing release with a maddening intensity. She'd shamelessly used him to get what she'd wanted, and had hoped he'd use her in return, but he'd escorted her to the bathroom and abandoned her when all she'd wanted was for him to stay and hold her.

Am I crazy?

To want a man who'd spanked her to hold her and comfort her after a mind-blowing orgasm brought on by being punished?

Yeah, definitely crazy.

Still, if he had stayed, she would have panicked. She needed her space, to reclaim herself again in whatever way she could. She was on the edge of falling off, losing herself to him and his world.

Despite her relief at being alone, the emptiness of the bathroom left her feeling oddly hollow. How had Emery's presence become more crucial to her than her privacy?

After forcing herself through the motions of washing, she got out and threw on some workout clothes. She wasn't a fan of competitive sports, couldn't even name more than five professional football teams, but she loved to exercise. Tennis would be a welcome distraction. And with Cody, she might get some answers to her burning questions.

He was waiting in the hall outside Emery's bedroom. He wore a gray t-shirt and black basketball shorts and running shoes. She bit her lip to hide a smile.

"What?" he asked curtly.

"I thought you'd be wearing a polo shirt and short tennis shorts. You look like you're ready to go play a pick-up game of basketball."

"Yeah...I'm not like the Bossman. He's old school, all class and East Coast money. I'm from inner city Chicago."

Cody lifted his chin. The shuttered, defensive expression on his face made her heart ache. He was as out of place as she was in this world of luxury.

She offered him a smile. "I'm from Manhattan, Kansas. I'm not exactly at home here either."

Cody's face softened. He handed her one of the two tennis rackets. "Let's do this so I can get back to work."

Sophie caught him by the arm, halting him. "Hey, you want to ditch tennis? I'd rather talk."

The fleeting moment of trust she'd established with him faded. His spine stiffened and he slid back a step.

"If it's about Emery, we don't talk about him."

He started walking. She rushed to catch up, trying to match his long strides.

She fisted a hand in his t-shirt sleeve to get him to look at her. "No. You will talk to me because last night he went into some sort of mental episode and locked me out."

Cody froze. His fingers clenched the tennis racket.

"Emery flashed back the second he heard the clock chime and talked to me as though I were Fenn."

"The chime? Of the clock in the hall? Shit!"

He tossed the racket and started running. Sophie dropped her own racket and ran after him.

Cody ran down the steps two at a time and skidded to a stop in front of the clock. He opened the wood panel at the base and ripped out several little pieces of metal, shoving them into his pockets. He studied the clock and the swinging pendulum with a deep scowl.

He flicked his eyes to hers. "Hans removed the parts from this clock years ago. It should never have been able to chime. I'm tossing these parts in the trash."

"So who put the parts back in?" Sophie reached out to touch the rich smooth wood of the clock's base.

"I don't know, but I have to find out. If you ever hear that clock or any other clock chime in this house, you get me or Hans immediately."

Sophie gritted her teeth. "Only if you tell me why."

Silence passed, and Cody breathed hard as he considered her. "Fine, but not here. Let's go to my office."

She followed him down another series of halls, ever more aware of the massive size of Emery's home. Cody paused in front of a gilded door with a keypad entry. He quickly punched in a code and the locks clicked. He gripped the brass knob and opened the door for her to enter.

Cody's office was a cornucopia of gadgets and computer gear. She'd definitely stumbled into Batman's cave.

"Welcome to the Larson Command Center." He pulled back a cushy chair and let her sit down, then shut the door and picked up a little black box. He flicked a switch and the blinking red light on the side changed to a steady green glow.

"What's that?" Sophie pointed to the box as he sat down in the chair next to her.

"Bug jammer."

"Paranoid much?" she teased, but Cody only stared at her, no trace of humor in his pale blue eyes.

"Trust me. Any paranoia I've got is justified."

"Okay, so what's with the clock chimes then?"

Cody slid his wireless keyboard onto his lap. Plinking away at the keys, he set up one of his monitors to reveal a large conference room. Nine men sat around the table. Emery was at the head, talking, but Sophie couldn't hear any voices so she figured Cody must have muted it somehow.

She leaned forward, squinting at the men on the screen. "Cody, did you mute them?"

He ignored her question and instead picked up his wireless keyboard and started tapping away. The computer monitor nearest her started rapidly flashing through various camera feeds. Room after room came up empty. Only when his scan was finished did Cody seem to relax. His shoulders rolled back and the tension tightening his features eased.

"The sound of clock chimes set him off. Hans and I think that wherever the kidnappers held him must have had an old clock. He goes back to the night he escaped. Hans and I have witnessed enough of the flashbacks to have put a few pieces of the puzzle together. Emery and Fenn were held somewhere close by for a couple of months. Then something happened and there was a chance to escape. We think Fenn distracted the kidnappers so Emery could get out. Fenn must have died that night. They must have killed him. Whatever happened, Emery won't talk about it."

Sophie hesitated. "He's going to tell me everything."

Cody's brows rose. "Does he know that?"

"Yes. It's why I'm here. We have a deal." Embarrassment heated her cheeks, but she had to explain the situation to him or he wouldn't help her.

Cody's face darkened. "So you bang the Bossman, and he shares his tragic details over pillow talk? To think, I was hoping you'd be different."

Fury spiked in her. "It isn't like that! You've checked me out. Why do you think I'm here? To hurt him? I have to talk to him. It's not just about the story. I have other reasons."

With a long sigh Cody sank back into his chair, his attention once more on the monitors. "It's about the girl abducted from the park?"

Her eyes burned with tears and she focused on Emery's face on the screen.

"Rachel."

There weren't words for anything else.

Cody's voice was rough when he pointed to Emery on the screen. "That man owns my soul. He rescued me and I can't even begin to repay him. I'd die for him. Hans, too. Do you understand that?"

Goose bumps rose on Sophie's arms. There was an odd sinking in her chest and she shifted restlessly. "I get it. Loyalty like that runs deeper than friendships, deeper than blood. It's soul deep."

Cody released a heavy breath. "Yeah. So you get me when I say if I think even for a second that you're a threat to him, I'll shut you out."

Sophie understood that sort of loyalty even though she'd never had it, not after losing Rachel. But she knew full well what it was like to believe in protecting someone else with every fiber of her being. The fact that she sensed Emery was still in danger made her want to protect him like that.

"If I have it my way, I'll be one of his greatest allies. Cody, I know you saw my life, pulled out all my dark secrets, but you seemed to have missed the big picture." Sophie looked him straight in the eye. "I'm an investigative journalist. The police let me help. I've solved twenty-five-year-old cold cases. I've been looking into Emery's case."

The chair creaked as Cody leaned forward, resting his arms on his knees. Hope burst into his eyes. "You think you can solve the kidnapping?"

Sophie nodded. She knew, just knew in her gut that if she could get Emery to talk, the details he'd give her would be the key to solving it.

"There are things that don't fit. I think it was an inside job. The ransom may not have even been the real goal. What he went through doesn't match up with ransom abductions, but rather resembles faked kidnappings to hide murders. I need Emery to talk to me, to give me those details he hasn't shared with anyone else. I think they might be the key. And if I'm right?" She paused and drew in a deep breath, making sure she had his complete attention. "He's still in danger. Whoever targeted the twins then will still want him dead. He's a ticking time bomb."

Cody was silent for a second. "But it's been twenty-five years. Who's to say the kidnappers are still alive? Or the person or persons who hired them?"

"One kidnapper. I've gotten that much out of him. Whoever the other two men were, they don't seem to be in the picture anymore. We're looking at one man, and if it's an inside job, we're talking family or friends of the Lockwoods. Emery's kept himself locked up here pretty well, but I have a feeling he may be targeted soon. I read that Lockwood Industries is planning to release a new product that will change private security. Is that true?"

The resident hacker coughed pointedly and gave a small nod. "It might be…I'm bound by confidentiality agreements not to say anything, but it will make a ton of money for the company in the coming months."

"And that's exactly the type of thing someone would want to capitalize on if they were planning to take him out. At the right time, Emery's death could make someone very rich. We just have to figure out who."

"One last question." He steepled his fingers, eyeing her sharply, like a falcon watching a field mouse.

"Ask." She knew he meant to test her, could see it in his eyes. He would kill to protect Emery and right now he was making sure she wasn't a threat.

"Why do you care about Emery or what happened to him? Why do you need to solve this case so badly?"

She didn't answer right away, but sorted through the truths that filled her like crystal water in a large stone basin. She'd peered into that water long enough, for so many years, that she knew what mattered and what he wanted her to say because it's what she would have wanted someone to say if she'd asked the question.

"The man who took my friend, the man who took Emery...they can't go free. It's a battle waged every day. Good people try to protect innocent lives, but we don't always win. When someone is lost...we have to find a way to pursue justice. We can't allow people like that to go free, to harm others. I never really wanted to be a journalist, but I owed it to Rachel, to give her justice. If not her, then the thousands of other victims whose lives were violently ended and too soon. Emery deserves to have peace and know he's safe, at least from the man who killed his brother. I wish I could have peace for what happened to Rachel. It's about righting the wrongs, fighting evil. It's my burden, my price. Do you understand?"

"More than you know," he replied in a low voice. He focused on her intently. "What do you need from me?"

She was slightly surprised at his abrupt agreement. Whatever she'd said must have swayed him, and for that she was grateful. "First, I want you to get me everything you know about the Lockwood family. I need every police report, witness statement, anything you've got connected to that night."

"You got it, babe." Cody winked and picked up his keyboard again. "Let's catch some bad guys."

* * *

Emery leaned back in the massive cherrywood chair at the end of the large conference table. Brant and seven other board members watched him. They'd just spent the last thirty minutes discussing whether the latest GPS locator was ready for its launch. The board would sometimes get their feathers ruffled when Emery went over their heads to get gadgets out on the shelves faster. To him it was simple. If the product had passed the safety and warranty tests, then it was ready to go. There was no need for large-scale delay and massive release parties to build hype around the product. Lockwood Industries had been founded on one concept: get a good product, make it affordable, and get it out into the hands of the consumer.

In essence, Emery built products that could rescue people. Waterproof GPS locators, cellphones with satellite connectivity options, ground-penetrating radar. The goal for the devices to help people was of key importance. After everything that had happened to him as a boy, he'd wished he'd had something like the products he made. He'd have given anything for a cellphone that his parents could have traced to find him, but there hadn't been anything like that then. Now, he made product that saved lives. And to Emery, that's what mattered. Not a huge launch party for a product that might reveal massive defects only a month after it hit the market.

"Gentleman, I think you'll find releasing the Black Widow locator a week early will generate more interest and increase profits."

The murmur or reluctant agreement made him nod and stand. "I thank you all for coming."

The board members filed out of the room until only he and Brant remained. Morning light bathed the walnut-paneled room in rich gold. Emery was content to stay in the sun for a moment, absorbing its warmth. After last night, he felt as though the chilly rain had sunk deep into his bones.

"What is it, Brant?" he finally asked.

Brant placed his palms on the edge of the chair he'd been sitting in and looked Emery in the eye.

"The board is concerned about you. You need to start coming to Manhattan for the meetings. They're breathing down my neck about your reclusive tendencies again. A little mystery is all fine and well, but if the general public ever got wind of your…well, that nasty little club you frequent, things could go south for you very quickly. Spending more time with the board might win you support if that were to happen. We need to be meeting at the LI offices in Manhattan, not hopping on planes to come to you. I know you have issues…"

Emery laughed, the sound bitter. "Come now, cousin, let's not bandy words about. We both know you think I'm crazy."

Brant scowled. "I've never said that. You're eccentric, that's all."

"Uh huh." Emery knew his cousin well. Sadly, it was only a matter of time before Brant would try to oust Emery from the CEO position.

"Look," Brant said, "I'm sorry to bring it up. We can talk later." He glanced down at his watch and then attempted to make conversation again. "I suppose you aren't coming to your parents' costume ball, are you?"

Emery started to shake his head but paused at the sound of musical laughter drifting down the halls. It stilled his heart for a mere instant, then it fluttered to life with the wild thrum of a hummingbird's wings. How long had it been since he'd heard that? Laughter filled with innocence, joy, pleasure?

Not since the kidnapping. Twenty-five years.

His eyes closed. Time spun back on a gilded spindle, unweaving the span of dark years to a moment in his life when he had no fear, no pain.

"*Emery, look!*" *Fenn grinned and pointed out the window of their father's study. The sun teased Fenn's unruly locks, casting a shimmering halo of gold over his head. He splayed his hands on the window pane and pressed his face flat against the glass, making faces at Todd, the young gardener. The man laughed, a rich sound that had Emery laughing too.*

He joined Fenn at the window and pressed his face against the glass, making faces at Todd. Todd grinned wickedly and raised the garden hose he'd been holding, aiming it at the window. Water splashed right at the glass in front of their faces. Both Emery and Fenn leapt back before realizing they couldn't get wet.

"No wonder it takes Todd so long to water the flowers." A deep rumbling chuckle came from behind them.

Emery spun, finding his father watching them from the doorway of his study. His father was a handsome man. His dark brown eyes warmed like the black coals and orange flames in the grill when he cooked hamburgers during the summer.

"Dad!" Fenn ran to their father, catching his arm. "Mom says we can go outside since we've finished our lessons. Wanna come?"

Emery joined his brother, grabbing his dad's other arm. "Yeah, Dad, come on!"

Their father laughed and shook his head. "I've got some work to finish, but I'll join you in an hour."

Emery smiled up at his father. "Promise?"

Dad patted his shoulder lightly. "Promise."

If only he'd known that was the last night he and Fenn would spend with their father before their world of safety and comfort would be torn asunder.

The memory dissolved like morning mist evaporated by the rising sun, leaving behind a hollow ache, as if someone had punched him in the chest and stolen something vital.

Somewhere in the house Sophie was laughing.

His Sophie.

A tremor of melancholy rippled through him, the epicenter of his sadness growing larger. *He* wasn't making her laugh; someone else was. She was happy with whoever she was with, and it wasn't him. The thought wounded him, a knife sunk deep in his stomach, wrenching painfully to expose his insides. In that moment Emery hated being hurt, hated that the mere sound of Sophie's laugh caused him to feel this way. He should have known the price would be too high when he'd kissed her. She'd penetrated his carefully guarded heart, made him feel things he'd sworn never to feel, made him weak when he'd sworn never to be vulnerable again.

There was a shriek of feminine laughter, a booming bark of a man's laugh, and Cody went zipping by the doorway, a blur.

"Bring back my cell phone! Hey!" Sophie was shouting. The sound of running steps preceded Sophie by mere seconds and she slid into view, halting in the doorway when she saw Emery. Wearing soccer shorts and a loose t-shirt that said "Train through the pain," she held a tennis racket. Her cheeks were pink, sweat dewed on her brow, and damp spots on her sleeves evidenced she'd been wiping more sweat from her face. She had been working out, just as he'd asked. The faint sound of her panting breath kicked his body into a whole new level of need. He couldn't help but imagine what she'd sound like as she raced toward a powerful climax with him thrusting into her.

Emery's heart leapt into a sprint. He wanted to pull her into his arms, smother her with kisses, fuck her senseless, then carry her to the shower, bathe the sweat from her body and take her all over again. He took a step toward her, every intention of doing just that when Brant spoke, reminding him they weren't alone.

"Emery, you didn't tell me you had a visitor." Brant swept past him and held out a hand to Sophie. "Nice to meet you, Ms...."

"Ryder. Sophie Ryder." Sophie's cheeks flamed, the blush adorable.

He smiled. "I'm Brant Lockwood, Emery's cousin."

Emery clenched his fists as he recognized the look of hungry intent on Brant's face.

Sophie smiled at Brant, but the look was forced; not a hint of warmth gleamed in her eyes. Her reaction pleased Emery. He didn't want Sophie to be interested in his cousin. She belonged to him, not Brant. As if answering his thoughts, her hand moved to her wrists, touching the gold cuffs almost absently.

"Those are lovely bracelets," Brant said.

"Thank you, I got them from a—" her eyes darted to Emery then to the floor— "friend."

"Ah, I see. My cousin has spoiled you, then. He doesn't usually give cuffs to his women unless they're fully tamed."

Brant's comment made Emery's blood run cold. What did Brant mean? He'd never cuffed a woman before. Sophie was his first. The women he'd been with in the past always had their official club cuffs, and took them off once they left the club. Not Sophie. She wore *his* cuffs, at his command. Because she was *his*.

The look of hurt that slashed across her features and the triumphant shine in Brant's eyes told him everything. He'd said that just to upset Sophie. The bastard.

"I should go." Sophie backed out of the doorway. "I'm sorry to interrupt your meeting, Mr. Lockwood. I thought you might be interested in the picnic Hans and Cody prepared. But I see you're busy." She spun on her heel as though to leave.

Emery lunged, catching her arm and tugging her fully into the room and into his arms. He angled his body and hers so that her back was to Brant. He dropped his head, touching his nose to hers.

"There have been no other women, Sophie. You certainly aren't tamed. I'd never want you to be. Do you understand?" He cupped her chin. "Do you?" It was an intimate confession, one better suited to his bedroom without his cousin looking on, but he didn't want her to think for one minute that she was like any other woman he'd met.

Sophie blinked back tears and gave a shaky nod.

"Good. Now what's this about a picnic?"

"We thought we'd dine out on the patio. What do you think?" Sophie prodded hopefully, reaching out for his hand. He met her halfway, taking her hand in his and curling his fingers around hers.

Now this was more like it. The silver of her eyes was alight and sparkling like the sea at sunrise, emotions rippling through her gaze in bright patterns. He held the key to her happiness in his hands, and the power of knowing he could and would make her happy was exhilarating. Sophie's happiness meant everything to him. Even though he knew they were wrong for each other and would eventually part ways, he couldn't help but immerse himself in the here and now and give her what she wanted.

"A picnic?" He pretended to think it over, running a palm across his jaw in contemplation.

"Please Emery. The weather is perfect and I made us some sandwiches."

"Very well, lead the way." He linked his arm in Sophie's, kissing the tip of her nose. She laughed and pushed at his chest. How odd that he couldn't keep from touching her, kissing her, even in the most tender of ways. All his life he'd kept women at a distance, only with them during planned seductions. But with Sophie, he needed to show her affection, chaste and simple as it was. He just needed to feel her. She was flinching less and less, overcoming what appeared to be an aversion to physical contact. How alike they were in so many ways.

When his cousin coughed, Emery sighed. "Brant, you and I will talk later," he called over his shoulder. He didn't miss Brant's irritation and something darker, but Emery didn't care. His cousin's temper needed little provocation. He was constantly unhappy.

Now Emery on the other hand…he was happy. Too many years of guilt and sorrow had rendered his heart incapable of joy. But at that moment, he felt good enough to forget the past, if only for a few hours.

He brushed a kiss against Sophie's temple as they walked down the hall. She gave a sweet little sigh as they emerged into the light outside.

Chapter 9

THE LOCKWOODS HAVE DECLINED TO GRANT
INTERVIEWS OR MAKE COMMENTS TO POLICE,
ASIDE FROM THEIR PLEA FOR INFORMATION.
THIS IS THE SECOND TRAGEDY SUFFERED BY
THE LOCKWOODS THIS YEAR. IN FEBRUARY,
RAND LOCKWOOD, ELLIOT LOCKWOOD'S ELDER
BROTHER BY TWO YEARS, DIED AFTER A LONG
BATTLE WITH PANCREATIC CANCER. RAND LEFT
BEHIND ONE SON, BRANT LOCKWOOD, AGE
EIGHTEEN.
—*New York Times*, June 10, 1990

Sophie nibbled on the last of her turkey sandwich before lying back on the thick, red fleece blanket. The sky overhead was a rich cerulean blue that seemed to go on forever, unmarred by clouds. Beside her, Emery was sitting up, long lean legs stretched out and crossed at the ankles as he talked to Hans about something. She didn't really pay attention to the conversation, something about a man named Wes, Emery's friend, and a woman named Corrine. Apparently there was drama there. A lot of drama. But nothing seemed urgent.

The entire afternoon felt like a dream. Sunshine, warmth, the low rumble of male voices. It made her homesick for Kansas. Her father had three brothers and they were always around. She'd spent her entire childhood waking up to the deep reverberation of male voices in the kitchen below. Usually the owners of those voices were gently teasing her mother. It was a happy memory. Nothing had changed since then but at the same time everything had. She could never go back to those days, sleep in her old bed and hear her uncles' and father's voices, and enjoy life with the innocence that she'd lost.

She was grown. With her own life, living her dreams. But now, in this moment, with Emery, she was creating new memories. The comfort of that removed nearly all of her determination to remain distant. She rolled onto her side and curled an arm around Emery's waist the way she used to cuddle her favorite stuffed bear, Mr. Nesbit, when she'd been a child. Emery kept talking, her action not disrupting his conversation for a moment. He laid his arm over hers. The skin-to-skin contact was delicious and soothing at the same time. Her stomach flipped and her heart bounced against her ribs when he laced his fingers through hers, holding her arm to his waist.

Comfort grew inside her, a slow blooming peony that unfurled its petals and stretched in the sun, finally unafraid to let go of itself, for just a few blessed moments. Sleep called to her and she yawned and rubbed her cheek against Emery's jeans-clad hip. Somewhere in the deep recesses of her brain she marveled at the level of intimacy he'd gotten her to give him. And thinking of that led to memories of that spanking.

Dear lord, she'd be wicked and disobey him every day to get that punishment. He'd known just how to hit the right spot and rub away the sting, leaving her burning only with insatiable desire. A more shocking thought came to her: she knew the intensity of being with him would only increase. What would it be like to let him remove her clothes, restrain her and take what he wanted? He'd spread her thighs wide, thrust into her hard, mercilessly, exactly like she needed. His fingers would stroke her clit, make her come just before he finally unleashed his own animal needs. She needed him to feel that way, to want that as much as she did.

But that need terrified her. Going there with him, bearing her soul, could ruin her. She'd never been able to do that with another man. She'd vowed to submit to him, wanted to, but knowing it wouldn't last…when it ended…

Am I strong enough for that?

Sophie had no answer. Only the hint of an ache in her chest.

"You want dessert?" Emery asked, stirring her from the light sleep she'd almost given in to.

"Hmmm?" She made no other reply.

He laughed and patted her bottom. She jumped as her sensitive skin leapt at his touch. Finally she opened her eyes, blinking several times. Emery leaned over her, a strawberry in his hand. He'd cut the green top off and held the fruit to her lips. Sophie opened, letting him feed her. She'd always loved strawberries, and it was delicious. Licking her lips, she savored the sweet juices, then opened her mouth for another. He watched her take each bite, eyes burning with each little nibble she took from his fingers.

In between bites she spoke. "Have you ever read *Tess of the D'Urbervilles?*"

Emery nodded. "Yes, a long time ago. In college, I think. Why?"

She shrugged, but he caught her chin, the action forcing her eyes up to his.

"Why?" he repeated.

She swallowed thickly, a little nervous. "There's a scene where Tess is seduced by Alec, the antagonist. He feeds her strawberries before he ravishes her."

"So I'm the villain now?" Emery's tone frosted slightly, his once warm eyes cooled.

She kicked her lips up into a devious smile. "The word I was hoping you'd focus on was *ravish.*" She leaned up and nipped his fingers before sucking the juice off them.

I shouldn't bait him.

He was a tiger prowling the edge of his cage of control and she was pulling him by the tail. She was asking for trouble, but logic failed her and hormones took over.

"You offering?" His own lips parted as he touched her mouth with strawberry flavored fingertips. The rough pad of his thumb made her shiver, and heat sparked through her like a thousand pinpricks of desire. Her entire body—every cell—called out to him, compelling him to take what she was offering.

She struggled to find her voice. "I might be."

Heat flared in her cheeks. Want and need throbbed between her legs, beating like a drum she had to answer.

It made no sense, her obsession with him. They were as different as could be and she'd never believed opposites attracted each other. She'd especially never been drawn to bad boys, or brooding men. But maybe that was because she'd never looked deeper. Beneath the wicked glint in Emery's eyes and the layers of his seductive smiles, there was a storm in his heart. One born of passion, loss, pain, and tragedy—all churning together, on the verge of devastating everyone and everything around him. Could she find a way to get into the eye of that storm? Nothing mattered more to her in that instant than finding a way to him, and maybe then she could escape her own nightmares and guilt.

Teach me. Teach me to be strong. It was all that she'd wanted for so long. Peace and strength. To be able to shrug off the talons of her past digging deep into her heart.

Emery bent his head to hers and nuzzled her throat. His lips left ghostly kisses. The world shuddered, light flashing and dimming, as she was lulled into the enchantment of his touch, his kiss. Any wish, any command, she'd obey so long as he never stopped touching her.

When he made as though to move away, she whispered, "Please don't stop. Please…"

A cool breeze teased her hair, tugging strands into her eyes, reminding her they were outside and might not be alone.

"What about the others?" she murmured. She brushed her fingers through his thick, soft hair. She threaded through the strands and tugged lightly to get his attention. He lifted his head and she met his molten gold eyes.

"They went back inside while you were dozing. We're alone." The odd, rough note to his voice sent a whisper of a thrill through her and it scared her at the same time. What if she wasn't ready? He'd take everything she'd give and maybe more. What would remain of her, if she gave him all that she was?

Sophie jerked back, suddenly desperate to escape him. She couldn't do this, wasn't ready to surrender.

"You're not getting away. Not after begging me not to stop." He captured her hands and pinned them on either side of her head on the blanket.

Her pulse spiked again with the fluttering rush of a humming-bird's wings. She hovered, indecisive, knowing she had no choice but to let her passion sweep back in and carry her away.

"You like it when I take control, don't you?" He flexed his hands, tightening his grip a little on her wrists.

"No." She lied, knowing it would bring out the dominance in him. Never had she had the slightest urge to play with fire until now. There was something about Emery that made her wild, reckless. Now she saw the appeal of teasing the flame with her hand, to taste the edge of pain and revel in the delicious burn.

The sharp lines of his face softened with a lazy grin. Like a lion who'd just captured a little mouse, his devilish look of enjoyment said he loved to feel her struggle. And she wanted to struggle, wanted to be chased and caught. Sophie was fast becoming addicted to the rush of fighting and surrendering.

"Let me go." She pushed up at him as though to get rid of him, but she rolled her hips up, pleading for him to keep her pinned. The dance of fight and giving in was an erotic fantasy she'd never expected to crave.

Emery dug his fingers into her skin, not enough to hurt, only to keep her down. He used one knee to push hers apart so he could thrust his thigh against her core, and pressed down. A little moan escaped her, unable to be held in as he slid his thigh against her in a rhythmic motion. The thin material of her soccer shorts offered no real barrier to protect her from the onslaught of sensations and desire from the contact of his leg. She threw her head back, eyes locking on the endless skies.

Her vision tunneled as he licked a path from her neck down to her collarbone, exploring sensitive spots and places that made her shudder and gasp. He moved her wrists above her head, and held them both in one of his hands before he slid his free hand down past her stomach and beneath the waistband of her shorts. He toyed with her simple cotton underwear before he delved deeper.

Panic exploded through Sophie. Her heart battered her ribs like a wild stallion against a fence post. He'd find her slightly rounded belly and be repulsed. She wasn't thin, wasn't flat stomached and trim like other women. Her face flamed and she whimpered. He'd discover how plump she was and lose interest. It was over.

But Emery didn't stop. His hand curved over her lower abdomen, stroking her skin before moving down to cup her mound. He pressed hard and then when she arched her back, he eased up. She dropped her hips in frustration until he teased her clit with his fingertip. He circled it, teased it, tormented it. She'd never touched it herself; it had always been too sensitive, almost painful, but when he brushed over it, the near-pain became something altogether different. Her core throbbed in time with her heartbeat, answering the bolts of lightning shooting out from her clit.

"What are you thinking about?" he asked.

Thinking? She couldn't think past the fact that his hand was between her legs, creating devastation and raw hunger.

When she didn't answer he thrust one finger into her. "I'm waiting for an answer."

"I don't know!" she gasped, hips shooting up to push his finger deeper.

He dropped his head to her neck. The warm rush of his laughter should have upset her but it didn't. He nipped her skin, biting and holding fast to her neck like a tiger with its mate. The sharp but minor flash of pain made her womb clench.

"Oh god!" Her head thrashed. The pain was exquisite, divine…like nothing she'd ever felt before.

Through the haze she heard his voice. "Tell me something secret about you. Something you hide from the world." He licked the sore spot on her neck, then rubbed his cheek against hers like a possessive tomcat. The faint prickle of his jaw gave her shivers. She loved it when he dominated her, even gently.

"Something secret?" She wondered what secrets she had worth telling.

"It can be anything you want. Just talk to me." He kissed her in a melding of mouths, soft and sensual yet packed with erotic delight. When he drew back, she saw the corners of his eyes crinkle with amusement at her inability to talk.

"Umm. My middle name is Eugenia," she blurted out, then smacked her hand over her mouth and shut her eyes in horror at the confession.

The rush of warm laughter over her forehead made her eyes open again. "Eugenia?" Emery didn't even try not to laugh.

"My mother's fault. She wanted something sophisticated. She's never quite gotten over marrying a Midwesterner. She was from Boston. My dad wanted names like Katie, Stephanie—you know, something normal. My mother fought for something more traumatizing, but not intentionally, I don't think." Sophie scrunched her nose up. "God, it made my middle school years awful. Girls can be so mean." She knew she was rambling but she couldn't stop it.

Emery stalled her words by moving his hand, which he still had between her legs. He slid a second finger inside her. All conversation vanished. She fought for air as he started pumping his fingers deep inside her.

"You've been such a good girl, Sophie." He murmured in her ear and rocked against her in time with his fingers, until he became as breathless as she. The thin edge of control hung between them, swaying provocatively and waiting for one of them to give in first.

"Tell me something secret about you." She needed to hear him talk. The rich cadence of his voice did something to her insides, made her core throb and her heart seize.

"Something secret," he rumbled teasingly against her ear.

"No." She tried to speak but he quickened the rhythm of his fingers. "I want you to actually say something secret…"

Lights starting flashing behind her eyelids as she sank into a dark sea of desire rimmed with longing.

"Emery! Oh god!" She screamed as she climaxed, something she'd never done in her life. Pleasure like nothing else, a ghost of near pain as he pressed his thumb on her clit.

Beautiful. Glorious. Devastating.

How apt the words were for this moment. For him.

He panted against her ear, the sound ragged and wonderfully human. Too often she'd thought of him as inhuman, too perfect to be real. But this man—losing control and catching his breath against her—he was real. He didn't say a word. He'd been just as affected as she was. For a long moment they were connected by the lingering scent of passion, the crisp aroma of oncoming rain and the distant chatter of birds.

"Thank you," she finally said.

Emery lifted his head and removed his hand from between her thighs.

"I don't think anyone has ever had that reaction to me giving them an orgasm before."

A telltale heat crept across her cheeks. "You're not upset, are you?"

"Upset for you thanking me? No. Just curious. Why the gratitude?" He helped right her clothes and urged her to sit up. A shiver rocked her, and he wrapped the picnic blanket around her shoulders. "Only the truth, remember?"

"I've never…" She gulped and ducked her head, dropping her forehead onto his shoulder, foolishly hoping to hide from him. "I've never had a climax like that before."

Emery moved fast, sliding her into his lap. He wrapped his fingers around her ponytail and tugged, forcing her head back. His lips brushed hers, and then he pressed his forehead to hers, eyes closed.

"You're killing me, Sophie."

"What?" she whispered.

"You are so sweet. It's killing me. I want so much to—" His words were cut off and she would never get to hear what he meant to say because he lifted his head and sniffed the air.

"Do you smell that?" he hissed and surged to his feet.

Sophie inhaled, and the heavy, acrid scent stung her nose. "Smoke!" She jumped up and promptly stumbled as her legs gave out. Apparently mind-blowing orgasms were not good if she had to run anywhere quickly.

Emery spun, his eyes darting around the grounds, looking for the source of the smell. The curling tail of smoke rising in the sky in the distance told them where the fire was.

"It's the stables." He grabbed her hand and they started running. "We've gotta get the horses out!"

The stables were about a quarter of a mile away from the back of the house. Legs pumping, Sophie managed to keep up with Emery's long-legged sprint through the back gardens and across the lawn. When they finally reached the stables, the waves of heat from the fire almost kept them from getting closer. The wood-paneled building had easily contained a hundred horses at a time in the past. But now the building was mostly empty, Sophie guessed.

"There." Emery pointed to the left side of the stables, where a fire was blazing in a room next to the stalls.

Through the orange inferno and the dark smoke, they could see flames devouring hundreds of golden trophies and shiny blue silk ribbons hung along the far wall of one room where a door had been left open. All evidence of the glorious equestrian history of the Lockwood family was turning to ash. Before she could fully absorb the tragedy of that loss, something exploded in the room and the fire rushed outward. Emery spun and tackled her to the ground, and the air was knocked from both their lungs as an explosion rocked them.

Horses started screaming.

Sophie shoved at Emery, pushing him off her as the flames retreated momentarily. "Get to the horses. Go!"

"Stay back. I'll get them out." Without a backward glance he rushed toward the flames.

She sat there for only an instant, in awe as the red and yellow blaze silhouetted him. In that moment he seemed no mere man but something else. Someone of strength, courage, and compassion. Everything she'd ever wanted to be. Everything she'd ever wanted in a man she hoped to fall in love with someday. Somewhere deep inside, her rational brain screamed at her to get up and go save Emery before he went and got himself killed being noble.

She ran headlong after him, straight into danger. When she ran to the next stall down from where he was and threw open the door, he flashed her an incredulous look before growling about punishments coming her way. He got his horse loose and headed outside while she ran to the next door. When he returned back into the smoke, she went after him.

"There's two more," Emery's shout came through the gloom before horse darted past her and out onto the lawn, free of the fire.

Two more. They could do this. She believed in him, even as her lungs singed inside with the heat of the flames and her eyes burned with smoke.

Just as she and Emery got the fifth and final horse out, the wood around them shuddered, groaned and gave way. She fell to the floor mere feet from the burning stable door. Hands lifted her up and pushed at her backside, hard. She ducked her head just in time, barely missing a collision with a fallen beam, and fell onto soft, cool grass. Emery followed, coughing violently.

They both lay there for a few seconds, clearing the smoke from their lungs, before he wrapped an arm around her waist and dragged her farther away from the burning wreckage. When they were about fifty yards away, he collapsed onto his back, eyes closed, one palm on his chest as he breathed. Sophie recovered a little more quickly and sat up, watching the stable burn.

Flecks of ash floated up around them, caught in the faint breeze and swirling in dizzying circles around the yard like snow from storm clouds. Much farther away, the five horses they'd rescued were watching the fire with nervous eyes. Every one had been saved. Relief flooded her veins, dulling her senses like morphine. Adrenaline left her system and she wanted to curl up in a ball and sleep.

The moment her eyes started to close, she saw a man standing on the other edge of the flames. He wore all black and had a ski-mask over his face. She scrambled to her feet and started running, despite her legs buckling. She lost sight of him when she skirted around the burning stable. He disappeared from view in the thick trees.

"Sophie?" Emery was behind her, one hand settling on her shoulder as he turned her around, face etched with worry lines. "What's wrong? What are you doing?"

"I thought…I saw someone disappear into the woods."

Cody and Hans suddenly burst from the house at a full run. Both men were armed. Cody had a Mauser 9mm, but Hans had an AR-15 pistol ready as he ran. Had she not known Hans a little better, from what Emery had told her, she would have been terrified. His gaze was cold and calculating as it swept the stable and the surrounding woods before he checked on her and Emery.

"I smell gasoline." He commented so quietly she could only just hear his voice over the roaring blaze behind them. "Someone set this fire. I want everyone inside the house. *Now*."

Emery got to his feet. "It's a distraction, isn't it? Set fire to the stables, draw us out."

Hans gave a curt nod and then paused. "Or they wanted to draw us out, knowing we'd rush back in a few minutes later. Could be a trap. Stay behind me until I figure out what we're dealing with here."

They moved as a unit to the back entrance that led to the kitchen. The door was ajar.

Sophie swallowed, her throat sore from the smoke. She bumped into Emery's back, which made Cody run into hers with a grunt. She rose up on tiptoe to peer over Emery's shoulder.

A black box with a red bow on top sat on the kitchen counter. It was about the size of a shoe box.

"What's that?" Cody whispered.

Sophie glanced at him, surprised to find the usual spark of humor in his eyes had faded.

Hans entered first, setting the pistol on the counter with care, flicking the safety on. Then he approached the box, studying it from every angle.

"Doesn't appear to have any weight sensors. It might have something inside that will be set off with movement."

"What? Like a bomb?" Cody asked.

With a low growl of warning, Hans pulled out a small device the size of a smartphone and waved them all back. He clicked on the device and moved it over and around the package. A green light flashed and the device beeped.

"No bomb. Must be organic or something nonmetal." He pocketed the device.

"What was that thing?" Sophie asked Emery.

"A handheld metal detector I created." He started toward the counter, holding her behind him.

"Emery, I don't think..." Hans trailed off when Emery ignored him and undid the bow and eased the lid off the box. Whatever was inside made him freeze. Blood drained from his face, leaving him as pale as alabaster.

"My god," Hans breathed, his eyes wide. Fear shadowed the man's eyes briefly and that scared Sophie more than anything.

She drew closer, needing to see what had frightened two of the bravest men she'd ever met. Inside the box lay a little boy's sneaker. It looked old. A puzzle piece snapped into place and she flinched.

"It's one of Fenn's, isn't it?" She already knew the answer, even as Emery's eyes closed and he sucked in a breath and nodded.

Seeing the reminder of Emery's twin's promising life cut short instantly became one of the worst moments in her life after losing Rachel. The shock sunk deep into her bones. The sudden drop, the fall into darkness and uncertainty, then the understanding dawned like a sun over a barren wasteland.

"Someone set the fire so they'd have time to plant this here." Such a simple plan, yet incredibly effective. It had left the house vulnerable. "Hans, I saw a man when Emery and I got out of the stables. I saw someone in black, wearing a ski mask. He was on the other side of the stables."

Hans bowed his head a moment as though in thought. "He's gone by now. He set the trap and laid the bait. The question is now, what does he want us to do? And how can we avoid it?" Hans balled a fist and slammed it down on the counter. "Damn! We played right into his game. He knew how I'd react. He could only know that if he's been watching us." Hans turned his attention to Cody. "Check the monitors. Find out if we have any angles on him entering the premises. And find out if we have any bugs in this house. If we have to do a room-by-room sweep, then we will."

"This is bad," Cody muttered. "Real bad." He shifted restlessly.

Only Emery remained still. He held the shoe up, his long elegant fingers tracing the shoe's designs and stroking the laces.

"He's baiting me. What does he want me to do?"

No one said anything. All eyes remained fixed on the shoe.

"Should we call the police?" Sophie finally asked.

Emery and Hans both shook their heads and Emery spoke. "No. No police. The more men we allow inside the grounds the more we put ourselves at risk. We need to avoid media attention. Hans, call my parents. Ask if we can send the horses to their stables down the road."

Hoping to hide how badly her hands were shaking, Sophie shoved them in the pockets of her shorts. "So what do we do now?"

Hans looked at Sophie. "We keep quiet and calm. It'll force the man to act again to draw us out."

"You stay here with Hans. Eat and relax. I have some things to see to." Emery picked up the shoe and strode from the room.

"Wait—"

Hans caught her by the arm, halting her. "Let him go for now. He needs some time to banish his ghosts."

Chapter 10

BRANT LOCKWOOD, THE LOCKWOOD
CHILDREN'S COUSIN, VOLUNTEERED TO SPEAK
FOR THE FAMILY AND MADE A PUBLIC APPEAL ON
TELEVISION AND THROUGH THE LOCAL PAPERS
TO THE BOYS' KIDNAPPERS. "PLEASE BRING MY
COUSINS HOME. WHATEVER YOUR PRICE IS, WE
WILL PAY IT FOR THEIR SAFE RETURN."
—*New York Times*, June 10, 1990

Ghosts.

Was he always to be haunted?

Emery walked down the long hall leading to the library. This part of the house was modeled like a French chateau, with stone walls covered by large decorative tapestries. Most of them depicted the Hunt of the Unicorn, his mother's favorite image. The hall was dark enough that the colors in the cloth remained rich. Emery had long ago hated unicorn tapestries. As a boy he'd found them girly, and had rooted for the hunters in the murder of the beautiful beast. But now...

He paused before the scene of the unicorn in captivity. The rich white threads woven in the shape of the mythical beast gleamed in the low light, a glimmer made with a hint of silver thread amid the snow white. The simple wood fence sewn around the beast didn't seem powerful enough to hold the unicorn. It was a marvel that something so wondrous and beautiful, a creature born of magic and moonlight, could be contained by the mortal-made fence.

He stared at the tapestry for a long moment before realizing what was so captivating about the unicorn. It wasn't that the creature was trapped, but rather that it allowed itself to be held captive. It surrendered to the destiny of the tale, giving itself over to the hunters. Emery felt something in his chest tighten and his respect for the unicorn grew. It was submissive. *Like Sophie.* He reached out, touching the unicorn's blue collar, held by a clasp of gold thread that wound around the unicorn's neck.

Innocence captured. Innocence tamed.

Immortality made mortal.

It reminded him of something his mother used to say whenever she'd find a lone Monarch butterfly trying to migrate during a storm, surviving the rain to keep flying against all odds. She'd hold Emery in her arms, point toward the colored wings and say, "Not all wonders are endless. Some last only for a breath of time, but are no less magnificent than the mountains that have stood for millennia or the seas which shape the shores with their waves." Then she'd kiss him on his cheek and send him off to play with Fenn.

Emery's hands clenched at his sides. Fenn's shoe burned his palm. The sting of that long ago night was returning. The old secrets clawed their way up from their graves, churning the soil with decayed hands, as they were resurrected by old evils. Emery shut his eyes briefly, and then continued walking down the hall into the massive library.

The polished walnut bookshelves hummed with life and light. The room was two stories tall. A circular staircase led to the upper level, where a catwalk allowed access to the higher shelves. Red brocade chairs were angled toward the large fireplace and reading tables were placed throughout the room near the shelves. Two tall French doors allowed light to stream through from one side of the library to the other.

The tension that had coiled tight in Emery's body eased almost instantly. Books, especially these books, could calm any storm inside him. So many of the novels were old friends that had kept him distracted and entertained when depression would have weighed him down. In the years following the kidnapping, he'd sought solace among their pages.

Setting Fenn's shoe on the table by the two chairs near the fireplace, he walked to the nearest shelf. His fingers trailed the titles by Robert Louis Stevenson. *Kidnapped, The Black Arrow, Treasure Island.* When his whole life had flipped on its head these stories had kept him breathing. He'd begun to view his kidnapping from a distance, as though it hadn't happened to him, but instead he'd simply read about it in a book. It was the only way Emery kept moving, kept living. So he'd spun a tale to himself about two princes who'd been taken, and one whose life had ended, one life destroyed. And he'd locked the truth away in his heart, deep in the dark recesses where no light could ever shine.

He wasn't sure how long he stood staring at the faded spines with the glimmer of the gilded letters of the titles winking back at him in the afternoon sun. He'd reached a road with two paths ahead.

It was time to stop hiding, at least from himself. He had to tell Sophie everything, let her have the story come what may. If he shared it, the burden on his shoulders would have to ease, and maybe, just maybe, he wouldn't hate seeing his brother's face in the mirror every day.

The headache struck without warning. He doubled over and the light around him flickered, and that other sense, that distant echo of a ghost soul connected to his, stirred.

A work-calloused palm rubbed a jaw lined with stubble. A heavy sigh. Gotta shave. Jeans hung low on the man's hips, the black boots a snug fit. Should be fun to ride the new bull tonight for the crowds. Dangerous as hell. A wicked laugh of excitement escaped him. God, he loved rodeos.

And then just as quickly the image sank below the surface of his consciousness. Emery blinked and rubbed his temples as he straightened. For that single instant he'd sworn he was somewhere else, living in a dream amid mountains where he was himself and yet...not.

He had to talk to Sophie before guilt drove him mad, or madder than he was right now. But first, he needed to do something that was long overdue. He dug his cell phone out of his pocket and dialed his mother's number. He hadn't just hidden from the world all this time; he'd hidden from his own parents. Shame and guilt had erected a wall between them. How could he face them on a day-to-day basis when he'd left Fenn behind to die?

Miranda Lockwood answered after the first ring, her voice soft and worried.

"Emery? What's happened? Are you okay?"

Deep breath in, deep breath out. He could do this, talk to her, like he used to as a child. "I'm fine, Mom. I would like you and Dad to come to dinner tonight."

She laughed lightly, but he could hear the hope mingled with hurt in her tone. "Of course we will. We haven't seen you in nearly five months."

Five months? He'd really let it go that long without seeing them? That made his guilt all the stronger, until the emptiness and loneliness was so deep he couldn't feel the bottom. Like dropping a stone into a dark well...It made no sound, only fell forever into the abyss.

There was a pause as her voice wavered and then she breathed out and spoke again. "What time should we be there?"

"Seven."

"Seven it is. I can't wait to see you, Emery," she whispered, still sounding shaky, and the line disconnected.

His throat tightened and he swallowed several times. Hearing his mother's voice this time brought more comfort than the agony, but the pain didn't fade. His need to be protected, to hide from everything he was afraid to lose, had already cost him his own family, what little he had in life. The last twenty-five years of his life had been wasted while he'd closeted himself away in this house. His parents had lost two children that night, not just one, and he'd brought that pain on them, not his kidnappers. The realization left a bitter taste in his mouth.

"Who were you talking to?" Sophie's voice drifted across the library.

She was standing in the doorway, still wearing her exercise clothes marked with soot from the fire. Her eyes were wide, dark gray, like summer storm clouds with a hint of blue. They were eyes that saw too much, understood too much. He wanted them to see him. He didn't want to use words if she could see the secrets he needed to set free.

Moved by the need to hold her, he held out a hand. She hesitated, and then walked to him. Wrapping her arms around his neck, she drew his face down to hers to kiss him. Surprised, it took him a moment to react, but then he banded his arms around her lower back to hold her close. She felt so right in his arms, as though some great force had made her for him.

"Who was on the phone?" she asked again when they broke their mouths apart. She rested her hands on his shoulders, the touch light, yet still it made him fight repressed shivers of need for her.

"My mother. I've invited my parents to dinner tonight."

Sophie's brows winged up over her eyes. "They're coming here? Tonight?" Her lashes fluttered and she licked her lips.

"I want them to meet you. And I haven't seen them in several months."

"Okay." She rubbed her cheek against his shoulder, still holding him.

Secrets weighed him down, the past a thousand stones in his pockets, pulling him to the bottom of the lake. But if he told her, shared them, he wouldn't have to keep them alone anymore. He curled his hands around her lower back and lifted her up. Her legs parted, going around his hips as he walked them over to a large couch by one of the windows.

Emery toppled backward, letting her fall on top of him as he sprawled the length of the sofa. He cupped her face. Sunlight wove through the pale gold wisps of hair which had escaped her ponytail. She looked rumpled, wind tussled, alive. The women he'd been with before had never had a hair out of place, never had an ounce of sweat even in the midst of passion. Sophie was different. She lived in her body; she didn't keep it pale and starved. She was real, and real was what he needed. The time for facades was over.

"I'm going to tell you what happened."

The heat, which had lit her gray eyes with silver lightning, softened and her smile faded.

"Oh...should we...er...move?" She gestured to their position, where she lay on top of him.

"No. I like you right where you are. You keep me grounded and the nightmares away."

She relaxed into him and laid her head on his chest just below his chin. Emery curled his arms around her and took a deep breath as he readied himself to plunge into the turmoil of memories.

"Three men came in through the back door leading to the kitchen."

"The door we came through after the fire today?" she asked.

"Yes. One of the few blind spots for the cameras. Of course, back then we didn't have cameras." He rubbed one palm over her lower back, stroking her.

"Tell me everything you can remember. Shut your eyes and picture it. Sometimes that helps."

He tensed, every muscle in his body instantly freezing. He didn't want to relive the worst moment of his life, not so vividly. But he knew she was right. She had a point about it being easier to picture. Weren't his nightmares always so real?

"Okay...but..." he trailed off. What could he really say? *Stop me if I start to panic or shush me if I cry like a child?* No. He wasn't a child any longer and he couldn't show such a weakness.

"I'll be here with you. Every step of the way." Her hands on his body tightened, the pressure comforting. She would be there, she'd pull him back from the brink of despair.

Letting his lids close was one of the scariest things he did. But he had to. It was time to let the memories out, free them so they wouldn't weigh him down a moment longer. Twenty-five years was long enough.

He took a breath and began. "I spent the early evening catching fireflies. There were so many of them that summer…"

Light.

Darkness.

Light.

Darkness.

Eight-year-old Emery Lockwood curled his hands around the thick glass jar, gaze fixed on the firefly that buzzed and bumped into the container's sides. The bottom part of the insect's body flashed a pale green and then went dark. The pulsing glow brightened then faded, surging back to life before dying again, like a phoenix from the ashes. It was easy to get lost in the rhythmic pattern of the firefly while the house was quiet and his room was dark. The aroma of fresh cut grass from the gardeners' early work still lingered. The almost tangy scent of it was calming. The bedroom floor was littered with grass clippings from when he'd tracked them in on his shoes after a successful day of bug catching.

He'd spent nearly an hour hunting down the brightest glowing firefly. He grinned.

"Emery!" The whooping shout of his twin brother disturbed the quiet peace of their bedroom.

With a heavy sigh, he pressed his nose against the cool glass of the jar. He wasn't in any particular hurry to answer his brother's shout. He'd much rather spend the evening watching his bug glow.

A second shout echoed up the hall, accompanied by the sound of foot-steps ricocheting off the wood floor outside the room.

So much for being left alone to enjoy his firefly in peace.

"What?" he hollered back.

Fenn stomped into the room, hands on his hips, golden eyebrows slanted over hazel eyes, a nearly exact mirror to Emery's.

"Mom says to come down and get your dinner before the guests get here."

Emery set the jar down and rolled off his bed. "Why didn't you just bring mine up here?"

On nights when their parents didn't host parties, the family ate in the dining room, but when their mother and father had guests over, they were allowed to eat up in their room.

"Nana says we have to eat in the kitchen tonight," Fenn said. "She said we made a mess last time and she doesn't want to find a trail of ants leading to our room again. You were the one that spilled your Coke, not me."

Emery punched Fenn's shoulder. Although younger by three min-utes, he couldn't let his brother boss him around. Fenn always thought he was in charge, and though Emery didn't mind most of the time, an occasional punch to the shoulder reminded his brother that Fenn was not in charge of him.

Fenn plopped down on Emery's bed and cradled his chin in his palms. He prodded the firefly jar with an index finger, grinning as the bug's tail lit up. "So, you coming down or what?"

His brother's smile was infectious. He had a way about him, and Emery couldn't help but smile too.

A flicker of movement outside their window caught Emery's eye. Their room overlooked the thick army of stalwart oaks that bordered the property. Their sheltering darkness was penetrated only with a smattering of glowing, winking lights as fireflies wove through the trees. Emery was certain he had seen something aside from the lazy glow of the Chinese lanterns hanging on strings leading to the gardens.

Drawn by his own curiosity, he leaned toward the window, placing his small hands against the glass, which was still warm from the long gone afternoon sun. His eyes flitted across the bank of trees, looking for whatever he'd glimpsed moments before.

A shape slithered out from behind the edge of the trees, the lights from the lawn just barely illuminating the outline of a terrifyingly tall man, clothed in black, with long limbs like a spider.

Emery gasped, heart slamming violently against his ribs, as though Fenn had knocked the breath out of him with a baseball bat to the lungs.

His twin sat up, hazel eyes suddenly alert, bright and wide with worry. "Emery?"

Wordlessly, he raised a hand and pointed at the figure. Fenn turned, and in that second whatever Emery had seen was gone.

"What?" Fenn scanned the trees, leaning on the window ledge.

Goose bumps dotted his skin and infinitesimal shivers crawled like ants up to his neck and down his spine. "I saw something."

His brother rubbed palms over his own arms, as though plagued by the same sense of unease. They'd always shared feelings. Sometimes he was convinced they shared thoughts.

"Should we tell Mom?" Fenn's voice cracked as he whispered the question.

Emery hastily shook his head. He didn't want to look like a sissy. Their mom was great for rescuing them from some things. She could kill the nastiest spiders, and even got rid of icky girls at Fenn and Emery's birthday parties when the frilly dressed little villains descended upon them during the cake eating. For that alone, she had his and Fenn's undying loyalty, even if she was a grown-up and a girl.

But she didn't need to know he was scared by shadows in the woods.

Fenn crossed his arms and his face settled into a stern expression, eyes narrowed. "You sure you don't want to tell her?"

"You kidding? I'm not messing their party up, no way." He raised his chin. "Besides, I'm not scared of shadows."

"You were scared! I felt it!" Fenn accused.

"Nuh uh!"

Sometimes Fenn was such a blockhead.

"Were too!" Fenn leapt from the bed and socked Emery.

*Retaliation was only natural. Mom always said, "Love thy brother,"
which Emery now silently amended to "Punch thy brother," and tackled his twin.*

They collapsed, kicking, pulling t-shirts, and laughing.

*"Emery! Fenn! Honestly!" A half-exasperated laugh froze them in
mid-battle.*

*The twins turned their heads to the doorway. Their mother stood
there, wearing a pale blue gown with a skirt that billowed out like the
petals of a flower. Her blond hair rippled in long waves down her back,
like a mermaid come to life from the book of fairy tales Nana read to
them.*

*One pale brow was arched as she showed her disapproval. "You're
supposed to be eating dinner, boys."*

*Even though she tapped the toe of her silver shoe like an impatient
princess, a smile hovered at the corners of her lips. Emery's heartbeat
jumped and twisted over and over, like a bird with a broken wing.
More goosebumps pebbled his skin and a chill worked its way up his
spine with the ghostly touch of spider legs.*

*He needed to touch her, to be held by her. Pushing away from Fenn
he ran the few short steps to his mother and hugged her. With a soft
laugh of delight she returned the embrace.*

*Her fingers threaded through his hair, the contact simple yet so
full of love. He squeezed her tighter, desperate to hold onto her. Some
primal instinct warned him things were on the verge of disaster. He
rubbed his cheek against his mother's silk dress before glancing at Fenn.*

*Fenn was watching them, his body captured in the frame of the bed-
room window. The forest below was lit up with Chinese lanterns as
servants carried them out to the trees. The bobbing lights cast multicolored glows over where the shadow had once been. Rather than be*

reassured, Emery's worry grew, gnawing at his stomach like a ravaging pack of wolves.

"Mom?" Fenn opened his mouth, but Emery silenced him with a faint shake of his head.

"Not now." Emery mouthed. Even if he was worried, he didn't want to ruin Mom's party. Even though Fenn hadn't seen the shadow, didn't believe, he, as the eldest, often saw it as his duty to care for Emery. Emery hated that sometimes, but he wasn't going to let Fenn's sense of duty ruin the party.

Fenn sighed.

"Come here, Fenn." Their mother held out an arm and Fenn joined in the embrace. Boys shouldn't like hugging their mothers, but Emery didn't care, not in that moment.

"Now. Both of you, downstairs. Eat your dinner and be nice to Nana."

Mom shooed them down the spiral staircase. Emery raced Fenn into the large kitchen where a dark-haired woman a little older than their mother was setting out plates with sandwiches.

Nana's dark hair was pulled back in a loose bun. Wisps threaded with faint silver, like Christmas tinsel, hung loose against her cheeks. Her eyes were black, the irises so dark that they blended with her pupils. She always had a ready smile, one she kept just for them.

Nana smoothed her hands over her pants and pointed to the barstools. "Sit, you two."

"Nana, can I have a Coke?" Fenn asked, crawling up the tall wooden stool to sit at the huge marble island. Emery joined him, so their elbows knocked together. On the verge of scuffling again, they shot each other mutinous looks and simultaneously balled their fists.

"Emery," Nana warned. She'd knocked their heads together more than once when they stepped out of line.

His cheeks flushed with heat. "Sorry."

He and Fenn settled down to eat, sipped their sodas from the bottles and watched the guests pass by the kitchen windows. The Lockwood mansion's kitchen had an ideal and rather unusual location in the house. One entire side of the kitchen had large windows that faced the gardens, giving the cooks something to watch when taking breaks between meals. There was one door that led directly outside to the gardens and it was on the left side of the room, near the walk-in pantry.

Outside, strains of music filtered through the air, mixing with the cicada songs and cricket symphonies. Muted laughter warmed Emery's ears with the pleasant melody of happiness. Dad. Something was making him laugh.

Fenn's eyes locked on the windows facing the gardens. "Nana, can we go outside? Puh-lease?"

"No Fenn, sweetheart. You boys ought to be in bed. You have tennis lessons tomorrow at eight-thirty." Nana ruffled a hand through Fenn's golden hair. He wrinkled his nose and pulled free of her touch like a disgruntled puppy. Emery snickered at the expression on his brother's face.

Fenn narrowed his eyes and glared at Nana. "I'm not a sweetheart." He used the imperious tone their father employed when answering his work phone in the study, sounding very stern, all businesslike and no nonsense.

Nana only grinned. The laugh lines around her mouth and eyes crinkled.

"So like your father. No wonder you drive your mother crazy." She picked up the plates and set them in the sink before heading to the pantry. Fenn followed her, ready to argue his case.

Emery turned his attention back to the windows facing the gardens. Women danced on the marble patio, their gowns swirling around their ankles in bright colors. Men in suits held them, spinning them around and around, in a whirling world of light and life.

Suddenly the door leading in from the gardens opened and the only warning he had that something was wrong was Nana's gasp and Fenn's muffled cry. Emery turned just in time to see three men dressed in black and wearing masks enter the kitchen through the open doorway. The world around him came to a grinding halt. He was suspended in terror *as he saw Nana rigid and scared. Fenn, eyes wide, was held prisoner by one of the men. The music from the party muted into near silence; the only sounds were the raging thunder of Emery's heart and the scuffle of boots behind him. He tried to flee but a gloved hand clamped around his mouth, and an arm curled around his throat in a chokehold as he was hauled back into a huge body.*

"Please!" Nana was gasping. "Please don't hurt them. They're only children!"

The man holding Emery swung around in the direction of Nana's voice. Emery glanced wildly about, seeing his brother being held by the scruff of his neck, a hand silencing him too. A third man strode toward Nana, a black gun in his hand.

Cold black eyes, like onyx stones, fixed on Emery. The gun barrel pointed at him for a moment before the man turned back to Nana.

He was going to hurt her. Bile rose in Emery's throat and he swallowed it down. He had to do something, anything.

An ancient instinct to survive surged through Emery. He clawed, hissed and fought like an angry bobcat. The arm around his neck tightened. Black spots grew in slow increments across his vision until he was on the edge of darkness. Aching pain swept through his arms and legs, then they went numb. Emery had no strength left to fight and only then did the hold on his neck ease. Glorious air flowed back into his lungs, and he gasped like a goldfish that'd accidentally leapt out of the bowl.

"Why are you doing this? What do you want? Money?" Nana's arms were raised up in surrender, but her gaze kept flashing to the boys, checking to see if they were all right.

Emery wished he could tell her that he loved her too. But the hand around his mouth prevented any sound. Tears stung his eyes, and he blinked them away, his vision blurry.

The armed man strode right up to Nana and without so much as a warning, struck her temple with the butt of his gun. She went down like a rock, blood splattering the white tile floor by her head.

Emery's throat burned as his strangled scream was silenced by the gloved hand.

"Stupid bitch," the man with the gun muttered. "Come on, we've got the brats. Let's go."

He flicked the gun barrel toward the back door. Emery was lifted off the ground and held tight. Ahead of him he could see his brother was being carried the same way. They were halfway out the back door when Fenn somehow got loose and dropped to his feet. He scrambled backward and reached the knife block on the counter, pulling a blade out to swing at their attackers.

Fenn didn't hesitate. He struck, sinking the knife deep in the leg of the man who'd carried him. The man bellowed and swung at him like an enraged man-eating black bear. Fenn ducked, and the man's hand swiped the soda bottles off the counter.

The sharp explosion of glass made everyone freeze.

Everything happened so fast after that. The man with the gun skirted around the counter, caught Fenn by the throat, and ripped the knife away from his hand.

"You little bastard!" He backhanded Fenn, but didn't release him. Fenn's head snapped to the side. A red hand-shaped mark quickly formed across his cheek.

Trapped, immobile, silenced, Emery couldn't scream, couldn't move. He was unable to defend his brother. It was, to that point, the single worst moment of his life.

The lively sounds of the party offered a haunting backdrop to the horror before him. Their parents and guests were only a short distance away, yet all were unaware of what was happening. His captor moved outside, walking past the other man, who once again lifted Fenn.

Emery freed one hand, reaching for his brother.

A brush of fingertips, the reflection of agony and pain in his brother's eyes, and then they were ripped away from each other and stolen from their home.

They left behind their last refuge, their world of adventure. Emery's *eyes blurred with tears as he fought for one last look behind him. The green glass from the bottles glinted and sparked in the waning light like emerald gemstones sprinkled with ruby drops of blood.*

* * *

Emery's lashes opened slowly. He had the strangest sense he'd awakened from a dream, rather than having just confessed the secret horror he'd suffered for the last twenty-five years. His gaze sought Sophie's. Her chin rested on his chest, and large, diamond-sized tears hung precariously on the tips of her lashes. She blinked rapidly, cleared her throat, and spoke. Only a tiny waver betrayed the emotion she seemed desperate to hide.

"What did the men look like?"

"Two of them looked average. White men with brown hair and brown eyes. Could have been brothers. The third man…He was huge, or at least he seemed that way to a couple of eight-year-olds. He had dark hair with a hooked nose and black eyes. He had an accent. I couldn't place it then, but now I know it was Italian. His name was Antonio. I never caught his last name, but I heard the others call him that when they thought Fenn and I were asleep."

Emery closed his eyes. He concentrated at first on Sophie. She felt good on top of him. The air was thick with the mix of her natural scent and the shampoo from her hair. But he had to let it go. Had to focus on the memories.

"Where did they take you? Do you know?"

"One of the crumbling mansions about eight miles from here. It was abandoned, condemned. No one would look there for us, or have a chance of seeing us."

"Tell me about the place they kept you."

He summoned the memory and spoke aloud as it unfolded.

The walls were empty shells, the paint peeling and faded with the barest hint of color left. Trees grew between the cracks in the marble floors, the force of nature challenging the man-made structure. Ivy snaked up the crumbling banister of the stairs. Much of the second floor had been obliterated by the elements after so many years. Even as terror clamped vicious claws around his heart, Emery mourned the loss of the grandeur. It was like finding one of his favorite toys broken, knowing it could never be fixed, and the games he'd loved to play were forever ended.

The thick scent of rotted wood and decay filled his nostrils, the pungent combination further tainted by the smell of Fenn's blood as their captors dragged them to a door beneath the stairs.

"Should we put them in here, Antonio?" One man asked the dark-haired leader.

"Yes. Throw them inside," Antonio barked.

Emery and Fenn stumbled into the darkness and the door slammed shut behind them, a lock clicking into place. He immediately felt around until he bumped into Fenn, who sat on the floor.

"You hurt?" he whispered.

"My arm hurts a little." Fenn lifted his arm in the dim light and Emery saw a streak of blood beneath the torn shirt.

Both boys were quiet for a long while. A single shaft of muted light slid through the crack by the door.

"I'm scared, Fenn," Emery whispered, a shiver slithering the length of his spine.

"Me too."

"Do you think Mom and Dad will look for us?" Emery wanted to believe their parents would search for them. He prayed they wouldn't think he and Fenn had run away. If Nana was alive, she could tell them what had happened. If she was alive…

"They'll look. I know they will," Fenn said calmly, but Emery could feel his brother shaking next to him.

Emery forced his eyes open. The library ceiling was awash with an artist's rendering of Mount Olympus and the Gods and Goddesses. It was such a contrast to the confined darkness he and Fenn had lived in during their captivity.

Funny. He'd rarely looked at this mural over the years. It was only now, lying here with Sophie, that he noticed the painted heavens.

"You must have been so scared." Sophie shifted her head, bumping his chin. Her arms tightened around his chest.

Scared? He'd been petrified. Terrified out of his mind. Thanks to that damned closet he became unhinged at the thought of being in an enclosed space, couldn't sleep in any room with closed doors where there weren't light switches within easy reach of his bed.

"They kept us in the closet for the first two weeks."

Sophie gasped and raised her head. "They never let you out in all that time?"

"They did. Separately. Just to go to the bathroom and to wash with cold water from a bucket. We only ever had a few minutes."

Icy water, the thick cold sponge raking over his skin. The piercing sunlight so sharp and painful after hours in the darkness.

"The worst part was at night." His skin crawled from the mere recollection.

"What happened then?" Sophie's eyes were wide, full of sorrow and worry. The emotions swirled like blue clouds over the silver of her eyes.

"The bugs and rats came. Cockroaches got under our clothes, rats crawled over us while we tried to catch a minute or two of sleep."

Tiny paws scampered over his bare arm, the squeak of a rat shocked him and the painful pinch of tiny teeth sank into his forearm.

A scream tore from his throat. Fenn grabbed his arm, hushing him.

"S'okay, Emery," he murmured. "Did it bite you?"

"Uh-huh," Emery replied in a half-whimper.

"It'll be okay. I'll watch for them. Go back to sleep."

Even though it was too dark to see his brother, he found Fenn's hand and clasped it in his own, the touch a simple and vital reassurance. They were together.

"I got bit. A lot. After…after I got home, they took me to the hospital. The doctors were worried about infections and I remember getting several shots."

He shuddered at the memory of the way the hospital nurse had jabbed the needles repeatedly into his skin without warning. He'd cried. Cried for his mother, his father, for Fenn. He hadn't been able to stop. And when he'd finally run out of tears and was only sucking in ragged breaths, he'd been forced to stay all night in the sterile hospital room. His mother had curled up around him on the hospital bed, holding him, while his father had slept next to him in a chair. Even though he'd been safe, he hadn't slept a wink that first night. It was only when dawn arrived, washing the room out with its glow, that he'd drifted off to sleep and slept for nearly two days without waking.

"Don't drift away from me." Sophie cupped his face in her hands, her elbows resting on his upper chest. "Keep talking, but don't let the memories drag you back."

Her request sounded so easy, but it was impossible. He could no sooner stop the tides from pulling the sea out each night.

"We've opened a can of worms, Sophie. I've spent years trying to bury these memories. You wanted them; now you've got them." He hadn't meant to snap at her, but his reply came out clipped.

Her flinch made his chest ache with regret. Determined to apologize, he curled his hands around her wrists just beneath her cuffs, his thumbs stroking the delicate skin of her inner arms, where he could feel the rapid fire of her pulse.

"I'm sorry. It's not easy to relive this. When I was a kid I convinced myself it was just a story, that all that happened wasn't really to *me*. But telling you...it brings it right back inside me. I *can't* stay distant."

Her lashes dropped, spiking over her cheeks as she closed her eyes. She sighed. "I know how you feel."

He laughed bitterly. "You don't. People always think they understand. They don't."

Her lashes flared up, revealing aggressive gray eyes. "Actually, I do."

"What?" He tightened his grip on her wrists.

"I guess you haven't read the file that Cody gave you?"

Emery blinked. "No. Not yet. Why?"

"Well, you should. It's a real pager turner." Sophie tugged her wrists free and rolled off him. The second her feet hit the floor, she walked away from him.

The instinct to chase her down was strong, but his mistrust got in the way, kept him where he was. He sat up and rested his elbows on his knees as he watched her.

Sophie paced the length of the library, her gaze taking in the room.

"This place is so beautiful. Every room is like something out of a fairy tale." She stopped before a shelf by one wall where a gilded picture frame sat. Inside was a picture of Emery, Fenn, and Brant. Brant stood in the middle, his arms locked around their necks in a fake chokehold. At eighteen, he'd been older and stronger, and he'd always pushed his younger cousins around.

Thankfully Brant had outgrown his headlock phase. Of course now he was all about creating deadlocks with the company board. If it wasn't one thing, it was another. Damn. Today was a string of disasters between the meeting with Brant, the fire at the stables, finding Fenn's shoe. A moment of peace with this unique and haunted woman. That was all he wanted.

He focused on Sophie, tracking her every move. Her breasts bounced just the slightest bit as she set the frame down and walked back a few steps. Hunger for her, for the pleasure she could give them both, made his body taut.

"Sophie, come here," he commanded.

She eyed him warily and then walked over. He parted his legs and motioned for her to step between them. She came, obliging him, even if she was reluctant.

"Straddle me," he demanded.

Rebellion warred with desire on her face, but desire won out and she complied. She placed her hands on his shoulders for balance as she lowered herself. Her knees parted, her legs sliding around to hug his hips. The action brought her close to him, their pelvises bumping. He didn't miss the flare in her eyes, the spark of heightened awareness. He cupped her bottom, squeezed as she rocked forward with a tiny gasp.

"Tell me what happened to you. What's in your file that I should know about?" He leaned forward and when she tried to lean back, he put a hand on her shoulder blades, keeping her in place. She was at the perfect height for him to nuzzle her throat. He flicked his tongue out, relishing the faintly salty taste of her skin, even though he tasted soot as well. She needed to shower before dinner tonight. But right now he needed answers.

"Talk to me." He kissed a path up her neck to her mouth. Her body gave a little shiver, as though she were on the verge of coming undone.

"Read the file." Her tone was probably supposed to be impertinent but he chose that moment to smack her bottom and her words came out in a rush of fast breaths.

"We are sharing, remember? I tell you something, you tell me something."

She wrinkled her nose and glared down at him. "I'm not ready to talk."

When she tried to distract him by grabbing his face and planting a kiss on his lips, he nearly laughed. Her attempt to dominate him was cute. But he was the dominant one. Clearly she needed a reminder.

Emery snagged her wrists and wound them behind her back, pinning them there, and used his other hand to take hold of her neck and pull her face down to his. She squirmed, only making him more restless and hungry for her.

"Stop wriggling or I'll take you on the floor. With the mood I'm in you'd be in for a hell of a ride, and trust me, you wouldn't like getting carpet burns," he warned with a low growl.

She tugged her wrists, but his hold didn't let up. "I think you say things like that just to shock me."

She didn't believe him? Her mistake.

Holding onto her, he lifted her up as he stood and then he dropped to his knees on the thick carpet by the couch, efficiently pinning her to the ground beneath him. She was trapped chest to toes and couldn't move, except for her head.

"Still think I'm bluffing?"

Sophie had the good sense to look hesitant before replying. "Okay, so obviously playing strip poker with you any time soon is out of the question, because I can't read you at all."

"Strip poker? That's an excellent idea for later. I'm damn good at cards." He couldn't resist leering down at her, and she laughed.

"Oh good lord, you'll be the death of me." She blew out an exasperated breath and tried to dislodge his body from hers.

"Hmmm," he chuckled, enjoying her half-hearted struggle. "I'll be preoccupied during dinner tonight, thinking of all the ways to get you naked. Whether it be cards…or otherwise."

"You'll be thinking about sex with your parents right there?" The shock in her eyes and the delightful way she parted her lips made his erection harden to painful proportions. Seeing his chance for relief, he dropped his head and kissed her. Open-mouthed and hard, his tongue conquered hers. He swallowed her little sounds of pleasure. It was impossible to keep his hands off her. Dinner was a few hours away and he was already regretting calling his parents. Seeing them could have waited until tomorrow.

Have to have her, now. He'd gripped the neck of her t-shirt, ready to rip it right down the middle to get to the feast of her breasts and stomach, when a voice disturbed them.

"See, Hans? Like I said, humping like bunnies. Better get a hose and spray 'em down," Cody sniggered from the doorway of the library. Hans, rather than looking amused, was frowning in obvious disapproval.

"Get off me," Sophie hissed, shame tinting her face as she shoved at his shoulders.

Emery kept her pinned beneath him a moment longer, pushing his hips down, reminding her that he had every intention of staking his claim on her later. He bent, stole a kiss rough enough to leave her blinking in dazed surprise. Then he got to his feet and helped her up, loving the way she wobbled and fell against his side.

"Why don't you get cleaned up?" He swatted her behind and prodded her toward the door. When she left he made eye contact with Hans and flicked his head to indicate that the bodyguard should follow her. Hans returned the signal with a nod and trailed off after her.

Cody leaned a hip against the nearest chair, looking entirely too smug about interrupting Emery's seduction.

"Cody, get me her file. It's time to read up on my guest."

"You got it, boss."

Chapter 11

IN THE THREE MONTHS SINCE EIGHT-YEAR-OLD
TWINS EMERY AND FENN LOCKWOOD HAVE
GONE MISSING, NO RANSOM CALLS HAVE COME
IN. NO ONE HAS SEEN ANY EVIDENCE OF THE
CHILDREN SINCE THE NIGHT OF THEIR PARENTS'
PARTY.
—*New York Times*, September 12, 1990

Another shower. Sophie had taken one only a few hours ago, yet so much had happened since then. She looked a wreck. Soot blackened her nose, forehead, and neck, and her eyes were red from the smoke. She still wore her exercise clothes from tennis that morning. It marveled her that Emery had wanted to touch her, let alone kiss her. The man was unpredictable.

And hot. Burning hot and dangerous. She wanted him bad, so bad she had the shakes, like an addict during withdrawal, when he wasn't nearby.

If Cody and Hans hadn't come in…they might have done the horizontal tango on the library carpet.

Damn Cody. Then again, did she really want her first time with Emery to be on the floor, sweaty and covered in ashes?

No.

Sophie showered quickly and did her best to style her hair.

Naturally it didn't want to cooperate. It had to be a universal truth: a woman's hair never cooperated when she was about to meet the parents of the man she was seeing. Well, she wasn't technically *seeing* Emery. How *was* she supposed to define their relationship?

She imagined the look of horror on his parents' faces if she said, "Hi, I'm Sophie, I'm letting your son seduce me and in return he's telling me about the worst moments of his life."

Yeah, bad idea. Perhaps she should leave the explanations to Emery.

When she left the bathroom she was surprised to find a midnight blue dress lying on the bed, along with a pair of red flats with silver buckles on the toes. She picked the gown up and couldn't help but admire it. The cut was A-line and the skirt flared out like a dress Grace Kelly might have worn, only there wasn't a scratchy crinoline underneath. Instead it had a built-in, multilayered, silk underskirt. The bodice looked fitted and the waist would be trim. Sophie checked the tag and blushed when she realized it was her size. Who had purchased the clothes? And more importantly, how had they known her size? It was then she noticed the small note tucked inside one of the shoes.

She pulled it out and read it silently.

Sophie,

The shoes and dress are my gift to you tonight. Wear them and nothing else. It will please me. Disobey and you will face punishment. I have been lax in letting you take control. Tonight I will remedy this.

~Master Emery

Master Emery. It sounded so dark and sinful. It reminded her of that first moment she'd met him in the club. Domineering, sensual, powerful. She eyed the note thoughtfully. So he didn't want her wearing anything underneath the dress?

A smile curved her lips and she fought off a giddy little laugh. She glanced around the empty bedroom, then hastily dropped her towel and donned the conservative black bra and panties she'd retrieved from her suitcase. So he thought to order her around. Well, he had another think coming. She wasn't going commando under this dress. If he found out and punished her? Well, she did like the spanking and wouldn't mind at all if they repeated that little activity.

She slipped into the dress and was relieved to find the material stretched a bit, which meant she could reach back and tug up the zipper herself. Once done, she peered at her reflection in the full-length mirror, surprised to find she looked good. Really good. Emery's gilded cuffs gleamed against her skin. She touched them, admiring the way the light from the window caught the bracelets and they glinted with promise. He'd put a sign of his possession on her. For some insane reason, she was happy. Another unexpected smile snuck up on her.

She wanted to find Emery and thank him for the dress. No one had ever spoiled her before, or treated her like this. It made her feel girlish, hopeful. Like a woman her age should feel. But she hadn't felt this young and happy...well, ever. Sometimes she worried she'd spent so much of her life trying to fix past mistakes that she'd never given herself a chance to have a life, to just be herself without any baggage weighing her down. Unable to resist giving in to one small temptation, she swirled around in a slow circle, watching her skirt poof out in a blue cloud around her knees.

With a delighted sigh, she left the bedroom and wandered down the hall. Rather than going back down to the kitchen or to Cody's command center, she took a new route, picking a hallway at random. Some force inside her pulled her in this direction like an invisible string, drawing her closer to something important. The farther she walked the dustier the paintings and side tables were. Tiny cobwebs hung on the high wall sconces lining the hall. Why hadn't the maids cleaned this part of the house? It looked abandoned.

She paused in front of one door, the only one along the long hallway that wasn't closed. The force that whispered silkily in her mind entreated her to look within. She set a palm against it and pushed. The door creaked on its hinges as it opened, revealing the sight within.

Her heart shot up into her throat and her blood chilled.

Emery stood only a few feet away, between two twin beds. One lay bare, the other was strewn with toys and knickknacks like small marbles and baseball cards. Sophie held her breath as Emery knelt on one knee and set the single tennis shoe at the foot of the bed that was covered with toys.

It's a shrine. For the brother who'd died.

Without looking at her, he spoke. "A part of me always expected him to come back. I kept our room the same, but…" He bent his head and rested his forehead in his palms. "He's never coming back. I'm a damn fool for hoping otherwise. He's dead."

Sophie was too upset to breathe or to make a sound. He was hurting, a kind of hurt she was intimately familiar with and it was breaking her heart to see him like this.

Finally he got to his feet and faced her. Dark circles hallowed his eyes, making his features look gaunt and haunted.

"Don't you want to know how I know he's dead?" The edge in his voice was razor thin.

"How?" she croaked out on a harsh breath.

"Because I left him to die. Fenn distracted our captors while I escaped. I was outside the house when the shot rang out. I was the *coward* who ran and left him behind with those monsters." The raw agony in Emery's eyes ravaged her soul, but he kept talking, even when she didn't want to hear anymore. His hands were clenched into white-knuckled fists.

"You know what they say about twins. There's a connection. When the gun fired, I felt it. Like it exploded out of the back of my own skull. The pain was so bad that I tripped and busted my chin on a rock." He ran a finger over a small scar on his chin; it matched the placement of a wound she'd seen in a photograph of him when they'd found him.

Sophie started forward but Emery turned away. "It went dark. The little voice in my head, the pulsing light that was my brother. It went dark."

At his words, her own soul seemed to sink below the surface of a deep, cold sea. It would be so easy to surrender to her own pain, to allow his to join hers and drown them both in a tide of misery.

He raked his hands through his hair before he put his palms on the window sill. He hung his head.

"Sometimes I get these flashes, these instant glimpses of someone else, a life so different from mine. It feels like him, but it can't be. He's gone. Otherwise he would have come home. I feel like I'm going insane. The world is pulling me apart from the inside out."

She knew exactly what he meant. There were moments when she felt like an old tapestry with its edges frayed and torn. All it would take to unravel her was a tug on the right thread.

She inhaled slowly and went toward him. When she touched his shoulder he flinched but didn't pull away. "Is that why you locked yourself away?"

"It's a fitting punishment. I ran, left him behind to die. Now I wait for a boy that won't ever come home, a brother who will never grow up."

Sophie wrapped her arms around his waist and laid her cheek against the back of his shoulder. He was trembling, but he wasn't alone anymore and neither was she.

"You asked me what happened, what made me understand you. My best friend Rachel was kidnapped. We were only seven. A man stole her from the playground. I was the only one who saw him.

They never caught him. They never found her body. And I couldn't give them any information—no license plate, no details, to catch him. I *failed* her, my best friend."

Emery went utterly still. He turned around in the loose cage of her arms, wrapping his body around hers, crushing her to him as though she were precious.

"What could you have done? You were practically a baby," he murmured in her ear. His lips teased her sensitive skin and his warm breath was soothing as he nuzzled her hair.

"So were you." She stroked his chest, feeling the rich fabric of his dress shirt slide beneath her hands. "Even though it's the truth, it doesn't ease our guilt."

He tilted her chin back to peer down at her in all seriousness. "Is that why you came here? You hoped I had some secret answers, some way of coping?" He laughed softly, full of sorrow. "Sophie, I locked myself away in this place. I have no more answers than you."

He was right. She hadn't been willing to accept that tragic truth until now. Suddenly an idea struck her.

"Why did you never tell anyone what happened? Why not take the police to the mansion where they held you?"

"The man in charge, Antonio, said he'd kill my mother and father if we ever breathed a word of what happened. Of course, he told us this while still pretending to ransom us. I thought if I just stayed quiet, he'd leave me alone, not harm my parents."

"Wait. You just said 'pretending.' He wasn't really intending to ransom you?" If that was true, her research on the case had been leading in the right direction. The real intent could have been to murder the boys. A purpose like that often was connected to an inside job.

Emery shook his head. "After the first three weeks, Fenn and I overhead him talking to the other two men. They were making plans for our disposal, but had to wait for the signal from whoever was in charge. Apparently, the ransom was a ruse. Someone must have hired him, otherwise his waiting so long to finish us off doesn't make sense. Now it's happening again."

Sophie narrowed her eyes, peering over Emery's shoulder out the window as she puzzled over this new development. Just as she suspected. Planned, carefully planned murder of the Lockwood twins.

"Maybe whoever hired him was waiting for something to happen and killing you had to be postponed. He might have gotten scared about being exposed if he had Antonio make another run at you once you were safely home again." It made sense. A third party could have hired Antonio and the others to take the twins, kill them, and make it all look like a botched ransom. But once Hans had been hired it would have made Antonio's job harder, and he'd probably been advised to wait until Hans and Emery lowered their guard. Even if it took twenty-five years.

"Antonio never spoke of anyone else. He was a cruel bastard and spent most of the day finding ways to torture Fenn and me."

"Emery, who could benefit from your death?" It was a risk to ask him something so sensitive, but she could feel the puzzle pieces were so close to coming together. She felt as though she were in a heavy cloud, and although she could feel shapes a dense fog wrapped around them, cloaking them from view, making them appear different from the truth.

"No one. I don't have any enemies. Not even my business competitors hate me enough to try to kill me. My parents are retired, my uncle dead. Brant has fifty percent ownership of Lockwood Industries."

At the mention of Brant, Sophie's hair rose on the back of her neck. Something in her gut warned her he couldn't be trusted.

"Through his father?"

"No, Uncle Rand didn't leave anything to him in his will. He sold everything he held back to my father. Brant had to buy his way back into the company. When I took over from my father, I let him in pretty cheap."

"That was nice of you," Sophie murmured.

He shrugged. "I offered him the company, full out ownership five years ago. He didn't take me up on it. Said he liked his position on the board and didn't want me to leave as the president. Brant's not perfect, but he's no murderer." Emery cupped the back of her neck and held her still as he bent his head to her, stealing a soft little kiss.

She rose up on tiptoes to return his kiss, letting all of her worries go for the moment. Cupping his face, she stroked his cheeks and licked at his lips, begging him to open his mouth to her. Emery curled his fingers around her waist and lifted her up against his body. With a gasp, Sophie clung to his shoulders before smiling at him and claiming his mouth again. Years of inner wounds—lonely aches, pain, and sadness, all of the things that had weighed her down and punctured her soul since she was seven years old—ceased to matter.

The feel of Emery's mouth on hers, his arms around her body holding her protectively, flooded her with strength and hope. So long as he held her, kissed her, wanted her, she could do anything. She couldn't think about when this kiss would end. That someday she'd have to go back to her own life. Leaving him would cleave her soul in two, and she'd have to use every bit of her willpower to stay alive. For now…she had this moment.

Beautiful and bittersweet.

* * *

His world was reduced to one single action. A kiss. Who was this woman who plucked his heart from his chest? He was a dominant man and should be in charge. Yet she stripped him of years' worth of armor. Once more he was naked before her, telling her his every secret, his shames, his failings. And his dear, sweet Sophie had told him her own secret.

Rachel.

Her confession forced him to admit a disheartening truth. *We do blame ourselves for the past.* When you loved someone you signed on for the worst moments, the darkest hours. Some battles were obvious. Soldiers went to war on battlefields, giving their lives for their friends. There were other struggles where people were just as brave, though more quiet in their suffering. Mothers who held sick children in cancer wards, parents gazing at the empty bed where their child should be, or a little girl on the playground, watching a gray van drive away, leaving only a black cloud of pollution behind, as her friend was stolen from her.

It was all the same in the end. Some lives were snuffed out too soon, but many of those lives had been filled with love, surrounded with those who stayed and fought to support them till the bitter end. It was those survivors who were faced with the hardest battles. They had to forge ahead without their loved ones and exist with the pain of loss.

Shame burned through him like a roaring fire, searing his insides. He'd hidden from the people who cared about him. His parents hadn't been able to break through his carefully erected defenses. He'd kept them out. And he might have continued to do so until he died, if it hadn't been for Sophie. She'd dragged him kicking and screaming out into the light, and he couldn't go back. He didn't want to.

She broke free of his mouth and buried her face in his neck. A cold dampness soaked through his shirt where she'd tucked herself against him.

Tears. Sophie was crying for him. Another wall was obliterated inside his heart. His own eyes burned and he blinked rapidly. Her empathy for him, her own suffering, told him she wasn't anything like the cold-hearted journalist he'd wanted to paint her as. She was so much more. Sophie Ryder was all heart, and right now her heart was bleeding for him. He wasn't worthy of her tears, yet they filled him with a sense of healing reverence.

"Shush." He rubbed her back in slow, smoothing strokes. "Don't cry, please, Sophie." He tightened his grip on her body as she inhaled a ragged breath.

"I'm okay." She insisted, sniffling once or twice. She pushed at his chest as if determined to separate herself from him.

With a heavy reluctance he let her go, feeling as though his entire existence was ripped to pieces at the distance she put between them. She stepped back, dabbing at her eyes with her fingers, rubbing stray tears away. "I'm sorry I lost control." She looked as though she wished to say more but he fixed her with a stern glare.

"No apologizing for showing me your heart. Never apologize for that." He cupped her shoulders in his palms and pressed a kiss to her forehead. "Come on, I need to fetch something from my room. My parents will be here soon." He led her from the room and back down the hall.

Her eyes widened. They paused outside his bedroom door and he waved a hand for her to enter.

Understanding flooded his senses. Her faint trembling and shimmering silver eyes spoke of fear. "Don't tell me you're afraid of them?"

"Well...yeah. They're your parents. I...What exactly will they think of me?"

"That you're lovely, intelligent, and entirely mine." *That's all that matters to me.* "Did I tell you how enchanting you look?" He brushed her hair back over her shoulder, reveling in its silkiness.

"No, you didn't." She crossed her arms and looked up at him expectantly.

"You are beautiful. I must admit I chose your dress well."

Sophie's lips parted on a gasp. "You picked these? How?"

"I had Hans take me into town while you were cleaning up. There's a little boutique there. The woman who owns it is a close friend. Do you like what I've chosen?" Unable to resist he fisted his hands in the dark blue skirts, loving the way he held her captive. Earlier at the store he'd seen many different dresses but this one had seemed so Sophie.

The conservative cut, but the lively flare and bell shape of the skirts gave her comfort and mobility, and for once he found those two qualities appealing. The women he'd been with before had worn tight, restrictive clothes. While outwardly they'd appeared sexier, he'd had a damned hard time getting their clothes off. With Sophie, he could get his hands up her skirts and find her center with ease, and have no trouble taking what he wished, giving her what she needed. As his friend, Madeline, had packaged up the dress, all he could think about was how at dinner he could slide his hand up her inner thigh, stroking her to a slow burning passion, all without any suspicion from the others. And Sophie would have to control herself, or else reveal what his touch was doing to her. It would be a wonderfully wicked game.

"Of course I like it. I guess I expected that if you were picking something you'd make me wear some slinky black dress."

He cocked an eyebrow at her, surprised she'd assume something so wrong. "I want easy access to you and for you to feel comfortable. A woman has stronger orgasms if she's comfortable. Slinky dresses hold no interest for me."

Her blush told him everything and it was too much to resist. He caught her wrists by the cuffs and removed a slender chain from his pocket, connecting the cuffs together. With a panicked gasp she struggled to get free but he lifted her arms above her head and hung the tiny chain connecting the cuffs to the small brass hook sticking discretely out of the wood on the left bedpost at the end of his bed.

"Hey! Let me go, Emery. Seriously." She struggled to stand on tiptoes to pull the chain free. It was no use. Just the way he wanted it to be, Sophie at his mercy.

* * *

Emery stepped back and crossed his arms, studying her with a satisfied expression. "Beautiful and tempting." He walked a half circle around her, eyes skating over her appreciatively. Her body responded with a flush of heat from her head to her toes. Finally he came back to her and cupped her cheek, his thumb tracing patterns over her lips, while his other hand settled on the back of her lower thigh. He coasted his hand up, and the erotic and playful stroke made her core throb. His hand froze when it met the silk of her panties. Emery's brows drew together in displeasure.

"I specifically told you to wear the dress and nothing else. Did you misunderstand the instructions or did you rebel on purpose?" The dark carnal gaze he covered her with made her thighs clench tight together.

"Uh...I misunderstood?" she answered in a breathless whisper.

His hand holding her cheek moved around to tangle in her hair and he tugged her head back. "Try again."

Sophie licked her lips, noting the way his eyes tracked the movement with fascination.

"I rebelled."

His hold in her hair eased the slightest bit, but his breath quickened. Suddenly he dug the fingers of his other hand into the silk of her panties and ripped the fabric. The small garment dropped to the floor at her ankles. She was bare, completely open now. She felt more vulnerable to him than ever, as though the destroyed undergarment had provided some defense to his wandering hands.

Emery shaped the curve of her bottom, clenching the rounded flesh once before dipping his fingers lower, to the folds of her sex. He brushed them, teased them apart and sank one finger deeply into her. Sophie arched up, pleasure zinging through her limbs like bolts of electricity. He swirled his finger, then thrust it deeper, repeating these two actions as he moved his lips to her neck. Starting with soft kisses, he worked his way down to her collarbone, then back up to her ear, mixing licks and nibbles as he commanded her attention with his mouth and hand.

The power of his hold over her was like a spell. He used her body, plucking at it like strings on a harp, until she was quivering and aching to sing for him in a melody of pleasure and need. She tugged hard on her bound wrists, trying to free herself so she could touch him, feel his muscles ripple beneath her body. A twinge of pain circled her wrists but it faded in the wake of Emery's skilled kisses. The rush of the oncoming climax built like a storm gathering high in the clouds and Sophie sucked in a breath, her eyes closing as she awaited the explosion of passion.

In an instant, Emery robbed her of the orgasm that had been so close. He withdrew his hand from between her legs and released his hold on her hair. When he stepped back, she saw the victorious gleam in his eyes. He raised his hand to his mouth, sinking one of his fingers between his lips. The action was so subtle, yet so seductive. Her knees knocked together as she watched his full sensual lips suck her honeyed essence from his fingers. The blood still pumped in her ears, violent and hard, as though she'd climaxed and she was still hanging on the edge. Watching him lick his fingers, clean them of her taste, made her crave his mouth between her legs, even knowing it would probably kill her if he ever licked her there.

The dark and flirty smile he flashed at her was blinding. He knew exactly what his actions did to her—unwound her from the inside out and spun her back wildly into his world where she had no control. Without a word he turned and walked into the bathroom to wash his hands. Sophie's arms and legs shivered with the near release. She squeezed her thighs against each other, feeling her slick juices coating her legs.

Damn! She wanted to scream with frustration. He'd done it on purpose.

When Emery returned a minute later, he carried a small damp hand towel. He knelt at her feet and raised her skirt with one hand while he washed her clean. She parted her legs, humiliation coloring her face and flooding her with heat as he washed away the remnants of her unfulfilled desire.

He dropped the cloth onto the floor and pushed her skirts out of the way even more. He rubbed his cheek against her right thigh, the prickle of his stubble burning her skin deliciously. With a heavy sigh, he pressed a kiss against her inner leg, close to the apex of her thigh, and then moved back, dropping her skirts. When he stood, he once more towered over her. He slid his hands up her arms, massaging her muscles before he reached her wrists and held them doubly imprisoned between him and the cuffs.

"I know you're angry with me. But you deserved far worse than that for your punishment. I am feeling lenient and grateful to you for comforting me today. So I went easy on you. In the future…" he shut his eyes and rested his forehead against hers. "The more we come to know each other, trust each other, the less I'll let you get away with. Don't disobey me again."

The words "or what?" died on Sophie's tongue at the strange mixture of shame at her behavior and comfort from being held by him. It was an odd contradiction, and her heart and mind were unable to process it. She had disappointed him and it left her feeling restless and anxious. The more time they spent together, the more they seemed to become attuned to each other. Sensing the other's needs, not just their desires. He was craving her just as much as she craved him, and it wasn't just sexual anymore. They were relying on each other emotionally, something she'd never thought would be possible for her, and he acted as though it hadn't been possible for him either.

Yet, as he held her, she knew he wasn't angry; perhaps his disappointment was only temporary. She would make it up to him. She'd promised to be submissive. It was part of their bargain, but somehow it was more than that. She wanted to submit, not because of some agreement they'd made, but because of how pleased he was with her when she successfully surrendered to him. She wanted to see approval gleaming in his eyes, feel the touch of his hands in pleasure rather than in punishment.

Emery unlocked the cuffs and brought her wrists down, rubbing at the reddened circles left behind. Neither of them said anything for a long moment as he massaged her wrists.

"Time to go meet the parents?" Her smile was strained and tension tightened her face.

"My mother is sweet, and my father…well, just don't let him intimidate you. His bark is worse than his bite." Emery chuckled at the pale look of fear on her face. "Trust me. You'll do fine. Be yourself."

Sophie walked with him outside the room and down the hall before she spoke. "That's what worries me. Be myself? With my job, I doubt they'll find that endearing."

"Endearing? No. But they might be relieved." He tucked a lose coil of her hair behind her ear.

"Why?"

Emery and Sophie reached the stairs that led down to the main entryway.

"I've never told them what happened that night. They deserve answers. They deserve the truth. And you are going to help me give it to them."

Chapter 12

MIRANDA AND ELLIOT LOCKWOOD ARE LOSING
HOPE. STILL NO SIGN OF THEIR MISSING SONS.
—*New York Times*, September 20, 1990

The sound of voices reached Sophie long before she saw the source. A soft, lighter voice, slightly husky, merged with a rich baritone one. Sophie shot a glance at Emery, who walked calmly beside her toward the door, but his hand gripped hers so tightly she thought her bones might break.

"They're early," he noted with surprise.

Panic swept through her. Her muscles cramped and her lungs seized.

"Oh God, I can't do this." She started to back away but Emery caught her by the waist with one arm, the gesture outwardly relaxed, but his hold was firm.

"Sophie, calm down, or I'll take you back to my room and bend you over my knee..." He let the sensual threat sink in. She forced her lungs to open and her tension to fade.

"Okay." She meant only to glance at him, but that one look held her locked in place.

"I need you to be with me. I haven't…" he cleared his throat. "I kept myself apart from them for so long that I feel like I'm a stranger lost to them."

Lost to them? She wondered at his choice of words. Wouldn't he feel *they* were the strangers? Then again, he'd been a lost little boy so long ago, perhaps he'd never been able to escape that feeling and was finally now confronting it. She squeezed his hand back.

"I'm here. As long as you want me."

With a little nod, he seemed to relax. "As long as I want you," he echoed.

They rounded the corner at the bottom of the stairs and Sophie caught her first glimpse of Miranda and Elliot Lockwood, talking with Hans and Cody. Sophie was struck instantly by Miranda's beauty. She was in her late sixties, but the woman's ageless face made her look not a day over forty. She wore a knee-length, white and black striped dress and black sandal wedges. Her gold hair was swept back in an artfully styled bun, threaded with fine hints of silver.

Emery's father was dressed exactly like Emery, in an expensive suit and an ice blue tie over his crisp white dress shirt. He was incredibly handsome. Laugh lines bracketed his mouth and crinkled the corners of his eyes as he shook Hans's hand and grinned with warmth. Sophie's heart clenched. Emery's features were a masterful blend of his parents': the twinkle of his mother's eyes, the relaxed but even-tempered smile of his father. Emery's face bore his mother's features honed to masculine perfection, and his body carried the muscular build of his father.

The welcoming hubbub grew silent as Miranda and Elliot noticed Sophie and Emery for the first time. Miranda's eyes tracked them uncertainly and she raised a hand as though to reach for her son before she dropped it back to her side. The tension was palpable.

"Emery…" she began hesitantly. Hurt and loneliness carved aged paths over her face, showing twenty-five years' worth of misery and heartache.

When Emery made no move to go to her, Sophie reacted and jabbed him in the lower back, hissing just softly enough for him to hear. "Hug her."

He moved immediately and caught his mother's hand to press a kiss there, a formal reaction. But his mother tugged him into her arms for a tight embrace.

"After all this time," she said just loudly enough that Sophie heard. "I will not let you pull away from me." There was anger and hurt hinted at in the soft cultured voice, but Sophie heard it. Miranda Lockwood had missed her son. *Deeply*. Even though he only lived a few miles away, he must have made it seem like an ocean separated them. Her heart went out to Miranda.

"It's good to see you, Mother," he murmured.

Miranda held him, her eyes closed as she kissed his cheek, her body shaking against him.

Elliot gently tapped his wife's shoulder. "All right, Mandy, let the boy breathe. I want him to introduce his lovely guest." He didn't hug Emery as his wife had. Instead, he held out his hand and after a second, Emery took it.

Miranda wiped her eyes and released her son, her gaze zeroing in on Sophie.

Emery quickly stepped back and curled a supportive arm around Sophie's waist. "This is Sophie Ryder. She's my—" He looked down at her and then with a wicked glint in his eyes he finished, "girlfriend."

Standing behind Emery's parents, Cody's eyes popped wide and Hans's lips quirked.

"Girlfriend? I know we haven't seen you in months, but I wasn't aware you were…seeing anyone." Miranda assessed Sophie with a critical eye that had her wanting to blush and bury her face against Emery's chest to hide. Instead she smiled and held out her hand in greeting. She had to seem confident now; that's what Emery needed. Her support.

"It's a pleasure to meet you both."

Miranda and Elliot were still hesitant but finally they each shook her hand, as though surprised that Emery had finally introduced them to a woman. He'd confessed earlier that day that he'd never introduced them to a woman he'd been seeing before.

"Dinner should be ready." Emery cut in when his mother opened her mouth, likely to start in on questions.

They proceeded en masse to the dining room, where the salad course was already set out. Sophie was oddly relieved to have Hans and Cody there. They acted like buffers against what would have been an extremely awkward dinner with just the Lockwoods. Hans and Cody were her allies now and it might be handy to have witnesses present if the Lockwoods decided to interrogate her. Given the calculating look she was receiving from Elliot, she thought she might already be tied to a chair and getting questioned beneath a single lamplight in a dark room had Emery not been present.

Elliot pulled out his wife's chair, allowing her to sit, and Emery mirrored the action for Sophie. His palms settled on her bare shoulders for just a moment. The touch was a fleeting comfort and a sign of support she desperately needed.

When she found the courage to face Miranda, who sat directly across from her, she managed a nervous smile. Emery carried on a polite conversation through dinner about other family members, mutual friends, and the status of the company. Sophie noted with interest that while Elliot had surrendered his role as president to his son years ago, he still kept up with the latest news.

"Is it true that the Black Widow GPS locater is virtually untraceable by metal detector scans?" Elliot asked. He toyed with the stem of his wineglass, rotating it in small circles over the white tablecloth as he spoke.

Emery swallowed his food, took of sip from his own wine and

then leaned back in his chair. "Yes. The device is small enough to fit in any cell phone. It's designed to piggyback off the motherboard of any device and it blends in like a chameleon. You can't detect it with any metal detector devices. It also has a tracking range of 500 miles." Pride was reflected in his tone.

Sophie perched on the edge of her chair, fascinated to hear Emery talk about his company and the products he made. It was the first she'd seen of the infamous businessman, but it was also the first time she'd seen passion in him outside of their bedroom activities. His enthusiasm excited her. What he described would be groundbreaking.

"I heard Brant was trying to push back the release date," Elliot remarked.

Emery chuckled and set his napkin on the table. "As usual, Brant is all about theatrics. I told him no. We've set a date and we're running with it. LI doesn't need release parties and all of the hype our rivals resort to. It's unfortunate that Brant disagrees but it's still my decision."

"True enough," Elliot agreed. "Brant doesn't understand what our company is really about. He's always loved the power, not the purpose."

When chocolate mousse was brought out for dessert, Miranda finally spoke up.

"Now, Sophie, my son and husband have thoroughly monopolized the evening. I would like to get to know you better. Tell me, what do you do for a living?" She leaned forward in her seat, a determined cast to her lovely eyes.

"I…uh…" Sophie really believed now was not the time to discuss her occupation.

"She's a journalist." Emery cut in. "She's actually here to write the story of the kidnapping. It's how we met." He captured her hand as it crept across the table toward her wineglass. Raising her fingers to his lips, he kissed her knuckles.

"I see," Miranda said slowly. Her eyes narrowed on her son in a mixture of concern and then distrust as they flashed to Sophie.

"When you mean the story…" Elliot set his wineglass down and fixed Emery with a meaningful look. Worry formed hard lines around his mouth and eyes.

"*Everything*. I'm going to tell her everything. She'll write it down and the world will finally have the story it's longed for." There was a bite to Emery's tone that made Sophie wince and shift restlessly in her chair.

Miranda shoved her chair back, knocking her wineglass over. The burgundy liquid stained the white tablecloth, seeping in a steady pool.

"You should have talked to us! Not a journalist!" Miranda threw her napkin and fled the room. Hans was instantly on his feet to follow, but Sophie waved a hand and announced to the men she'd go. She had made this mess by being there and she would help make things right. Miranda had a right to know why Sophie wanted the story of the kidnapping, and more importantly, she needed to understand that Emery wouldn't be hurt; not by her.

It wasn't hard to find Miranda. She was in the drawing room across the hall, standing before the large window that faced the back gardens.

"Mrs. Lockwood…" But now Sophie was at a loss for words. Seeing Emery's distance from his parents had hit home. She'd pulled away from her own parents, rarely spoke to them or saw them anymore. It hurt too much to see the disappointment and sadness in their eyes. She'd let them down, let Rachel's parents down. Emery felt the same, she knew that, had somehow known deep in her bones they were so alike in this.

"Come here, Ms. Ryder." Miranda said, pointing to the floor by her side.

Sophie obeyed silently, musing over whether Emery had gotten his need to control from his mother. It was probably a genetic trait.

"Do you see the gazebo over there?" She pointed to the beautiful marble gazebo at the back of the garden. "Twenty-five years ago, I was there, dancing with Elliot. He was waltzing me around in circles. I remember how safe I felt. We had *everything* we could ever want. I should have known that I could never trust such good fortune."

Sophie held her breath until her lungs burned. The silence stretched uncomfortably as Miranda continued to stare at the distant structure, her lips trembling as she seemed to struggle to compose herself.

"It was there in that gazebo I first heard the screams. Francesca, the boys' Nana, came running out into the gardens screaming about the boys being taken. Blood was dripping down her face and she was screeching hysterically. My first thought was that my boys were dead. Why else would there be so much blood? I couldn't process her words. She was telling me they'd been taken, but all I could hear was the echo of her screams. All I could see was the blood all over her clothes." Her eyes closed for a moment before she continued. "Children are so small, Ms. Ryder, like tiny little birds with fragile wings, so easily wounded or broken. A parent's job is to protect their babies, even when they are old enough to no longer need our protection. When I saw Francesca the only thought in my mind was they were dead. With that much blood, they couldn't still be alive."

Sophie shut her eyes, fighting off the sudden wave of nausea at thinking about how terrifying that moment must have been for Miranda and Elliot. Her own past speared her straight through the heart. Images of things she could never erase.

Rachel strained for her hand as the man dragged her off the swing. "Sophie!" Her frightened cry was piercing as he dragged her away, kicking and screaming. Running, crying, Sophie tried to catch up, to follow, but the van was too far away and the man's long-legged strides too fast.

"Rachel!" She'd screamed the name until her voice was hoarse and finally, only then did grown-ups come out of their houses.

The lonely swing moved back and forth; the metal hooks at the base of the swing set creaked.

Rachel was gone.

"When you realize something has happened to your child, everything seems to slow down and speed up at once. Every protective instinct inside you claws to the surface. In that moment I would have done anything to save my boys. Only...they were beyond rescue." Miranda focused on drawing her fingertip along the windowpane before looking back out of the window. "A child vanishing is, in some ways, worse than a child dying. Do you know why, Ms. Ryder?"

Sophie couldn't stop the tears that leaked from her eyes, and her nose started to burn painfully. She knew. God, did she know. It had been her own living nightmare since she'd lost her friend.

"It's worse because you have hope." Even a sliver of hope could be more powerful, more devastating when finally all ability to hope died. When Rachel had been taken, Sophie had hoped every day for a year that they would find her. Then she'd lost hope and prayed they'd recover her body, if nothing else. Something in her died as the years passed and Rachel was never found.

Sophie was so lost in her thoughts that she only realized after several minutes that Emery's mother was staring at her.

"This is more than just a story for you," Miranda observed. "Will you tell me what it is you're trying to hide? I see the tears clinging to your lashes." Her keen gaze missed nothing. "I will tell you everything I remember about the night my sons were taken if you agree to tell me what drives you. Do you agree?"

"Yes." Sophie swallowed thickly. "When I was seven, my best friend was abducted and never seen again. I was the only one with her when the man took her. Just me." Her voice shook and her throat was so constricted it felt as if she was swallowing glass shards. "I couldn't stop him. I couldn't remember his face, or his license plate—nothing. We never found her body. We never caught him, either."

There. It was out. She couldn't take back her confession, but would Miranda understand why this mattered so much? She and Emery shared a type of tragedy that thankfully few people ever experienced. It was as though they were drawn together by that single thread of pain, and yet their connection over the last day had grown into something infinitely more than that: something intangible she was too afraid to name but hoped would continue. Between them there were no secrets—not the ones that kept them both from the rest of the world. Together they were free.

"Ah." Understanding transformed the cool, distant expression on the other woman's face. Sorrow and concern were there as well. "Emery knows about your friend?"

Sophie nodded. "I told him about Rachel. I wanted him to know that this isn't just a story to me. This is…" How could she possibly explain? "Emery survived. He's alive. It's a miracle to me. So many other children are taken and never seen again, but he got away."

"How did you meet my son?" Miranda asked. "He said you're going to write about what happened." There was still a wariness in Miranda's eyes, but she no longer seemed hostile.

Sophie tucked her hands in her skirts, trying to hide their trembling. She wasn't used to telling someone her darkest truths, or discussing herself so openly. But Miranda needed to hear it.

"After losing Rachel, I devoted my life to stopping people like the man who took her. I'm a journalist, yes; but I'm not here to focus on his pain, or his trauma. I'm here to solve the mystery of who was behind it. Mrs. Lockwood, I'm good with puzzles, I see patterns in things. I came here to find Emery and get all the details he wouldn't share with police or even you. If—" she drew in a shaky breath— "If I get the right information, I might be able to see something everyone else couldn't. I want to find who was behind this and stop them."

"But it's been so many years. What good would it do now?" Miranda asked.

"Mrs. Lockwood, in cases like your sons' abduction, there's always something off. No ransom calls or letters were ever made or delivered; no one ever came forward. Your sons were hard to target, and an average person wouldn't have bothered with them unless they had another motive. Like money. So why then did no one call for a ransom?"

Emery's mother was watching her, a cunning glint in her eyes as she puzzled over Sophie's words. "You think someone didn't want a ransom?"

"Yes. I think the kidnapping was a ruse. Someone wanted to kill Emery and his brother, and make it look like it was done for a ransom. But that no ransom was never arranged because the boys would have accidentally died before a call could be made. Yet there was so much time, a three-month gap. They were waiting for instructions from someone."

"But who..." Miranda trailed off, her gaze distant. "Who would want to do that to my babies?"

"That's what I want to know, Mrs. Lockwood. I want to find that person and stop them. Because I think that the danger isn't gone. Even after all these years, Emery's life is still at risk. I feel it in my bones."

"I wish he would have told Elliot and me what happened. What if he had and we'd learned something that could have stopped this years ago?"

"As a mother, you don't know who to mourn more. The boy who perished, or the one who lives with the guilt of surviving."

Miranda smoothed her dress, the motion slow and measured. "And Emery wasn't the same when he came home. He was..." Emery's mother blinked rapidly, but a stray tear slipped down her cheek. With a hasty move, she brushed her fingers over her cheek, trying to hide the evidence of her tears. "He was still my son, but he seemed broken. Without Fenn, he withdrew from us, from the world. In so many ways, it's as though we've raised a stranger. I barely know him at all and I want to, Ms. Ryder. I want my son back. When he called today, I didn't know what to think, but then when I saw you with him, I realized you had something to do with this."

That didn't sound like a good thing, and Sophie waited for Miranda to accuse her of hurting Emery, but the accusation didn't come. The other woman was smiling, even if her eyes were a little watery.

"I don't understand," Sophie admitted quietly.

Miranda held out her hand and took one of Sophie's between hers, holding it tightly. "I see my son again, the one that seemed lost to me. He's there, just a faint but steadily growing presence. Because of you. I saw how he looked at you throughout dinner, the way he touches you so protectively, affectionately. It's how his father is with me. He trusts you and if he trusts you, then so do I."

She squeezed Sophie's hand in a silent show of support and Sophie held fast. This was not how she'd foreseen meeting Emery's parents.

"You're not upset that I'm here?" she asked.

"No, I'm not. If Emery can open up to you, that's what matters. Whatever happened that night has weighed on him and I only wish I knew why."

Sophie bit her bottom lip. "He wanted to tell you both what happened but he feels responsible. I think Fenn forced him to escape and made him leave alone. I can't imagine how that must have felt, to abandon your brother, even though he told you to. I think Emery fears you'll blame him for leaving his brother behind."

"What?" Miranda's face paled. "How could he? We would never...oh, my poor boy!"

Without another word to her, Miranda rushed from the room, crossed the hall and went back into the dining room. Sophie started to follow but froze in the doorway as she saw Miranda hugging Emery fiercely and whispering softly to him. The stark pain in his eyes soon turned to quiet grief and then relief and love before he shut them. Elliot joined his wife and son, arms curling around their shoulders.

Never in her life had Sophie felt more like an outsider. She was intruding on a reunion that was twenty-five years overdue.

It was time to leave.

She didn't want to stay any longer, even if her heart begged her. They'd only just learned to talk to each other, to open up. To know that something might have come from such intimacy—to turn her back on it felt like a betrayal, but her own sorrow was too great to bear alone. Too many years spent repressing that pain had finally caught up with her. Seeing Emery achieve what she could never have—peace—made her want to run away, like the child she always seemed to be inside.

Rachel's parents would never have such a moment. It was her fault. If she hadn't been so scared, she could have screamed for help sooner. But she'd failed. Failed her friend, her friend's parents, and herself.

Emery's story had seemed like the answer to everything, but she was wrong. It wasn't the answer. It was the acceptance by his parents. That moment when he could open himself up, wounds and all, to his parents and not be judged. That was an absolution she would never get.

She had to go upstairs, pack and leave. Her editor would want the story on the kidnapping soon, but Sophie couldn't afford to stay here. She'd get the copies of the articles from Cody and do a phone interview with Emery in a few days. He needed time with his family now and having her underfoot would be the least helpful thing for him. There was no point in her staying. If she found any hard evidence of who was behind the killing, she had Cody's information, and could contact him immediately. She wanted to put as much distance between herself and the past as possible.

When she got back to Emery's bedroom she grabbed her suitcase and dropped it on the bed. She started throwing clothes in and rushed into the bathroom to gather her toiletries. Hurrying back into the bedroom, she stopped dead when she saw Emery leaning casually against the door frame, blocking the only exit. His arms were crossed over his broad chest and a scowl darkened his face.

"What do you think you're doing? You can't leave, not after you've given me my family back."

She gulped and remained silent. Her heart thudded loudly enough that she was shocked he didn't seem to hear it.

"Sophie," he growled. "I'm not letting you walk out of this door."

"But—"

He was across the room in seconds and with a quick swipe of his hand he knocked the suitcase to the ground. The move wasn't violent, more decisive than anything else. She stared numbly at the clothes she'd hastily shoved into the suitcase. They were now scattered in a heap on the floor. Emery seized her attention by clasping his hands around her wrists and trapping her hands at the small of her back. All she could do was gaze up at him, wide-eyed, her body humming with muted pleasure at the domination swirling in his eyes.

"I put cuffs on you. Even if they aren't on you all the time, the symbolism is the same." His voice was passion-rough, as though he held onto his control by a whisper-fine thread. "Do you know what cuffs on a sub means in my world?"

Her mouth was as dry as sandpaper as she struggled to speak past the lump in her throat. "Cuffs represent a claimed sub. A dom cuffs a sub he wishes others to know belongs to him. The next step up is to collar a sub during a ceremony." She knew that much from what Hayden had briefly explained over the phone when she was giving Sophie some inside tips on the club and the D/s lifestyle.

Emery licked his lips, his body tense against hers. "To me they are a sign of commitment. If I were to take you to the club wearing these, everyone would know you were mine, that I owned you as sure as I owned my own soul. A cuffing is not always temporary,

Sophie, especially not for me. I've never cuffed a woman before. I want you like I've never wanted anyone, and I don't want just one night." His confession was a ragged whisper and the echoing wildness in his eyes had her heart racing to a tempo it had never beat before. He released her for a single moment, to retrieve a set of leather cuffs from his dresser before he came back and secured them to her wrists.

The cuffs on her wrists seemed to burn her skin deliciously. They weren't just pretty jewelry. They meant something important to him, and that in turn made her feel their presence all the more strongly. He wanted her for more than one night? She'd never been wanted like that. No one had ever…She closed her eyes a moment, trying to regain control. It was all she'd ever craved, in the darkest, loneliest part of her soul. One wish: to be wanted. And he'd uttered those longed-for words with the hunger of a starving man.

"I know I should give you a choice, let you walk away if you're frightened…" He lowered his head to hers, teasing her lips with his, but not kissing her. "But I can't. *You're mine.* You're not free to leave me, or this." He feathered his lips over hers.

Sophie marveled at how different this kiss was. Each time he touched her, kissed her, held her, she was struck with a deep sense of wonder. So much of his soul, his heart, his very being seemed to flow from his mouth to hers. For a man so determined to separate himself from the world and hide behind the bars of his gilded cage, he wore his heart not on his sleeve but on his lips.

"Say something," he begged in a low growl of frustration. His grip on her wrists tightened the faintest bit.

Foolishly, she couldn't say everything that burned at the tip of her tongue. "I'm not going to write the story. I can't. I didn't see before now how much I had intruded on your life, your privacy. It wasn't right."

He sighed against her cheek, his dark golden lashes falling down over his tanned skin.

"For such a brilliant woman, you never cease to amaze me with your silliness. I don't give a damn about the story. We can discuss it later." Emery opened his eyes again, fixing her with a cinnamon gaze pierced with shards of forest green. "Right now, all that matters is getting you beneath me in bed. If you don't want that, then use your safe word. Say apricots and I won't touch you tonight. But if you don't say it…" His eyes flicked to something behind her. Belatedly she realized it was the bed, mere inches away.

Her breath hitched and she had to resist the urge to sigh in relief and lean into him. Finally. He was taking control, telling her she couldn't leave, that there was something between them worth exploring. She could let him take over, let him rule her as he wished, and be free to enjoy the passion he'd promised in every heated touch and fiery caress since she'd met him.

"What about your parents?" she asked.

"Gone. Hans took them home. We're going to attend their party next week."

"Party?"

"Their annual costume party," Emery said as he released her wrists and moved back to his bedroom door, shutting and locking it. The click of metal into metal shot a bolt of excitement through her, shocked by the strength of the desire that followed.

All thoughts of the party or his parents faded. She was caught up in the panther-like grace of his movements as he came back to her, pausing to open the drawer of his nightstand. He pulled out the pair of leather cuffs she'd worn in the club and placed them on the bed near where she stood. Then he turned back to the drawer to retrieve two more leather restraints and several short lengths of chain no more than three feet long apiece.

"Come here," he ordered. The short tone was intimidating but not cruel.

When she hesitated, the frown on his handsome face turned into a brooding scowl. She hastily walked to him, eyes dropping to the carpet at his feet.

"Wrists," he prompted.

Sophie held out her wrists and he removed the gilded cuffs and replaced them with the leather cuffs, taking a second to slide a finger under each leather cuff to make sure they weren't too tight. He didn't link the cuffs together yet, but kept her wrists unbound. Then he knelt at her feet and secured the second pair of restraints to her ankles.

She stared down at the tousled halo of soft wheat-gold hair. It was one of the features she adored about him. He wore it longer than was fashionable and he always looked deliciously rumpled, as though a woman had been running her hands through his hair. It made him look so thoroughly male, so virile and attractive. She wanted those to be her hands. To leave her mark upon him, much in the way he left his mark on her body with each kiss.

As though aware of her gaze on him, he raised his head, his eyes tracing a searing path up her body before reaching her face.

"Tonight, you fulfill your bargain. We play by my rules. Do you understand?" The change in his tone, the darker hints of domination and control, teased the words, and she couldn't repress an excited shiver that flashed through her body like quicksilver.

"Yes," she whispered.

"Yes, what?" he growled. One hand cupped the back of her neck and he massaged the tense muscles, but his expression was stony and almost cold. This was Emery, the dom. A side of himself he'd kept hidden until now. It didn't frighten her. It excited her. Her nipples pebbled at the rough feel of his hands against her skin as he continued to stroke.

"Yes, sir?"

A momentary wink of amusement colored his eyes into a deep honey gold. "Are you asking me a question, little sub?"

Sophie nearly started to explain, but realized that would get her spanked. As much as she liked the idea, she wanted to prove to him she was learning about his world.

"Permission to speak, sir?"

A jerk of his head and he dropped his hand from the back of her neck. She mourned the loss of his touch instantly, but struggled to focus.

"I was confused, sir, about whether to address you as sir, or master. Which would you prefer?"

Approval gleamed in his eyes and his lips twitched slightly.

"Your thoughtfulness is pleasing to me. For that you will be rewarded. Later. Most subs call doms 'Sir', but in cases where a dom and a sub are more deeply connected, 'Master' is a better form of address. I would prefer to be called Master." He hadn't ordered her to call him Master; the phrasing seemed to hint she might have a choice. There was no denying, though, that the idea of calling him Master, in the bedroom, was erotic. It made her inner walls slick with desire and her senses heightened. Surrendering to him would be the most sensual and arousing thing she had ever done and she couldn't wait.

"Thank you, Master."

"Say your safe word. Practice it. I want to know you can say it." He crossed his arms over his chest, waiting patiently, but the pose was still intimidating. He oozed raw power and sexuality, like a large jungle cat waiting to pounce.

"Apricot," she replied instantly.

"I've been meaning to ask." He suddenly grinned, with an expression so potent, so blatantly full of masculine arrogance. "Why that word?"

Before she could reply he knelt before her and focused on her red shoes, easing them off her feet. There was something so intimate, so erotic about being barefoot in front of him. He drew a finger along the inside of one arch and she stifled a giggle. He glanced up, one brow arched.

"I'm allergic to apricots," she choked out when she realized he was waiting for her answer.

He said nothing to her response, but merely stood up and stared at her for a long moment before he finally spoke. "Put your hands flat on the bed and lean forward a little."

With a tremor of excitement, Sophie complied. His palms settled on her shoulders, then slid down her arms across to her back. The zipper of her dress moved down inch by inch. Her breathing lightened when the gown gaped open and he could undo it no further. Emery stepped close behind her, pinning her thighs to the bedside with his own. Heat lanced through her body and she fought off a shiver as he glided his hands beneath the straps on her shoulders and pulled them down. The dress dropped to her waist, caught between their bodies. Emery stepped back, allowing the fabric to fall to the floor.

Even though she had her back to him, the heat of his gaze on her made her flush and tremble.

"You are beautiful." Simple words, yet they evoked a raw response of pleasure in her. She knew if he said them, he meant them.

"Turn around and look at me."

Naked except for her bra, she resisted every instinct to cover herself and pivoted to face him. She bravely raised her eyes. The feeling of being so exposed was overwhelming. Her breath quickened and her cheeks flamed. Sophie wanted to curl her arms around herself and hide.

He stepped close again, hands settling on her naked hips, fingertips teasing her skin in slow patterns.

"Take off your bra."

"Emery," she uttered his name in a shameful plea. The scars. They were always there, a reminder of her ugly secrets. If he saw them, it would be all he'd ever see and he'd never truly look at her again. It was too intimate, too personal to reveal her suffering to him. It had been easier to tell him, but show him? That was verging on the impossible.

"Now." The growl came from the back of his throat, animalistic and so dominating it made her shake.

She dropped her chin, eyes falling to the floor as she reached behind her back and undid the bra clasp. With painstaking focus she slid it off her arms and let it fall to the floor.

Silence. Awful silence. She'd expected a gasp, an exclamation or some other logical reaction to her scars. Nothing.

"Please, say something, anything," she begged, her throat constricting as she fought to swallow her fear. She couldn't cry; she had to stay in control. This had been bound to happen. He wouldn't be attracted to her now that he saw how imperfect her body was.

One of his hands resting at her hip moved up to touch the three long, jagged scars that ran diagonally across her body, over her breasts. Her skin was marred with the light brown and slightly raised lines of the scars. She'd hoped they would turn pink or white, but the damage to her skin had been so complete that the marks remained dark and angry looking.

"You told me these were from a surgery," he reminded her.

"They are…sort of. I didn't get them from a surgery, but a doctor did sew me back together." She drew a breath, trying to focus on the feel of his fingers. They brushed over the numb skin. She could barely feel his touch; the nerve endings hadn't ever reconnected after the horrible damage to her chest.

"What happened, Sophie?"

At least that she could tell him. Now that he'd seen them, it didn't matter how they'd come about. No shame there, thankfully.

"I was doing a story on a man who thought he was the next Jack the Ripper. He'd killed three women in Missouri. The police had a suspect but no proof and not enough evidence to get a warrant to get into his house. I figured I could help out. Rather than stay on the sidelines, I got a little cocky. If I could get inside and find something I could call the cops and then they'd have a reason to enter the premises. I waited for the man to leave and snuck in to look around for evidence. He came back a few minutes later. I guess he'd forgotten something. He found me…We…er…fought. He was pretty good with a hunting knife."

She shut her eyes. The memory of that encounter had lost much of its horror over time. In truth, she'd been far less scared of him than she was of the man who'd taken Rachel. By the time she'd tangled with the serial killer she was well aware how full of evil the world was, and she'd expected it around every corner.

Chapter 13

ONE MISSING LOCKWOOD BOY FOUND ALIVE!
ON SEPTEMBER 29, LOCAL POLICE OFFICER SEAN
O'MALLEY WAS DRIVING ON THE BACKSTREETS
OF A NEIGHBORHOOD APPROXIMATELY SEVEN
MILES FROM THE LOCKWOOD ESTATE WHEN A
SMALL BOY STUMBLED OUT OF THE WOODS AND
INTO THE PATH OF HIS VEHICLE.
—*New York Times*, September 30, 1990

What happened?" Emery was still stroking Sophie. Each touch made her less ashamed of the scars and more aware of his body and his hands on her, and the way he made her feel beautiful, desirable. His fingers traced the knotted flesh and she reached up to cover his hand with hers. He turned his palm away from her chest to catch her hand, linking their fingers. He squeezed gently, a tender reassurance from compassion rather than pity. It made her eyes burn and she blinked back tears.

"I got him back for the scars with three shots to the chest from my .22."

For the first time since earlier that day, Emery laughed.

"There's my girl." He cupped her chin with one palm, his gaze stealing hers.

She was startled at the warmth, rather than heat there. It was different. Sensuality surrounded her with his fully clothed body so close to hers, but that look—it was million miles away from lust. It was softer, sweeter and it made a storm of butterflies flutter wildly in her stomach.

He was seeing her, not the scars. His gaze was a promise of so much more than pity, more than even compassion. Rather she saw an understanding. His scars weren't on the outside, but they were there all the same. It reminded her of an old poem by John Donne about two loves being so alike that they could not die. The hairs along her forearms stirred and her body and heart moved as one toward him.

He dropped his hand and tenderly grasped one of her breasts, kneading it. His fingertips strummed over the nipple, bring it to an erect peak before he plucked the bud. Delicious pain shot straight to her womb and she arched up on her toes. She had only moments to enjoy the teasing of her breast before he doubled her need by pressing his hand against her mound and squeezing softly. The pressure on her mound made her suck in a breath as desire slammed into her.

"Does any of this hurt?" he whispered as he continued to play with her breast, tweaking her nipple again and again.

"No, Master." The word 'Master' came instinctively, and she barely had time to laugh inside at her own desire to call him that. To give him control even in that single syllable.

"You please me, Sophie. I didn't even have to remind you. If anything I do hurts in a bad way, say your safe word immediately."

"Yes, Master." Since the attack, her breasts had not been sensitive, but beneath his touch they seemed to come awake.

Her lashes lowered and she simply focused on the feel of his hands. It had been so long since she'd been touched there. The contact between them was physical, yet with each stroke, each caress, he was entering her mind and heart. There was fire and carnality in him, barely restrained beneath his tense muscles. He abandoned all decorum and indulged in every animal urge: rubbing his cheek against her aching breasts, licking the tender tips before suckling them. Emery shed every shred of restraint and she couldn't help but want to join him and become a creature focused solely on sensual discovery. Sophie fought the urge to shift restlessly beneath his stroking.

Emery pulled her flush against him, the smooth fabric of his expensive suit sliding erotically against her bare skin, making her tingle wherever it touched her. The sense of utter wickedness, the sinful bliss of being exposed and naked while he remained fully clothed, was decadent. She was vulnerable and he was in charge. He smiled against her lips as he held her face between his hands and kissed her. It was a slow leisurely exploration of her mouth that left her hot and aching. She curled her fingers into his lapels, dragging him close so she could kiss him back.

Their connection seemed to last for hours, and he broke away from her all too soon. What she saw in his eyes terrified her. Gentleness. Desire. Hunger. Excitement. The blur of emotions was too overpowering. He couldn't possibly feel all those things at once, not for her. Sophie struggled to stay on the surface of her own emotions. She couldn't let herself fall too deep, too hard, into him. She'd never be able to stop from drowning in him.

"You still don't believe I desire you?" A slight frown wrinkled his brow.

How could he? She wasn't thin, wasn't beautiful. She was a plain, dumpy girl from the Midwest. Men like him dated models from Milan or Paris.

"Whatever you're thinking? Stop," he ordered sharply. When she didn't immediately meet his gaze, he fisted a hand in her hair and jerked her head back. "Do you want me to prove it to you, little sub? I know exactly how I would. Tie you down to my bed and show you just how hard you've made me. I'd punish you with climax after climax until you'd screamed yourself hoarse, and you wouldn't be able to sit down for at least two days." That wildness was there, lurking in his eyes, and coloring his tone. He was angry with her, because she didn't believe he desired her.

Her mouth dry, she gasped. "It doesn't make sense for you to want me."

"It makes perfect sense, and if you argue with me I will redden your ass with my hand until we're both hurting. Do you understand? I won't accept those thoughts, not from my sub. Do not disappoint me, Sophie." He waited for her to protest, but she didn't dare. Only when she kept silent did he continue. "I love your luscious figure. You have full breasts, perfect to fill my palms, hips made for the span of my hands to grip. And don't get me started on your ass. I have very wicked thoughts about that particular body part." He shot her a crooked grin.

A breathless laugh escaped her. "What about my ass?"

He dropped his hands to the body part in question, clenching the soft flesh, which caused her hips to jerk into his reflexively.

"It's the perfect cushion for me to pound against when I take you from behind. It's just the right size for me to hold when I lift you up to take you against the wall." He pulled her impossibly tighter against him, his pants-clad erection rubbing over her throbbing core. If he kept talking like this she wasn't going to last the rest of the night, and his slow seduction suggested he planned to play for the next several hours.

"Aren't you going to get undressed?" She tugged at his coat but he caught her hands.

"When I wish to. First, I have to do what I've been aching to do since the moment I first saw you." Without a warning he scooped her up into his arms and carried her to the bed. He set her down and retrieved the chains. The sight of them, and knowing he would restrain her completely, made her heart skip a few beats and rush to catch up.

She remained still, only moving her body when instructed. After a few minutes he had her arms and legs tied to each corner of the bedpost. The chains were snugly fastened to silver rings on her wrist and ankle cuffs.

Emery knelt on the bed between the V of her thighs and simply looked at her.

"You are stunning. Like no other woman I've been with. You are real." His soft murmur made her writhe against the restraints. His eyes narrowed on the small struggle and he grinned wolfishly. He settled his hands on her waist and leaned over.

Her body vibrated with need, with excitement. And yet she was scared. Not of being hurt. He would never hurt her. But she knew on some level that being with him, truly and completely, would change her forever. No other man's touch would drive her mindless with sensual hunger. He would possess her totally and she would never be free of the memories of him. She didn't want to be free. She wanted to melt into him, merge with the passion he drew forth from her, and be the wild, wanton creature he summoned with his smile, his kiss, and whisky-rough whispers of what he was going to do to her. Bad things. Deliciously bad.

He sat back on his heels and slipped his coat off, tossing it on the back of a nearby chair. Then his hands settled on his tie. He loosened and slid it over his head and then, with a truly sensual and wicked twist to his lips, he slipped it over her head and down around her neck. He tightened it enough for her to feel the knot against her throat. He stroked the tie flat between her breasts and then tweaked each nipple back to life. Sophie moaned, trying to raise her hips. The chains were tight enough that she had no real ability to move. The sounds of her slight struggle against the bonds was mixed with the sound of his harsh breathing. She strained up, meeting his hooded gaze, knowing the depth of her power over him in that instant. She had the ability to control how much he enjoyed being with her; it was as she'd been told. The submissive had the power, not the dominant because a true dominant could only find pleasure when his partner had submitted willingly. The way Emery's eyes glittered with passion and hunger as well as pleasure was the only proof she needed to see that her surrender heightened his desire. He wouldn't have enjoyed this if she wasn't enjoying it too.

"I like it when you wear my clothes." He bent his head and licked and nibbled a path up from her belly to one breast, taking the nipple in his mouth. His teeth sank into the tender flesh around the nipple and his tongue flitted out, laving the peak.

Sophie threw her head back, bowing with sheer pleasure as he started to suck hard on her breast. She thrashed wildly as his mouth worked miracles on her breast and his hand shaped the curve of her hip before settling on the back of her leg where her bottom met her thigh. The skin there was soft and sensitive and his fingers teased her, gliding back and forth, drawing closer and closer to her center from behind.

When he reached her slick inner folds he drew his fingertip in lazy patterns, spreading the moisture that pooled there. Before she expected it, he slid that same finger into her sheath. Sophie arched off the bed, gasping. Her reaction spurred him to a quicker pace. He added a second finger, pumping them deeper inside.

"So tight," he ground out between clenched teeth. Emery moved, looming over her as a third finger joined his other two. He worked them slowly and gently, but he was firm, preparing her.

Her inner walls clenched around his fingers, trying to pull him inside her. "Emery, please…I'm not going to last much longer."

"All right, sweetheart," he breathed against her lips. She had only a moment to be surprised at the gentle ardor with which he'd spoken before she heard the whisper of a zipper and the rustle of clothes. Then the head of his cock was nudging at her core.

She wanted to kiss him, wanted to have his mouth on hers, but he was watching her, his lips parted as his breathing hitched. Then he was inside her. The thrust was sharp and hard, and they shared a moan of pleasure when he withdrew and thrust in again, his hips inching closer and closer to hers. The entire time he worked his way into her, their gazes were locked.

A lock of burnished gold hair fell into his eyes and lent him a boyish look, not like that of the hardened wealthy recluse who'd insisted he'd never let her inside his heart and soul. That wounded man had vanished. The man above her in bed was fresh with passion and emotion. His hazel eyes were warm as honeyed chestnuts and his lips were just as sweet as he murmured sweet nonsense. Each time he pulled back, then moved into her again, it was like coming home. Frissons of pleasure began to radiate out from the point where their bodies connected. Her arms strained against the restraints, but he covered her completely and the skin-to-skin contact satisfied her need to touch him for now.

Heat rippled beneath her skin in response to each movement of his hips. Like a symphony, they moved in time with each other, finding a rhythm that spiraled them together down a road they'd both been afraid to travel. Sophie kept her eyes on him, memorizing the shadows and moonlight and the feel of his heart beating wildly against hers. He jerked, his pace suddenly more frantic, more desperate.

"Come for me, sweetheart, I'm not gonna last, I..." He cursed at the same moment her own body unleashed the wild passion that had been locked inside for years. It exploded out of her in every direction and a little cry of shock and delight escaped her trembling lips. Her body clamped tightly around his, clinging to him as he followed her over the edge.

They'd made love. It had been the most blindingly intense thing she'd ever felt. Emery dropped his head in the crook of her shoulder and neck, kissing her skin delicately. She shifted his semi-hard length still inside her. What they'd done... it could never be undone. What had she been thinking?

Tears welled up in her eyes and she blinked them back. Emery lifted his head and frowned. His brow knitted and he cupped her cheek.

"Was I too rough?"

She managed to shake her head.

"I meant to last longer, Sophie. I'm sorry I didn't." He ran his thumb over her bottom lip, his cheeks slightly flushed.

"No," she distracted him. "It was fine, you were…" A smile teased her face. "You were the best I ever had…*will* ever have," she added more quietly.

"And that's worth tears?" He caught one stray drop by her cheek and wiped it away, rocking his body gently at the same time, and Sophie moaned. Her sheath continued to clench and quiver around him in the aftermath of the most devastatingly perfect climax ever.

"What will happen when we're done? We have to go our separate ways, you know that. I will hate knowing I left this behind," she whispered.

Emery's face clouded with a dark emotion she couldn't read, then it was gone and he lowered his head to take her mouth.

Right before his lips captured hers, he spoke again, "Hold on to this moment; don't think about tomorrow. Just be with me."

She surrendered herself, her heart and everything in her that she'd held secret all her life. He owned her and she couldn't find the strength to care, not tonight.

Chapter 14

THE OFFICER STOPPED HIS CAR AND
APPROACHED THE BOY, NOTING HIS BONY
APPEARANCE AND THE SEVERE BRUISES ON HIS
FACE, AS WELL AS A DEEP CUT ALONG HIS CHIN.
—*New York Times*, September 30, 1990

Cody lounged back in the driver seat of his car, debating his next move. People filled the sidewalks as they explored the seaside village for late dinner and other evening entertainment. He turned his attention back to his phone. Earlier this afternoon he'd found a bug in his office. The tiny tracker on one of Emery's new bug-detecting prototypes had gone off. Cody had been tinkering with the new device and had located the bug, lodged in a tiny crevice of wood near the window. Cody took his time removing it so as to not give a clue to its installer that he'd found it. It was time to quit playing nice with the other side. Whoever this bastard was had blown up Emery's stables and nearly killed Emery and Sophie.

Naturally Cody did what he did best: he'd reversed the signal's connection and set up a tracking program on his phone. It led him into town, but then the signal had cut off abruptly. Cody wasn't like Emery and Hans. He didn't think defensively, but rather offensively. He was a tech man. His understandings of people were based on what technology they used. *Take this guy, for example*, Cody thought. *He plants a bug, then the signal stops... why?*

He couldn't understand it. Why plant a tool if you quit using it?

Something wasn't right. To be honest, nothing had felt okay since Emery had brought Sophie home. From nearly the moment she'd arrived, Emery's nightmare flashbacks had returned, barns had been burned and threats from the past seemed to have resurfaced. He'd personally gone over every inch of her personal life from the moment she was born to now, and he'd found no connection to Emery's kidnapping. So why had her arrival started a string of bad events? Cody had learned to read people at a young age and he didn't think Sophie was in on a plot to kill Emery or anything like that. According to her, she was here to save Emery's life. But he couldn't dismiss the feeling that her showing up had started something bad.

The light plink of rain on his car window made Cody shudder. He'd rather be back in the mansion than out in the rain. The sign of a nearby bar caught his attention. He could get a drink and keep dry while he waited to see if the signal would come back on.

He pocketed his phone and got out of the car. People hustled by him on the street, trying to get inside as the rain came down harder. He merged into the throng of bodies moving into the bar. Inside it was hot and noisy. A man with a guitar strummed lazily and sang a classic rock love song while couples milled about the tables. Harried waitresses, burdened with trays of glasses and bottles, fluttered between the tables. Cody spotted an empty seat at the bar and snagged it. He put his hand up to signal the bartender. The tall, dark-haired man with a hooked nose came his way ready to take his order.

"What'll it be?" The man's tone was gruff, as though doing his job was an irritation.

"Scotch on the rocks."

The bartender grabbed an empty glass, filled it with ice and poured two fingers of Scotch before passing it to Cody.

Cody leaned back against the bar and took a drink. The place was filled with happy tourists and restless locals. The combination filled the atmosphere with a charge of energy. He longed to join in but he didn't know anyone. As much as he loved his private world behind the Lockwood gates, he needed to get out. Get a life. Hans always teased him about needing to get a girlfriend. Maybe he was right. If nothing else, getting laid once in a while would be nice.

He took another sip. Frowning, he licked his lips. A heavy taste numbed his tongue. Funny, he hadn't had Scotch in a while but he didn't remember it tasting like…

The world around him suddenly spun on its axis. The tilt caught him off guard and he fell back against the bar.

"You okay?" The bartender's gravelly voice seemed to bounce around in his head, the sound deafening.

Cody blinked, straining to bring his blurry vision back into focus. The guy had come out from behind the bar and was peering down at him.

"Can't…can't…" Cody's tongue was too thick to form words, his limbs suddenly too heavy.

"Let me help you. I'll get you a cab." The bartender bent and threw one of Cody's arms around his shoulders and hoisted him up onto wobbly legs. Shouldering his way through the crowd, the man dragged him to a black sedan.

It wasn't a cab. Nausea ate away at his insides, and the sick feeling doubled when the man opened the door and shoved him hard. Cody pitched forward into the dark interior and landed on the backseat. The man lifted his legs and shoved them inside before slamming the door shut. Cody struggled to stay awake, but darkness and silence pounded at the insides of his brain repeatedly and then everything went black.

* * *

Cody woke to the intense pain of a rope slicing into his wrists and ankles. Head throbbing and neck aching, he swore softly and forced his eyes to open. His eyelids scratched over his eyes like sandpaper and his mouth was dry and sticky.

"Welcome to the party, Cody," a rough voice rumbled from somewhere to his right. Cody swiveled his head heavily in that direction, raking a bleary gaze over the bartender.

"Who the hell are you?"

"I'm a good friend of Emery's." The man threw back his head, tossing long wavy black hair from his cold dark eyes. Cody wasn't afraid of much, but those eyes…like peering into the fires of hell.

"You're the asswipe who set fire to Emery's stables." It made sense. This prick was toying with him to get back at Emery.

"Any more insults and I will lose interest in being courteous."

A laugh gurgled up unexpectedly. "Courteous? You motherfu—"
Crack!

Cody's head snapped back with the blow. Blood trickled down his face and the headache which had only just started to dull came roaring back to life. Hacking up the blood which drained down the back of his throat from his nose, he tried to get hold of himself. He took stock of his surroundings. It was a sterile room lit by one hanging ceiling light. There was a laptop open and on, sitting on a cheap table that had been shoved into the corner. The glow of the screen taunted him. His one ally was out of reach.

His captor sat straddling a metal chair beside him, forearms resting on the chair back, within easy smacking distance.

Bastard. Fucking bastard.

"Too scared to talk, Cody? I had a feeling you were all chatter and no action." The way the man spoke his name was almost obscene, as though he enjoyed using it. Well, newsflash for him, Cody wasn't a pansy and unless this guy started to cut off body parts, he wasn't singing like a canary any time soon.

"Okay. I'll talk. You'll listen. My name is Antonio. I know a lot about you, Cody. You are quite the hacker. My bug showed me just how skillful you are. Does Emery know you regularly hack into government databases when you're bored?"

Cody blinked. The bug had been impossibly small, yet Antonio implied that he was getting video feed. It was the only way he would know how Cody spent his off-hours.

"So you got into my office after you left that sick little calling card in the kitchen." Maybe if he could keep Antonio talking, he'd learn more about the man's end game.

Antonio shrugged. "A little theatrical, I admit. But it was well worth it. I only wish it had been covered with Fenn's blood. Pity it wasn't." He stood and walked over to his desk, where a huge metal mallet sat. He picked it up, tapped it into his other palm thoughtfully and turned back to Cody with an evil grin. With slow, measured steps he moved back into the sickly yellow circle of light from the single overhead lamp.

"Now, I have a few questions I need answered. Cooperate and we'll be great friends. Keep quiet and I'm afraid your typing career will be short-lived." Antonio's black gaze dropped to Cody's hands.

Oh, hell no! Cody jumped in the chair, only to feel the ropes around his wrists cut deeper. This creep was going to pulverize him with the mallet!

"Who is the girl sharing Emery's bed?"

Cody hesitated only a second, weighing the odds of whether the information would hurt Sophie. Her job was public knowledge.

"She's an investigative journalist."

Antonio digested this with apparent interest as he scrutinized Cody's face. "And Emery knows what she is?"

Cody nodded. Who the hell was this guy? Antonio was tall, built like a linebacker, and he looked dangerous enough to give Hans a run for his money. But while Hans carried himself with a quiet sense of power, this man seemed to glory in it. With each twist Cody made in the ropes, Antonio's lips twitched, as though he enjoyed watching Cody struggle.

He had to think of something fast. "Can I ask you a question?"

His captor stroked the head of the mallet thoughtfully. "Go ahead."

"What happened to Fenn the night Emery escaped?" There was a high likelihood this question would get him killed sooner rather than later, but he wanted to confirm his suspicion that it was Antonio who had kidnapped Emery and Fenn.

"That is actually a question I would like answered as well. I cannot finish the job I was hired to do until I find both of the twins. I have put off killing Emery for years, hoping Fenn would contact him, reveal his whereabouts. But now I don't have to worry. I've finally found him."

Cody's ears filled with a sharp ringing and the words tumbled out. "Fenn's alive?"

Antonio's face darkened, his eyes narrowing. "Enough questions. Why did Emery bring home a journalist? He never takes women home. What game is he playing?"

Cody calculated the risk of telling more than he should. There was a chance he could get more questions answered. Like the fact that Fenn Lockwood might still be alive…

"Emery's going to tell her about the kidnapping. In return he's getting lucky."

Antonio laughed. "Such a poetic answer, Cody. Are you hoping the lovebirds will stay together? Like a fairytale?" His laughter turned harsh. "Don't you know that fairytales are gruesome things? Violent, bloody? The charming prince always loses his companions in the last battle. He goes on alone. And you are not the prince of this tale."

Those words were the only warning he got before the mallet swung down on his right hand.

A primal scream tore from his lips and his bones seemed to explode out of his hand and shatter. Adrenaline spiked, flooding him with more panic, and he fought for breath. He flung his head back, sucking in air as pain radiated from his hand. Blood crashed against his eardrums, dulling his awareness to any sound beyond the steady roar in his head. It was only when the other man's hand dug into his hair, wrenching his head back, that he realized Antonio was talking to him. The man's lips moved and Cody stared hard at them, trying to understand what he was saying.

"We have a long night ahead of us, Cody. I suggest you stop screaming or you'll go hoarse long before midnight."

His scream, which had apparently kept going, cut off abruptly at Antonio's words.

"What happens at midnight?" he asked with a gasping breath as the pain in his hand continued to scream silently all on its own. He wanted to throw up...no, he *was* going to throw up...The pain worked its way upward, spreading through his body. His hand was a bloody mess and he couldn't stop staring at the odd way white shards of broken bones poked out at odd angles from his skin.

"Carriages turn back to pumpkins, horses to mice, and I slit your throat and leave you somewhere for Emery to find."

Shit. What the hell do I say to that?

Cody's churning insides went still as a single-minded focus he'd never experienced before took over him. *Separate pain from thought,* Hans's voice echoed in his head.

"What time is it?" he asked, amazed at the steel in his own voice, even if the words did come out between panting breaths. Hans would be proud.

Antonio checked his watch. "Eleven o'clock."

Cody looked over at the computer and smiled through the shattering agony zinging through his limbs like an electric current. "One hour? A lot can happen in sixty minutes."

"Indeed. A lot." Antonio picked up the hammer.

Cody shut his eyes. *Forgive me, Hans, but I'm going to scream like a ten-year-old girl.*

* * *

Hans paced the empty space of Cody's command center. Years of protective service left him with a natural sixth sense for danger and everything in him screamed that something was wrong.

Very wrong.

Cody had been gone for almost two hours. He never left the house without telling Hans where he was going.

The kid's desk was cleared of its usual clutter and on it sat one single device. A tiny bug the size of a pinhead. Hans was no whiz like Cody was with all of this tech stuff, but he knew that bug wasn't a product of Lockwood Industries. Which meant Cody had found it. That bug could be connected to whoever had set fire to the stables and left the package with the shoe. Logically it had to be, but Hans wouldn't jump to any conclusions.

Hans's cellphone buzzed in his back pocket. He retrieved it and answered.

"Yeah?"

"Hans, it's Royce. We've got a problem. Cody's been kidnapped." Royce Devereaux explained hurriedly. Hans had only a moment to think how lucky Emery was to have such a loyal friend who viewed this as his problem too.

"What's happened?" he demanded.

"I happened to see Cody at the Dockside Pub. He was having a drink and then he sort of seemed out of it all of a sudden. Like he'd been roofied. I started to go to him, but the bartender looked like he was helping him. But then I saw him walk Cody outside and throw him into a black sedan. I tried to get to them, but the crowds in the bar were rowdy and I got into a fistfight trying to get out. By the time I got outside the car was gone."

"Damn." Hans pulled the phone away from his ear to hold it to his forehead as he shut his eyes and drew in a calming breath. He put the phone back to his ear.

"Royce, can you be here in ten minutes? I'll talk to Emery. We need someone to keep an eye on Ms. Ryder. She'll want to come with Emery and me and he won't let her."

"I can babysit her. I'll bring Wes. Between the two of us, we'll keep her safe and sound."

"Good." Hans hung up.

* * *

The bedroom door burst open and Sophie lurched upright in bed, blinking away sleep. Emery was on his feet in an instant, a gun in his hands, aimed at Hans's chest. He immediately cursed, clicked the safety back on, and set the gun down.

"Damn it Hans, knock next time." Emery laughed softly, and reached for the covers as though to climb back into the bed. Sophie was still trying to swallow her heart, which had jumped into her throat in sudden panic.

"Royce called. He said he saw Cody get abducted from the Dockside Pub in town."

Emery cursed. "I'll get dressed. Do we have any leads?"

"Yes. I found a bug, not one of yours, on the kid's desk. I need you to reverse the signal and track it to the owner. Maybe we can find whoever took him."

Sophie struggled to grasp what Hans was saying, but Emery was already up and at his closet. He jerked on a pair of worn jeans that hung low on his lean hips. He slipped a black t-shirt over his head and tugged it down before reaching for his leather motorcycle jacket.

"What was he doing when they got him?" Emery asked.

"Don't know. Royce said he was just taking a drink and it looked like someone must have slipped a drug in his glass, because he started to stumble. Apparently the bartender was the one who escorted him to the car and drove off with him. Maybe this has to do with the bug I found on his desk. Royce tried to get to him but he got tangled in a bar fight on the way out."

Holding the bed sheet around her, Sophie climbed out of bed, looking for her clothes as she listened. They'd have to get moving fast and that meant she needed to get dressed immediately.

"It's Antonio, isn't it?" she asked Emery softly as she bent to pick up her own jeans and a top from her suitcase on the floor.

The dark expression on Emery's face was all the answer she needed.

"Probably." Despite the harsh flashes of fury that swept over him, his skin was paler than before.

She touched his shoulder, curling her fingers into the leather of his jacket.

"Don't worry. We'll find Cody," she promised.

He finally looked at her and then grabbed her wrists and dragged her back to the bed. What was he thinking taking her back to bed at a time like this?

"Hey, what the heck are you doing?" she demanded as he shackled her to the headboard and tucked her beneath the covers.

"Sorry, Sophie, I've got to know you'll be safe and the best way I can do that is to leave you here."

"Emery!" she screamed. "Please, don't leave me here!" She fought, tugging on the cuffs until her arms ached and she was exhausted from shouting.

Hans looked between her and Emery and said, "Royce and Wes have volunteered to come and watch over her while we find Cody."

"Good." Emery pressed a kiss to her lips before he exited the room with Hans. The last sight she had was of Emery tucking a gun into the waistband of his jeans and dropping his t-shirt and jacket over it. Something about that made her stomach turn.

He'd left her behind.

"Emery! How could you!" She continued to scream until she was hoarse.

He didn't come back.

The silent house around her was eerie, and she felt as if she was trapped in a tomb. Torn between anger at Emery for forcing her to stay here and worry about Cody, she didn't hear the sounds of movement downstairs right away.

Masculine voices drifted up the stairs and down the hall. Sophie tensed. Royce and Wes must be here.

"Knock, knock," Royce announced as he and another man entered the bedroom. She recognized the second man instantly. He was the redheaded dom at the Gilded Cuff Club. He'd had the lovely submissive sitting at his feet and he'd been stroking the woman's hair and watching Sophie with mild interest. Not with sexual interest, but he'd definitely been curious. So this was Wes. Unlike Royce, who had an all-American rugged handsomeness about him, Wes had a sharp, dangerous look to him that reminded her of Emery.

"Well, well, we meet again." Wes's voice was low, silky, and seductive. "Officially, this time. I was admiring you the other night. You were such a breath of fresh air in the club. It's a pity you're Emery's. I'd have been happy to tutor you in the ways of submission."

I'll just bet you would, she thought dryly. Sophie sank deeper into the bed, trying to ensure that the covers wouldn't slip down and expose her nakedness to the two men.

"Can you please let me out of these cuffs?" she asked, attempting to sound plaintive and sweet. She had a feeling that demanding her release would get her nowhere with these two men.

They shared a meaningful look that boded ill for Sophie's plans. Then Royce shook his head.

"Sorry, sweetheart. We've got orders straight from Emery. You are to remain right where you are."

Royce and Wes seated themselves on opposite sides at the foot of the bed. Royce's lips twitched at Sophie's little growl of frustration. Wes, however, propped one leg up and rested his arms on his knee and stared at her thoughtfully.

"Royce said you're writing Emery's story."

"Well…I'm actually not planning on writing it anymore. Emery and I have to have a little talk about that."

Royce's humor faded and he focused on her. "You've had a change of heart?"

"I came here intending to solve the kidnapping, not just write about his story. But yesterday some psycho burned Emery's barn to the ground and left one of Fenn's shoes inside the house as a present. The story doesn't matter, at least not the revealing of what happened. What matters now is solving the case and catching this bastard. Emery's in real danger, more danger than I even realized. I thought I would have time to track down the man responsible, but he's already here and going for the kill. I'm sure he's the man who took Cody tonight. Which is why I should be out there helping, not tied to the damn bed!" she snapped.

The two men exchanged glances. "Do you think it would be wise to go out there in harm's way where Emery will be worried about you? The kidnapper might get hold of you and use you against him. Did you ever think of that?"

Stupidly, she hadn't. She was so used to taking care of herself that the idea of her being used against anyone seemed so…unlikely.

"Well, that's what worried Emery, and that's why he called us. So relax," Royce chuckled. "I'm sure we can entertain you for a few hours." He waggled his eyebrows teasingly, but Wes's gaze was still frank with interest.

Needing to change the subject and the sensual intensity of their stares, she tried another tact. "Can we watch TV or something? This is extremely awkward with you both just staring at me."

She prayed it might give her time to figure out how to escape them, or at the very least convince them to set her free and take her to Emery. There was no way she wanted to sit on the sidelines, not when she knew she could help rescue Cody. It wasn't just that. She had a bad feeling. A chilling sense of dread crawled into her chest, burrowed into her heart and weighed her down.

"I guess that would be okay. Football's on tonight," Royce replied.

Wes was still watching her with far too much interest. Her body was all too aware of it. She was naked beneath the sheets, her wrists were chained to the headboard, and she'd been left alone in a room with two completely masculine men, both of whom made it clear they were interested in her. Why hadn't Emery given her time to get dressed before he'd chained her to the bed if he knew these guys would be coming over?

She hadn't forgotten Royce's comment about a ménage. She tried not to think about what it would be like trapped between him and Wes, sweaty bodies straining, and the soft rush of panting breaths. But as soon as the image was there, it faded beneath a more powerful image of Emery. His hands on her, his body trapping hers, sliding into her, silky and hard, invading her again and again.

"She's blushing," Wes announced. One of his dark reddish-brown brows rose.

"It's probably because you're staring at her like a hungry wolf, Wes. Ease up on her. She's far too modest for you. I made a play for her, and she wouldn't have it. She's all for Emery." Royce got off the bed and headed for the massive flat screen TV mounted on the wall opposite the bed.

"Pity." The dark focus of Wes's cobalt blue eyes was as rich as the night sky and just as endless. He licked his lips, the action so positively seductive that her insides flipped and knotted uncomfortably.

Save me from gorgeous sexy men. Sophie focused on slowing her breathing and trying to banish the heat from her cheeks.

Royce was looking about for the TV remote when the door to the bedroom burst open.

Faster than Sophie could blink, Royce and Wes were facing the door, guns raised. They had guns? She hadn't even seen where they'd been keeping them. When she finally turned her head to the doorway, she grinned in relief. Both of her watch dogs muttered curses and put their guns away.

"Hayden, what the hell were you doing? We could have shot you." Wes started toward her. His handsome features were a mirror of Sophie's friend's, and she realized with shock that they had to be related. Brother and sister?

Hayden Thorne kicked her lips up into a grin and strode in. She was all fire and sass, everything Sophie wished she was. Hayden had the luscious body of a 1940s starlet, with high cheekbones and expressive eyes beneath graceful winged brows and a tumbling mass of red hair that made her look like Rita Hayworth. She was the sort of woman that Sophie couldn't even be jealous of, because she was too nice and too loyal, and still an ass kicker at the same time. She was one heck of a girl, and from the moment she'd bumped into Sophie in town a few weeks ago, they'd liked each other instantly.

Hayden tossed her hair over her shoulders, ignoring the furious glares of both men.

"Hi Sophie, I heard you needed rescuing from my brother and his pal." Only then did she flick a scathing glance at Wes and Royce.

"Hey, I'm not some pal. I used to babysit you." Royce glowered thunderously. Hayden shot him a wicked grin, as though she'd spent all her life teasing him.

"Babysit? You didn't babysit me. You just sat on me. I distinctly remember you shoving my face into the dirt and pulling my hair. You'd never know you were eleven years older than me, not by the way you acted." She stomped past them and put a knee onto the bed to reach Sophie's wrists.

"Now wait just a damn minute—" Wes grumbled low and warningly.

Suddenly Hayden had a Taser aimed at her brother's chest. "Don't try to stop me, Wes. I've had a long day and tasing you and Royce would bring me too much pleasure."

Royce backed up a step, moving out of range. "Your sister sounds serious."

"Hayden, you'll regret making me angry." Wes's tone was silky and dangerous. He crossed his arms over his chest, a move that reminded Sophie of Emery, and her heart kicked back into the rapid fire pulse of panic. They were wasting time arguing. They needed to get to Emery and Hans.

"Oh yeah? What are you going to do, Wes? Nothing is more important than getting Sophie free and helping Emery. You men are too pigheaded to realize this is a trap. He and Hans are going to get killed unless we can get there in time."

"And how do you know what's going on with Emery?" Wes demanded through clenched teeth. Sophie wasn't often scared, but she admitted that Wes made her a tad nervous. Hayden simply shrugged off her brother's obvious anger.

"I bugged your phone months ago. Interesting phone sex, by the way. *Ick.*" Hayden shuddered theatrically but kept her Taser pointed at him while she used her other hand to unlock Sophie's cuffs with a small key. Sophie couldn't help but wonder why Hayden had a spare key ready.

"I'll be sure to start every conversation with something inappropriate," Wes muttered.

Royce laughed, a charming lopsided grin on his face. "So Hayden, I always had you pegged for a feisty submissive. Don't tell me you're secretly a domme?"

Wes sent a dark, blazing look at his friend. "What are you talking about?"

All of Hayden's bravado wavered in the wake of her brother's thunderous question. Her creamy skin turned ashen. Royce gulped and looked away guiltily.

"Hayden, what's he talking about?" Wes started toward his sister, punishment gleaming in his eyes.

Sophie chose that moment to intervene. "Um, Wes, not to be rude, but can we talk about this later? Emery's in danger, remember?" She slid off the bed, collected her clothes, and held the sheet with a curled fist at her shoulders.

The second she closed the bathroom door behind her she heard Wes yell.

"What do you mean my sister's a member of the Gilded Cuff?"

Sophie winced in sympathy for Hayden.

So much for keeping that little secret locked tight.

As she scrambled into her clothes, hoping someone would know how to find Emery, the empty hole in her gut screamed disaster. Something awful was going to happen.

Chapter 15

THE BOY WAS QUICKLY IDENTIFIED AS EMERY
LOCKWOOD. THE OFFICER WRAPPED A BLANKET
AROUND THE BOY'S TINY SHOULDERS AND PUT
HIM IN THE BACK OF THE SQUAD CAR, SECURING
HIM SAFELY INSIDE BEFORE SEARCHING THE
SURROUNDING WOODS FOR SUSPECTS AND THE
OTHER MISSING CHILD.
—*New York Times*, September 30, 1990

I'm impressed, Cody. You've lasted much longer than I expected. A lesser man couldn't talk with a leg, a few ribs and a hand broken." Antonio's accent had thickened after the heat of torture. "Perhaps I should have started slicing rather than smashing." He lifted up a bowie knife. The yellow light from the overhead lamp flashed over the gleaming silver blade.

Cody didn't like that he'd impressed the bastard. Pain fogged his brain, making him wish he'd died an hour ago. But damn it, he kept finding strength somewhere. Between every crushing blow, he'd somehow rallied and stayed coherent. Of course, he was more aware of the pain he was in.

If Hans had been here, he'd have told Cody to find his Zen place. *Bullshit.* Hans was a dead man if Cody ever survived this.

Tears leaked down his cheeks, joining the cold sweat that had broken out over his body in the last ten minutes.

Was he going into shock? He hoped so; anything would be better than how he felt right now.

"Half an hour to midnight." Antonio checked his watch and rose from his chair. "Well, I have something to see to before the grand finale." He gaze dropped to Cody's restraints and lingered. He flashed a malevolent smile. "Don't go anywhere." The look was so cruel, so full of evil, that Cody's frantic pulse shot straight into hyperdrive. He had to remain calm.

"Ha-ha," he croaked. He'd lost his voice screaming a long time ago.

Antonio pushed away from the table he'd been leaning against.

"I would say it's been a pleasure to know you, Cody, but I'm afraid you were always a means to an end. Emery will come for you. No doubt he's tracking the bug you left behind. And when he gets here, my trap will snap shut." He snapped his fingers, the sound echoing loudly off the empty white walls.

"What?"

"Oh, didn't I tell you?" His captor's face composed itself into one of mock innocence. "This warehouse is rigged to blow ten minutes after midnight. Emery will arrive just in time to find you and you won't be able to warn him. He'll think he has a chance to save you and get you out, but he won't. It will be my greatest pleasure, killing him with hope."

Cody couldn't breathe. His lungs burned when he dragged in a gasp. "What happened to the slit-my-throat plan?"

"This is better. That little bastard has kept me busy for the last twenty-five years. Finally I can make my move. I know where Fenn is now and after Emery dies, I can leave this island and get on with the original plan."

Fenn? Cody dared not believe what he was hearing.

"Since I'm going to die, just answer me one question. Where is Fenn?"

Antonio studied him a long moment. Cody felt like a cow heading to the slaughterhouse.

"Colorado."

"Holy shit," Cody muttered. Emery's twin was alive. Fenn was alive! Hope welled up in him like a clear spring filling with cold, crisp water. He had to survive, had to tell Emery.

"You will die, Cody Larson. Do not be foolish enough to think you'll come out of this alive. I would stick around to watch the fireworks, but I've got a flight to Colorado first thing tomorrow morning."

Cody sucked in a breath. After all the pain, the agony, the excruciating torture, he was getting somewhere, yet he was going to die before he could warn Emery.

Fate was a cruel, two-faced bitch.

Antonio gave him one last look of malicious glee before he left the room. Cody counted five minutes before he tried to move. During the torture, Antonio had retied his hands behind his back with the rope that bound his waist, and left his feet free. With a broken leg, it was probably smart to do at the time; Antonio probably figured Cody couldn't kick out or run. Cody focused on wriggling until his left hand slid into the back pocket of his jeans. His fingers closed around his small Swiss Army pocket knife. He flicked open the largest blade and shifted his hold to start cutting the ropes binding his wrists. He cursed as the blade nicked the heel of his broken hand. Finally the rope loosened and dropped around his waist.

He was free. He stifled a moan as blood rushed back to his injured hand. Using all the strength he had left he dragged himself to his feet, trying not to look down at the crooked angle of his shattered leg. Cody collapsed in the chair by the table and tapped the power button on the computer, bringing the screen to life. There was no time to look through whatever Antonio kept on here. Taking his pocketknife he tucked the blade back in and flicked out the USB memory stick. It clicked into place and he opened the drive. There was only one file on the memory stick. A program he'd designed called "Echo." It would copy the entire hard drive at a rapid pace and back it up to a cloud. He'd be able to see everything Antonio had been up to.

"Come on," he growled as the program started to run. He checked his watch and grimaced. Ten minutes to midnight.

The second the program was done he jerked the USB out. It was only then that he noticed the small icon at the bottom of the screen. Another program was running. He clicked on it and his breath whooshed out of his lungs. A countdown clock was ticking away. Only it wasn't counting to midnight, but to detonation.

Five minutes.

"Shit!" He lunged from the chair, biting back a shout of pain as his broken leg gave out beneath him. If he could drag it behind him, he might be able to limp out of here. Antonio wasn't coming back. No one would be here to stop him, if he could just get out in time…

Tears blurred his eyes as pain and fear raged inside him like the fires of his own personal hell. His damn leg…couldn't…couldn't…

His body betrayed him just outside the door and he went down.

I'm sorry, Emery.

* * *

"What is this place?" Emery asked as he and Hans pulled up in front of a dark two-story factory on the edge of town. The windows were all smoky gray with the haze of the factory's pollution. One pale yellow light stood out in the sea of dark glass. A figure moved past the light, catching both Emery's and Hans's attention.

"It's one of the old breweries, I think." Hans pulled out his gun.

Emery glanced at his cell phone, focused on the blinking dot. The signal from the bug on Cody's desk was coming from inside.

"Let's go. We don't have time to waste. Cody could be in there." Emery didn't say what they were both thinking. He might already be dead and they were too late.

He and Hans stepped out of the car and started toward the

darkened brewery. The main door was locked but Hans aimed his Beretta at the lock and shot it out. They had wanted the element of surprise in case Cody's kidnapper was still around, but there was no time.

The main floor of the factory was empty and quiet. A solitary set of stairs led up to the upper floor, where they'd seen the light coming from when they'd gotten out of the car. Hans led the way, gun up and ready. They moved together, silent as predators tracking prey. After years of living with Hans, Emery had picked up his bodyguard's ability to move soundlessly and quickly. They both knew that any sound they made could betray their presence and get Cody killed.

At the top of the stairs they caught a glimpse of light at the end of the hall. Bathed half in light and half in shadow, was a body.

"Cody!" Emery cursed softly and shoved past Hans. All instincts fled, all rational thought vanished.

Cody. He was the only thing he could think about. He skidded to a halt and knelt by his friend's side. For a brief, heart-stopping second, he thought the young man was dead. Then Cody groaned softly. Emery turned him over and took in the sight of Cody's bruised face, torn short, bloody hand, and the unnatural angle of his leg.

Whoever had done this would pay. Dearly.

"Damn, kid, what happened?" Hans growled as he assessed Cody's injuries.

Cody's eyes fluttered open, bleary and unfocused as he looked between Hans and Emery. Pain fogged his expression as he struggled to speak.

"Gotta…go…guys." Then his eyes rolled back into his head.

"Shit, he's in shock. We've got to get him out of here." Hans grabbed Cody's body and with a mighty heave, lifted him up over his shoulder in a fireman's hold.

"Get him to the hospital and come back for me," Emery said as he checked his own gun and eyed the open door where the only source of light slithered out from the shadows.

Hans paused, hesitation and wariness in his gaze. "Emery…"

"Hans, we always knew it would come to this. I'm not asking you to save him. I'm *telling* you. So get the hell out of here."

In that silent moment, Hans studied him with a mixture of pride and regret. After twenty-five years, this could be the end of the line and they both knew it.

"See you on the other side, Emery."

"Yeah," Emery sighed, and turned his back on his bodyguard and his wounded charge. He raised his gun and stepped into the room, clearing the corners first, as Hans had taught him. It was empty, save for a table, two chairs and a computer. A single lamp hung low from the ceiling, the only source of light in the room except for the computer. It wasn't one of Cody's machines, which meant it belonged to whoever had taken him.

Emery didn't stop to think, but rushed to the computer and started pulling up files. A red blinking icon at the bottom of the screen distracted him. He attempted to close the program but the window opened. Blaring red numbers showed a countdown.

Twenty-eight seconds.

To what?

The pit of Emery's stomach dropped. The hairs on the back of his neck rose in warning and the memory of Cody's gasping, "gotta go guys" echoed through his mind.

It was a trap.

He dropped his head back and looked up at the ceiling, taking a deep breath. What he saw above him made his heart stutter and stop. A ton of C-4 packs were attached to the metal beams above.

Twenty-one seconds.

"Damn!" He shoved the chair back and surged to his feet, finally able to move again. He wasn't going to get out of here in time. He ran into the hall, looked at the narrow stairs. It would take too long.

His head flicked in the other direction. There was a window at the end of the hall about fifteen feet away. Emery approached the window and looked down. There was a giant vat of water below the window.

With a grim smile he jogged back to the end of the hall and without another thought he ran straight at the window. A second before he reached it, he jumped, tucking his body into a protective crouch as he shattered through the window. Glass and wood from the panes sliced through him and he ducked his head and raised his arms, clenching his eyes shut.

The explosives detonated. Fire, glass and stone tore into him from behind as he fell. Before any pain could register he was plummeting into the water. It swirled round him, tugging him into its depths, as the fire of the explosion lit the world above him. He struggled to hold his breath, fighting the choking sensation. With strong strokes, he swam deeper and deeper, trying to escape the debris that were crashing into the water around him. A heavy metal beam shot straight down and he barely avoided it. It snagged his jacket and tugged him downward, pinning him to the bottom of the metal vat. He gasped, air bubbles escaping his lips in pale white quivering shapes as they fluttered up to the surface. Emery fought to free himself of the jacket, but his limbs were heavy and cumbersome. His vision wavered, and flashes of shadows crept in at the corners.

To be anywhere but here... Hans and Cody were safe; they had to be. And Sophie. She was safe at home in his bed.

A silent scream tore through his mind at the thought of never seeing her again. What he wouldn't give for one more touch, one more smile. To see her silver eyes looking at him with passion, with something more, something he'd been too afraid to hope for. It was the only thing that mattered now, to see the love shining from her eyes. Was dying really like falling asleep? He was barely aware of drifting away.

Chapter 16

After radioing in the discovery of Emery Lockwood and requesting backup, Officer O'Malley searched the woods. Several squad cars, an ambulance and reporters descended on the scene. The accompanying photo depicts the world's first sight of young Emery Lockwood after being rescued.

—*New York Times*, September 30, 1990

The hellish glow of the flames made the horizon look as though it was on fire. Sophie's world zeroed in on that one raging inferno.

"Drive faster!" she shouted at Royce. He slammed his foot on the Maserati's gas pedal.

She prayed they'd get there in time.

"Oh god," Hayden gasped from the backseat. "It's the old brewery."

Royce screeched to a halt on the street where the factory had been, far enough away to keep the car from becoming part of the inferno.

As she jumped out of the car, Sophie raised a hand as if to shield herself from the scorching heat. Her insides clenched and her instincts screamed that Emery was somewhere inside the brewery.

"That's Emery's car," Wes shouted as he pointed toward the Mercedes parked twenty feet farther up the street.

Sophie sprinted toward the warehouse, but nearly tripped over two smoke-tinged bodies. Dropping to her knees, she turned them over.

Cody and Hans.

Royce, Wes, and Hayden joined her, helping to lift the bodies and drag them away from the fire.

Cody's eyes opened and he fought for breath. "Sophie... bomb..." He coughed violently and couldn't seem to get out anything else before he slipped back into unconsciousness.

"Bomb?" Sophie and Hayden spoke at the same time. They all turned to look back at the burning factory.

Something wild and ferocious rose up inside her. A beast of rage and pain roared deep in her heart. She knew Emery was still inside, dying, perhaps already dead. But she couldn't stand by and watch.

Never again.

She would find him, or she would die trying to get him out.

Sophie stood and ran toward the burning edifice. Black smoke curled amidst the flames, which were licking destructive paths to block her way. But it didn't matter. She'd cross the fires of hell for him.

The others were shouting, their voices distant and muted. She didn't listen. The brewery door hung open, half hanging from its bottom hinge, and she was so close.

Strong arms banded around her waist and hauled her back several feet. She screamed, clawed, fought savagely to get free. Emery was in there. She couldn't leave him alone to die. She had to get him out; she had to save him.

She hadn't saved Rachel. There was no way she'd survive failing someone else.

In the midst of her panicked fighting she realized it was Wes who held her captive.

"Damn you! Let me go!" she screeched, throwing her legs and arms out to shake herself free, but he didn't release her, even when her elbow hit his eye.

"You'll get killed. He'd never forgive me," he snarled back as he fought to contain her flailing limbs.

"No! I have to find him. He can't…he can't be alone."

She tried to ram her elbow into his side but he twisted his body and she missed.

The brewery shook and part of the roof collapsed, blasting her with a cloud of thick smoke. He dragged her back another ten feet and only then did she run out of strength.

All around them the fire raged and smoke swirled in smothering clouds.

Darkness, such awful darkness. The one person she'd ever truly trusted with herself, since Rachel, was gone. Somewhere in the crumbling, burning rubble lay the man she loved.

Loved.

Yes. She loved him. She'd never loved anyone else the way she did him. She'd spent her whole life being an outsider, with the weight of secrets and tragedies holding her down. Then she'd met him. He'd sent those secrets tumbling off her shoulders and stolen her heart with his tender yet fierce, unrelenting passion.

Before Emery, life had been a pretty dream, like walking through a museum and seeing the world through the lovely scenes and painted, false faces. But there was no truth in that, only imaginings.

Emery was real. Each smile, each husky laugh, each ragged breath he'd drawn against her neck as they'd made love the night before. That was real, that was true. He was so much more than anything she could have dreamed of. He had wanted her, all of her, even the parts of herself she'd tried to hide. She'd never forget the way his eyes had flashed with desire and pride as he admired her naked body. So wounded, so scarred, yet he'd still needed her.

There had never been any illusions with him. He saw her for what she really was and still wanted her. How often was someone fortunate enough to find a soul so attuned to theirs that they were accepted and wanted without any pretenses or expectations?

He was her guiding star and she'd lost him. How could she go through life without the light of the stars to show her the way home?

"I'm so sorry, Sophie," Wes whispered. His voice broke and his grip on her body tightened as though he had to cling to someone. Strange how death could unite two strangers. They both mourned the man lost among the ashes.

Wes slid a hand over her face, brushing back her hair, the touch soothing, brotherly. That comfort only made the pain worse. His arms around her vibrated, as though the tragedy of losing his friend had forced him out of control. The dancing flames played with the shadows on his handsome face, creating hollows around his eyes and below his cheekbones that made his features look like a macabre skull. He inhaled a slow deep breath and dropped his gaze from the fire. She raised her eyes to his, seeing her own pain mirrored in his gaze. She opened her mouth to speak, not even sure of what she could say.

"Wes," a hoarse voice growled, "get your hands off my woman."

They both turned to stare at the man who emerged from the smoke and gloom at the side of the brewery. For a second she couldn't move, couldn't think beyond what she was seeing. Wes dropped his arms from her body.

"You're alive!" she gasped.

Soaking wet, cut and bruised, Emery was the most wonderful thing she'd ever seen. The sobs came without warning and she could barely see him as tears blinded her. He started toward her but she was already there, throwing herself against him. They fell back to the ground. He grunted softly beneath her, and curled his arms around her waist, keeping her against him. Sophie buried her face in his throat, inhaling his scent. She continued to choke down little sobs, hiccupping and feeling pathetic but unable control herself.

"Shh..." He smoothed his large palms over her back, rubbing her in slow strokes as he tried to soothe her. His chest was warm and damp against her cheek. The rapid double thump of his heart against her ear was the sweetest sound she'd ever heard. This wasn't a dream. He was here, alive—how she didn't know.

"What the hell happened, Emery?" Wes knelt next to them and looked Emery over in obvious concern, his eyes taking in the tattered state of Emery's clothes. Sophie curled her fingers in his shirt, holding on to him. Two pairs of legs appeared as Hayden and Royce joined them.

"Hans and I found Cody. He said something about getting out of there, but it was only a minute later I found the bomb."

Emery drew in a slow breath, the action raising his chest and Sophie along with it.

"It was a trap. Whoever took Cody meant for me to come here so they could blow this place up with me inside." Emery stroked her hair and she listened as he talked about finding Cody and the laptop.

"The bastard put C-4 all over the ceiling. I jumped through the window and landed in a huge vat of water just as it exploded. Lucky break for me. I almost didn't make it. One of the beams had me pinned. I nearly drowned before I got my jacket off." Emery's grip around her tightened. She pressed her lips against his throat, tasting cold water and his slightly salty skin.

"So let me get this straight." Royce chuckled. "You narrowly escaped being blown to bits all over Long Island and you were worried about a little drowning?"

The laugh that escaped Emery's lips was filled with relief; the tension in him seemed to dissipate. Sophie found the ability to breathe again.

"Well, when you put it that way..." He lifted himself up to sit and he took Sophie with him, tucking her in his lap as they faced the others. Hayden's eyes were wide with worry. She talked a tough game, but it was obvious she'd never suffered through something like this before. A sheltered life often left one unprepared for harsher realities. Sophie offered Hayden a weak smile, which seemed to calm her friend somewhat.

Emery glanced around. "Are Cody and Hans here? They went out a few minutes ahead of me, but I don't know if they got out."

"They're pretty banged up." Royce helped Emery and Sophie stand. "They weren't as close to the blast, but they didn't have the water to shelter them. Cody's in bad shape; looks like someone gave him a serious beat down."

Hayden held up her cell. "I called an ambulance. It should be here any minute." No sooner had she spoken then an ambulance came roaring up the road, sirens blaring and lights flashing.

"Damn, Emery, you are one lucky son of a bitch. I'm glad you're okay." Royce slapped Emery's shoulder, making him wince. "Sorry." Royce laughed.

Emery smiled as he nuzzled Sophie's cheek and hugged her tight. She burrowed into him again, unable to resist the need to touch him. So long as she held him, he couldn't die, couldn't vanish, couldn't leave her alone. Last night had forged a connection between them that would take years to undo. The fear and panic she'd felt at losing him had nearly destroyed her, would have if he hadn't walked out of the smoke and taken her into his arms. Like a phoenix from the ashes, he had returned to her.

* * *

Afternoon sun cut through the windows of Emery's bedroom. The pale gold curtains pulled back on either side glowed and cast warm colored shapes over the bed. Emery had slept only a few hours before waking again. Plagued by worries and memories, he couldn't stay asleep or even rest. It felt all too familiar—the trauma, the tragedy, wounds. They'd spent half the night at the hospital with the police, giving statements about what had happened. Only then had he been able to bring Sophie home and take her to bed.

She'd trembled and clung to him as he'd simply held her for several long moments, breathing in her welcome scent and feeling her heart beat against his chest.

"I thought I'd lost you," she whispered. "I was dying inside. Then you came out of the smoke and I could breathe again." He saw the fear in her eyes, the stark pain and the slow realization that she wasn't emotionally distant from him, and that seemed to scare her just as much as the thought of losing him.

Cupping her face in his hands, he rubbed his nose against hers in a sweet little Eskimo kiss, trying to get her to smile. But when she did, it was tremulous.

"I'm okay, sweetheart. I'm right here, just a little battered, but fine. And you're safe here with me. We'll get through this." He dropped his hands to her waist, holding her close, wanting every bit of his body to touch hers. The connection between them was so strong, he felt invisible threads twining around his heart and securing him to this brave woman he'd come to think of as his, *only* his.

Sophie feathered her lips over his and his blood rushed to all the right places. God, he needed her, needed to hold her, to possess her, to share himself with her. After thinking he'd die in that dark vat of water, pinned helpless, drowning, he vowed the first thing he'd do was get her alone and brand her as his and seek comfort in her kiss and her touch.

"Sophie, I want you." He murmured in her ear as he traced her spine with gentle fingertips. Her response was to tug at his t-shirt, lifting it up from his waist and over his shoulders. He let her remove it and then he pulled her shirt off as well. They were stripping each other piece by piece, not rushing, but not delaying either. His jeans, then hers…When they were completely naked, he lifted her up and she wrapped her legs around his waist, her calves resting high on his buttocks as he walked the few feet to the wall by the bed. Using the wall and his body, he trapped her against it, holding her up with one hand on her ass. The other he used to position his cock. When he was ready, he thrust in hard. Her head fell back and he leaned in, kissing and nipping the exposed skin of her neck and shoulder as he hammered his hips against hers.

The feel of her around him—silken heat, breathless sighs, and husky moans—was a fantasy he'd never imagined with any woman before. He claimed her, marking her with his love bites, and proving to himself and to her that he was very much alive. She came first, crying out his name, and it was nirvana to his ears. He shouted when his body seemed to melt from the inside out; his balls drew up tight and he spent himself inside her. With any other woman, that would have been enough; he'd have let her go and walked away.

Not with Sophie. A deep contentment filled him as he remained connected to her, feeling her wild heart beat in rhythm with his, their shared breaths and souls seeming to whisper to each other through the portals of their eyes.

"Take me to bed," she pleaded and sealed her request with a tender kiss that was more heart than heat. His legs shook as emotions rolled through him, but he carried her to his bed and set her down. With quick but unsteady movements, he shut off the lights and joined her in bed.

The second he had her in his arms again, he made love to her a second time. Slow and deep. He buried himself inside her again and again, his eyes locked on hers as he lost himself. She'd taken him over, ripped his soul out and replaced it with something strange: heat, compassion, hunger, a need to never be without her. She was his and he'd never let her go. Like a wolf with his mate, he would protect her with his last breath.

He loved the way she fell asleep while he was still inside her. She purred softly, like a pleased kitten, and drifted off. He kissed her cheek hugged her close. He managed a couple hours of rest, but he couldn't really sleep.

Every part of his body hurt like hell. Glass shards had cut into him, and between the explosion and hitting the water hard, he was bruised all over. The hospital had attempted to keep him overnight, but since the only outward signs of trauma were some minor cuts and bruises, he battled the doctors and nurses, fighting for the right to go home. All he needed was some time to rest and recover and he wouldn't do that in a damn hospital bed. He wasn't sure whether jumping through the window, falling into the water, or the explosion had done the most harm. Still, it was nothing compared to what Cody had suffered. Cody was lucky to be alive after the torture he'd endured and it was all Emery's fault.

Thank God for Sophie. Wherever she touched him, the pain seemed to fade. She was warm and soft, a healing presence. He couldn't forget the look on her face when she'd seen him come out of the smoke at the brewery. When she'd torn free of Wes's arms and flung herself at him, he'd wrapped himself around her, clutching her to his chest like the precious thing she was.

Sophie Ryder. Journalist and sweet seductress.

She'd crept into his heart and carved her name there.

His lover stirred, nuzzling into his neck, her breath fanning his skin as she sighed and drifted back to sleep.

If only they never had to leave his bed again. He shifted his body so that he faced her. Her beauty was intoxicating. She had creamy skin, pale rather than tan, and her long lashes looked as if they were tipped with dark gold. Her light, wheat-colored hair tumbled in a gleaming mass around her face. Her slightly upturned nose animated her face when she wrinkled it in displeasure. Her lips were a light pink shade with a hint of dusk that matched the tips of her breasts. He could spend years stroking her mouth with his fingertips, just to feel their silky texture.

Sophie licked her lips, her pink tongue swiping delicately over his finger. He swallowed a laugh at the puzzled look she gave him when her lashes drifted up.

Last night could have gone so differently. He could have died. Funny; it was his second brush with death and he hadn't realized how long he'd been expecting it to happen again. As though he'd lived years in an awful stasis, just waiting for the other shoe to drop. Even though they'd all survived last night, it wasn't over. The man who'd taken Cody was on the loose. Sophie had come to him at the Gilded Cuff, warning him he might be in danger and he hadn't taken her seriously. She'd been right. Antonio was back and wanted to finish the job. Everyone he loved, especially Sophie, was now in danger because of him.

Panic hit him like a punch to the gut. They were all still exposed, too vulnerable. He had to get Sophie out of here. She'd never leave willingly. She was too stubborn. If he told her to go, she wouldn't leave unless it was for a good reason. The woman thought she could protect him. Maybe she'd stood up to those other criminals she'd battled, but he wouldn't let her stick around and die for him.

Emery kissed her temple and she cuddled deeper into the curve of his body. He liked her tucked into his side, the way they molded together.

How was he going to protect her?

She shifted restlessly against him, her eyes closing again, and she gave a little sigh. Her arms tightened about his chest, causing his body to stir. Never before had a woman tempted him to the point of mindless madness. She'd reduced his world to one tiny yet infinite universe. Half of him wanted to send her away, remove the source of confusion which had upset his carefully controlled environment. The other half of him refused to let her leave his sight for even a moment. She belonged to him, and he never relinquished what was his.

As much as he craved staying in bed with her forever, he needed to get back to the hospital and check on Cody. Hans, fortunately, had only suffered a concussion from the blast and they'd kept him overnight for observation. Even though the police had posted a guard, Wes and Royce had volunteered to take turns watching over the rooms until Emery could get Cody and Hans home. If there was one thing Emery had learned from his bodyguard, you never left yourself exposed. Policemen could be bought off; so could nurses and doctors. Only Royce and Wes could be trusted to keep watch over his other friends.

Emery carefully disentangled himself from Sophie and headed to the bathroom to shower. Already naked, he stepped into the stall and turned the hot water on.

His hands shook slightly as he rubbed his sore muscles and let the water work its magic. Shutting his eyes, he struggled against the memories of the moment before the explosion, which ran rampant behind his eyelids. The blaring red digital numbers counting down. The rush of heat and pain as the explosion chased him into the dark water. He sucked in a breath and forced himself to focus. The police had questions and had agreed to meet him at the hospital at four p.m. That gave him two hours.

Dizziness swamped him and his entire body went rigid in an attempt to quell the spinning sensation. It was as though something was stabbing at the base of his spine, sending violent shivers up the length of his back. That sense of a self outside him took hold.

His face, in the mirror, days old stubble. Flickering fluorescent lights painted thick shadows around his eyes. Pain radiated out from his shoulder, an old injury from a bull kicking him. Another day, another day to work until his palms cracked and bled, another day to pray the bank wouldn't foreclose on his dream...

Emery surged back into himself with a sharp gasp, his chest burned with the lack of oxygen until several deep breaths later. He had to stay in control. These dreams, these...visions, his descent into madness, it had to stop. Everyone he loved was still in danger. The question was, what was he going to do about it?

* * *

Sophie woke to an empty bed, reaching across the vast expanse of the sheets for Emery. A hint of warmth lingered beneath her palm.

Emery's dented pillow looked lonely. It was the man that should have been next to her that she missed. She sat up and searched the room, hungry for a glimpse of him.

Even though he'd flinched with pain and shouldn't have exerted himself, he'd made love to her—slowly, sweetly. When she'd protested, telling him to wait until he was better, he'd murmured that he had to touch her, kiss her, be inside her, with such desperation she couldn't deny him. It was in that moment when he'd slid home inside her, and she'd cushioned him with her body, that she'd come undone. He hadn't moved at first, only gazed down at her, the entire world shining from his eyes. Her breath had caught in her throat, and she'd ceased to exist outside that embrace, outside him.

All of it was terrifying but enthralling at the same time. Like Alice before the looking glass, she'd marveled at the change in the way she saw the world. She'd chased a white rabbit down an unexpected trail and met the King of Hearts. She was still Sophie, still the same woman, but something inside her had been set free, unleashed from a cold, dark prison. The fire of her passion and the need to love and be loved burst from her without the strict restraint she'd once had.

The sex that had followed Emery's brush with death had been nothing short of mind-blowing. They'd both collapsed in a tangle of limbs, gleaming with sweat. He'd taken her into his arms, and covered her face and neck with soft, teasing kisses that held so much raw emotion she'd had to rub tears from her cheeks.

Yet neither of them had been brave enough to speak.

I love you.

Three words heavy with consequences. Until she was brave enough to say them, she'd breathe life into them with her kisses, her caresses, and hopefully he'd feel what her heart wanted so desperately to tell him.

She closed her eyes, breathing deeply. The faint whisper of water

on tile drifted to her ears. Curious and also shy, she slipped out
of bed, wrapping the sheet around her body. Holding it tight with
one fist above her breasts, she walked toward the bathroom. She
eased the door open and padded inside on bare feet. Inside the glass
shower stall, Emery had his back to her. His tanned skin was riddled
with hundreds of tiny cuts and bruises. He pressed one forearm on
the wall, his head resting on his arm as he drew in slow breaths. He
looked so broken, so wounded. An invisible fist clenched her heart
and squeezed.

She dropped the sheet and reached for the door. She needed to
touch him, hold him in her arms. Never in her life had she had
someone who belonged to her, someone she could reach out and
touch whenever she wished. She'd envied lovers who had such free-
doms. To be so open with another person that you could hug them,
brush your lips over theirs and link hands. It was a gift often taken
for granted. For the first time, she felt brave enough with Emery to
be open.

When she laid a hand on his left shoulder, his tension eased and
he turned around to face her. Hot water ran in tantalizing rivulets
down his well-toned chest and the rippling cords of muscle that
formed his abs. Unable to resist, she smoothed her palms over his
pectorals. His muscles leapt beneath her touch and his gaze zeroed
in on her mouth.

"May I touch you like this, Master Emery?" she asked, almost
teasing him, as she continued to stroke him. He curled his hands
around the flare of her hips and pulled her deeper into the shower,
closer to him.

"You may always touch me, unless I order you not to." His gruff
response and the heavy-lidded gaze he gave her shot her full of desire
and fresh hunger.

His words lit a fire in her. She unleashed every decadent thought
and fantasy she'd ever had. A man to touch, to kiss, a beautiful body
to lay her hands upon, to explore in delight and satisfaction. Not

that she would ever be satisfied. Being with Emery was as addictive as any drug. She'd never get enough of him.

He remained still, his hands resting on her hips as she explored him. When she took his length in her hand, stroking and squeezing the impressive erection, he sighed. His head fell back against the shower wall. He was hard as marble yet the skin was silky, and she marveled at the way he felt in her hand. He was nothing like her other lovers. Those had been hasty fumblings in the dark—quick, momentarily satisfying. None of those nights compared to even one minute with Emery, amorous or not.

"Harder, grip me harder!" His voice was a low growl that gave her body goose bumps.

She forced her gaze up to his face, startled by his pained expression. He met her stare and nodded in silent encouragement. Sophie tightened her hand around him and continued to stroke. His fingers dug into her skin. She rocked forward, teased by the water droplets trickling down his neck. She licked the water away to kiss her way up to his mouth. He dropped his head to hers, to give her easier access to his mouth. The kiss was slow, deep, full of heat and tenderness and something she was too afraid to examine closely.

Emery tensed in her palm and jerked away. A wave of embarrassment and disappointment tore through her with devastation. Had she done it wrong? Then she glimpsed the passion in his face as his jaw clenched and he tossed his head back, inhaling a ragged breath. He rotated their bodies, putting her against the tile, and then he turned her to face the shower wall.

"Put your hands on the wall and bend forward," he instructed in a guttural whisper.

Sophie did as he commanded. The water from the showerhead struck her back, making a waterfall of blissful heat down her ribs and backside. He was behind her, shoving a strong thigh between her knees, kicking her feet apart. He positioned the head of his cock at her entrance and thrust home. She rocked up on her toes at the power of their union and the delicious vulnerability. A moan of need escaped her lips as he withdrew. His hard length dragged against newly awakened nerve endings inside her and she tried to push back against him. He curled the fingers of his right hand around the nape of her neck, holding her in place while his left hand roamed from her breasts to her mound to her thighs where her hips met her legs. The way he held her made her helpless, but she trusted him. When he slammed into her with such force that stars burst behind her closed eyes, she cried out at the sudden unexpected pleasure of the hard penetration.

Emery made a rumbling, purring noise of pleasure as he rode her hard. The intense pleasure between them built into an almost tangible force. Then he slid in a sharp, slow rhythm as though he had all the time in the world to possess her. The feel of their slick bodies meeting, the soft sounds of flesh upon flesh and the heat of the water and the silken hardness of him inside her made her lightheaded. The climax she so desperately needed hovered at the edge of her awareness. His hard thrusts, digging fingers and their shared moans surrounded her, filled her.

"Who do you belong to?" Emery demanded in a husky whisper that bounced off the tile and wove through the spray of water to caress her ears. Sophie's arousal spiked and her body clenched around him.

"Who?" he rasped again, his own control seeming to shred. He punished her with a deep pumping movement and smacked her bottom. The combination of pleasure with the zing of pain set her spiraling toward the rush of ecstasy that awaited her.

"I belong to you, only you," she gasped and he sank deep, hard into her hot willing flesh. Her knees buckled under the weight of her climax. She collapsed against the shower wall. Dimly, she was aware of him as he cursed, thrusting once more into her spasming sheath before he joined her in the rush of bliss. His arms locked about her waist, and he held her up, even as he shook around her. He pressed his lips into her neck, nibbling and nuzzling while he held her in the gentle prison of his embrace.

"God, Sophie...God." He groaned and finally withdrew, turning from her body, and turned her to face him.

Sophie covered his mouth with hers, preventing him from saying anything else. He met her kiss with raw hunger which soon softened. The electric tingles that sparked to life between their every touch seemed to intensify with the simple kiss.

"I'm so glad you're okay," she breathed between kisses. "I couldn't bear to lose you too." Could he hear what was hidden in her gasping breaths? She *loved* him. "You're not allowed to do something like that ever again."

His rough laugh teased her ears, sending a flurry of shivers dancing down her spine.

"So you're giving me orders now?" He spanked her hard, and she jumped against his body.

He was not going to distract her. "You're damn right I am."

She dug her nails into his shoulders in retaliation for her stinging bottom.

Leaning into her, crowding her against the tile, his lips curved in a smile against her mouth as he stole a kiss. When she tried to deepen it, he pulled back.

"Not that I don't want to continue this *discussion*, but we've got to get to the hospital. I need you to watch over Cody while I talk to the police."

Finally, Emery would allow her to carry part of his burden. Her love for him only strengthened, like an ever growing oak tree, the roots sinking deeper, lodging in the rich soil.

"Okay." She smoothed her hands up his arms, over his shoulders and around his neck, pulling him back down for one more kiss.

Chapter 17

THERE WAS A TEARFUL REUNION OF THE
LOCKWOOD FAMILY WITH THEIR MISSING
CHILD AT ST. AUGUSTUS HOSPITAL, WHERE THE
BOY WAS TAKEN FOR EXAMINATION AND POLICE
PHOTOGRAPHS. EMERY'S SUFFERED FROM
SEVERE DEHYDRATION, BRUISED RIBS,
STARVATION AND BITE WOUNDS FROM VERMIN.
—*New York Times*, September 30, 1990

Sophie had never been a fan of hospitals. The pungent aroma of
death and the scent of sterile disinfectants made her stomach churn.
Emery walked with long purposeful strides beside her. His face was
a mask of stone, betraying no emotion, but his jaw popped once
or twice as they headed down the hall to Cody's room. The last
time Emery had been here must have been when they'd brought him
in after he'd escaped Antonio. Sophie's throat burned as she imagined the little boy, scared and hurt, with his brother dead. Her hand
sought his as she laced her fingers through his, tightening her hold.
He didn't react except to shut his eyes for a second before opening
them again.

At the end of the hall, Royce sat in a stiff-looking metal chair
with a stack of papers in his lap. A red pen cap jutted out from
between his lips as his pen skated across the top of the page. He
glanced up through weary eyes. Relief softened the stress that tight-

ened his features as he watched them approach. He blinked, scrubbed his face with his hands, capped his pen and dropped the papers on top of a worn leather briefcase next to his chair. He stood as they reached him.

"How is he?" Emery asked in a hushed tone.

Royce grimaced. "Not good. He's quiet, which isn't like him. The doctor said he's out of the woods, but the healing will take time..." He rubbed his neck, glanced away before his eyes returned to Emery. "The man who took Cody...he shattered his hand with a metal mallet. Most of the bones were broken, even the small ones. It may be years before he gets control back over his hand, if ever. The doctor is worried about nerve damage, too."

"Christ." Emery hissed under his breath.

"Yeah. That's not all. He's got broken ribs, a broken leg, bruising all over his body. The kid took one hell of a beating. If I ever get my hands on the bastard who—"

"He's mine. You can finish off whatever pieces I leave behind." Emery growled low, like an alpha wolf issuing a challenge. A storm brewed behind his eyes. Tension emanated from him like static sparks.

Desperate to distract him, Sophie spoke. "Is Cody allowed to have visitors?"

Both men focused on her. After a moment Royce nodded. "Yes. Go on in."

Emery pushed the door open, then put a gentle hand on Sophie's back as he ushered her into the room first.

Cody was in a bed, blankets tucked around him, except for one of his legs, which was in traction. White wires and clear tubes were everywhere, connecting to bags and IVs in Cody's arms. A saline bag hung from a metal rod by the bed and several machines beeped, sending numbers skipping across their black screens. Cody's head was angled toward the window, but he turned to face them as they approached.

It took everything in Sophie not to cry out, not to run over and hug him. Black and purple bruises covered his face, and one eye was swollen shut. She could barely recognize the handsome carefree man she'd come to care so much about.

"You start to cry, babe, and we'll have a problem." Cody's raspy voice ended on a rough chuckle.

She answered him with a watery laugh and went to him, pulling up a chair by his bedside. She blinked away the stinging tears, refusing to let them fall, and smiled.

"Well, I'm sorry, but you look like crap," she teased, knowing humor would make him feel better.

Cody cracked a grin, even if it was one obviously faded with pain. He switched his attention to Emery. "Hey, bossman."

Emery reached out as though to touch Cody, but froze inches from his shoulder and pulled his hand back. His hazel eyes swirled with a torrent of greens and browns, matching the array of emotions that warred on his face.

"You had me worried." Emery finally spoke.

"I always worry you." Cody winced and flattened a hand over his chest. "Emery, could you get me a cup of coffee? Nurse Ratchet won't let me have anything besides water, but I need caffeine."

"I'll go." Sophie started to rise, but Cody's left hand, the unbroken one, caught her arm, the grip surprisingly tight for someone so wounded.

"Stay, Sophie. Looking at you makes me feel better." Cody shot a more energetic grin at his employer and friend.

"Why?" she asked.

"You're hot, babe." Cody shot a wicked smirk at his boss.

"Cody, find your own hot woman to drool over." A war of looks began between the two men, half sneers and mockingly threatening scowls.

"Can't. Stuck in this damn bed. So I'll borrow yours."

Sophie found herself wanting to laugh as she watched them engage each other. It was like watching two brothers feinting back and forth in a play fight.

Emery's face softened. "I'll get your coffee. Don't think you can seduce my woman from me while I'm gone."

Emery left the room, much less stiff than when he'd entered.

The second the door shut behind him, Cody was even more alert, more like his old self. He fished through his blankets, cursing when his right hand, so heavily bandaged that it looked more like a giant white bear paw, kept getting in the way. Finally, near his hip he found what he was looking for and pulled out a Swiss Army pocketknife.

"Here, take this. Show it to no one. Especially not Emery."

Her heart dipped low, the beat erratic as she stared at the small pocket knife.

"What is it?" She opened her palm as he set the knife in it, closing her fingers protectively around it.

"There's a USB flash drive on there. Antonio had a laptop in the room where he held me. After he left me to die, I got on the computer and copied the hard drive. Whatever was on there, we have it now. The computer was destroyed when the place blew to hell."

Sophie's lips parted as she drew in a quick breath. Blood pumped wildly in her ears.

This was huge. Beyond huge! They had a chance to anticipate Antonio's next move. Maybe even figure out where he was getting his intel on Emery, assuming they could get anything from the flash drive.

"Why can't we tell Emery?" Surely he should be the first to know…

Cody's face drained of color. His gaze floated to the ceiling, then slowly drifted back down, reluctantly, to her.

"Fenn may be alive. Antonio said he'd been looking for Fenn for years. Why would you look for a dead child, unless that child wasn't dead?"

Her throat stopped working and she forced an uncomfortable swallow as more shock rocketed through her. Fenn alive?

"Oh god!" Her hands flew to her mouth, stifling her cry of shock. "If we tell him and it turns out Fenn is dead or if Antonio gets to Fenn before we do and kills him, then it will be the last straw for Emery. I know he wouldn't be able to survive losing Fenn a second time."

Cody was right. They couldn't tell Emery. There was only so much devastation and tragedy a heart could withstand. If Rachel were suddenly alive and taken yet again before Sophie's very eyes, Sophie would never be able to get past that. *Never*. Hope could bring the most horrific trauma to a soul, more so than any other torture someone could endure. It reminded her of the story Granny Bells used to tell about Pandora's box. The box had unleashed all of the world's worst nightmares, but it always also released hope into the world.

Emery needed hope, but Sophie wouldn't dare give it to him, if there was even one chance he'd have it ripped from him.

"If we can find Fenn and get him to safety, then we could tell Emery, right?" she asked. "I could go, since you need to rest and Hans needs to watch Emery's back."

"Great plan in theory. But you're forgetting Emery won't let you out of his sight," Cody pointed out with a knowing grin.

The momentary rush of optimism at her plan faded. "True. He's a little overprotective." She tucked the pocketknife into her purse, mulling over the dilemma. Then it hit her.

"Royce or Wes could go. I bet one of them would jump at the chance to help out."

Cody brightened. "That could work."

The strain in Sophie's shoulders eased until Cody spoke again.

"We have to work fast. Antonio was supposed to catch a plane to Colorado this morning. That's where he thinks Fenn is."

"How do you know that?"

Cody shrugged. "I got him to talk. Villains love to ramble. He figured I'd be dead and wouldn't be able to repeat what he said. Plus, that dude was making mincemeat of my body parts and I needed to have something else to think about besides the pain."

Neither of them spoke for a long moment, the weight of what had almost happened seemed a tangible force, pressing down on them. If Emery and Hans had been there a moment later…if she'd begged him to stay or to take her with them it might have cost them those few precious seconds and they would have all been dead. It was a sobering thought.

Their gazes met and held just as Cody opened his mouth to speak, but the hospital room door was opened and Emery strode in, his hands full with three coffee cups.

"Coffee for you." He set one cup down on the tan tray table that stretched across the hospital bed.

Cody lifted up his bandaged right hand, cursed and switched so his left hand caught the coffee. He downed a large gulp, and then set the cup aside with a blissful sigh of relief.

"Nectar of the gods," he said dreamily. Emery and Sophie exchanged relieved looks. Cody was a mess, but he'd be all right.

"Sophie, I got you some hot tea." He handed her the second of two cups, which she took gratefully. The hot Styrofoam warmed her hands, dispelling some of the October chill which seemed determined to keep her fingers frozen.

Emery took a sip of his coffee. "I spoke to the police." His brows lowered as he seemed to be mulling over whatever he'd said to the officers. "There wasn't much to say so it was a short conversation. I told them you were kidnapped. They'll want a description of the man who took you, Cody. Tell them the truth, but leave out any connection to my kidnapping."

"Okay," Cody agreed quietly.

Sophie pursed her lips. No matter how short his conversation had been, talking to the police had obviously unsettled him. She didn't like the faraway look in his eyes just then, or how the knuckles of his free hand were white where he gripped the frame of the hospital bed.

She turned her attention back to Cody.

"When do the doctors think you'll be ready to come home?"

Home. Funny, she hadn't expected to fall so in love with Emery's home to the point that she thought of it as hers, too. But it was true. She'd never felt more connected to a place in her life. The apartment back in Kansas had never been home. Instead it was a rest stop on the way to where she was meant to be. Arriving at Lockwood Manor that first night…that had been like coming home. Emery had been right beside her, his body pressed flush to hers as they'd passed through the gates and entered the realm of her dreams, a world where she could be happy, she could belong. She suppressed a shiver of longing. If only it were true. But Lockwood wasn't her home. She was there only for a story and only for a short time. Emery hadn't been interested in keeping her around for long, and certainly not forever. He'd given her no indication that he wanted her to stay with him. Sophie was a fool for wishing he'd change his mind.

Cody's groan brought her back to reality.

"The doctor said three weeks at least, plus therapy. Boss, work your magic and jail break me. I can't stand much more of the food in this place. And Nurse Ratchet keeps taking my cell phone away and says I shouldn't be texting with my one good hand or I'll get carpel tunnel." Cody's eyes widened slightly and he lifted his lips in a hopeful smile.

Emery set his coffee down and crossed his arms over his chest, giving the younger man a commanding look. "I want you here at least another full day. After that we'll see about getting you out."

Cody moaned dramatically and dropped his head back onto the mountain of pillows. "You're a cold-hearted man, boss."

Despite his attitude, Sophie could have sworn a smile flickered across his face for an instant.

While she felt bad for Cody having to remain here, she was relieved Emery was being protective. With the extent of the young man's injuries, it was still unwise to let him leave. Another day under the doctor's watchful eyes couldn't hurt.

Emery's mouth kicked up in a crooked smile. "Just think of all the Jell-O you get to eat." As he spoke he picked up a plastic spoon and nudged a green Jell-O cup in Cody's direction on the tray table near the bed.

"I'd rather be at home with my laptop and a cheeseburger," Cody grumbled, but he picked up the Jell-O. His eyes flicked to Sophie, a flare of meaning blooming for a split second as he reminded her of the USB flash drive in her pocket. She shot a glance at Emery, her heartbeat cantering madly as she prayed he wouldn't notice her reaction to Cody's silent message.

"Well, we should go." Emery rose, stretched long arms over his head, a yawn escaping him as he turned in her direction. "Hans is ready for discharge and Wes is going to follow us home to just to keep an eye on things. Cody, Royce will be outside if you need anything."

Cody opened his mouth, a wicked glint in his eyes, but Emery cut him off. "And no, he's not bringing any women, alcohol, or electronics. You need to sleep."

"Well damn," Cody moaned and collapsed back on his pillows. "You sure know how *not* to show a guy a good time. I'll die of boredom before they ever let me out of this hell hole."

Sophie rose from her chair, kissed Cody's cheek. "Rest up."

He caught her elbow, as though embracing her gently so he could whisper. "Keep me in the loop."

Emery gave a warning growl, but it had little bite to it. "Get some sleep."

He gave Cody a commanding glare. It was stern, but layered just beneath were softer emotions—love, concern, the determination to protect. He was forever shocking her with his tenderness. Emery wanted the world to see a stoic, reclusive man with no weak spots, no vulnerabilities. But he gave himself away in every breath, in every touch and look for those he loved.

"Come on, Sophie. Wes is waiting on us." Emery slid an arm around her waist, his grip possessive but gentle as he tucked her into his side. She craned her neck over her shoulder, glimpsing Cody as he shut his eyes and seemed already to be sleeping.

She looked forward again, leaning more into Emery's sheltering hold. She had to figure out how to get Wes alone to tell him what she'd learned. How on earth was she going to do that without Emery noticing? Bile rose in her throat at the thought of deceiving Emery. She swallowed the unpleasantness back down. It was wrong to lie to him, knowing what she knew, but telling him could potentially be so much more hurtful. The last thing she ever wanted to do was hurt him.

* * *

"You told me you were going to take care of him," the cold voice whispered over the phone.

Antonio clutched the steering wheel and glowered at a family walking past his car. The little children wheeled small luggage bags, laughing and shoving each other as they followed their parents toward the airport entrance for departing flights.

"He should be dead. I timed it perfectly." He had. The entire night had gone off without a hitch, until he'd arrived at the airport early this morning, ready to catch a flight to Colorado when his client called him. It seemed Emery had survived the blast in the brewery.

The man on the other end of the line snarled. "Perfect or not, you failed. It seems the bodyguard got the hacker outside before the explosion. Emery jumped through a window into a vat of water. So you failed, completely." There was a deadly pause. "You know how I feel about failure."

Antonio resisted the urge to shout back at his client. He'd never had a problem carrying out a hit before, but these damn twins were his undoing. It was still a mystery as to how the boys had escaped twenty-five years ago. He had come back to the abandoned mansion that night to find one of his two accomplices dead of a gunshot to his stomach, the two boys gone, and the second accomplice missing as well. The puzzle had only grown when the next day he'd learned only one twin had found his way home. The other was gone...and he hadn't been the one to kill him, which meant that boy might still be alive. His boss had told him to leave Emery for now, and to concentrate on finding Fenn. It had only taken him twenty-five years and the invention of the Internet to track down one little boy. A boy that had grown into a rather dangerous man.

"I'm tired of you fucking this up. You've got one more shot before I call in someone else. Twenty-five years is a long time to mess up something like this." His client's voice was smooth again, dangerous. Antonio smiled grimly. He was dangerous, too, especially when his reputation was on the line.

"I have a flight to Colorado in an hour. Fenn is going to be in a bull riding competition tomorrow night. I'll take care of him."

Silence on the other end.

"Mr. Lockwood?" he queried. Surely his client hadn't hung up.

"You will stay here. Take care of Emery. He's more of a threat. He's the one who remembers. Fenn would have come home if he knew his identity. You can always take care of him later. I want Emery gone, and take out that damn reporter. When he dies, she'll suspect foul play. Remove them both and make it look like an accident. I don't want any police interest."

Another group of people paraded past Antonio's car, heading to the terminal. He wanted to finish this damn job and leave. It had been one hell of a disaster. His client had been displeased. Very displeased, and that wasn't good for his business.

So Antonio focused on watching Emery for any signs that Fenn had contacted him, or revealed where he was. Apparently that had been a vain hope. If he hadn't come across a ten-year-old picture of Rookie Rider of the Year for bull riding last month, he might never have found Fenn. At eighteen years old, Fenn had become a real expert at the rodeo. And since Antonio discovered Fenn was going by another name he was able to track his movements by the competitions he entered. It was almost laughable. The eldest child of one of the wealthiest East Coast families in America was living in an old run-down trailer in rural Colorado.

"Finish the job, D'Angelo, and I'll double your final payment."

"Consider it done. By tomorrow night Emery and the reporter will be gone."

The line went dead.

Antonio flipped the phone shut and tucked it into his jacket pocket. Even though the money was a nice bonus, it had long since ceased to be about the money. Emery and Fenn had made a mockery of his life's work.

It was time to end this.

* * *

Sophie's hands trembled as she logged on to her laptop. The small pocketknife rested on her thigh, looking oddly harmless. No one would have guessed it held secrets that could crush or bring back the soul of a tortured man. Emery's redemption could be at this very second on the flash drive.

She had to work fast. She'd only been able to tell Wes in a few brief minutes that he needed to occupy Emery for an hour while she checked out the information.

Jamming the USB drive into the computer, she immediately opened the files and scanned over the folders. Her heart stuttered to a stop when she saw one titled "FL." She clicked it open and started sorting through the PDFs until she saw a birth certificate with the name Fenn Smith. It was classified as a replacement document for a lost birth certificate.

"Fenn Smith," she murmured, reading over the details before moving on to the next documents. There were pictures. Hundreds of them. All of them had the same person, a boy who looked exactly like the one from the photo of the night Emery was found by the police. She clicked photo after photo, watching this other boy grow into a man. Her breath hitched as the reality of what she was seeing sank in.

It was Fenn. He was exactly like his brother, a living, breathing copy of the man she cared so much about. Fenn's long unruly hair nearly reached his ears, calling for a woman to run her hands through it. It was tousled, a wild reflection of Emery's more tame style. She stopped to gaze at one particular picture, of Fenn leaning back against a paddock fence, wearing faded worn blue jeans that hugged his legs enough to show his lean, muscled figure. Brown cowboy boots crossed at the ankles, a Stetson tipped back on his head, and a rakish grin stretching his lips wide. He was so alive, so vibrant. The build and shape of his body were a perfect mirror to his twin's. Their faces had the same chiseled beauty that had her body melting and her brain fogging with desire.

Fierce tears stung her eyes.

And then there were two. She couldn't stop smiling.

Fenn was alive.

The news hit her again, as the shock began to finally wear off. Then the panic set in.

The assassin sent to kill Emery was on his way to Colorado this very second to finish off Fenn. She couldn't delay a second longer. She grabbed her phone and texted Wes. Fenn was in Walnut Springs, a small town in Colorado mainly famous as a resort town for skiers in the winter. She sent Wes the directions and emphasized how important it was that he get on the first flight out of Long Island. He'd have to make his excuses to Emery and leave right away.

They couldn't tell Emery, not until they were sure Fenn was safe. He couldn't lose his brother twice. No one was strong enough to survive that. Her heart twisted at the guilt of not telling Emery, but it was better this way, and hopefully he'd never know she'd kept the truth from him, even for a short time. He'd never understand why she had to deceive him. Someday soon she'd be able to tell him Fenn was alive and help reunite him with his brother.

Her cell phone vibrated with a text message from Wes.

On it. Will text when I find him. Booked flight for tonight.

Tonight? She wished he could leave sooner.

Her phone rang and she picked it up, expecting to hear Wes's voice, but it was his sister Hayden.

"Hey girlie, I've got to get out of town for a few days. Wes is pretty upset about the club thing."

Sophie grinned. "He's mad, huh?"

"Yeah. He's acting like I'm some sort of depraved lunatic for going there. This coming from the man who is dating one of the subs from the Cuff, and he goes there practically every weekend. I swear he should have 'hypocrite' tattooed on his forehead."

Hayden's husky laugh cheered Sophie up.

"So you're leaving?"

"I figured I'd take a quick vacation. We have a house on Lake Michigan and I thought I'd go and spend a week there, let him cool off before I come back. You don't need me here, do you?" Hayden's tone turned odd and almost worried.

"I'll be okay." She hoped to God that was the truth. Although she and Hayden had only known each other a couple of weeks, she felt connected to the other woman and their growing friendship was deep.

"You don't sound too sure. I guess if it was me I'd be nervous if left alone with all these men. Talk about a testosterone overload. Emery can be a dominating tyrant, Royce just a dominating ass, and I won't even get into what my brother is."

Sophie laughed, surprised at how easily Hayden could make her feel better. She'd never had many girl friends. She'd always been a loner and had never understood most of the women back in Kansas. Hayden was like her, different somehow.

"I think I can handle them, Hayden," Sophie assured her.

"Okay, well call me if you have any problems. I'll set them straight."

"Thanks. Have fun on your trip."

"Don't worry, I will. Bye, Sophie."

Sophie started to say good-bye but the line disconnected. A deep-seated ache settled in her chest and she felt suddenly very alone. It had always been hard to connect to people in general. With the dark history of Rachel's abduction always looming large on the horizon, she'd stayed clear of people, except to write stories. As a journalist she could talk to people, interview them and stay distant. Emery, though, was her own personal sun—intense, overpowering—and he pulled her into his orbit. It was only a matter of time before he burned her up. She wanted nothing more than to be in his arms and turn to flames as long as his lips were on hers, his body pressed flushed to hers.

As if summoned by her thoughts, the bedroom door opened and Emery stood there, dressed in his dark suit, a blood red tie against his white shirt. Heat flooded her cheeks as she remembered that same tie around her own neck, his hands smoothing it down her bare chest between her aching breasts. It had been the only thing he'd allowed her to wear except for her cuffs, in their bed. And it had been so erotic, decadent, to wear something that was so uniquely his.

His immaculate clothes were his armor; she knew that now. Her eyes dropped to the screen of her computer for a second, seeing Fenn's face and a pain knifed through her ribs. She forced herself to feign a casual manner as she smiled at him, logged off her computer, and set it down.

"Hey." She hoped her face showed more warmth than her suddenly rough voice.

"What's wrong?" He crossed the room and joined her on the bed, curling one arm around her shoulders. He cupped her cheek and turned her to face him. "Talk to me." Emery dropped his hand to her hands, his fingers gliding over the gold cuffs still locked around her wrists. They didn't match her clothes, but that wasn't the point. They were his mark of erotic ownership and she wanted to show them to the whole world.

"It's just everything that's happened. I think it's starting to set in, you know?"

"You've been in shock. It's only natural."

Sophie shivered as guilt slithered up the length of her spine where it nested at the base of her neck and sank its fangs there, making her shoulders tense. Why did he have to be so perfect and understanding? It made her silence about Fenn seem so much worse. She did the only thing she could do to keep her lips sealed. She kissed him, praying he wouldn't taste her betrayal when her trembling lips met his.

Finally he drew back and cupped her cheeks. "I want to take you somewhere." He dropped his hands and took hold of her arm.

"Where?"

"A place I go to think sometimes." He led her from the room.

* * *

Hayden zipped up her suitcase and checked her phone one last time. No new messages. That was good. Her brother Wes had arranged a flight to Colorado tonight. She'd called their family's private pilot and gotten him to take her to their destination first, beating her brother's request by a mere minute. She smiled with glee. Her bug on Wes's phone was still intact and she knew everything that he knew.

Including the biggest news of her life.

Fenn Lockwood was alive, in Colorado, and in danger. She was going to get to him before Wes. She was tired of being his little sister and not her own person. No one liked being a shadow, especially not her. She would prove she was a woman to be reckoned with. She would rescue Fenn and bring him back and earn the respect of the community she'd been raised in. Returning to Long Island with the long-lost boy everyone believed dead, she would in a way return the innocence of her world. The northern shore of the island had suffered greatly after the kidnapping because the Lockwoods, a strong social and economic force in Weston, had withdrawn almost completely from life for at least a decade after losing Fenn. The golden gleam of promise that the mansions had basked in had long since been shrouded in the mists of the tragedy and it was time she burned away the heavy cloak of fog.

Maybe then her parents would stop pressuring her into situations that would leave her married to a wealthy man, who would start sleeping with a mistress the second their vows were spoken. Every girl she'd known in prep school seemed stuck in a bitter, loveless marriage and suffering the plights of mothers with spoiled children. Such would be a fate worse than death for Hayden. There had to be a purpose to her life, something that motivated her. She only wished she knew what that was.

She dropped her phone into her purse and gripped the handle of her luggage to lift it off the bed. She was ready to get out of here. Colorado would be a blessed change of scenery from the choking closeness of the elite community on the island. She loved it with all of her heart, but the people in it seemed determined to drive her insane with their petty concerns for money, clothes, and pride. Hayden would be happy to do without the glamour.

Twenty minutes later, she was easing back in the cushy seat of her family's private jet. Her brother, Wes, wasn't due to leave until an hour after her, thanks to her flight. The pilot was sure he could get her to Colorado and then get back in time to pick up Wes without her brother ever suspecting she'd gotten there first. He'd figure it out eventually, but she'd take the advantage of the head start while she could. If the pilot didn't get back in time, Wes might have to fly commercial. Hayden sniggered at the image of her brother trapped in standard first class.

Hayden loved her brother, but as any person with siblings understood, you could love someone who drove you insane half the time. Wes was overbearing and overprotective. She had every right to explore her passions at the Gilded Cuff, just as much as he did. She was twenty-four years old, old enough to make her decisions and live her own life. If it took rescuing Fenn Lockwood to prove to Wes she could handle herself, then so be it.

Her head fell back against the pillowed headrest and she shut her eyes. She tried to imagine what Fenn would look like. He was probably as handsome as Emery was. She prayed he wouldn't be as stubborn and frustrating as his twin. Sleep crept in at the corners of her consciousness as the exhaustion of the previous day caught up with her. Her images of Fenn were soon tainted with flames, the roar of an exploding brewery, and the terror of thinking Emery was dead. She had to find Fenn. She couldn't watch Wes endure through that pain again. She hadn't even been born when the kidnapping occurred, but she'd grown up with beneath the cloud of sorrow and the distance her brother put around himself because of losing his friend. She shivered and slipped deeper into dark dreams of Fenn and the fate that awaited him if she couldn't get there in time.

Chapter 18

POLICE ATTEMPTED TO GET THE SURVIVING
CHILD TO SPEAK OF HIS CAPTIVITY, HIS BROTHER,
AND THE THREE MEN WHO HAD HELD HIM. THE
BOY WAS UNRESPONSIVE TO ALL INQUIRIES.
PSYCHOLOGISTS BROUGHT IN TO EXAMINE HIM
HAVE STATED THAT EMERY LOCKWOOD IS
SUFFERING FROM SHOCK AND WILL LIKELY SUFFER
FROM POST TRAUMATIC STRESS DISORDER. AT
THIS POINT, IT IS IMPOSSIBLE TO DETERMINE
WHETHER EMERY WILL EVER BE ABLE TO SPEAK OF
WHAT HE ENDURED.
—*New York Times*, September 30, 1990

The graveyard was a few miles from the Lockwood estate, nestled in a secluded part of the woods well away from paved roads. Sophie sat next to Emery in the front seat of his car of choice, a dark gray Porsche Cayman. Its engine purred seductively low as he turned the vehicle off the road and onto a gravel path heavily infiltrated with rebellious grass. The smooth ride turned jarring as they rumbled along. Sophie rolled her window down, letting the wind tug her hair wildly in different directions as she studied the surroundings. Thick copses of trees dotted the sides of the path, making it impossible to see much beyond the forests to any part of the land beyond them.

Wherever they were going, it wasn't a place frequented by cars, or people. Emery kept his gaze straight ahead, his jaw set as he switched gears in the Cayman, slowing it down to a gentle roll. The thick scent of rain and wildflowers teased her nose. Turning the car around a narrow bend of trees, Emery stopped in front of a massive wrought-iron gate. Dead ivy vines clung to the gate's elaborate scrollwork-styled entrance. A massive padlock hung around the gate's connecting points.

Emery shut the engine off and unclicked his seat belt. "We'll walk from here."

Sophie joined him at the entry. Through it she could see about a quarter of a mile of land serving as a private graveyard, with a large, light gray stone wall sealing it away from the wilds that surrounded it.

"What is this place?"

"My family's private cemetery. The Lockwoods have been here since the pilgrims set foot on North American soil." Emery pulled a set of keys out of his pocket. He made quick work of the padlock and let it drop to one side of the gate as he opened it. The hinges creaked loudly, protesting the movement, but he pushed hard and they opened enough for them to slip through.

A chill settled into the base of Sophie's skull and that ancient animal instinct of awareness that she was not alone took over. She slowly turned her head, seeking the eyes she felt were focused on her and Emery, but she saw no one in the woods. Only trees and shadows.

"It's this place," he whispered. "You always feel as though someone's watching you." He reached over and took her hand, gripping it firmly in his.

"Did I ever tell you about my Granny Bells?" she whispered back. Strange as it was, she felt safer whispering, as though it wouldn't wake the dead.

"I know very little about your family, Sophie." His eyes met hers as they walked. The implied *I'd like to know more* came with a gentle squeeze of his hand around hers.

She sighed. "I'm so used to asking everyone else about their lives, I forget to share my own."

"I can see that," Emery chuckled. They were walking down a worn path in the grass where dirt was more prominent from hundreds of years of feet stamping along a singular route.

"Well, I was born in Kansas. That's where my dad's family's from. They're farming folk, lots of brothers, sisters, hardworking types. My mother's family is a little more blue-blooded. East Coast based. My mother's mother, Grandmother Belinda—everyone called her Granny Bells—moved out with Mom to Kansas when she married Dad." She couldn't help smiling at the memory. Her father hadn't been all that eager to share his wife with his mother-in-law, until he met Granny Bells. She was, as her father put it, a rare and unusual breed of cat, which was a polite way of saying the woman was a bit on the crazy side but more interesting than disruptive.

"And you liked her, your Granny Bells?" Emery's eyes were warm as he paused in their walk. He leaned back against a tall monolithic tombstone and pulled her close so their waists and hips pressed together. He wrapped his arms around her, his fingers locking loosely at the small of her back.

"I loved her. She was a queer sort of woman and many people thought she was crazy, or that old age had made her that way. But I don't think so. She used to tell me about our ancestors, the ones who lived in Salem at the time of the witch trials." Sophie remembered the light in the old woman's eyes when she spoke of magic and spells. "We used to talk, Granny and me. She'd tell me things that would sound crazy to repeat out loud, you know? But I swear, deep down I think they're true. Like I was born with a sixth sense that sometimes surfaces when I need it to. I always knew which man was guilty of a crime when I started investigating. The police would have me come down to the station to see the suspect and I could just tell who it was. I'd get this feeling, like spiders were crawling all over me, and I'd just know. The police would have to have more than a gut feeling to find proof, but I didn't. I'd do some digging of my own and then find a way to get the police involved when I found enough evidence, since I wasn't bound by the law like they were."

Sophie, who'd been looking away as she spoke, turned back to Emery. He was studying her, curiosity and understanding mingling with interest on his face.

"Sounds crazy, right?" she joked, but it came out a little forced.

He shook his head. "No more crazy than if I were to tell you that Fenn and I used to talk to each other in our heads. Not with words exactly, but more like images, sensations. I…" This time he looked away. "I never told my parents about it. But that's how I knew he was dead. I felt that connection die the night I escaped."

Sophie inhaled a breath. The old prickling on her neck began again, as it often did when she was close to a revelation.

"What is it?" Emery asked, his gaze astute on hers.

"So you can't feel him anymore…Do you ever get a sense of anything, though? Something you don't recognize?"

"Well…yeah…" He stared at her, hard, as though his brain was sifting through the evidence of something important. "There have been times when I've had these…I guess you could call them glimpses. I see myself in a mirror, but it's not me, or I hear something that's not actually hearable. I'm not explaining this well…" His cheeks turned ruddy.

"Emery, what if there was an explanation for that?" It had to be Fenn he was seeing and feeling. God, she wanted so badly to tell him the truth. His brother was alive.

"Oh, there is. I'm going crazy. It's probably some form of PTSD or something." His self-deprecating laugh sliced her heart.

He gestured for them to start walking again. "This way."

He led her through a maze of both ancient and modern grave stones until they reached a place at the back of the cemetery. There was a lovely little area surrounded by three willow trees. Their long branches swayed low, rustling over the soft grass. Despite the breeze moving through the trees, there was a stillness to the place. Sophie shivered, very aware of the spirits that still lingered in the earth below her feet.

There was something ancient in the way the willows drifted, as though their branches were alive. Even when there was no wind, the trees would often seem to move of their own accord. The power that dwelt in nature was so often overlooked or drowned out by the modern rush of the day. But here, in this moment, it was impossible to ignore the rhythmic pulse in the ground and the trees speaking in hushed whispers of secrets belonging to the earth and the earth alone. Sophie remembered something her Granny Bells used to say. "Man has no power here, where spirits of the soil dwell."

Sophie shuddered and the knot of tension in her stomach grew tighter.

There was one large tombstone in the center of the willow trees. An angel had been carved so that she was kneeling behind the headstone, her arms folded over the top of the grave marker and her forehead resting on her arms. Her wings were spanned out but the tips touched the ground, making her look like a wounded dove with injured wings. The scene was powerful, the angel looked as if she was weeping against the headstone, showing her deepest grief for the bearer of the stone.

FENN LOCKWOOD.
BELOVED SON AND BROTHER.
AND THE DEAD SHALL RISE . . .

"We never had a body to bury. I couldn't bear to lead my parents back to the place where they kept us. I doubt we would have found him, even then. The men probably buried him somewhere else. My parents had to have a place for him, though. Funny, they never come here. I do, though. I talk to the stone sometimes. Other times, I don't talk; I just remember."

The gravity in his voice made Sophie's eyes burn with tears. He reached out and touched the stone angel's head.

"It's nice to think angels are weeping for him, that he was loved in this life and the next. But nothing eases the guilt in here." He tapped his chest above his heart. "I cost him his life. Me. It doesn't matter that I was only a kid. He's dead and I'm not. Survivor's guilt or not, his blood is on my hands."

It won't be for long. She wanted to say the words, but she bit her tongue and held back. She had to, or he'd rush off to find his brother and get killed. She had to be patient, or else she'd lose him too.

Just hang on, Emery. Soon you and Fenn will be together. She vowed it in the deepest part of her soul. She would reunite them with her last breath if she had to.

* * *

Emery was sick of being in the hospital. The sickly sweet smell of death and illness filled his nose and the chill of the cold halls made his hands clammy. It made his skin crawl and horrible memories kept shoving to the forefront of his mind. He forced them back down, buried them as deep as he could. They'd come crawling back to the surface, refusing to stay dead. But everything was changing, after so many years of silence, and worrying about it all coming out in the open. People he cared about were getting hurt. He had to stop it, but how could he? It wasn't as easy as just handing himself over to the man who'd kidnapped him. And he sure as hell wasn't going to just surrender to the sick creep that had obviously come back for more.

He approached the nurse's station next to Cody's room. A middle-aged nurse was filling out a report and smiled when she recognized him.

"Mr. Lockwood, it's good to see you back so soon. Mr. Larson is getting restless and your visits seem to calm him down."

Emery smiled, even though it was a bit forced.

"Good to know I help." *Considering I got him into this mess.*

The nurse grinned. "Go on in and see him. He should be awake."

"Thanks." He walked past her and nudged the door to Cody's room open with his shoulder. Cody was sitting up, a small netbook on his lap. His uninjured hand was pecking away at the keyboard and from the dark look on Cody's face it wasn't going so well.

"Damn it!" He slapped the small laptop lid down before he noticed Emery.

"Oh…hey, boss." He set the computer on his tray table and fisted his good hand in his blankets as he tried to pull the sheets up higher on his waist.

There was something awful in the flash of pain on Cody's face. It exploded through Emery's chest, tearing a hole in his heart, hitting him with dark rage. Emery wanted to wrap his hands around the neck of the man who'd done this to his friend.

"Take it easy, kid." Emery moved quickly to the hospital bed and pressed him back down into the thick stack of pillows. The body beneath his hand wracked with a sudden violent shiver and Cody sucked in a breath and clamped his eyes shut.

"Hey, you okay?" Emery was ready to hit the nurse call button, but Cody opened his eyes and blew out a slow breath.

"I'm good. Just dizzy for a sec."

Emery stepped back, eyeing the room, and found the nearest chair. He fell back into it and put a hand on Cody's knee.

"Breathe through your nose and lean back. It helps." A man didn't like to own up to being dizzy, but he'd had his share of nasty spells when he'd been held captive all those years ago. Whether it was from the beatings, or from starvation, he'd had to learn to find ways to overcome it.

After several exaggerated breaths, Cody's nostrils flared. He seemed to get better.

"I know what you told the police, but was there anything you left out?" Guilt ate at his insides. He didn't want to make Cody relive those moments, but he had to know if Cody had learned something useful, which could save them all in the future. He had to do it to protect the ones he loved.

Cody was silent for a long while, so long that Emery thought he wouldn't say anything.

"It was him, Emery. That sick freak who took you and your brother."

Emery stiffened, dread and anger sharpening their claws on his spine. No. It couldn't be true. He didn't want it to be true. The bogeyman that had haunted his nightmares since the day he'd escaped couldn't still be alive, still waiting to get Emery and kill him once and for all…

"You're sure?"

"Yeah. He said things…personal things. This wasn't a copycat." Cody's eyes went from lively to glassy, as though he was lost in bleak memories.

"What did he say?" Against his mind's wish to control, his body burned with anger and fear. Half of him wished Cody's story was true. The man who stalked him was out there and could be found and dealt with. Emery would kill him with his bare hands.

Antonio D'Angelo. The things that man had done to him and Fenn…A shudder rattled through him with the jarring impact of a train clattering over ancient tracks.

"Look, Emery. I'm tired. We can talk about this later, right?" Cody settled back into his pillows and pressed the pain button on his little handheld pain pump. A couple of the machines connected to his IVs beeped loudly in response.

As much as Emery wanted answers, he didn't want to push Cody too far. Emery had been there in that hospital bed, hurting and scared, too full of devastating memories. He knew better than anyone what needing a break was like. He could give Cody a day to regroup before he asked his questions. He got up from his chair and patted Cody's shoulder.

"See you later. Call me if you need anything. Royce will be outside."

"Thanks, bossman." The reply was a whisper as Cody's dark blond lashes fluttered and he surrendered to sleep.

Emery paused as he reached the door, looking over his shoulder at his friend. Something felt wrong. Something deep in his bones was stirring, churning like the hands of the dead clawing their way out of cold graves. It was only a matter of time before the ghosts resurrected themselves and the awful truth of the night he'd escaped from Antonio came out.

God help me. God help us all.

* * *

The costume lying on Emery's bed was stunning. Sophie nibbled her bottom lip before succumbing to the urge to run her fingertips over the gown. It had a black underdress with a netting of golden lace sprinkled with tiny diamonds. A black satin sash tied loosely around the hips. She lifted it up and smiled. It was a retro style dress, like something a flapper would have worn in the 1920s. Sophie loved it. Any man with money could buy an expensive dress for a woman, but not just any man could find that one dress, so unique, so splendid that the woman was seduced merely by the touch of satin beneath her hands and excited to live the adventure wearing such a classic dress could bring. Emery knew just how to seduce her.

A pair of black closed-toed pumps sat next to the dress on the bed. The heels were high enough to make her legs look sexy, but not too high so as to be uncomfortable. She lifted one shoe, speculating on when he'd had time to shop for her yet again.

"You like it? Mother's party theme this year is *The Great Gatsby*. You know the novel was set on Long Island, don't you?" Emery was suddenly behind her, his hands spanning her waist. Soft lips rained kisses down on her cheek and neck. His natural tendency toward gentleness always surprised her. It was so at odds with the brooding man who'd threatened to bend her over, spank her, and bring out her dark side with wicked pleasure. Yet he was both the dominant master and the gentle lover. They were the same man and she was in love with all of him.

"So I'm Daisy Buchanan. Are you Gatsby?" She turned in his arms, tilting her head back to peer up at him. She loved that he was so tall. It made her feel safe and secure when she leaned into him. Yet at the same time, he could give her that look, the one so hot it made her melt. His lashes were long and dark like burnished gold, dropped to half-mast, softening the primal heat in his gaze.

"Yes, assuming you'll be my Daisy and belong to no other man. Will you?" His palms slid up her back under the thin navy blue cotton sweater she wore. She ducked her head under his chin, releasing a breathless giggle as he struggled with the clasp of her bra.

"Having trouble there, Casanova?" She gave in to the desire to kiss his chin along the length of the faint scar. What she wouldn't give to remove the hurt, take away the memory of what caused it.

"And you wonder why I insist on no undergarments? These things are impossible," he growled in her ear.

Laughing, she reached back, her hands meeting his as she guided him to undo the clasp. Even though the bra still hung on her shoulders after he'd unclasped it, he spun her to face the bed and dragged her back against his body. His hips ground into hers and his hands moved under her sweater and loosened her bra to cup her breasts. Her nipples pearled beneath his teasing fingertips.

"You like that?" he murmured low and soft.

"Uh huh." She finished on a gasp as he pinched the sensitive tips.

His hands dropped to the zipper of her jeans, and the buzz of the metal teeth as he dragged it down was loud. He eased her jeans down off her hips and hooked his fingers in the edges of her panties, tugging them down until her ass was fully exposed.

"Bend over," he commanded.

She complied without thinking. The rustle of cloth was her only warning before he pushed the head of his cock into her swollen sex. He kept one palm on her lower back, holding her down as he worked himself deeper through a series of slow thrusts. Sophie buried her face in the coverlet of his bed, her hands clenching and unclenching in the soft fabric. With each thrust he filled her, stretched her, and she basked in the spreading bliss. He leaned over her, his arms caging her shoulders, his panting breaths spreading over her neck. He pumped into her, changing his strokes, teasing her, keeping her pinned and only able to beg in breathless gasps for more or harder. He always gave her what she asked for, but always pulled back when she was ready to explode.

"Emery, please!" she begged.

He leaned back, gripped her hips and started pounding into her. The slap of flesh on flesh and the sounds of their lovemaking filled the room. Sophie could barely think beyond the moment. His possession, his passion. It was everything she wanted and needed. There was no separation between them, not an inch of distance. They were as close as two people could ever be.

Her climax was so close; she was ready to burst. If he slowed down one more time she'd die. Emery suddenly changed his position and penetrated her from a different angle. She buckled under the supernova of pleasure. He came seconds after, uttering a harsh cry of his own release. He collapsed on top of her, and both of them bent over the bed, but his weight wasn't an unwelcome one. His ragged pants by her ear increased the tingling of her aftershocks, enriching the small ripples of the tiny climaxes that followed. He was still buried deep inside her and semi-hard.

"Ready for round two?" She couldn't resist the urge to tease him and wiggled beneath him.

Emery let out a half-laugh, half-groan. "You're going to be the death of me." His chuckle vibrated against her back and she couldn't resist a feline smile.

"Me? I'll be lucky if I can walk after this," she half-heartedly protested.

"If you can't, I'll carry you." He brushed her hair back from her neck and placed a kiss where her pulse beat beneath her skin.

"I wish we didn't have to go to the party. I'd rather stay here, just like this," he murmured. Her heart gave a funny flip in her chest. The truth of his words filled her with warmth, yet it was tinged with disappointment that it wouldn't come to pass.

Emery finally straightened and pulled out of her. Sophie, sweaty and loose-limbed, quickly darted into the restroom to clean up. A smirk curled her lips and she restrained the urge to laugh. He'd turned her inside out, made her a wild and wanton creature, and it suited her. She could never go back to being the quiet, reserved woman she once was. That old Sophie Ryder was gone and she was never coming back.

Thank God. She was finally getting to live her life. Emery refused to let her keep herself hidden away. Funny...he was the recluse, but he'd opened his own heart, dropped his walls to let her in and she'd been forced to do the same in order to love him.

"Come on, Sophie." His voice echoed across the bathroom marble.

He appeared in the doorway, already fully dressed again and looking devastatingly handsome. If a person really could look like a million dollars, he could, in the best way. The refined, tailored suits and the silk ties, made him a thing of masculine perfection enhanced by the natural virility and sensual appeal hidden just beneath the layer of clothes. She'd seen him naked, gloriously so, and he was all man, all primal energy suffused with the sexual appeal of natural warriors of old, like the sort of man who'd throw her over his shoulder and haul her to bed. After seducing her beyond her sanity. He was so damned good at that.

A smile flirted on her lips and he noticed.

"What's that for?"

"Hmm?" she asked.

"That little grin."

"I was just thinking, it's so easy for you to get dressed." She grumbled as she finished cleaning up and walked back out to the bedroom. She was completely naked and yet for the first time she didn't feel vulnerable or exposed. She didn't have to worry about disappointing him with her scars. He'd kissed each and every one with a tenderness that had nearly ripped her in two.

"It may be easy for me, but I guarantee you'll look better." He leered until she burst out laughing. She was still giggling when she reached for her panties and bra. He was suddenly behind her, surrounding her with his strength as he caught her wrist, stilling her.

"No underwear. I want you bare tonight," he whispered into her ear. His husky tone was like drinking whisky when it burned in all the right places.

Her body burst into flames all over again. She released the lacy pair of panties and fingered the barely there bra. It wouldn't have provided much cover anyway. The dress's fabric was thick enough that she supposed she could get away with going braless.

"Thank you, Master Emery," she teased.

He smacked her bare bottom, leaving a little sting that he rubbed away, which only made her want him back inside her.

"You know…if I was more of a dom, I'd demand that you call me that with respect and expect it. You're lucky you're not dating Royce or Wes. They're both far stricter about those things. I know you're not submissive enough for that."

"Lucky me." She wrinkled her nose.

"Yes, lucky you…" he murmured. "I do like the sound of that. I think I'll start insisting you call me Master more often." He moved away from her as he picked up her dress and held it out.

Sophie raised one brow at him. "Oh? I bet that won't last long."

She took the dress and slipped it on, then slid her feet into her black pumps. Emery whirled a finger in the air to indicate she turn around. She spun. His hands were at her lower back, tugging the zipper up. A shiver tickled her spine.

The intimacy of this moment was wonderful. She and the man she loved were getting dressed for a party, helping and teasing each other the way serious couples might. She and Emery had known each other for such a short time, yet she knew him on some level better than she'd ever known her own family. And soon it would be over. He'd told her his story, but soon they'd find his brother and then there would be no other reason for her to stay. But she wanted to, God how she wanted to.

Sophie turned to face Emery and flung her arms around his neck. He stumbled back a step in surprise, wrapping his arms around her waist with a surprised laugh. She buried her face in his neck, breathing in his unique scent of man and musk with a hint of his cologne. He was strong, warm and playfully tender as he held her close. She shuddered, unable to contain the emotions flooding through her. He made her alive in a way she'd never been before. Weak with desire, but strong somehow, too, like she could conquer anything, do anything. She'd never felt that way before, as though she were capable of anything. Sophie had always believed in herself and had confidence in most of her abilities, but this ran deeper.

"Hey...hey, Sophie." He tightened his arms and murmured soothingly in her ear. "What's wrong? I was only joking." His large palm cupped her cheek and she leaned into that touch, nuzzling his palm, feeling so safe and so cared for that it made knowing she was leaving soon even harder.

"It's not you...I'm fine." She relished his hold a moment longer before forcing herself to pull back. With her fingertips she wiped away the remnants of moisture from her eyes.

Emery looked doubtful, and his eyes focused on hers with a patient intensity that made her look away.

"We'll talk about this later. I want to know what's upset you, but we're running late." He pressed a soulful kiss to her trembling lips, threaded his fingers through hers and led her by the hand. He picked up her shiny gold purse and held it out to her as they headed down the hall.

Hans was waiting for them by the front door, dressed all in black, a serious expression on his face. A gun hung on his hip and Sophie had a feeling there were other weapons concealed in other places on his body.

"The car's waiting outside," Hans said as he handed Emery a small handgun.

"Wait a second. You think we need guns?" Sophie swallowed hard. The kidnapper was still out there, ready to kill Emery. It was easy to forget this when he overwhelmed her with passion in his bed.

"I need a weapon. Not you. Hans will keep you safe." Emery pulled her close and kissed her right temple before slipping the small pistol in his coat pocket. Hans went to the coat closet, retrieving a black fur coat.

"You like it?" Emery held it out. "It was my grandmother's."

Sophie blushed as she slid her arms into the soft silk-lined sleeves of the luxurious fur coat. It was warm and snug. She felt like a million dollars. And it was all wrong. As they descended the stone steps outside to the car a haunting chill overtook her. For a second, she couldn't breathe. It was as though someone had stepped over her grave. Pain tore through her and she cried out. Emery's arms were around her, catching her, and just as quickly the pain was gone. The vision she'd glimpsed, the black world covered in a spray of ruby red was gone. Her Granny Bells's voice echoed in her mind, a memory from long ago.

The devil comes for you. He comes for us all someday. Be ready, sense him and raise your fists, Sophie girl.

She could almost feel her Granny's wrinkled hands grasping her child-sized fists, clenching her fingers and raising them up in front of her face like a seasoned boxer. No one had listened to Granny back then; she'd been an old woman with Alzheimer's, but Sophie had listened. She had remembered.

"Sophie, what's wrong?" Emery's gruff tone made her speak up and say what all of her instincts were screaming for. She turned in his arms.

"Please, Emery, let's forget about the party. I want to stay here, all of us. I have a bad feeling."

Emery cupped her chin and raised her face. His hazel eyes were dark in the purple evening light that crept through the windows.

"You really are worried," he observed, his face softening.

"Yes." Relief coursed through her and her shoulders dropped as the tension eased. He would listen to her, and they'd stay, safe from whatever her instincts were screaming was going to happen.

"We have to go, just for a little while. I promised Mother. Hans will be with us. Everything will be fine. I promise you."

"No! Emery please!" She tugged on the lapels of his black coat.

"You can stay here, if you're too upset. Hans will be glad to stay behind and keep an eye on you."

Her jaw dropped. "Are you crazy? With that assassin running loose? He doesn't want me. He wants you. Hans has to stay with you." She still held the edges of his coat and she rubbed her fingers absently on the expensive material as she hoped in vain he'd change his mind.

His sigh gave her just a flicker of hope before his words killed it. "Then come with me, Sophie. We'll stay half an hour and come straight home. Scout's honor."

She managed a weak smile. "You were a boy scout?"

"Eagle scout." He grinned.

"Of course," she muttered, but she felt a little better. Even though her entire body still seized at the thought of heading into certain danger, she knew she wouldn't talk him out of it and she had to trust him.

Her shoulders slumped and she dropped her hands from his chest. There would be no winning this argument. She let Emery escort her to the Mercedes and help her into the backseat. They both slid across the black leather. Hans got into the front passenger seat next to the driver and rattled off directions. Sophie tucked herself into Emery's side and tried to banish the worry from her mind. She knew she would fail. The devil was out there. He was coming for them. She had to be ready.

Chapter 19

IT HAS BEEN TWENTY YEARS SINCE THE INFAMOUS LOCKWOOD KIDNAPPING. EMERY LOCKWOOD IS NOW PRESIDENT OF LOCKWOOD INDUSTRIES, THE COMPANY HIS FATHER ELLIOT AND HIS UNCLE RAND CREATED MANY YEARS AGO. DESPITE THE NUMEROUS SOCIAL FUNCTIONS ELLIOT AND MIRANDA ATTEND, EMERY HAS REMAINED RECLUSIVE, KEEPING WELL OUT OF THE PUBLIC EYE.
—*New York Times*, January 7, 2010

Emery's parents' mansion was packed. Expensive foreign cars lined the mile-long walk from the gate to the house, and valets in tailored suits bustled about the arriving guests. Japanese lanterns lit the grounds. A big brass band filled the air with old school jazz inside the ballroom. Everywhere people danced and laughed. The shimmer of jewels and expensive costumes made the room sparkle and shine. He wanted to enjoy the occasion. He hadn't come to a costume party since he was a boy. But his heart wasn't in it tonight.

He glanced across the ballroom to where Sophie was. Her ashen cheeks and haunted eyes wounded him just as much as her silence toward him all evening. She seemed to have withdrawn into herself, silencing her only guardian against whatever had upset her before they left his home. Her face was pale, almost sheet white, and she kept nibbling her lower lip in anxiety. Something had set her to this mood and had disrupted the sweet, sensual creature he'd made love to only an hour before. She'd been so wonderful then, teasing him as they'd dressed. The moment between them had been charged with electricity he'd never felt before with a woman. She soothed him, teased him, and lit a fire in his blood at the same time. She was everything he could want or need in a woman...in a wife.

The realization hit him like an avalanche, knocking him sideways. Christ. He cared about her. No...He loved her and wanted to spend the rest of his life with her. His own thoughts shocked him. As a child he'd never imagined sharing his life with anyone except his brother, but now he couldn't imagine another moment without Sophie. Of course it was too soon to talk about that sort of thing with her. She was bright and independent. Hell, she might not want to get caught in a long term relationship with him. She had her entire life ahead of her, and he'd spent most of his hiding in the shadows. But he couldn't let her go, not this one. She was everything to him.

After losing Fenn, he'd lost his sense of direction, like a painter losing his sight. Losing his other half had torn him apart, unmade him, until he was nothing but a speck of dust in the creator's mind. Without Fenn, there was no Emery, but Sophie had restored him to the ranks of the living when he hadn't even realized he'd been dead. She'd breathed life into him. She'd taught him to love, to laugh, to trust his heart again.

A sudden need to see her, to touch her, filled him at that moment. He scanned the crowd, finding her dancing with his father, the worried expression still lingering on her features. Her head was cocked at a small angle as she listened to whatever it was that his father was saying and she laughed. A pretty blush stained her cheeks, the sparkle of life temporarily restored.

"I hope you plan to keep her, Emery. She's a special girl." His mother's voice made him start. He turned to find her standing there smiling up at him. He opened his arms and she hugged him, pressing a kiss to his cheek. It was getting easier and easier to let his mother through his crumbling guarded walls. Maybe someday they could be as close as they'd once been before...He didn't want to think about the past. He wanted to look forward. Fenn was his past. Sophie was his future.

"I want to keep her, Mother. I do. I will make her mine."

"A woman wants to know when she's loved, Emery. That one doesn't want money or jewels. She wants your heart. Can you give her that?" Miranda asked. The tragedy of losing Fenn had left a stark melancholy in her eyes that broke his heart, and that old guilt still ate away at him deep inside.

"Mother, I need to tell you about Fenn. What happened that night...?" His voice broke. She shushed him.

"I know what happened. You got separated...and he didn't make it. Your father and I don't blame you. Emery, I miss Fenn with every breath I take, but I am so thankful you survived. *So thankful.*" Tears filled her eyes and she brushed her hand over his cheek. The motherly stroke made the awful ache in his chest deepen.

"Look at us," his mother chided. "This is a time for happiness. Now go steal that girl of yours back before your father woos her away from you." His mother smiled, eyes still bright with tears. She patted his arm and turned away to speak to her other guests. He started to walk forward when someone bumped into him.

"Emery! So you decided to come after all." His cousin Brant, dressed in black pants and a black shirt, slid his black mask off his face.

"Yeah, I figured I should." Emery didn't want to stop and chat, but it seemed Brant did.

"And your lovely little conquest? Where is she? Don't tell me the bloom's off that particular rose so soon." Brant's tone was teasing, but his eyes were anything but. The hardness there gave Emery momentary pause.

"She's here." He didn't elaborate. For whatever reason, Brant wanted to throw him off and he wouldn't allow his cousin to play mind games.

"Ahh...still taken with her? Well...have a lovely night, cousin." Brant slid his mask back down over his face and vanished into the crowd of bodies.

His phone buzzed in his pocket. He would have ignored it but he never put his phone on vibrate. He slid a hand into his pocket and pulled out a cell phone. He frowned. It was not his phone. His was *gone*. The hairs on the back of his neck rose and something pitched south in his stomach.

The caller ID read unknown. "What the hell?" He answered it. "Who is this?" he growled.

An all too familiar voice came through the line. "Hello Emery," Antonio D'Angelo said.

"You piece of shit—" he started.

"Now, now, Emery. Is that any way to treat an old friend?"

"You burned down my stables, you killed my brother, you beat up my friend, and you tried to blow me to hell. I don't think you're running for friend of the year."

Antonio laughed, pleasure evident in the sound, and it made Emery's blood boil.

"Always so mouthy. I had such a delight in beating it out of you. But I do hate to correct you. As much as I wish I killed Fenn, I did not."

"What?" Emery's answer was a breathless gasp. His brain seemed to fill with a steady fog.

"Need I say it again? I was not there the night you escaped. My men were, but not me. I discovered your brother wasn't dead only a few days ago. I'm surprised your little reporter hasn't told you. She knows Fenn is alive. She and that hacker friend of yours have been keeping secrets from you, it seems."

Emery's heart stuttered to a rigid stop. The noise of the room faded to a distant buzz, his head cloudy with confusion.

Sophie. Sophie had been hiding this from him, something that meant everything to him. She wouldn't, couldn't keep that secret from him. It was another of D'Angelo's games.

"You're lying."

D'Angelo laughed. "You don't have to trust me, Emery. I can prove it to you. She wants the story of a lifetime and she kept the news of Fenn being alive to herself because she wants the glory of the story. She got your hacker to play along, for a price of course…They're too close, wouldn't you say? Perhaps they were lovers before you met her. She knew so easily where to find you at the club. I bet she and Cody have been planning this for months."

Emery gripped the phone so hard the plastic cracked.

"Try not to look so surprised, Emery."

Surprised? How the hell did Antonio…Emery spun around, eyes searching the crowd. He had to be here, watching him. There were too many people and the lighting was too dim for him to get a clear view.

"She was happy to fuck you for the story, for the money, but now she's spreading her favors out. Just like a woman."

Lies. Had it all been nothing but insidious lies?

"I'm hanging up," he growled.

"I'm sending you a video file. I'd suggest you watch it."

The phone went dead.

A second later the e-mail icon popped up. He tapped the e-mail and the file started to upload. He pressed play and watched.

It was a video taken from when Cody was in the hospital. D'Angelo must have planted a small button-hole camera in the room somehow. The thought filled him with cold dread. The man had been in Cody's room, close enough to finish off his friend. The video showed Cody and Sophie alone in the room, talking. He couldn't read their lips, but the body language was clear, furtive glances, shifty eyes, and then Cody slipped something small—looked like a pocket knife—into Sophie's hand. She hastily tucked it into her pocket as Emery entered the hospital room.

There was no way to be sure what Cody and Sophie had talked about, but the visual evidence was damning.

The blood in his veins was cold as ice as he replayed the video two more times. Emery felt as though someone had punched a fist in his chest and had wrapped cruel fingers around his heart, squeezing painfully. She had betrayed him. He'd given her his worst memories, told her the darkest secret in his soul, and she was using it against him and working with his friend—a young man he'd rescued and treated like a younger brother. The joy and elation of knowing Fenn might still be alive was soured by the manner in which he'd learned the truth…He couldn't trust her. He dropped the phone to the floor and smashed it beneath his boot. If Sophie wanted to play games, he would play.

Cold rage suffused him with an incredible sense of self-control. He walked across the ballroom floor, his heart turning to stone with every step. He reached Sophie and his father.

"May I cut in?" His frozen smile gave his father pause. His father glanced at Sophie, one brow raised in question.

"It's all right, Mr. Lockwood," Sophie assured him. His father stepped back and Emery slid into his place without missing a step. He captured her hand in his, and placed his other hand on her lower back, pulling her tight into his body. Sophie's eyes lit with sudden sensual hunger, a look he recognized instantly. Emotions whipped through him sharply. He'd never see that look again after tonight and it was tainted by knowing Sophie had secret motives with regard to him. His sadness was drowned in a rush of fury and yet he still wanted to sink into her body and find heaven. It was a cruel joke that the one woman he made love to, which felt like coming home, was the one woman that had betrayed him.

"Emery?" Such a sweet, innocent sounding voice. Damn, she was a hell of an actress.

He tightened his grip on her lower back as he leaned forward to whisper in her ear.

"Care to go somewhere private?"

"Why?" she whispered back.

He nipped her ear and pressed his erection against her belly. Sophie's lips parted on a soft, shivery sigh.

"You lead, I'll follow," she promised, eyes half closed as she linked her arm in his. A blush lit her cheeks as he led her from the dance floor. He had a perfect place in mind for what he needed to do. One last time, he'd pretend she was the woman he'd given his world to. One more night, then he'd cast her out and move on.

* * *

Sophie had that awful sense of doom. It filled her to the brim like smoke curling up from a deadly spell from a witch's cauldron. Yet Emery was distracting her with his endless passion. She couldn't refuse him, never wanted to refuse him. He'd made her feel more alive, more herself, than she'd ever been in her entire life. Emery pulled her into a room just off the ballroom. There was a large mahogany desk and a couple of leather armchairs. Behind the desk floor-to-ceiling shelves were lined with hundreds of books bearing gilded spines.

The click of the lock in the door had her spinning around. He leaned back against the door, arms crossed. He wasn't smiling, not with his eyes, even though his lips curved upward.

"Sit on the edge of the desk, spread your legs wide for me." The command was smooth and erotic but the stark flash of violent pain in his eyes confused her.

"Do it, or I'll redden that ass of yours with my hand," he warned.

Sophie lit up inside with a powerful stab of arousal and backed up to the desk. She stood on tiptoe and eased back on the desk, raising her eyes to his as she spread her legs. His gaze dropped and she knew he was remembering that she wore nothing underneath her dress.

Emery shoved away from the door and stalked over to her. She leaned back instinctively as he invaded her space. He caught the nape of her neck with one hand, squeezing slightly, the pressure a command the stay still. He tugged her hair and she tilted her chin back, exposing her throat. The first caress of his lips under her jaw was more an echo of a kiss given centuries ago. Her skin tingled and whispered with the faint sensation. Every single cell of her being focused on the contact, the brush of lips, a graze of teeth on her throat, the hot tip of his tongue tasting her.

The climax in her womb began to build—slow, faint at first, brought on by the feathering kisses and slight sting of her scalp where he fisted her hair. His other palm touched her knee, tracing patterns with warm fingertips before it slid along the outside of her thigh, pushing her glittering dress up until she was bare to her hip. She wanted his lips on her mouth, to feel the emotions he let pour from his mouth to hers each time they came together. But he didn't kiss her.

He pressed her down until she lay on her back on the desk, then he pushed her dress up to her waist and grabbed her hips. The sudden jerk that dragged her bottom to the end of the desk stole the breath from her body. Animal ferocity filled his every touch as he lifted her legs, curling her calves around his slim, powerful hips. The muscles of his ass were tight and she pressed against him, urging him closer. She shuddered with longing when he unbuckled his belt and undid the first button. His eyes lifted to hers, holding her captive as he unzipped his pants and freed himself.

There were a thousand things she should have said at that moment, when she saw the flicker of angry shadows in his eyes, but he didn't give her a chance to think. His hands went to his neck, loosening the burnished gold tie he wore. Working one finger in the knot, he slid it loose and reached for her hands. Using the tie, he bound her wrists together and pulled them above her head. He made some movement with his hand above her head, and although she couldn't see what he was doing, she guessed he'd done something to the desk's edge because her wrists were pulled tight and the tie was secured to something she couldn't see.

The cold glint in his eyes had her heart skipping wildly. What had changed since they'd arrived at the party? This was not the Emery she'd come to know; this was the Emery she'd first met that night in the club, the one full of fire and anger and defensiveness. All of his barriers were back, his fortress sealed against her once more. The progress she'd made in getting inside his walls had been unraveled.

"Don't move," he growled.

She was helpless...Her knees clamped together.

"Keep your legs open."

With a deep breath she forced herself to calm down and she let her knees fall apart, but she couldn't stop them from trembling. He leaned over and placed a fingertip on her lips. Then he trailed it down to the rising and falling of her breasts. She watched that finger as he gave the dress a gentle tug and freed her breasts one at a time. Her breath quickened and her nipples pearled. Emery circled one peak, eyes dark as though fascinated by the sight of her aroused body. His brow furrowed slightly as he concentrated on her other breast, cupping it, kneading it until both breasts were swollen and heavy. She arched her back, pressing herself into his touch.

Sophie wanted to ignore the warning her heart gave her in that moment, when their eyes met again and she saw the darkness gathering in him like some violent storm on the horizon. But the ability to think rationally evaporated as Emery bent his head and took one of her nipples in his mouth. She moaned as he sucked hard on the sensitive tip, laving the tip with his tongue before biting it.

"Ooh!" She couldn't contain the sound of pleasure/pain as it rippled through her. He moved to the other nipple and bit down on it while he slid his hand down between her thighs. One of his fingers dipped into her hot channel and her hips shot up, trying to push him deeper. His finger retreated instantly and she whimpered at the loss.

"Are you innocent, Sophie?" His question forced her eyes open.

"What?" she asked, confusion mingling with pleasure as he bent to her breast again, but he blew a soft breath against it rather than putting his mouth on her skin.

"Was everything about you a lie?" he murmured against her breast before he kissed his way up to her neck.

"A lie?" She could barely string two words together because he'd slid his fingers between her folds again and she clenched around him.

He shifted between her thighs, positioning the head of his cock at her entrance. The first few inches of him sank in easily but as he pressed deeper her body stretched, trying to accommodate him. They rocked together, the tie tightening around her wrists as she jerked when he thrust hard. A few seconds later he was fully inside her and his face loomed over hers.

"You lied to me," he whispered against her lips. The guarded expression on his face was gone. He was open to her, like a book open at the center page, revealing everything. Rage, hurt, desire, all because of something she'd done.

Her heart stuttered to a stop. He knew. Fenn was alive and Emery knew she'd kept it from him.

With aching slowness he kissed her, and she may as well have been outside the garden of Gethsemane after having kissed his cheek in betrayal. It went soul deep—the numbing, destructive feeling of her own powerlessness to explain why she'd kept Fenn's existence from him. But Emery didn't let her think long about it. He withdrew from her body only to plunge back in. They shared a moan of dark pleasure, but his trembling shoulders gave away his own lack of control. The dom inside him was demanding vengeance and she would pay for the hurt she'd caused him.

"Is that all I'm good for? A fuck and a newsworthy story?" He slammed into her and she bit her lip at the exquisite sensation of him punishing her with pleasure. It was wicked, it was the worst thing she could do in that moment—enjoy herself while she knew he suffered, and he was forcing her to feel this way on purpose.

"Emery…please, let me explain—" her words ended on a gasp as he pinched one of her nipples hard.

"You. Betrayed. Me," he hissed, each word punctuated with a thrust.

She raised her head, glaring at him. "No!" Whatever he thought, she'd explain, make him understand.

"You paid Cody off when you found out Fenn was alive. You didn't tell me because you wanted the story." His brows lowered, his lips parted on a snarl as he started fucking her hard and fast. He filled her and a rush of ecstasy stole her breath as she desperately fought to raise her hips to take him deeper inside her.

He was making love to her differently. There had always been a gentleness, at least in his eyes, or lips when he'd made love to her before. This was purely animal, purely about domination and control. Pleasurable yes, but it was only physical. The intimacy they'd struggled to establish with each other over the past several days was destroyed. The devastation of this realization hit her hard and she fought to push him away. He was removing emotion from his passion and it didn't feel the same; there was a hollowness to his actions that rocked her to the core.

"Emery, stop!" she hissed, jerking her wrists, trying to free herself. He was off her in an instant, pulling out of her body, his face dark as a summer storm. They were both still, panting, frustrated. Finally he shoved a hand in his pants pocket and got out a handkerchief. He wiped himself clean and tossed the white piece of cloth into the garbage can by the desk as he fixed his pants. He wouldn't look at her, and she couldn't look away from him. Like watching a train wreck, she was seeing the man she loved spiral away from her, in a crash of black smoke and death.

In that instant she had the strange sensation of being completely and utterly alone. He'd become nothing more than a trick of light, a play of smoke and mirrors, and she realized she'd been chasing a dream that was never going to be within reach. The flesh and blood man she'd come to love with every part of her soul was more shadow and illusion. Was she the same for him? Had they believed they could come together and make sense of the world they lived in? In truth were they merely dark silhouettes of ships passing through heavy fog in the night? Every kiss, every touch that had been shared between them would soon be blackened by betrayal.

He reached for her wrists and in one swift tug his tie slid off her skin. He held the tie for a long second, staring at the expensive gold fabric before he dropped it in the trashcan, too. When he turned away from her, the world came crashing down. His shoulders slumped, his head bowed.

"I gave you everything, Sophie. Everything that I had, everything that I am." He moved to the wall, resting one palm flat on it as he leaned against it. "Get the hell out of this house, leave town tonight. Hans will mail you your things first thing tomorrow. Don't ever set foot on my island again. Do you understand?" Her banishment was done with the barely controlled fury of a wronged king. He spun around and walked back over to where she still sat on the edge of the desk.

Sophie had no breath to utter a sound. When she didn't respond he gripped her throat, not squeezing, but the gesture was clear. She was at his mercy and he was tired of playing the game he thought she was playing. But there was no game, and she'd have to leave him forever.

Emery dropped his hand and stepped back, the space between them large enough to fill an entire galaxy.

"Get the fuck out. Now!" he bellowed. The shout had her moving fast, her body trembling with sexual frustration, her heart shattering as she tugged her skirt down and fled the study. She had to leave, but she couldn't think, couldn't breathe. All she felt was the splitting of her ribs as she tried to suck in air and the implosion of her heart in her chest. He hated her, never wanted to see her again.

Shock pulsed through her, numbing her to everything as she

stumbled down the hall. Her purse…She needed to find her purse so she could get out of here.

Tears burned at the corners of her eyes, but she refused to let them fall. There would be a time and place to grieve, but now wasn't it.

Be strong. Have to be strong. Or she'd never make it out of the house.

"Sophie? What's wrong?" Hans was there in an instant, wrapping an arm around her shaking shoulders. She couldn't get the words out, only turned into him and shook with silent sobs.

Never in her life had she felt so cheap, so used. Emery had screwed her and tossed her out like a whore.

"What happened? Where's Emery?" Hans demanded.

Finally she had the strength to say what she couldn't before. "He used me, Hans. He said hateful things and he *used* me…I need to leave right now."

The shock in Han's black eyes quickly turned to anger. "I'll take you back to town. We'll get your things first. After that I'll beat the shit out of him for being an ass." The last was more a muttered growl to himself than one meant for her ears.

"No, please don't. He isn't worth the bruised knuckles you'd get from hitting that rock hard head of his."

Hans laughed but it came out forced and rusty. She touched his arm, squeezing slightly.

"Please, don't do anything. I mean it. Just stay here and keep an eye on him. He'll need you more than ever."

Hans gripped her shoulders when she turned to leave.

"Hang on. What do you mean?"

"Cody…Cody found out that Fenn is alive. When Antonio held him hostage, Cody got into the man's files from his computer. He gave them to me when he was in the hospital. We agreed not to tell Emery, not until we were sure Fenn was alive and especially that he was safe. Antonio is looking for him and was planning on going for him after he'd killed Emery. I looked through the files Cody gave me and found Fenn's location. He's in Walnut Springs in Colorado. We sent Wes Thorne to find him."

"And Emery knew nothing of this?" Hans asked.

"No. I wanted to tell him. But I know him. He'd be reckless. He'd go running off to Colorado and get himself killed by Antonio. And we didn't tell you because you'd either have to tell him or lie to him and we didn't want to put you in that position. You're too important to him. He *has* to trust you when he can't trust anyone else."

Hans's dark eyes were full of worry but he seemed to understand.

"How did he find out? Is that why he was cruel to you?"

She nodded. "I don't know how, but he found out." She closed her eyes, took a breath, opened her eyes and met Hans's gaze. "I have to go. Please take care of him. For what it's worth...I still love him. I'll always love him and I don't want him to get hurt."

The usually stoic bodyguard cleared his throat. "Love is worth a lot, Sophie, especially from a woman like you. I'll keep him out of trouble for you."

"Thank you." She stood upon tiptoe and kissed his cheek. The smile she summoned trembled at the corners. She retrieved her purse from the coat check and left through the front door. The world was quiet outside. The noise of the party was muted. It was early yet, only just past six, but the skies were black with night. A color that matched her aching soul and battered heart. It managed to beat a steady rhythm, even though the pain.

Sophie took a few steps down the long gravel path leading to the main gates where the valets could call a taxi for her. The crunch of gravel behind her made her stop abruptly. A hand clamped down over her mouth. She dropped her purse and clawed at the gloved hand. Another arm hauled her back into a muscled body.

"Hello, sweetheart. We meet at last." The prick of a needle stung her neck like an angry wasp.

Her muffled cry went unheard.

"We'll set a nice little trap for our boy Emery." Something sharp sliced her arm and blood dribbled down onto her purse and the ground around it. The spot where the needle pierced her began to burn. Black spots bloomed over her eyes and heaviness stole through her arms. She struggled to stay awake, but it didn't matter.

Every nightmare she'd ever had, every horror she'd faced when she closed her eyes, was there.

She was back on the playground with Rachel. Rachel. Her small body was an easy target as the man grabbed her by the waist, hoisting her up and covering her mouth with a cloth. Sophie couldn't move, couldn't scream. She was rooted to the spot in terror. The man laughed, the sound grating in her ears.

"I'll be back for you, little girl, when I'm done with this one," he'd jeered, the crooked teeth and soulless eyes a sight she'd repressed in the blackest part of her soul.

"Rachel!" Her scream was too quiet, her voice hoarse as the man ran to his gray van and threw Rachel's limp body into the back. The tires screeched as he pulled away...

She'd never left that playground. She was trapped with the guilt and the fear, left alone as darkness closed in.

Chapter 20

EMERY LOCKWOOD, THE SOLE SURVIVOR OF A
KIDNAPPING THAT OCCURRED TWENTY-FIVE
YEARS AGO WHICH CLAIMED HIS TWIN BROTHER'S
LIFE IS ONCE AGAIN THE SOURCE OF NEWS IN
WESTON, LONG ISLAND. RUMORS ABOUND
REGARDING LOCKWOOD'S MEMBERSHIP TO A
NEWLY FORMED PRIVATE CLUB ON LONG ISLAND.
MEMBERSHIPS TO THE GILDED CUFF CLUB COST
IN THE TENS OF THOUSANDS PER YEAR AND
STRICT ENTRANCE REQUIREMENTS KEEP MOST OF
THE GENERAL PUBLIC FROM GETTING INSIDE TO
GLIMPSE THE HANDSOME BILLIONAIRE WITH THE
TRAGIC PAST.

—*New York Times*, October 31, 2014

Emery sat in his father's study chair, slumped over the massive desk. He dug his fingers into his scalp until it hurt. His chest felt as though it was on fire, as if some angry god had thrust his fiery hand deep into Emery's chest and ripped his beating, bleeding heart out and cast it into the flames. Breath didn't come easy, and his temples throbbed as he desperately tried to find some balance in his head. Only one thought pierced the gloom: Sophie was gone. The wound she left behind would never heal. Hell, it might kill him now, and he had done it to himself.

He was a fucking asshole and he knew it. He'd just screwed her and sent her packing. He should never have touched her, never gotten close to her. Even hating her, he still loved her, and he'd been cold to her just to have one more second of heaven. He had enjoyed it, been aroused as hell, but it wasn't the same, not like all of the other times he'd made love to her. Perhaps that was the difference. This time had been sex, just a quick fuck to get her out of his system, but she was deeper under his skin than ever. Already he missed her and wanted her back in his arms so he could apologize.

The door to the study crashed open. Hans was a black silhouette before the light from the hallway.

"Get out, Hans, I need a minute—"

His bodyguard moved fast, throwing a punch so hard that Emery crashed back in the chair and it toppled over. Pain exploded in his jaw. He groaned as he struggled out of the over-turned chair.

"What the hell, Hans?" He wiped a palm over his mouth, tasting blood from his split lip.

"Ms. Ryder just left here in tears…" Hans's reply was like a wolf's growl. It would have scared anyone but him.

Emery leapt to his feet. "Good—" Another blow popped his eye and he staggered back into the bookshelves behind him. Several heavy tomes crashed to the ground.

"Stop that!" he snarled, raising his fists in defense. If prepared he knew he could get the drop on Hans. He was the better boxer of the two, but if Hans's strength was coming from anger, Emery would likely get his ass kicked.

"You're a real piece of work, Emery. Sophie and Cody were saving you. They were going to tell you about your brother once Wes had found him and made sure he was safe. D'Angelo told Cody he was trying to find Fenn and kill him. If they'd told you, we both know you would have rushed off and gotten both Fenn and yourself killed. Is that what you want?"

Emery lowered his fists a few inches as Hans's words sank in.

"Why didn't she tell me?"

His bodyguard's glare knocked his feet out from under him.

"She loves you and she was only protecting you from yourself.

She wanted to tell you, but had to wait until you and Fenn were safe. Whatever you did to her, whatever sins you've added to that long list, you'd best get on your knees and pray she'll forgive you. Now get your shit together and let's go find her before she gets too far away."

Emery swallowed hard and followed Hans outside. The party was still in full swing and there was no sign of Sophie in the crowded room. Emery led the way as he and Hans pushed through the mass of dancing people. When they reached the front door Hans pointed to something at the bottom of the steps.

Sophie's purse lay on the ground, with a spray of blood over it. "Is that—" Emery's words died on his lips as he reached the purse.

A cell phone, one that he didn't recognize, was next to the purse. The screen lit up as an unknown number called.

"I'm beginning to hate cell phones." Emery said as he snatched up the phone and answered the call.

"I'm guessing you've discovered my little fib. I couldn't resist, you see…" Antonio chuckled. The sound brought back horrifying memories, ones he tried to shove back in the dark. Pain and fear always followed that sound.

"Where have you taken her?" His body trembled as adrenaline and rage swept through him in devastating tidal waves, but he forced himself to calm down as he put the phone on speaker. As he listened, he got into the cell's settings to locate the number and flashed it to Hans. Hans was already on his phone, texting Cody the number on the cell Emery had, no doubt asking if it was possible to put a trace on the call. He waved his hand to tell Emery to keep him talking.

"You don't need to trace the call," Antonio said matter-of-factly, as though he knew exactly what they were up to.

Emery glanced around, suddenly wondering if Antonio could see them. But the gardens seemed empty.

"I do need to, because I want to find you and put a bullet through your skull."

"I was wondering when you'd grow a pair of balls. I thought

maybe you'd always be a sniveling little coward like you were when I had you." The way he said 'had you' made Emery's skin crawl, as though hundreds of spiders trekked along his flesh.

"Name the place and I'll meet you there. We'll finish this."

"Indeed we shall. The way I like, of course. My rules. Leave your rent-a-cop at home. No one but you and me."

"Fine, I'll come alone. Cops would only stop me from killing you." He had every intention of stopping Antonio's heart and he'd do whatever he had to in order to make that came true.

"You know where to find me. The place where I owned your soul. I'll be waiting." Antonio hung up.

The place where I owned your soul. Emery's fingers curled into fists. The abandoned mansion where he and Fenn had been held as children.

Hans cursed. "Shit, only a few seconds more and Cody said he would have been able to at least get a ping on a cell tower to narrow down a possible location…"

Emery shook his head. "No need. I know where he is."

"Where?" Hans's black brows rose in surprise.

"The old Carlton mansion. It's ten miles from here."

"How do you know where he is?"

There was a long pause as Emery forced his heart to slow from its galloping pace. "It's the place where Fenn and I were held when he took us. He thinks it will rattle me, being back there." Emery dug his hand into his pocket for the small handgun, thankful for the reassurance it provided.

"Will it rattle you?" Hans's tone was quiet.

Emery smiled bitterly. "I guess we'll find out, won't we."

"Thank God. You're letting me come. I thought for a second you might let that bastard control you."

"He has Sophie. *My Sophie.* We play by my rules, whether he knows it or not."

Hans's smile was grim.

"Then let's get to it. We have a woman to rescue," Hans said.

And my soul to save. Emery knew that he'd never survive losing Sophie. He loved her and he'd wounded her, put her in the path of danger. This was not going to end with her dying. He wouldn't let it. He wouldn't allow Antonio to steal another life that mattered ever again.

* * *

The smell of rotting wood and mold burned Sophie's nose. Her body trembled as it struggled to shed the aftereffects of the drug. The memory of that needle plunging into her neck slammed into her head, causing a violent headache. It pounded against her temples with the force of a bass drum. She couldn't help the moan that escaped her lips as she came around. She was facedown on a ratty cot in a dark room. She turned her head and blinked, giving her eyes a chance to focus in the dim light. When she moved her arm, something sticky clung to it. , and pain lanced through her.

She gasped when she saw the five-inch cut that was still bleeding. It didn't look too deep, but it had bled quite a bit while she'd been unconscious. It burned like hell. Sophie struggled to sit up and glance about the room. It looked like she was in some sort of cellar. One out of a slasher film. Dark liquids of an unknown nature were collecting dust in rows of mason jars that sat on wooden shelves around the sides of the room. Electric lanterns hung from nails on the wooden posts supporting the ceiling. Dust and debris littered the floor where she sat and Sophie realized with a horrible sinking feeling that she had to be in an abandoned mansion somewhere. Emery had told her there were several empty, crumbling mansions not far from where he had been taken…

"Oh God…" She knew where she was. It was the only thing that made sense. She'd been taken to the mansion where Emery and Fenn had been held all those years ago.

The scuffle of boots on the wood stairs by the cot had her scrambling back. Boots and jeans came into view and then Antonio D'Angelo, the harbinger of doom for the Lockwood family, came into view. He paused at the bottom and leaned against the post at the base of the stair railing.

"Hello, sweetheart." He had that tone of voice, one she knew sadly too well. There was evil in it, a delight in creating terror. The flash of his predatory smile was one she'd seen years ago on another man's face as he'd taken away her best friend.

The primal part of Sophie was terrified, but the other half of her knew what to expect. He would do something to her, something that would hurt her in the worst possible way. But no matter what he did, there was a part of her that was untouchable: the part she'd given to Emery. The sacred barriers around her heart were strong as ever; not even Emery's recent treatment could undo the love she carried for him.

"You and I are going to get acquainted, get the party started before Emery shows up." He stripped off his black leather jacket and hung it on the post.

"Do you honestly think you'll get to me that way? That I'm so easy to scare?" She replied coldly, but her voice was too hoarse.

"Yes, yes, I think I will. See, I know about your friend. Rachel. That was her name, wasn't it?"

"Don't you dare say her name." Quiet rage filled her, giving her strength. She clenched her fists at her sides, restraining herself.

"Do you think she cried, when that man raped her? Maybe she liked it? I bet she liked it right up until he killed her and left her body in some shallow grave."

The words were daggers. And she bled with each breath. White hot fury seared her brain. How she remained grounded and in control, she'd never know.

Antonio laughed even though she had not given him the reaction he would have wanted. "You must not have cared much for her."

"I care, which is something someone like you will never understand."

She got to her feet, slowly and carefully. She wasn't going to let him do anything else to her, with his words or otherwise, not without a fight. Gone was the frightened child on the playground. There was no innocence left in her to destroy. For once she was pure strength.

Antonio's black eyes filled with wicked glee. "You aren't frightened, are you." It was a statement, not a question.

"What's there to be scared of? An assassin who couldn't even kill two eight-year-old boys? You had twenty-five years to kill Emery even though he's been here all along. Yeah, you're terrifying." Sarcasm dripped from every word. The flash of anger on his face made her grin inside. He reigned in his temper, though.

"You expect me to kill you quickly, if I lose my temper. You'd miss the fun of torture. Smart girl. I see why Emery is so anxious to get you back."

Finally something had gone right. Emery didn't love her and wouldn't be entering a certain deathtrap to rescue her. It was a small reassurance.

"He won't come." She relaxed, confident. Whatever would happen would be between the two of them. She could brave him and his cruelty, but Emery had to stay away.

"You're wrong. He's on his way. You see…I was the one who convinced him you'd been keeping the news about Fenn a secret to hurt him. And he hurt you back, didn't he?"

Her face betrayed her pain and the malevolent delight he took from her expression made her stomach turn.

"He's always been easy to manipulate. I used Fenn as a way to control him when I had both boys. They used to gang up on the two men I hired to help me. They were spoiled little brats and they fought so hard to escape, so many times. But I figured them out. All it took was separation. Emery would cower and do whatever I wanted if I hurt Fenn. It actually proved rather fascinating. I used to put Fenn in another room and torture him. He never made a sound, but Emery did. He had no way of knowing what I did to his brother but he would scream in pain each time I sliced his brother's flesh." Antonio pulled a hunting knife out of his boot and held it up for her to see.

"I've had my suspicions, you see, that those boys had some sort of connection to each other. I've spent the past twenty-five years fulfilling other contracts—"

"Kills, you mean," Sophie spat.

"Yes. I kept tabs on Emery. He never once showed signs he was communicating with his brother. It took me longer to find Fenn on my own. But I did. The funny thing is, he can't remember a thing. He's been raised by strangers and has no clue to who he really is. It will be so much easier killing him. He'll never see it coming."

Sophie slowly got up, easing out of her black pumps. The concrete was cold and rough beneath the soles of her feet, but it was better than being in heels. She'd break an ankle if she wasn't careful. *This is no different than the last time. You got out alive that time too.* Her inner voice tried to encourage her, but she knew chances of her survival were slim. Sometimes one had to go down fighting and take the enemy down with them if they could. If she died and took Antonio with her, it would be her last act to save Emery.

"Have you decided you'd like to play, then?" He flicked the knife in the air and caught it.

She kept her steady gaze. Over the years she'd learned how to deal with men like him. They enjoyed power, and their ability to hurt others. If she presented herself as weak, he'd kill her immediately and it wouldn't give her any advantage to die now. Any shift of her eyes, any slight indication of her thoughts or plans would be seen. He'd pick up on them and stop her. That left only a few options. She needed him to put the knife down.

"I think I'll leave you in pieces for him to find. Cut you up and scatter your little bloody bits all over the mansion. It will destroy him and when he's barely able to breathe, I'll come in and finish him off." Antonio studied her body like a butcher eyeing a fresh carcass.

Breathe in, breathe out. It'll be okay. She summoned her last bit of control and plastered a cool smile on her face.

"I guess the joke is on you, too. I never really loved him, you know. He was an easy target for my story." She crossed her arms over her chest, hiding her shaking hands with a false bravado.

He raised one brow in challenge.

She continued. "What, you thought I really loved him? You're just as gullible as he is. I played into his fantasy. A quiet, repressed submissive, looking for a master to open up her world to the darker side of the bedroom. It was only too easy and the poor sucker bought it hook, line, and sinker. He told me everything. I'll be famous when the story hits the papers." She eyed him speculatively. "I suppose I have you to thank for it. If you weren't such a pathetic psycho I'd be tempted to say we should team up. But I don't like you, so you'll forgive me if I don't offer to split the fame and fortune part of this deal." She continued to talk, her tone nonchalant, attempting to sound amused by the situation. Her eyes roved the room, using the momentary distraction of her voice to check for anything she could use as a weapon.

He still watched her through narrowed eyes, but he lowered the knife a few inches.

"You love him. I saw it when you looked at him tonight." He didn't seem as certain as before, though. His brow furrowed slightly.

Sophie pressed her advantage.

"Right, because women can't act." Her tone dripped with sarcasm. "You have no idea what I'm capable of. It was all a lie. He fell for it, and so did you. Never try to beat a woman when it comes to mind games. We're better at it. It's just simple evolution. Thousands of years of manipulating men to get what we want." She kept his attention by brushing a cobweb out of the way just a few inches from her face while her eyes swept the cellar, her gaze settling for a second on a large shovel. It was ten feet away, and she had no clue how to get past Antonio without him attacking. He held the knife loosely but that could change at a second's notice.

"Well, it doesn't matter whatever you've intended. He still loves you and killing you will hurt him, especially if he never knows your true feelings." Antonio's pronouncement forced her heart into her throat.

Time for plan B? Her inner voice was shaky. Sometimes no matter what you did, the deck was stacked against you. How often had her father said that when she'd get upset over something? She wished he was here now, so she could apologize for not calling more often, for not coming home to visit. There were too many things she'd failed to do in recent years…but she wasn't going to let this one man destroy her world so easily.

Screw the deck, screw the game. There was only one option.

She crouched as though to pick up her heels and the second her body was coiled tight, she sprang at Antonio's legs. He grunted as they collided and they both fell to the ground next to the stairs. She rolled and was on her feet running up the stairs. Her legs were weak and rubbery from the drug he'd injected but her desire to survive overrode the drug's effects.

He was too fast. Gripping her left ankle, he jerked and she tripped, smacking hard into the wooden stairs. She clipped her she rocketed up the chin and stars dotted her vision for a second. It was a second too long. Antonio, breathing hard, crawled up her body, knife in hand. In a frantic scramble of limbs she reared back, headbutting him. His agonized shout was the only urging she needed to ram her elbows into him and dislodge him from her back. Her skirt ripped up her leg as she crawled up the cellar steps. Adrenaline kicked in and remaining decaying wooden planks. She turned the rusted doorknob and plunged into the moonlight splendor of a crumbling ballroom.

Brilliant milky moonbeams burst through the high shattered windows of the mansion. Faint shadows formed spirals on the pale whitewashed walls. Ivy snaked up a staircase that led to nowhere and laced the edges of the broken window panes. Stone crunched ahead of her and suddenly Emery and Hans swept around the nearest doorway, stepping into the ballroom. Moonlight fell through the half-collapsed ceiling, striking the barrel of the pistol Emery aimed in her direction.

"Em—" Her warning shout was silenced as Antonio grabbed her from behind, the blade pressing against her throat. Her hands shot up automatically to grab his forearm, but when she dug her nails into it to drag it away, he pressed the blade deeper into her skin.

Hans and Emery froze, guns trained on Antonio, but she knew they didn't have a clear shot. He was hunched behind her, using her as a shield, and the cellar doorway behind them offered cover and prevented Emery and Hans from shifting to a better angle.

"Welcome home, boy," Antonio chuckled. "Did you miss me and our time together?"

"Fuck you," Emery replied coldly.

"Manners, boy, manners." The blade sank into her skin, cutting like butter. Blood oozed down her neck. Sophie met Emery's gaze, her eyes widening as she saw something on his face that made her go numb. His eyes glazed over, and he shook his head as though troubled with some inner demon whispering poison in his head. A man tortured…

* * *

The blood trickled down Sophie's neck and Emery couldn't breathe. The headache struck without warning and he fought to stay in control, but he could feel it crawling through his skin like a panther prowling through the shadows of the Amazon forest, seeking prey.

The presence of the other man, the one who'd drive him to madness, was back.

The black bull was massive and stood absolutely still in the loading pen, its eyes like twin pools of crude oil, unblinking and darker than the pits of hell. Its nostrils flared once, twice, a heavy snort. He was going to ride this beast even if it killed him. The prize money was his last chance.

Emery shook his head, ridding himself of the presence, if only for a second.

"Weapons down, you and your bodyguard. Kick them over to me."

"Shoot him!" Sophie gasped. "Kill him now, for God's sake!" She struggled and the blade at her throat cut deeper. The cry of pain that escaped her lips made his blood freeze. The memories, like ghosts, haunted him in his sleep, but this wasn't a dream. Antonio was going to hurt someone else he loved and the bastard would do it to torture Emery. He cocked the gun, held it ready for the shot to clear, but Antonio repositioned himself again, keeping Sophie in front of him.

"Don't test me, boy. You know I'll push back," Antonio cautioned but the jackal grin on his face said everything. If Emery crossed the line, Antonio would slit her throat in an instant.

This time when the blade bit into her, Sophie didn't make a sound. She closed her eyes as the trickle of blood deepened to a ruby line soaking the bodice of her gown.

"Hans," Emery murmured quietly.

"Yeah," Hans answered back, understanding his silent instruction. At the same time they lowered their guns to the floor and kicked them in Antonio's direction. They'd devoted years to preparing for scenarios like this, they were always working out every strategy and they were prepared to do whatever was necessary. Their guns skidded over the ballroom floor, clouds of dust billowing up in their wakes as they came to rest at Sophie and Antonio's feet.

Antonio removed the knife from Sophie's neck and then in a wicked jab, he sank the blade into her stomach and pulled it out.

"Sophie!" Emery bellowed and started toward them.

She jerked and then turned in Antonio's arms as though to fight off further attacks. He grinned at her and then shoved her away. She fell to the ground, coughing and moaning as she clutched her bleeding stomach. Antonio bent, grabbed the guns, and straightened, firing straight at Hans. The bodyguard jerked with the impact of the bullet to his chest and went down. Emery stood in the center of the ballroom, arms raised, palms empty as he faced down the man who'd ruined his life and taken his brother, his woman, and his bodyguard from him.

"It was always supposed to be just you and me, Emery. You shouldn't have gotten involved with her and I told you not to bring your rent-a-cop. What's a man supposed to do when you don't follow instructions?" Antonio's eyes were wild, his face so twisted that he looked even more unstable than Emery remembered.

Emery glanced at Hans, who lay facedown, unmoving. God...He prayed his friend wasn't gone. They'd planned for this, they'd planned...

Sophie moved, her body writhing slowly as she tried to drag herself away from Antonio. Blood darkened her dress just above her stomach and she pressed her hand over the wound to staunch the blood flow.

"She'll be fine, for now." Antonio was watching her too. "I know how to kill and I also know how to wound. I'm saving her for later, after I'm done with you. She'll get what's coming to her. She's a lying little bitch. She never truly loved you, told me so herself when she woke up."

"Yeah, I'll bet she did." Emery replied, his gaze shooting to Sophie's. She met his eyes, steady although pain-filled, and he could read the message there. He'd always been able to read her, and now was no different. He prayed she could read him the same way.

I love you. No matter what happens, I belong to you, Sophie.

She blinked. Tears slid down her cheeks and she gave an infinitesimal nod back.

Emery turned his attention back to Antonio. "Fine. You want to play, let's play. No guns, just fists. The way you like it."

"Ah, so you do remember our time together. I was beginning to think you were like your brother. Apparently he's a fucking head case, can't remember anything about his life before I took him."

The mention of Fenn made Emery hesitate a moment too long. Antonio fired his gun, and the bullet dug into Emery's shoulder. He grunted with the impact and then moaned as pain exploded in his entire body. It was like being hit by a freight train. His head seemed to jolt with the impact and something was shaken loose inside him. The other man was back in his head.

He settled on the bull's back, grinned at the other cowboys leaning on the metal railings, waving their hats in encouragement. The beast between his legs tensed, every raw bit of muscle rippling and tightening as it waited for the moment the gate would spring open and it could throw him through the air. The announcer's voice cut through the cheering crowds as he began the countdown to opening the gate.

Five…

"What's the matter, Emery, can't take a little gun shot?"

Emery breathed through his nose and resisted the urge to touch his arm. It burned like hell.

"Don't tell me you didn't like the odds, D'Angelo. Afraid I'd be more up to the fight since I'm not a kid anymore?" he challenged.

Antonio tossed the gun aside. It hit the floor with a heavy *thunk* not far from where Hans lay motionless. Emery raised his fists, ready to fight. He couldn't look in Sophie's direction, not when he needed to focus.

"Sophie, you okay?" he called out as he started toward Antonio.

"Yeah, hanging in there." Her reply was a little too breathless, but she seemed okay enough to respond.

"I want you to get out of here, if you can. You hear me, Sophie? Crawl if you have to, but do it." His tone brooked no argument. If she had any sense in her head she'd listen to him.

"But—" she began.

"I can't kill him if I'm worrying about you," he snapped.

Antonio raised his own fists and the two of them started to circle each other.

"Ready to die?" Antonio teased.

Emery glared at him and stalked forward. He wanted to end this now. He was so damned tired of living in fear, of having this man haunt his dreams and make him dread the shadows. It was time to be done with this.

"I'm ready for *you* to die," he growled and lunged at Antonio.

Antonio's first blow hit him in the jaw and he could feel the vibration of it all the way down to his toes. Emery swung and his fist collided with Antonio's cheek bone. A clenched fist sank into Emery's stomach and his breath rushed out in a whoosh, his head fogging with that other reality again.

The bull shuddered beneath him.

Three… Two…

"Emery, look out!" Sophie's scream cut through the haze and jerked him back from that other reality just in time for him to see Antonio holding another gun low and aimed upward at Emery's heart. He'd pulled it out as they'd fought. Before Antonio could shoot, however, Emery grabbed the other man's arms and they grappled wildly. He forced Antonio's hand away and the second it was pointed aside, the gun discharged.

Sophie cried out, and the sound was chilling as it ricocheted off the crumbling mansion's walls.

One…

The gate flew open and the bull shot out. He scrambled to stay on, but he couldn't focus, couldn't hear anything except the screaming of his own voice as terror he hadn't felt in years gripped him… he was… he was…

The bull reared and he lost his grip. The stadium lights spun in wicked patterns as he shot off the bull and was launched into the sky…

Emery ripped the gun from Antonio's hand and turned it on him, firing without hesitation. He unloaded the rest of the clip into the man before him, Antonio toppled over onto his back and blood oozed up from multiple chest wounds. Panting, Emery stood over him and watched the light in his eyes flicker out.

A gurgling laugh escaped his lips, blood flecked his mouth. "He'll send another...When I'm gone, another will take my place...He wants you dead." Antonio coughed and a splatter of crimson hit the concrete as he turned on his side, curling into a fetal position for a brief instant before relaxing onto his back again.

Emery bent and grabbed Antonio's shirt and yanked him up, shaking him.

"Who wants me dead?" He shook the man again, but his head fell back and a slow gasping breath escaped him before he went limp and his eyes clouded over.

Emery released the body and turned around. Sophie had crawled over to Hans, leaving a thick trail of blood behind her. She still clutched her side. Emery started toward her, his heart hammering. When Sophie reached Hans, she turned his body over. The bodyguard jerked and sucked in a breath.

Sophie screeched and fell back. Hans pushed up on his elbows and then with a groan sat all the way up. He looked around blearily then ripped his buttoned shirt down the front, exposing the Kevlar vest he wore. A small bullet was embedded deep into the vest.

"Damn it, I think I broke a few ribs. Don't tell me it knocked me out?" His face turned a ruddy shade as he looked around and saw Emery next to Antonio's body. "What happened?"

"He's dead."

"I can see that," Hans said, but then froze as he seemed to suffer a wave of pain. "This is going to be fun to recover from," he muttered.

Emery was so relieved he couldn't think past seeing Hans alive and breathing. He hadn't realized until now just how much the man had come to matter to him. In the frenzy of the fight, he'd been battling his own fears and worries for Sophie and Hans.

"Sophie, what happened to you?" Hans's question jerked Emery's focus back. Sophie blinked, her eyes glassy.

"She was stabbed. We've got to get her to the hospital," Emery's words escaped his mouth in a breathless rush as he ran in her direction. She was losing blood…and she didn't look good. He knew how serious knife wounds were. He wasn't going to let anything happen to her.

She tried to stand, but her knees trembled and knocked together like a shaky newborn foal. "I got shot too…when you were fighting…" Her hand dropped to her lower abdomen and she winced.

"Shot?" Both Emery and Hans were running to her as they repeated the word.

"Yeah…it doesn't hurt, though…" She collapsed right into Emery's arms.

Chapter 21

POLICE INVESTIGATED THE DEATH OF ANTONIO D'ANGELO, WHO WAS FOUND DEAD IN AN ABANDONED MANSION ON LONG ISLAND. A 911 CALL WAS PLACED BY EMERY LOCKWOOD, PRESIDENT OF LOCKWOOD INDUSTRIES. D'ANGELO ALLEGEDLY KIDNAPPED JOURNALIST SOPHIE RYDER FROM A PARTY AND LOCKWOOD PURSUED, HOPING TO RESCUE HER. DURING THE STRUGGLE, LOCKWOOD ALLEGEDLY SHOT D'ANGELO IN A CLEAR CASE OF SELF-DEFENSE. POLICE ARE NOT PURSUING CHARGES AGAINST LOCKWOOD.
—*New York Times*, November 11, 2014

Funny, she thought being shot would have been more of an event. But she'd not really felt it after the bullet had entered her and exploded out the back. The snap and burn as it impacted and exited her had left her panting for breath, but now a heavy ache filled her abdomen. Part of her knew it was bad…really bad, but she was so tired and couldn't' seem to think clearly.

"Sophie! Hey! Don't you dare shut your eyes!" Emery was shouting at her, but he sounded so far away, as though across a large field. His voice was drifting in and out as though a breeze teased it and she could only hear every other word. Her eyes swung up to his and she managed a weak smile. He was so beautiful, her sad, tragic love. A fierce wave of longing swept through her with the power of a vast wave crashing on a rocky shore. She wanted to stay awake, to gaze at him forever. She couldn't look away, but her eyelids were so heavy...

"Can't I just sleep a little? I'm so tired," she murmured dreamily.

Warmth was flowing into her from wherever his body touched hers. She liked it when he held her in his arms; she felt safe, protected, loved. She didn't have to be brave or strong, she could just be Sophie Ryder, a woman in love with a man. She didn't have to be anything else. Her head was too heavy now and she let it fall back. The world spun around her, moonlight in her vision like creamy streaks across the darkness. Heavy blackness descended, blurring the corners of her vision.

Pain spread through her with the force of a wildfire, so unexpected that she gasped a violent breath. Everything within her, around her, seemed to be slipping away. She clung to the world, the place she was, wherever it was, fighting to stay.

Suddenly above her the sky exploded with light. Sparkling fireworks burst in dazzling patterns, lighting up the dark blue expanse above. The shimmering sparks trickled down through the air, fading away into smoky outlines. A tiny hand slipped into hers, warm and familiar.

"My dad bought us sparklers, Sophie." The little girl's voice broke Sophie's heart. The world around her rumbled and shook as emotions within her echoed the earth's pain.

Rachel.

Another firework lit the sky and Sophie turned to stare down at the bright-eyed child, the best friend she'd lost all those years ago. Her cheeks were glowing a healthy pink, and when she smiled, she revealed one little dimple. They were both seated on top of a small hill overlooking a field full of other people stretched out on picnic blankets, watching the fireworks.

"Rachel," she whispered, the name as soft as a prayer spoken at midnight.

The little girl beamed up at her. "We've got sparklers, bottle rockets and a fountain!" The joy on her face made Sophie's heart clench. It was like finding an old photograph of someone you'd loved and lost, and seeing them smile, frozen in that one moment when their smile was genuine and their happiness was true. Sophie had left every photo of Rachel behind at her parents' home. She'd never been able to look at one without it killing her inside.

"Where are we, Rachel?" she asked as Rachel pointed a delicate finger up at the sky just as another explosion and an answering pop and crackle signaled more fireworks.

"We're home." Rachel gave a little unconcerned shrug.

"Home?"

The girl smiled at her. "You know that place, when you're just about to fall asleep and you feel yourself slipping away... that's where we are."

The tip of a sparkler burst into fiery bloom and a wash of silver sparks filled the air. Rachel's brown eyes were dark but they reflected the sparkler, making her eyes look like a pair of topaz gemstones.

It was all so familiar.

"Fourth of July," Sophie murmured. It had to be. Rachel held out a sparkler to her and she took it.

"Rachel..."

"Yeah?" Rachel lit a bottle rocket and fired it into the heavens.

"Rachel, am I dead?"

Her little eyes filled with sorrow. It was the sort of expression only a child was capable of. They understood loss so differently than adults. Their sorrow was more pure, untainted by bitterness and memories painted in shades of gray.

"You're not dead yet. I asked... I asked if I could come to you. They let me."

"They? Who—"

Rachel squeezed her hand. "I miss you, Sophie, but you can't come with me, not yet. Do you understand?" The little girl, still only seven years old, had a face full of love and peace. She tugged Sophie's hand, urging her to lean over so they could hug. Rachel was so small. Sophie had almost forgotten what it had been like to be that tiny. She curled her arms around her friend and squeezed her tight, wishing that Rachel could feel every emotion, every thought she'd ever had about her as the years had passed.

"Rachel…" Her throat constricted and she sucked in a ragged breath. I'm so sorry about everything. I couldn't catch him…" Tears filled her eyes and she could barely see so she dragged the back of her hand over them to wipe away the tears.

"What happened then…" Rachel's voice was gentle, so sweet. "It's over now." How she could be so strong Sophie would never know.

"I'll never forgive myself for what happened to you." Her broken whisper was barely audible.

Rachel reached up and brushed away a lone tear on her cheek.

"I'll wait for you, Sophie. I'll be here, always. Every time you close your eyes, there will always be fireworks and there will always be me."

"Fourth of July…" Sophie smiled. Waves of tears and sadness mixed with bittersweet love. It had been their favorite holiday, the one they'd celebrated together since their first birthdays.

"Don't cry." Rachel smiled and it was like the years that had passed between them vanished. They were children again, together. Secrets shared and dreams spun on golden threads wove tapestries of memories they'd always share. Whatever might have been, the things they might have done together, didn't matter. The past was sacred in that moment. An instant to be worshiped for what it was.

"Whenever I shut my eyes…" Sophie promised, hugging Rachel close again.

"Always," Rachel's answer filled her soul and she drew a deep shuddering breath. The night sky continued to be filled with glorious colors and brilliant bursts of light before it all faded around her.

Rachel's grip on her hand remained strong.

Sensations began to trickle back to her, piece by piece, and although her lashes felt heavy, she forced her eyes to open. Her tongue felt like sandpaper and her head hurt like the devil. A familiar and unwelcome smell invaded her nostrils. She was at the hospital.

The world around her was white—from the windows and walls to the hospital bed she lay in. Except for the man sitting in a chair next to her bed. Everything about him was so opposite to the stark, bland hospital room. The golden gleam of his hair, the sun-kissed skin. He was leaning forward, one of his hands clasping hers. Proud cheek bones, a faint scar on his chin, and the aquiline nose of a Greek god. A fierce tenderness filled her to the point of bursting when she saw the faint shimmer of dried tears on his cheeks as the morning light caught them. No one had ever cried for her before...She bit her lower lip, her own eyes burning. A lock of golden blond hair fell across his forehead. He was close enough for her to touch. She reached to brush it away, ignoring the stab of pain in her abdomen.

His eyes blinked, revealing their lovely shade of hazel. The world shrank in that single instant. She could see nothing outside his eyes and the same look of wonder reflected in his gaze as his lips parted in a soft rush of air.

"Emery," she rasped. Her throat was dry and raw but she found she could form his name without much pain. Seeing him here with her filled her with so much joy she could barely contain it. The warm feeling of happiness and relief cut through most of the foggy, drug-induced state she seemed trapped in.

"You okay?" He cupped her cheek and leaned in to brush her lips with his.

"I am...I think..." She chuckled and then winced as her stomach cramped and twisted in knots.

His eyes darkened with worry and anxiety formed tight lines around his eyes and mouth.

"You gave me a scare. I thought I was going to lose you."

"I seem to recall you kicking me out." She tried to tease him, but he scowled and looked away. She knew him well enough now to see his fury was directed inward.

"I was an idiot..." He met her gaze again. "If you won't forgive me, I'll grovel to get you back."

Sophie considered this. "How about I get to tie you up and punish you."

He snorted. "Go ahead and try."

"Well, I'll forgive you, but I'll tell you later how you can make it up to me." She paused, shutting her eyes, relishing the way he stroked her cheek with his knuckles. It was almost soothing enough to erase the pain. It was then she noticed his shoulder was heavily bandaged and in a sling.

"What happened?" she demanded.

"I got shot in the shoulder. It was a through and through, but my arm's out of commission for a while."

Sophie blew out a breath she hadn't realized she'd been holding. "What did the doctor say? How long will we be here?"

"At least a day for me. You have to stay a week, unless I can talk the doctors into letting me hire private care for you at home. The bullet passed through your stomach close to your side. They were able to repair the damage. The doctor said you were lucky you didn't bleed out and the knife wound was shallow, and mostly in muscle, which will heal easily. Hans and I rushed you to the emergency room in time and they were able to get you into surgery straightaway. It was a tough day yesterday; we thought you might not make it, but you did. I called your parents. Cody tracked them down. They're on their way to see us."

She warmed instantly at the way he said *us*. Her parents were coming here…Rather than dread their arrival, she was relieved. She missed them like crazy. After everything that had happened, she had so much she wanted to tell them.

"Now I know how you felt when you met my parents." He laughed softly.

"Oh?" She couldn't contain her smile. "Terrifying, isn't it?" The urge to tease him was impossible to resist.

"Yes, well, you had an easier time. As long as you don't tell your father that I seduced you, tied you to my bed and made love to you, then treated you like my personal sex slave, I'll probably make it through the meeting alive. Explaining dominant behavior isn't exactly easy. I'll be lucky if he doesn't kill me."

"I won't tell him. He'll only want to know that you love me. That's all he cares about. Besides, I love it when you get all dominant on me." She noticed her wrists were bare of the cuffs and she felt naked without them. "Where are my cuffs?" They'd come to mean so much in the last few days, a sign of her and Emery's commitment to each other.

"They're somewhere safe for when you're well enough to wear them." Emery frowned as he stared at the IV needle taped into the back of her hand. "But you needn't worry about wearing them anymore." She put her hand on his chest, feeling the steady beat of his heart kick up at his words. Was he done with her? After everything they'd been through, she couldn't believe it, not when he seemed so sweet and tender now. But what else could he mean?

"Well...actually I thought I'd get a ring, just to make sure you understand my intentions."

"Which are?" She raised her eyes to his, and her breath caught in her throat as she saw the depth of his heart in his eyes.

"To keep you. Forever."

His declaration demanded she face the guilt she'd been carrying. "Emery...I'm so sorry I didn't tell you about Fenn. I was going to, as soon as Wes said he'd found him and they were in a safe location."

His hand moved down from her cheek to cup the back of her neck. His fingers massaged her gently and she relaxed.

"I know. Hans explained what happened. You did the right thing. It's not your fault. I was an inconsiderate asshole."

"You were an asshole, definitely. But I have to admit, the sex was amazing." She blushed remembering the barely leashed ferocity of their coupling in the study on the desk. Even as weak and bruised as she was, that memory made her burn.

"Jesus, Sophie, I'm trying to be all gentle and caring and you're making me as hard as a rock. I feel guilty as hell about it. How can you even think about sex after what you've just gone through? A woman who's been shot and stabbed needs rest and relaxation." He laughed darkly and rested his forehead against hers as they shared her pillow.

"Sorry, guess it comes with the territory. I can't ever see myself not wanting you." She shut her eyes a moment, savoring the brief rest it brought before she spoke again. "Are you going to Colorado now?" Half of her wanted him to say no, but the other half knew he had to leave and bring Fenn home.

"No."

"No? Why not? Your brother is alive and we have to find him." She tried to sit up but he gently pushed her back down.

"We will. After you rest and heal. I'm not going anywhere without you. Fenn can wait until you're well enough to travel."

He was waiting for her. The knowledge of this made her feel all warm inside.

"If you're sure you want to wait..."

"Sophie, haven't you figured it out by now? I'd wait forever for you. You're mine and I'm yours. That's how it works when you love someone."

Her heart stopped, literally. The machines next to her bed chirped in alarm.

"You love me?" Her words were a hoarse whisper.

"More than anything." His eyes twinkled. "You better love me, too, or we'll revisit that particular punishment you like so well."

The flood of heat took her body by storm, momentarily erasing her pain. She rolled onto her side and scooted closer to him, ignoring the twinges of pain so she could tuck her head under his chin. When all the world seemed to have gone to hell and back, she took comfort in his embrace and the way it made her feel safe, secure, whole.

"Everything is going to be fine. We're together and I'm never letting you escape again." His words were a delicious burn, a promise, a vow, searing into her heart. She inhaled his scent, loving the dark masculine hint of musk and the fresh clean zing of his cologne. He'd showered and changed clothes.

"How long was I here?" She'd forgotten if he'd told her.

"A day. Royce watched over you while I got Hans cleared and he went home for a few hours. I stayed here and used one of the hospital room showers. There was blood and...well, I needed to get it off."

"It's okay," she assured him and burrowed closer.

They lay together for a long while, their breathing matched so perfectly she could have sworn they were one being, not two.

"Emery..."

"Yes?" His tone was so gentle, so sweet.

"I'd like to tell you about Rachel."

"I'd love to hear about her." His words were a little rough. "Why don't I bring you home and you can tell me all about her? I think I'll be able to convince the doctors to let you come home if I hire a fleet of private nurses."

"Home?" She eyed the whitewashed hospital walls. It would be nice to get away from here. It might be hard to heal in a place like this.

"Yes, our home. Lockwood is ours now, not just mine. Do you feel up to leaving early?" He shifted closer on his chair and let his fingertips linger on her cheeks, where he'd been gently stroking her skin.

"Yes. Take me home, Emery."

His full sensual lips curved in a bright smile that was nearly blinding. True joy lit every part of his eyes; no shadows lingered. He'd banished his demons, and she knew that loving him had been half the battle. The other half had been saving him and finding out Fenn was alive. She would share his heart with Fenn; it was the way of twins and she didn't mind. He was alive and he loved her. Love was all that mattered.

* * *

Sophie winced as she eased into Emery's bed. It had been three days since she'd come home from the hospital. Three days that had felt like a lifetime. They'd found out that Hayden Thorne hadn't gone to Michigan as she'd told them, but instead had flown to Colorado ahead of her brother in a feminine knight errant attempt to rescue the lost Lockwood brother herself.

Fenn was coming home soon. Once Fenn was here he'd be safe, and the brothers could come up with a plan for how find out who really wanted them dead. Sophie had an idea, too, and planned to make sure she helped.

They were going to be meeting Fenn in a day or two. He and Emery had talked on the phone. Emery had rushed into the room the first night she'd come home and he'd been flushed, excited, like a boy again. The memory made her smile.

"Sophie, you wouldn't believe it. He sounds just like me!" He'd laughed and stalked toward the bed, and her, tossing the phone at the foot of the bed as he stripped out of his coat and crawled toward her, grinning.

"Just like you, huh?" She laughed and tipped her head back, letting her tired body rest on the pillows as he caged her in, carefully, and stole a deep, seductive kiss.

The taste of him, so addictive, went straight to her head, and she couldn't remember that she'd been hurting moments ago. There was only him and his wonderful lips, loving her with little nips, sensual caresses, and that ragged breathing that told her he was just as lost to their passion as she was. A universe only for them. Just the two of them. She would never have guessed it could be like this, not between them. Sexy, yet sweet. He'd made plenty of delicious threats that once she was fully healed, Master Emery would be back and expecting his little sub to please him, but until then, she had this other side of him, one she loved as equally as his dominant side.

When their lips finally broke apart, he sat back and held out a pair of familiar bracelets. Her gilded cuffs.

"My cuffs!" She reached for them, but he lifted them out of her reach, a wicked flirty grin teasing his mouth.

"What are you willing to do to earn them back, little sub?" he demanded, but his tone was light and sweet.

She lowered her lashes, and peeped up at him impishly, knowing it would undo him. "Whatever my master wishes."

He dropped the cuffs onto the bed and leaned over her again, this time kissing a path to her ear, where he licked the inner shell and she arched up, ignoring the twinge of her sore body. She wanted him, wanted him so much that the ache for him replaced most of her other hurts.

"Easy, sweetheart," he scolded. "Don't hurt yourself. There will be plenty of time later for that." He eased onto the bed beside her and carefully pulled her into his embrace, holding her. She sighed and rested her cheek against his chest.

"You promised you would tell me about Rachel," he said. "Are you ready? I would like to hear about her." Emery rubbed her hip with one hand and pressed a kiss to the crown of her hair.

She was ready. There was a flicker of old pain, like when one has a scar that sometimes aches. But she ignored it and started to talk.

"Our favorite holiday was the Fourth of July. She used to get tons of sparklers…We always managed to set fire to something…"

Emery's laugh vibrated through her and she laughed too.

"One time we chased away her brother and his friend with a bunch of bottle rockets after they'd teased us. They stayed clear of us after that."

"I'll bet. Fenn once shot me with one of those. Burned like hell. I couldn't sit down for a week."

Sophie giggled at the mental image of Emery as a boy wincing as he sat down, only to hop back up again.

"I wish you could have known Rachel." Her best friend would

have loved him, and she knew deep down that somewhere deep inside herself, that part of Rachel was still there, smiling at the thought.

"Me too."

"She would have liked you, too."

"Sophie, I have something I would like to ask of you."

A little laugh escaped her. "Ask me? Since when, oh Master Emery, do you ask anything of me? I seem to recall you like giving me orders."

"Only in bed, my heart. Only in bed." His chuckle vibrated her body but he turned serious. "I know you like your job as a journalist." He didn't wait for her to disagree. She did love her job. It had become a driving force, a crusade she wanted to fight for the rest of her life. Saving people had become second nature to her.

"I've spoken to my father." He hesitated now, his words a little short, a sign of his nervousness.

"Yes?" She focused on him completely, trying to hide her intense curiosity.

"Well, some of the devices Lockwood Industries have been developing over the last few years are ideal for law enforcement. I was thinking of working out several private contractor deals with police forces and the FBI in order to supply them with these devices. We could help them. You know, like the small GPS devices. They could plant them on ransom money to track down kidnappers. There are a dozen other devices I've got that would help them. I want to help you save people in whatever way I can."

He waited for her reaction, and she saw the fear of rejection in his gaze. Her big, intense dom was afraid she wouldn't like his idea. But she did, oh she did. It was wonderful, it was…perfect.

She curled her arms around his neck and gazed deeply into his eyes. "That's a wonderful idea, Emery. You will help save lives. I know it. I have contacts for departments all over the country and could help you arrange those contracts with law enforcement."

"You don't mind my helping?" he asked.

She shook her head vehemently. "Don't mind? Emery, I love it. I *love* you. We can do this together."

Emery wrapped his good arm around her and kissed the crown of her hair. "I figured if we work together, there will be fewer victims."

She blinked away tears, trying not to let her sadness at missing Rachel ruin such a wonderful moment. "Are you excited to see Fenn after all these years?"

He nuzzled her cheek. "I can only imagine what Fenn is like. I wonder how changed he is…if he's like me at all or…" Emery's face reddened and he let his words trail off.

She wrinkled her nose and then smiled. "Cody didn't tell you? Apparently, he's a professional bull rider."

Emery stiffened. "A bull rider? No, he left that part out. That…no…God, I'm not crazy after all."

Sophie raised her head, watching his eyes and the myriad emotions that flitted across his face. "What do you mean?"

"You remember me telling you about those hallucinations I get sometimes?"

"Yes." Sophie raised herself up on one elbow and bit her lip against the pain.

"My connection to Fenn wasn't totally lost. I've been feeling him and seeing through his eyes for years. I just didn't realize it until last night. I think he was thrown from a bull the night we faced Antonio. I'll call Wes as soon as I can and ask him to check it out."

"What's he like? Fenn, I mean?"

"Seems like he's desperate…and wild."

Sophie leaned forward and kissed him before replying. "Sounds a lot like you."

Emery's gaze softened. "I'm not desperate anymore."

This time when their lips met it was both sweet and potent, like a love spell. He leisurely parted her lips and thrust his tongue inside her mouth in a slow deliberate rhythm. Her body flushed and her brain short-circuited, just like it had the first time she'd seen him in the Gilded Cuff. But now she knew every part of him and loved him with a depth she'd never dreamt possible. That was the beauty of living a dream. Emery was a living, breathing dream, and he was all hers, every wicked, dominating inch of him.

"What's that smile for?" He ran a fingertip down the length of her nose and tapped the tip. Her grin simply widened.

"Kiss me, then maybe I'll tell you."

"Bargaining again? I might have to punish you after all, little sub." He rolled over her slightly, just enough for her to get breathless and feel a little dominated.

"Death by kisses sounds nice," she suggested.

"I think that can be arranged." And with that he bent his head to hers, delivering more than one kiss she would die for.

Epilogue

Emery Lockwood, 33, reclusive billionaire and survivor of the Lockwood kidnapping of twenty-five years ago, is once again in the news. Lockwood has announced he is engaged to be married to crime investigative journalist Sophie Ryder, 24, of Manhattan, Kansas. No wedding date has been set.
—*New York Times*, February 3, 2015

Hayden Thorne sat in the front row at the arena, staring straight ahead at the long-lost Fenn Lockwood. He was settling onto the back of a black bull named Tabasco, a ten-gallon hat set low on his head. He bent to stroke the bull's neck and it tossed its head, furious. She could hear Fenn's rich laugh even though she was twenty feet away. He turned his head, smiling at something one of the cowboys perched on the railing said, and his teeth flashed white with a cool, predatory, and sexy smile.

Fenn was gorgeous, Hayden thought, in the way only a rough cowboy could be. Damn, he could wear a pair of blue jeans. A woman could lose herself in thoughts of digging her heels into that tight ass while he thrust into her—hard, wild. Hayden worried her bottom lip as the announcer started counting down to the gate release.

"Three…two…one…"

The crowd roared as the gate sprang open and Tabasco rushed out, Fenn on his back. Hayden held her breath as she counted the seconds. If he could get past eight seconds, he'd have a chance at winning the $50,000 prize money. At seven seconds, the bull turned and Hayden caught a glimpse of Fenn's face. It was white and strained with stark pain.

Something was wrong.

When the bull jerked and kicked again, the glazed look of pain was still etched on Fenn's face. And it cost him his control.

Tabasco sent him flying through the air. Hayden leapt to her feet as did the other people around her. Fenn hit the sand and his body didn't move. The bull was still leaping and rearing, trying to remove the flank strap around its lower body. It spun around, caught sight of Fenn's prone body, and charged.

Hayden shoved past people, screaming for them to move. She hadn't a clue what to do, but she wasn't going to let him die. She reached the front railing that circled the arena, keeping the crowds at a safe distance from the activity taking place in the center. Fenn was still stretched out on his belly on the sand. His hat had rolled a little ways away and was rocking slightly in the small night breeze. The bull was about sixty feet away.

"Fenn!" She didn't stop to think. She just acted.

Hayden kicked out of her Jimmy Choo heels and hiked up her dress and then started climbing the railing.

"What the hell are you doing, lady?" One of the cowboys in charge of the crowds was racing toward her. "Get down! We're sending in the rodeo clowns, they'll distract him."

She got to the top of the railing just as the cowboy jumped to grab her leg. He missed, spat a curse as she landed on the other side of the arena. Her feet sank deep into the sand. She put two fingers between her lips and whistled.

The sharp sound cut through the hushed crowd and the bull

slowed, whipped its horned head in her direction. It stared at her for a long second before it turned back toward Fenn. Hayden took a few shaky steps closer and whistled again. The bull, irritated, snapped its head back in her direction.

"Come on, you walking steak. Chase me, not him," she muttered. If she lived through this, she'd put her fortune to good use and buy the damned bull, then eat it.

The bull rotated its massive body, its hooves kicking up sand as it pawed restlessly and started to trot in her direction. A movement flickered out of the corner of her eye and she glanced to the right, seeing several strapping cowboys and easing open one of the gates close to Fenn. One of the cowboys raised his hand in Hayden's direction, motioning for her to look the other way. She turned to the left, where a couple of seriously pissed-looking cowboys were opening a chute.

"Work him this way, honey. Get him in this chute and we'll get you out. The crew on the other side will get Smith out." As he said this, three rodeo clowns, dressed in ridiculous clothes were running out onto the field, waving at the bull and whistling.

Smith. Fenn's new last name. She nearly smiled. An ordinary name for an extraordinary man.

Hayden jerked back to herself as Tabasco started to speed toward her. She started to run and nearly tripped. A skin-tight dress hadn't been the best choice of attire for running away from a charging, pissed off bull, but she'd come straight from the party back home and hadn't had time to change. She also hadn't expected to get into a rodeo ring to run for her life.

A cowboy to the left of the chute waved her on as he called out, "Faster, honey! We won't be able to get you out if you don't pick up the pace."

Hayden ran like hell. The thunder of hooves behind her made her feel like she had hellhounds on her heels. She reached the chute's opening and the cowboy, who'd climbed up the side of the chute, leaned down and grabbed her, jerking her up into his body. They toppled back into the stands just as Tabasco ran below them into the chute. The other cowboys slammed the chute closed.

"Well, hello, honey," The man she was sprawled on top of grinned at her. He was cute, just like every other damn man in the city she'd come across since she'd arrived here. She pushed hard against his chest. He fell back to the ground with a grunt and a laugh as she got to her feet.

"Damn, I love me a feisty woman."

Hayden ignored him.

Where the hell are my shoes? She realized she'd crossed half the arena and would have to go back to the other side and get them. Leaning over the railing edge she watched as Fenn was helped to his feet. He was limping, leaning heavily against one of his fellow riders, but he was walking. He turned, looking over his shoulder, and his gaze fell on her. The second their eyes met she nearly fell face forward over the railing. The world seemed to go white hot inside and around her, like she'd been hit by lightning.

It took her a few more seconds to realize he was scowling at her. She couldn't help but imagine him pulling her over his lap and spanking her. Her knees buckled and her lips parted on a breathless sigh.

Had she finally found a man who'd be strong enough for her? A real dom?

"Nice to meet you, Fenn," she whispered. She smiled back at him, loving the way storm clouds gathered on his brow as he turned away and limped out of the arena.

"What the hell are you doing here, Hayden?"

She was grabbed by her arm and spun about. She gulped as she realized it was Wes.

"Hey Wes…"

"Don't you 'Hey Wes' me! Explain what the hell is going on?"

"Um…I came here to rescue Fenn."

Her brother was pissed, super pissed. The only comfort she had was that he was her brother and wouldn't touch her; otherwise she'd be in real trouble.

But then again, she was already in a heap of trouble. She'd taken one look at Fenn Lockwood and she knew she was a goner.

Please see the next page for a preview of
Book #2 in The Gilded Cuff series,

THE GILDED CAGE

Chapter 1

The bull charged down the metal rail-lined run and into the narrow chute. Fenn Smith gripped the rusted railing and pushed his hat down harder on his head as he studied the beast.

Tabasco. A black bull with the temper of the devil himself. Just the sort of brute that would give him one hell of a wicked ride. The crowds in the stadium shouted and hollered encouragement as he maneuvered over the top rail and onto the beast. The stadium lights created a glare over the tan sand and heated Fenn's body despite the cool weather. Sliding himself down over the bull, he carefully settled on its back. It kicked and fidgeted, but there wasn't enough room to buck.

Fenn tightened his gloves hands and wiped a fresh line of sweat from his brow. The beast between his legs tensed, every raw bit of muscle rippling and tightening as it waited for the moment the gate would spring open and it could toss him.

"Give him hell, Smith!" One of several bull riders hanging on the side of the chute called out to him.

He laughed and smacked his hand on the bull's neck. He planned to do just that. If there was one thing he could do, it was ride bulls.

Fenn gripped the braided bull-rope that was wrapped around Tabasco's flanks. The resin treated rope would be easier to grip the more heated it became during the stress of the ride. A good thing, because Tabasco was a notorious head down spinner. Like a whirling dervish, he threw more men off in any given rodeo season in the state of Colorado. Men traveled from all over the country to ride him.

Some bulls bucked straight ahead, others spun in circles. The key was to watch a bull a few weeks before you planned to ride him and get a feel for his style. Fenn had spent the last two months studying Tabasco. He couldn't afford to make a mistake tonight, not when everything depended on this ride.

Shifting his weight, he kept his dominant hand in an underneath grip on the bull-rope and sat as close as he could to his hands. He leaned forward so that his chest was almost over the bull's shoulders.

"Riding now is Fenn Smith, a Walnut Springs native. He's competing for the grand prize, a cash award of fifty thousand dollars. The bull is Tabasco, rated by our rodeo staff as one of the tougher rides here tonight."

Fenn ignored the announcer's opening speech and focused on the ride. The scents of cheap beer, hay, and manure, aromas he'd grown up with, were strong yet comforting. This was his town, his stadium. He could do this. He had to do this. Visualizing the ride, he pictured the way he'd have to read the bull's body language to stay on for eight seconds. Just eight seconds.

Fifty thousand dollars. It was enough to reinstate the mortgage loan on Jim and Callie Taylor's Broken Spur Ranch. He wouldn't have risked his neck on this bull for any other reason. Old Jim was in his fifties and his twenty-year old daughter Callie needed to be looked after. They were his family and he'd risk his neck if that's what it took to help them. He licked his lips, rolling his hips as Tabasco shuddered and huffed.

"The gate opens in five..." The announcer began the countdown.

Almost instantly, an awful creeping sensation rippled over his skin, like beetles were scuttling over his flesh. With a roll of his shoulders he tried to shake off the unsettling feeling.

"Four, three..."

The bull shuddered beneath him.

"Two, one..."

The gate flew open and the bull shot out. Fenn scrambled to stay on as it ducked its head, preparing to tilt-a-whirl. The uncomfortable flank strip infuriated the beast and it would do anything to kick it off. Tabasco's front feet came up off the ground and Fenn leaned forward, squeezing his legs and maintaining a tight grip. If he could keep his hips square and centered...

A woman's scream penetrated his mind, tearing through his skull like a knife. Flashes... strong and powerful images flickered like broken fragments on an old film reel. Cracked columns broken by moonlight cutting through shattered glass windows. Ivy crept along a staircase that led to the floor of a mansion that had long since crumbled to the ground below. A deep baritone laugh, the explosion of bullets, a sound from his deepest nightmares...

His stomach clenched and churned, and his dinner worked its way up through his throat. He couldn't focus, couldn't hear anything except the screaming inside his head as terror he hadn't felt in years gripped him. He was... he was... a lost, frightened little boy again.

"No!" The cry barely left his lips before the world went to hell around him.

Tabasco reared his head then dipped down, his back legs going straight up in an unexpected move. Fenn's grip on the bull rope slackened completely.

"He'll send another... when I'm gone, another will take my place... He wants you dead."

Words—not his—scratched across the back of his eyes and burrowed into his mind like scorpions, leaving only stark fear behind.

The stadium lights spun in wicked patterns as he was launched into the sky. Wind whistled past him, cutting across his face before he smacked onto the ground. Something in his leg stung with pain and he had no air to let out the choked guttural scream just on the tip of his tongue. Pain rippled through him, starting at his head and working its way south to his feet. He couldn't move, not even an inch. Every sound, every sensation, was dulled by the agony surging through his body.

The bull would charge, wherever the hell he was, and it was only a matter of seconds before Tabasco would trample him and gore him with his horns. His face was angled to the right, and he could see his favorite hat lying upside down ten feet away. The hat rocked back and forth. He blinked, feeling grains of sand in his eyelashes.

Images flashed across his vision again. Strange sensations filled his body. Hands that gripped uselessly at sand, felt more like they were holding a woman in his arms instead. But that was insane; he was facedown on the ground, not clutching at some phantom woman.

"Smith! Move your ass!" George Romano, one of his friends and fellow riders, shouted. He was directly in Fenn's line of sight, climbing the fence at the arena's edge.

Move? He couldn't. Not happening. A brilliant splash of red caught his eyes. A drop-dead gorgeous woman in a tight red dress, red hair flowing about her shoulders, was scaling up the arena fence in her bare feet. George dove for her, but she threw her legs over the side of the fencing and dropped into the arena.

Son of a—

"Fuck!" Fenn growled as adrenaline spiked through him. Tucking his arms under his body he pushed his chest off the ground.

This had to be a dream. A bad one. There was no way a woman in a slinky red dress was sprinting past him, waving her arms at…Tabasco. Fenn craned his neck so he could see over his shoulder as the charging bull slowed to a stop and seemed to consider the woman. The brute huffed and pawed the sand, brown eyes locked on her. After a few long seconds, it whipped its head back toward Fenn.

A piercing whistle cut through the air. The crowd had gone silent, except for the cowboys hollering for the rodeo clowns. They were usually a welcome distraction when riders got thrown and the bulls wanted to charge them, but the clowns were too late to save him now. The whistle sounded again and this time Tabasco must have decided the girl was more of a target than he was. It kicked up the sand and started a steady trot in the woman's direction.

"Smith! Get moving!" George bellowed. He and three of the riders had tossed their hats to the ground and were heading over the top of the railing into the arena. A few more riders were working on opening a gate a few yards away.

Fenn found enough strength to roll over and struggle into a hunched sitting position. His lungs still worked to suck in much needed air. His vision swam and a heavy pulse beat in his head. He blinked, the simple action feeling like sandpaper scraping across his eyes. Thoughts weren't forming quickly, and he could barely think beyond being dumbstruck at the sight ahead of him. The cute red-headed woman was flying across the sand, kicking it up in small puffs as she fled to the other side of the arena. The bull was picking up speed and running after her. When she reached the open chute, a rider reached down over the fence, and she grabbed his arms. With one quick jerk, she flew upward over the fence and disappeared from view and out of harm's way. The bull ran into the chute and the gate clanged shut, sealing him off from the arena and leaving Fenn safe.

"What the hell?" he muttered.

Two pairs of arms gripped him under the armpits and hauled him up onto his feet.

"That was way too close," George panted.

"Shit!" Fenn's ankle went electric with pain and his eyes nearly rolled back in his head.

Please let it be a sprain. He couldn't afford a broken bone.

"That crazy girl saved you," George announced with a mixture of amusement and relief.

"Tell me that really didn't happen," Fenn demanded as he accepted his hat when one of the other riders held it out to him. He smacked it roughly with his palm, creating a cloud of sand and dirt around it.

"Oh, it did," George chuckled. "A woman just saved your sorry ass. A hot one, too. She's probably a buckle bunny. Play your cards right and you might be riding that tonight. I hope you can last longer than eight seconds!" George whooped and slapped him on the back as they walked toward the open gate.

Fenn hobbled, leaning against George's shoulder every few steps. He threw one glance back to the other side of the arena and caught sight of the siren in the red dress standing behind the fence, watching him. Long waves of red hair danced about her shoulders, playing across her collar bone. Her full lips were parted as though surprised somehow. She was a real vixen. God didn't make many women who looked like her. Full curves, sculpted features, a mouth made for sin…And she'd been the one to save him. For some reason that pissed him off. *Really* pissed him off.

He turned his back on the woman and looked straight ahead.

About the Author

LAUREN SMITH, winner of the 2014 Historical International Digital Award, attended Oklahoma State University, where she earned a B.A. in both history and political science. Drawn to paintings and museums, Lauren is obsessed with antiques and satisfies her fascination with history by writing and exploring exotic, ancient lands. She is currently an attorney in Tulsa, Oklahoma.